For Colette

Chapter 1

Lying next to a blazing taxi cab, the victim was unconscious, only just clinging on to life.........

He could not know that had he been able to watch something that was upsetting to him, almost sickening, for five seconds longer, then, probably, none of this would have happened and he would not now be fighting to stay alive........ a fight that he was almost certainly going to lose.

....

In the early hours of Wednesday morning, the peace and tranquillity was broken by the sound of a fire engine roaring through the streets. They had received a call from a passing motorist who had seen smoke as he was driving along the motorway. As he was unfamiliar with the local area, his description of where he had seen smoke was vague; however the officer in charge knew exactly where to head for, as a set of new industrial units at the side of the motorway had become a popular spot for vehicles being dumped and set alight.

As they pulled up to it, the crew could see it was a taxi, but there was obviously no-one in it. This industrial site was nowhere near any housing estates and, as it was still under construction, was poorly lit, and there was no CCTV in place. As the crew leapt out of the fire engine, they could immediately smell petrol, and therefore knew the taxi had deliberately been set on fire - all London taxi type vehicles had diesel, not petrol, engines.

"Jane, far side!" shouted the officer in charge.

Jane Tunstall had only recently joined the fire service, and was aware that she was working in a very male dominated profession; she was keen to demonstrate her enthusiasm to her senior officer. Consequently, in her haste to comply with his order, she did not notice the body lying on the ground until she stumbled over it.

Jane dropped down to her knees, to check if there was any sign of life, but then she shuddered; she tried not to look at the face.

"Ambulance needed!" she called. "There's a man down here, and I've found a faint pulse!"

The firefighters were still tackling the blaze when the paramedic arrived. The fire crew directed him to the victim, then carried on with the job in hand. Shortly after the paramedic, an ambulance arrived, followed immediately by the police; two officers got out of the car, and came over to where the victim lay. As the ambulance crew were lifting the body onto a stretcher, the young Constable saw the victim's face; he turned away quickly, and could not stop himself from vomiting onto the ground nearby.

The other officer, Pete Jones, was a much older and more experienced Sergeant; he and the paramedic obviously knew each other.

"You need to get this taped off, Pete," said the paramedic, as they were lifting the unconscious man into the ambulance. "This is no accident, and I don't think there's much chance of this fella living."

....

The ambulance set off at high speed, but not in the direction the fire crew or police expected it to go; the ambulance driver had made the decision to take the victim to a hospital that was actually further away in miles, but he knew as far as time was concerned, he could get there quicker. Both he and the paramedic were aware that seconds could count as to whether the victim lived or died.

When the ambulance arrived, the team at the accident and emergency department were ready, and swiftly moved the stretcher from the ambulance to the operating theatre. It was immediately apparent to the doctor in charge that, because of the severity of the injuries, the patient would need to be transferred to a hospital in Liverpool which specialised in head injuries, as soon as possible; so, while the theatre staff were battling to keep the victim alive, the doctor rang the ambulance station, which was on the same site as the hospital, to see if Mike Bates was currently working.

Mike Bates was a legend amongst ambulance crews throughout the North West; anyone who had ever worked with him wondered whether he had made the wrong choice in becoming an ambulance driver, as it was felt he could have given the top Formula One boys a run for their money. He always carried a stopwatch with him and checked to see what his record was from this hospital to the Liverpool hospital; thus, as the patient was loaded into the back of Mike's ambulance, he gave a thumbs up to the theatre doctor, set his stopwatch, and took off.

Mike knew this was probably his best chance of breaking his record, due to the fact that it was early hours of the morning; so, as well as the streets being reasonably empty, he could get through the Mersey tunnel quicker than at any other time of the day. The paramedic in the back expected a rough ride, but she also knew Mike would get them there quicker than anyone else.

As Mike pulled up outside the main door to the hospital, he checked his stopwatch, and let out a resounding "Yes!"

……………………………………………

Back at the industrial estate, the fire crew were just dousing down the remains of the taxi as the police began cordoning off the area.

Gary Ward, the young Constable who had been first on the scene, was cursing his luck, as the previous night's shift was his last one in uniform. Gary had a degree in criminology from Durham University, and was being fast tracked to greater things; before that, however, he was obliged to do two years in uniform as a police Constable. Remembering the victim's face, he hoped that he would never witness a sight like that again in his future career.

Sergeant Jones had marked out where the body had been found; although the victim was still alive, the paramedic's remarks to him earlier suggested that they would soon be dealing with a murder enquiry. Two C.I.D. officers, Detective Sergeant Ronald "Tinny" Smith and Detective Constable Paula Wright, arrived minutes before Debbie Price, who was in charge of the crime scene investigation team; D.S. Smith and D.C. Wright remained outside the area which had been taped off, while Debbie investigated the crime scene.

"Brilliant" they heard Debbie cry, as she stood by the area where Gary had been sick.

"Next time you hear me complaining about our job, just remind me that at least I'm not in a profession where you can get so excited over a pool of vomit," remarked Tinny.

Debbie walked back to the two detectives, very pleased with her discovery. "Well, if that's not the victim's, and the D.N.A. is in the system, we're in business."

"I can guarantee it's not the victim's, and will definitely be in the system."

"That's an impressive boast, Tinny - it was quite close to where the victim was found, and you can't possibly have a suspect yet."

Tinny explained what had happened; from the look on Debbie's face, he was glad that Gary had left the scene, as he suspected there would have been a second victim.

"Do we know who the victim is?" asked Debbie.

"We're reasonably sure it's the driver," replied Tinny, "a forty-year old taxi driver called Neil Hughes."

"Reasonably sure?"

"From what I've been told, there was very little left of his face to make any sort of identification possible, even though he was still wearing his taxi badge which had his photograph on it. So, when a couple of uniformed officers called at his home, they checked with his wife what he was wearing when he went to work yesterday. Obviously, they avoided telling her too much about the facial damage; they just said that because the lighting near the incident was so poor, and the policeman who attended only caught a brief glimpse of her husband before the ambulance left, they needed to verify it was Neil Hughes. So," concluded Tinny, "unless it was someone between five feet nine and five feet ten, muscular build, who'd also borrowed the victim's clothes and badge, we're reasonably sure it's the driver."

"Okay, no need to get stroppy," smiled Debbie.

"Sorry Deb, but it's this bloody job. I was talking to Pete Jones before and, as you know, Pete's been round the block a good few times attending pub fights, glassings, stabbings and God knows what else; even he said that this was, by far, the worst he's ever seen."

As Debbie walked back to continue with the crime scene investigation, D.C. Wright murmured "Remember, Sarge, at least you don't have to be overjoyed at the sight of vomit...."

Tinny just smiled. Tinny Smith had been in the job for some years, and had not long to go before he could retire. He was a big man both in height and build, and was well liked and respected throughout the various police authorities that he had worked over the years. Originally from Scotland, Tinny had lived in the North West of England for most of his life, but had never lost his Scottish accent.

....

Caroline Hughes was in bed asleep when the police knocked on the door. When she awoke and heard the knock, she assumed her younger son Paul had forgotten his keys again. As she was walking down the stairs she was going to give him a piece of her mind because, no doubt, he had been drinking with his mates in some "dive" somewhere, and he was still only seventeen years old. She wished he could be more like her older son, Michael; but she knew she could not stay angry with him for very long.

As she opened the front door and saw the two police officers, a police Constable and a W.P.C. her stomach turned; as for the police officers, they seemed slightly confused, as Caroline looked like she could have been Neil's daughter rather than his wife. She was about five feet six inches tall, slim with shoulder length, wavy blond hair, and was very pretty; some would have said she was beautiful, but not in a glamorous sense - more of a natural beauty.

"Does Neil Hughes live here?"

"Yes, but he's still at work – he's a taxi driver."

"Would you mind if we come in?" asked the W.P.C, as the officers showed their identification.

Caroline said nothing, stepped back, and directed them into the living room. When they were inside, W.P.C Jill Rathbone was the first to speak.

"If I could just ask, are you Miss or Mrs Hughes?"

"I'm Mrs Hughes - what's happened?"

"Perhaps you would like to sit down, Mrs Hughes."

As Caroline sat down, her eyes started filling up with tears; Jill Rathbone knew she would have to be careful how she worded the information she was about to impart.

"Mrs Hughes," she began, "I'm sorry to have to tell you that your husband has been taken to a hospital in Liverpool with head injuries, due to an incident he's been involved in."

"Was it an accident? Is he badly injured?"

"I'm afraid I don't know the extent of his injuries, and at this point the cause is still being investigated, so I regret that there's little more I can tell you at the moment."

Caroline jumped up, wiping away the tears from her eyes. "I must get dressed and get over to Liverpool as soon as possible."

"We'll take you over to the hospital Mrs Hughes, you don't want to be driving yourself at a time like this," insisted the police Constable, speaking for the first time since they arrived.

Caroline looked at him gratefully; she nodded, and hurried upstairs to get ready.

The journey to the hospital was made in almost complete silence.

....

As they arrived at the hospital, W.P.C Rathbone effectively took charge, as she had been there in similar circumstances on a number of previous occasions. Jill Rathbone's colleague, police Constable Mark Walker, was more than happy to let Jill take charge; Mark was not at all comfortable in these situations, he much preferred sorting out fights outside a pub, or chasing burglars. He knew Jill had trained as a family liaison officer, and was far more experienced in dealing with family members connected to a victim of violence. Jill suggested that Mark take Mrs Hughes to the family room near to the operating theatre, while she spoke to the medical staff to find out what she could.

P.C. Walker was relieved when Jill joined them, as Caroline had been asking him questions, to all of which he had avoided giving a straight answer. Jill now sat next to Caroline.

"Mrs Hughes - "

"Please call me Caz, everyone else does...........except Neil, who always calls me Caroline," at which point Caroline broke down and wept.

Jill just used her eyes to signal to Mark to leave the room, which he was relieved to do. She waited for Caroline to stop crying before she spoke again.

"I've spoken to the staff involved since Neil was brought in, but all they're able to say, currently, is that he's critical but stable."

Caroline attempted to wipe away the tears from her eyes, and sat up straight.

"What exactly happened?"

"I'm honestly not sure, but first reports seem to suggest that your husband was attacked."

Caroline groaned. "I knew something like this would happen sooner or later. For the last few years I've been trying to talk Neil into finding another job." She paused. "Is he going to be all right?"

"Unfortunately, I'm simply unable to answer the question, as the medical people told me very little."

Jill was, again, being slightly economical with the truth, because she had been told that there was a very small chance of Caroline's husband surviving; however, she knew from experience that to tell Caroline the whole truth now would just be unnecessarily cruel. Jill knew she needed to get Caroline's focus away from the man on the operating table, to the man Caroline knew before the attack.

"You said before that everyone calls you Caz, except Neil; how did that come about?"

"From the first night we met - although I told Neil everyone calls me Caz, he said he preferred Caroline and did I mind if he used the full title, and I said that's fine, and that's been the case ever since." Caroline smiled as she remembered. "I love telling the story of how Neil and I met, because I always think it was quite romantic. Of course, I suppose it must sound boring to most people," she remarked, looking slightly embarrassed .

"There's nothing boring about romance," said Jill. "I'd love to hear the story, if you feel like telling it."

Caroline looked pleased. "Well, it began when my friends and I were on a hen-night in Liverpool. We'd travelled there by minibus from Cheshire and North Wales, and arranged a time for the minibus to pick us up later that evening and take us back. Would you believe it, somehow the minibus going back home had left without me..............."

....
....

.............and she had no idea know what to do, as she certainly did not have enough money for a taxi all the way back to Cheshire.

As she walked out of the ladies toilets, she saw Neil, who she had previously danced with. Neil could see she was obviously upset, and looked like she had been crying.

"Caroline.....is something wrong? Is there anything I can do?"

"It's my own stupid fault," she said, and explained what had happened.

"I can drive you home."

"No, I couldn't expect you to do that – I live in Cheshire!"

Neil smiled "That's okay, so do I. I travelled over to meet up with some friends from Liverpool, but brought the car, as I don't drink." He looked slightly embarrassed.

"Oh....... when we were dancing earlier on, and we were talking, I assumed you were from Liverpool - although your accent isn't very strong," she ventured.

"I was born in Liverpool, but I've lived in Cheshire for the last five years."

It turned out that Neil lived in the part of Cheshire closest to Merseyside; Caroline, however, lived further into the county, about fifty miles beyond his home.

"Look, Neil, I really don't want to put you out........."

"It's no problem at all."

Caroline, in many respects, was a young nineteen-year-old; whereas Neil both looked and seemed older, yet was actually two months younger than Caroline. When Caroline and her friend had danced with Neil and his friend, it was obvious to Caroline that he was not confident where girls were concerned, and did not have all the standard chat up lines she had heard so often in the past. After she had made sure they had a second dance, she found she was chatting Neil up, something she could not remember ever doing before. There was something different about Neil, but Caroline was not sure what it was, other than she felt completely safe and secure when she was with him.

....
....

"You know, that feeling has always stayed with me throughout the twenty years we've been married. When I think back, although I was sometimes naïve, I certainly wasn't stupid, and would never normally have considered going in a car with a complete stranger at that time of night. Yet where Neil was concerned, I didn't have a moment's hesitation. When we stepped out of the club, I remember I instinctively linked my arm through his."

At this point, Caroline paused, glancing at Jill.

"I'm not boring you with this am I?"

"Definitely not," smiled Jill, "please carry on."

"Well," said Caroline, "on the way home we talked about jobs, families, friends and so on; I felt like I'd known him for years........."

....
....

They did not speak for a few miles as they travelled along, then Caroline broke the silence.

"By the way, you're a very good driver, Neil; you don't tear round bends in the road like a maniac, compared to some lads I've known."

"Oh, well.......thanks," he said, diffidently. "I passed my test when I was seventeen, but I never did like the idea of driving too fast – I want to get where I'm going in one piece."

Caroline laughed. "Me too! I reckon some lads think that driving too fast somehow impresses women, but it certainly doesn't impress me....... I'd rather feel safe and secure, like I do right now," she finished, as she glanced at him, smiling.

Neil did not take his eyes off the road, but she could see that he was also smiling.

....

As they pulled up outside Caroline's house, everywhere was in darkness. Neil got out of the car first, came round to Caroline's side, opened the door for her, and helped her out of the car.

"Seeing as you've come so far out of your way, the least I can do is offer you a cup of coffee," said Caroline.

"Oh.......no, thanks all the same; it's pretty late now, and I wouldn't want your parents to be disturbed," began Neil; then he saw the disappointment on Caroline's face, and relented. "There again, a caffeine boost is probably a good idea for the drive home," he grinned.

"Exactly," agreed Caroline.

"You've talked me into it, then – but I won't stay too long."

....

"Years later," said Caroline to Jill, "Neil and I talked about that first night; he told me that, at the time, he thought I invited him in out of politeness, and then immediately realised that wasn't the case. I'd often regretted inviting lads into the house because, no sooner would I sit down, than I would find myself almost fighting them off."

"I can relate to that," said Jill, wryly.

"But with Neil I knew that wouldn't happen, and I was right." Caroline looked sad for a moment, then continued her tale.

....

Neil did not stay long, much to Caroline's disappointment. However, they exchanged phone numbers, then Caroline walked Neil to the front door.

"Thanks again for coming to my rescue. And.....well, be careful driving home."

"I always am."

Caroline opened the door, and Neil stepped outside; they both stood there uncertainly for a moment, then Neil stepped forward, carefully held Caroline's face and, gently, kissed her on the lips.

....

Considering Caroline had got to bed so late the night before, she was up early in the morning, waiting till she felt it was a reasonable time to ring Neil on any pretext she could think of.

"Oh, hello Neil…..hope I haven't woken you up….er…..just checking you got home safely last night."

"Yes, no problem; as it happens, I've been up for some time, doing some jobs on the car. As a matter of fact, I'm glad you rang - I was going to ring you to see if – well - if you had any plans for this evening………?"

"No, nothing at all planned, I'll be at home on my own," she lied; she had actually arranged to go out with her friends.

"That's great - well there's a nice restaurant I know in North Wales; I don't suppose you would like to……….go there with me this evening?"

"I'd love to."

....

The restaurant they went to was actually quite close to where Caroline was born, and yet she had no idea of its existence. After coming off the main road Neil drove down a small lane, then turned into an even smaller lane which brought them out by a river. Caroline was charmed to see an old, small restaurant, and nearby was an even older church.

"Neil, this is absolutely gorgeous!"

"I hoped you'd like it," said Neil, as they walked into the restaurant.

Although Neil had shown a lack of confidence where talking to girls was concerned, even a shyness, he certainly showed great confidence in every other situation, which really impressed Caroline. He seemed totally at home now, as he ordered for the two of them, and the evening flew by far too quickly. When they got back to Caroline's in the early hours, the kiss they shared was far more passionate than that of the night before.

....

One afternoon three weeks later, they went to the same restaurant; it was afterwards, when they went into the church, that Neil asked Caroline to marry him.

....

"……………and of course, I immediately said yes," finished Caroline, triumphantly.

At this point, Jill was beginning to regret asking Caroline how she met Neil because she felt that, if the doctor came in at that point to say Neil had died, Jill would probably forget her professionalism, and cry as much as Caroline; so when Jill saw the door handle turn, she could not stop herself from holding Caroline's hand. Fortunately, it was only Constable Walker returning. Caroline was still smiling from telling Jill her story; Mark looked at Jill with admiration and reflected how good she was in these situations.

Jill then spoke. "I noticed the picture on your living room wall of yourself, Neil and, I assume, your two sons. Was that taken recently?"

"Yes, we had it taken by a professional photographer a few weeks ago."

"I also noticed your wedding photograph, on the fire surround. That photo was obviously taken twenty years ago - what's your secret?" Jill smiled, and further confided, "I must admit, when you answered the door to us earlier this evening, we may have looked slightly taken aback – we thought we may have gone to the wrong address, as there was no mention of Mr Hughes having a daughter."

Caroline nodded. "Yes, Neil's mates often pull his leg when we're out with them by saying they thought he was bringing his wife, not his daughter! Fortunately, it doesn't bother him at all - he just says to them 'you're only jealous!'"

They probably were, thought Mark, hiding a smile. He was immensely grateful to his colleague, and her remarkable ability to deal with people in vulnerable situations. While he had been outside the hospital, he had received instructions to obtain as much information about the victim that he could from Caroline, but suspected it would be a struggle to get her to open up to him; however, thanks to Jill, he felt that there was now a much better chance of success.

"Mrs Hughes, I've been talking to one of the theatre staff……. Neil is obviously in very good physical condition for a forty-year-old, isn't he?" he began carefully, constantly watching Jill and hoping she would be able to show him a sign, possibly by shaking her head slightly, if he were to say or ask the wrong thing.

Caroline looked gratified. "Please, call me Caz. Yes he is. Neil doesn't smoke or drink, and does regular training to keep fit; in fact, over the last four years especially, he's got himself into a shape that even Michael and Paul are envious of."

Mark thus managed to obtain, with the help of Jill's prompting, far more information than he could possibly have hoped for but felt, like Jill, that the man on the operating table definitely did not deserve what had happened to him.

As Mark heard the door open behind him, he turned quickly to see Caroline's two sons. Jill looked on with admiration as she saw this woman, whom she had thought of as almost fragile, become a mother who immediately comforted her boys. Jill made a sign to Mark, and rose from her seat.

"Mark and I will be outside if you need us for anything."
…………………………………………………………

It was midday when, back in Cheshire, a major incident team had been hurriedly put together. The senior investigation officer was Detective Superintendent Graham Benton. As Tinny took his seat, he was surprised to see Gary Ward sitting at the back of the room, not in uniform.

Benton introduced himself as the senior investigating officer, and looked around at the officers in attendance.

"I'll get straight to the point. Although the victim, Mr Hughes, is alive, this is being treated as a murder enquiry, as it's very unlikely that he'll survive. I'm including Detective Constable Gary Ward in the team, as D.C. Ward was one of the first at the scene…….."

At this, one of the other Detective Constables produced a plastic bucket from under his desk and placed it next to Gary Ward.

"Just in case, Morse, just in case," said the D.C., as some of the others started sniggering.

Gary Ward went bright red in the face, which seemed to cause the laughter to get even louder. Benton, however, was not laughing, and looked accusingly at the officer who had produced the bucket.

"Sorry, sir."

From the outset, it had been an in-joke on the part of his fellow officers to nickname Gary "Morse", after the fictional detective; they knew of his university background, and assumed he did his degree at Oxford, given that he originated from there. Although he repeatedly told everyone he graduated from Durham University, this did not stop them using the nickname, much to his annoyance.

Benton continued.

"The victim's wife has been interviewed by a uniformed Constable, but as we all know from previous experience, family members can often be useless in these situations. As far as Mrs Hughes is concerned, her husband was obviously a saint, and didn't have an enemy in the world. We all know, from the injuries he received, that can't possibly be true. Detective Inspector Bill Erickson will sort out who is doing what, but our first jobs need to be speaking to the victim's fellow taxi drivers, checking all CCTV footage in the area, and speaking to anyone who knew Mr Hughes. As this is D.C. Ward's first day in C.I.D., I'm putting him with D.S. Smith, who's the most experienced officer present." He looked directly at Tinny.

Tinny did not try to conceal his displeasure at this announcement, as he returned Benton's look. Benton simply gave a suggestion of a smile, nodded to the rest of the room, and left the briefing.

....

After Benton's departure, several conversations seemed to break out at once. Gary used this opportunity to go to the toilets, as the sight of the bucket had reminded him of the previous night's events, and he thought he was going to be sick again. He hurried into a cubicle, and locked the door behind him.

Shortly afterwards, he heard the toilet door open, and two people walk in. Gary froze and desperately hoped that he would not be sick again, because he could guarantee that one of the people who had just walked in would almost certainly be the joker with the bucket. Gary recognised one of the voices as Tinny Smith, but did not recognise the other.

"Alright Dave, how are you doing?"

"Not bad, Sarge, not bad. How did you manage to get stitched up with the fast track fella?"

"That's just Benton being snide."

Gary was unsure what to do; he decided to stay put, and hope the conversation did not last long.

"I thought you and Benton were mates from years ago?"

"I can assure you that Graham Benton is no mate of mine. We started at the same time and were at training college together in Warrington. I think *he* believed we were mates; but he's very much mistaken."

"I've heard that "Detective Superintendent" Benton is punching a little above his weight, is that true?"

"He was punching above his weight as a Constable."

"So, how did he manage to get to Superintendent?"

"Don't you know the story of Benton's crafty career move? In the early days it was obvious to everyone, including the man himself, he was never going to get very far in this job, so he married the Chief Constable's daughter, an incredibly ugly woman. I accept everyone has the right to be ugly, but she has totally abused the privilege."

Dave laughed, but Gary winced at this.

"Since that day, he's never looked back." Tinny paused. "Personally, I think, in order to reach the dizzy heights of Superintendent he's paid a very heavy price. Other than being an ugly woman, she's particularly unpleasant. I've had the awful experience of meeting her twice. The first time was when they got married, the second more recently at their twenty-fifth wedding anniversary. Unfortunately, as it was a free bar, my wife informs me I may have made the odd derogatory remark about Benton and his missus."

"Do you think that's why you've been saddled with Morse?"

"Absolutely certain of it. Since the wedding anniversary, he hasn't missed an opportunity to either make me look incompetent, or just do something he knows will annoy me."

At that point, both men exited the toilets, giving Gary the opportunity to breathe normally again; he stepped out of the cubicle, and waited until he heard the footsteps of the two officers fading away along the corridor outside.

He had always dreamed of being a police detective, but could not have imagined a worse first day in the job. Other than the ridicule from the other officers at the briefing, it looked like he was now stuck with a bitter and twisted Sergeant, who was obviously jealous of his friend's success. Gary did not expect to learn much from Detective Sergeant Smith.

....

As Gary walked back in to the briefing room, Tinny waved him over to a desk at the back of the room.

"I'm Detective Sergeant Smith, and you will be working with me. I'll be blunt, because I generally am anyway, and I'll say now I'm not happy having to conduct an investigation with a Constable who has no experience at all. I must also say that I'm not a great believer in the fast track system; however, this will be your opportunity to prove me wrong." Tinny looked appraisingly at Gary. "I noticed earlier you weren't pleased with the nickname Morse, so I'll call you Gary, and you'll call me Sarge. Is that clear?"

"Yes, Sarge."

"There's just one more thing that needs clearing up - there's a rumour going round that you drive a Porsche. Tell me that isn't true."

"It isn't true."

"Then whose *is* that Porsche parked outside?"

"It *is* actually mine, Sarge, but you told me to say it wasn't true."

Tinny smiled to himself; at least this lad has a sense of humour, which he will certainly need in this job, he reflected.

"How have you managed to obtain a Porsche on a Constable's salary?"

"It was a bribe, Sarge."

Tinny raised his eyebrows. "That's it, I'm intrigued now – you're going to have to tell me the full story."

"Well, my father owns a very large and successful printing business in Oxford, and the firm has been in my family for generations. I'm an only child, so my father always assumed that I would take over from him; but, as far back as I can remember, the only thing I ever wanted to be was a police detective. That's why I did the degree at Durham. The Porsche was a twenty-first birthday present from my father – he hoped that the gift would change my mind about joining the family business."

"I see," said Tinny. "What's to stop your father taking it back?"

Gary shrugged. "He can if he likes; I'd sooner be a Detective Constable on a push bike than a printer in a Porsche."

Tinny grinned. "You'll never be rich working as a policeman."

"I'm already rich, so that doesn't matter." Gary returned the grin.

Tinny had to admit to himself he was impressed with this young man's confidence, and thought maybe the partnership might work, despite his initial reservations.

"May I ask you a question, Sarge?"

"Fire away."

"It's obvious why I've been nicknamed Morse; how did you get the nickname Tinny?"

Tinny adopted a superior expression. "If you behave yourself, and I think you have the makings of a good detective, I might tell you the story. Deal?"

"Deal."

………………………………………………

Caroline, Michael and Paul sat quietly in the family room at the hospital, bracing themselves every time they heard footsteps walking down the corridor.

Caroline looked at her two sons, and wondered how they would cope if Neil died. Although Michael and Paul were so similar in appearance, they were like chalk and cheese in character. Michael, who had just celebrated his nineteenth birthday, was more like Caroline in many ways. He had recently moved into his own apartment, but she had no qualms about his ability to take care of himself; he was very easy-going, level headed, and had never been a worry to either Neil or Caroline.

She was far more concerned about Paul's current behaviour, and certainly his choice of friends; even when they were growing up, whenever there had been trouble with other boys, it was almost always Paul who started it, and invariably Michael who finished it. Although Michael avoided trouble and would gladly walk away from it, he would always stand up for his younger brother; Paul, however, was more like Neil, because if someone said "fight", he would stand and fight anyone. Paul still lived at home; although he spent most of his time at his girlfriend's house, his mother saw more of his dirty clothes than she did of him.

As the door opened, all three were surprised, as they had not heard anyone walking along the corridor; they were relieved to see that it was only the two Constables who had been standing outside. Jill explained that she and Mark were going off duty, but would be replaced by two new uniformed officers and that, at some point, a C.I.D. officer would be over to speak to them; as for Neil, Jill told them that, as far as she knew, he was still in the operating theatre.

Shortly after, the replacement Constables arrived, and introduced themselves. Constable Susan Yates was very impressed to note that, as she entered the room, the two young men stood up; she thought that these standards of manners and courtesy had long gone. She immediately liked this family, and understood why Jill and Mark had been so concerned about them; Constable John Swift, however, looked at Michael and Paul, and decided then that, if he had to arrest either of these two young men, he would like to have plenty of backup.

As the officers left the room, the sound of footsteps could be heard heading their way. When the door opened again, the man who entered introduced himself as Dr. Hargraves, the head neuro surgeon.

Caroline was the first to ask what they were all wondering. "Is Neil still alive?"

"Yes, but he's still critical. Your husband is in a coma which we have induced in order to stop the brain from swelling. We can take him out of the coma when we feel it's safe to do so."

"Do you know exactly what happened to him?"

"Someone has attacked him with a weapon of some sort," he began, but before he could finish the sentence, Paul was on his feet, glaring at him.

"Someone! It wouldn't have been one, pal, it would have had to have been a good few of them to get the better of my dad!" Caroline could see the tears in Paul's eyes. "He can stand his ground against anybody, and doesn't back down!"

Caroline looked at Michael, who nodded slightly, put his arm around his brother's shoulder, and said "Come on, kid, let's go and have a breath of fresh air." Paul glared at the doctor again, almost as though it was he who had attacked his father, as the two boys left the room.

"I'm so sorry," said Caroline, as the door closed behind them. "It's his way of coping with this situation."

"Please don't apologise, Mrs Hughes; the fact is, what your son has just said is music to my ears." Caroline looked puzzled. "I'm sorry, I should make myself clear," the doctor continued. "We can do no more for your husband at the moment; but to hear that he's a fighter, hopefully both mentally and physically, tells me that he has a better chance of surviving. The next twenty-four hours is crucial, and it may be that only your husband's will to live may keep him alive. I don't want to give you false hope in any way - with the severity of his injuries, I would have expected most patients not to survive; but, remarkably, he's still with us and, hopefully, will remain so."

The doctor paused for a moment. "This was a particularly vicious attack and I hope the police catch whoever did it," he said seriously; then he smiled. "I also hope they get to the attackers before your son does, otherwise I suspect I could be very busy."

At this, the doctor rose from his seat. "Would you like me to call the police Constables to sit with you, Mrs Hughes?"

"Thank you, doctor; but I think I'd just like to be on my own for the moment."

The doctor nodded. "Of course."

Shortly after he left, Paul and Michael came back into the room. Caroline waited for them to sit down; Paul knew by the expression on her face that he was in trouble.

"Look, Paul," said Caroline, "save your anger for the people who did this to your dad, not the people who are trying to save his life." He was about to speak, but Caroline held up her hand. "I haven't finished yet. Those people in the operating theatre have homes and families, but you don't see them knocking off at their end of their shift halfway through the job. You're not in the playground now. Grow up!"

Michael smiled and winked at his mum. "You should give him a smack on the back of his legs."

"I will, if he does it again!"

Paul had been staring down at the floor; but, when his mother said that, he looked up at her and smiled. Once again, Caroline knew that she would be unable to stay angry with him for long; after all, he was too much like his father, and she had never, ever been able to get angry with Neil.

....

A short while later, Paul went out to the coffee machine, and saw Dr. Hargraves; Paul approached him, holding out his hand.

"Sorry about before," he said ruefully. "Sometimes I don't think before I open my mouth."

"No need to apologise; I'd be angry if someone attacked my dad." The doctor smiled. "If your dad's like you, then he's in with a chance."

"My dad's ten times tougher than me."

The doctor put his hand on Paul's shoulder. "Good. Then that gives him an even better chance."

As Paul walked back to the family room with the coffees, he realised his mother was right, he did need to grow up.

....

When Paul got back to the family room, there was a middle-aged man speaking to his mother and brother, who Paul assumed was a plain clothed police officer. Detective Inspector Eriksson was not there long before he left; he was disappointed, as he had assumed he would be able to gain more information than the uniformed Constable had earlier, but had failed to do so.

Paul turned to Michael. "Is he in charge of the case?"

"No; the police class this as a major incident, so the senior investigation officer is a Detective Superintendent Graham Benton."

"Why don't you two go home for a while?" suggested Caroline. "There's nothing you can do while your dad's still in a coma, and I gather that won't change anytime soon." The two boys protested, but Caroline was firm. "Some of your dad's family will be here shortly, so I won't be on my own; besides which," she pointed out, "if we don't know how long your dad will be kept in a coma, it's not practical for all three of us to stay here all the time."

Michael and Paul reluctantly agreed, and left; but they had no intention of going home.

....

The brothers drove back through the tunnel, and headed back to Cheshire, straight for the taxi rank where their father usually ranked up; there, they saw some of the taxi drivers whom they knew to be friendly with their father, and went over to speak to them. As they were explaining what had happened, a great many more taxis arrived, as the word had been passed around on various taxi radio systems; however, none of the drivers could think of anyone that had caused Neil any problems, although they promised to find out what they could, and let the boys know.

Michael and Paul tried the same approach with all their father's other known friends but, again, they drew a blank; disappointed, they headed back to Liverpool.

....

The brothers walked into the family room at the hospital, to find their mother asleep on a couch; with her was their father's brother and sister. Ian, Neil's elder brother, put his finger to his lips, and motioned to the boys to step outside.

As they stepped back into the corridor and closed the door behind them, Michael turned to Ian.

"Has there been any change?"

"Your dad's still critical, and is in intensive care. As far as I can gather, as long as he's in a coma, that's keeping him alive."

Michael told his uncle where he and Paul had just been.

"Mike, just let the police do their job," advised Ian. "You're no good to your mum or dad if you get banged up for dealing with someone who could be totally innocent."

"I can't go into intensive care and make my dad better - I have to do something."

"That's right," said Paul. "Our dad has stood by us all our lives, now it's our turn to stand by him."

Ian sighed. He had never married and had no children, and had always envied his younger brother; he had seen the boys develop over the years, and knew them well. He was concerned; if Michael and Paul got to their father's attackers before the police did, he knew that Paul would do a lot of damage to them; but Michael would kill them.

"What you can do is concentrate on supporting your mum, she needs you now more than ever."

When they went back into the family room, Caroline was awake and was chatting to Neil's younger sister, Sally. Caroline looked apprehensively at Ian.

"Any more news yet?"

"Neil's still with us, which doesn't surprise me - he always was a stubborn little bugger."

Ian felt he should try and take Caroline and the boys' minds off the current situation, so he asked the boys what they were doing at the moment as far as their jobs were concerned. They all seemed to welcome the opportunity to talk about something else. Michael had gone into business for himself as a joiner, and was doing very well; Paul had started working in a solicitor's office, but left to take a course in plumbing with the intention of working with Michael. When Paul was at school, he had done very well in his exams and had always wanted to be a solicitor; however, he found he was not enjoying the job, and was far happier when he was helping Michael.

A little later, Caroline and Sally had just gone outside for a cigarette, when Ian turned to Paul and said:

"Your mum tells me you've been getting into a few scrapes because you're drinking too much."

Paul shrugged. "I like the odd glass from time to time."

"Whatever you do, don't end up like me. The drink ruined my life, don't let it ruin yours." Ian put his hand on Paul's shoulder. "Sorry, this isn't the time and place for a lecture. Look, I've got to get home now, but tell your mum I'll come back later, okay?" Paul nodded, and Ian went out into the corridor, smiling back at both boys as he closed the door behind him.

Caroline and Sally came back into the room shortly afterwards.

"Anything more yet?" asked Caroline.

"No, mum, nothing," said Michael. "I know this is an expression often used, but in this situation, no news really is good news."

Everyone was silent for a few minutes, lost in their own thoughts. Then suddenly, Sally remarked:

"That's the nearest I've seen our Ian sober than I can ever remember."

Caroline and the boys looked at each other; they had thought the same, but had avoided saying it.

Chapter 2

First thing on Thursday morning, as Detective Superintendent Benton entered the briefing room, everyone stopped talking and gave him their full attention.

"Dave, what did you get from the taxi drivers?"

"A certain amount of abuse and a great deal of animosity," replied Dave Lloyd. "The general consensus of opinion amongst the cab drivers I spoke to is that the police are a waste of space, and we're all a bunch of names which I'll not repeat in the company of ladies." He glanced at Paula Wright and smiled.

"And what's brought this on?" asked Benton.

"The drivers say that, in the past, whenever there have been problems and the police have been called, either we don't turn up at all, or not until well after the matter is resolved - usually by the taxi drivers themselves."

"In what way?"

"Most of the taxis have radios and, when there's a problem, the driver informs the taxi office, who in turn relays the message to all other taxi drivers; they call it 'blowing a thirteen'. If any driver says, for example, 'thirteen at the train station', as the other drivers hear this message from the taxi office, they all head straight to the train station. As one of the drivers put it, the five drunks or druggies in the cab who are being aggressive with the lone taxi driver aren't quite as brave when a few more drivers appear. The problem we have in this case is that Neil Hughes didn't have a taxi radio in his cab so, if he'd had a problem, he was very much on his own."

Dave paused. "By this time, the word had obviously gone round the other taxi drivers and more started to appear; there are some big lads working those cabs, and we felt it would be safer to leave it at that." He looked over to Tinny. "Even you would've backed down."

Benton then turned to Paula. "Where are we up to with the CCTV footage, Paula?"

"The images we have aren't very good, but there's someone coming over from Manchester University who may be able to help. The last sighting of the victim appears to show him picking up two people from the town rank, but as he turns off the High Street, there's no CCTV coverage in the direction he drove."

"Are we still looking at this as a murder enquiry?" asked Dave.

Benton nodded. "Yes, the most recent reports from the hospital are that the victim is only alive now because they put him in an induced coma. It's felt that, when he's taken out of the coma, it's unlikely he'll survive."

The Superintendent looked to the back of the room. "D.C. Ward, you looked like you were about to say something."

Although Gary had slightly raised his arm, because of the previous morning's experience, he was unsure of making any comment for fear of more ridicule; however, he now felt committed to say something.

"Could it be mistaken identity sir? Maybe the victim wasn't the intended target."

"Yes that's always a possibility; you and D.S. Smith can follow up on that line of enquiry. However," Benton remarked, "did anyone know that the victim has a villa in Spain?" There was silence in the room; Gary looked confused. "No, I thought not. We are talking here of a detached villa with a swimming pool, a few minutes' walk from the beach. I don't think there are many forty-year-old taxi drivers with villas in Spain." He turned to Dave. "You're the expert on finances; check bank accounts, not just the victim's, but those of his wife and sons, to see if there are any large sums being moved about."

Benton looked around at the other officers and continued.

"It wouldn't be the first time a taxi driver has supplemented his income by selling drugs from his cab. As we all know, a lot of the youngsters out nowadays appear to be using cocaine in the same way as they drink alcohol. As they're being ferried round from pub to pub or club to club by taxi, it's very convenient to be able to buy their drugs from the taxi driver who's taking them. Possibly the victim in this case has fallen out with the wrong people.

"Speak to your informants, see if the victim's name comes up regarding drugs and, particularly, the supply of drugs. So far, we've drawn a blank as far as motive is concerned. As it's unlikely the victim will survive, we need to dig deeper if we're going to catch whoever did this."

....

As the Superintendent left the briefing room, Tinny turned to Gary.

"Mistaken identity? Where did that one come from?"

Gary shrugged. "As I was knocking off last night, Mark and Jill were just starting their shift. They told me everything they'd found out from Mrs Hughes, and it just struck me that, possibly, he wasn't the intended target. However, I didn't know he had a villa in Spain, or that he could be selling drugs."

Tinny held up his hand. "I'll just stop you there. For all we know, Neil Hughes may well have acquired the villa by perfectly legitimate means and, as far as the drug dealing is concerned, that's just pure speculation. Your theory could well be right, so let's keep an open mind on this. I must also point out there are some people in this headquarters who own properties abroad, but no-one is suggesting that they are in some way on the take."

Gary wondered if Tinny really believed what he was saying, or was just dismissing the suggestion because it had come from Superintendent Benton. He also thought that, in future, he would certainly wait till the end of the briefing before he made any comment or suggestion.

As D.S. Smith and D.C. Ward were leaving the headquarters they bumped into Debbie Price from the crime lab.

"I believe this is the young man who tried to mess up my crime scene."

As Tinny smiled, Gary said "I am sorry Miss Price, but I did try to avoid looking at the victim's face. I can only apologise."

"Well," said Debbie, "you've partly redeemed yourself with the "Miss"; I just wish we had photographs of the victim before the ambulance took him away."

"Then hopefully, this may help," Gary offered, handing his phone to Debbie. "As I arrived, but before they put the victim onto the stretcher, I walked round the body with the phone set on video."

Her eyes lit up when she examined the top of the range smart phone and, turning to Tinny, she remarked "Remember when I was on that seminar in New York recently? All the CSI teams over there are issued with these."

"As I'm sure you know," continued Gary, "the video footage can be broken down into stills. What you'll find, however, is that some of those stills may be of the ground near to the victim, and of the back of the paramedic's head. I was looking away while I was filming, because I didn't want to look at what I thought, at the time, to be a corpse. It was only because the paramedic said "Constable" that caused me to turn round, which was when I saw the victim's face."

"This is brilliant - can I keep hold of this, until I can find the proper connection for it?"

"Keep it as long as you like, no-one ever rings me anyway," said Gary ruefully, "I've got no mates."

"Well, you have now; any time you're near the crime lab I'll put the kettle on," she grinned. "How did you manage to get one of these? They cost an absolute fortune."

"It was a bribe."

Debbie looked confused; "I'll tell you another time," said Tinny confidentially.

As Tinny and Gary walked along the corridor, Tinny glanced shrewdly at his companion.

"*Miss* Price? Debbie's at least mid-thirties and been married for over ten years, as I'm sure you knew," remarked Tinny.

Gary just smiled. "I know, it works every time."

Tinny was warming to this young man, not just for his confidence but also his sense of humour. In spite of his misgivings of the fast track system he was beginning to feel that, after all, he should keep an open mind about Gary's capabilities; even so, he decided, there was no harm in keeping the lad on his toes.

Consequently, as they were walking down the corridor, Gary got the distinct impression that, for some reason, Tinny was not best pleased with him. He realised he was right when Tinny remarked:

"The problem with the mistaken identity line of enquiry is that it'll be very time consuming. We'll need to check, not only the taxi drivers who work locally, but the surrounding authorities as well. You heard what Dave said before about the taxi drivers' attitude towards us; that'll make this even more difficult."

"Do we need to speak to the taxi drivers? Surely all we need to do is to go to the respective local authorities, and check their records. They have photographs of the drivers on file, as well as general information including age, etc., so if there are any other drivers similar to the victim, we should be able to get that information quite quickly."

Tinny glanced at him and smiled. "You're getting quite good at redeeming yourself."

"I'd prefer to get things right in the first place, so I didn't have to redeem myself."

……………………………………………………

Gary's suggestion certainly proved to be a good one, as they were able to cover a large area which included a number of different taxi authorities; however, they had no success in finding a driver who Neil Hughes could be mistaken for. Gary was very disappointed to find that this line of enquiry, being his idea, had come to nothing. Tinny obviously realised this.

"You'll find in our job that a number of lines of enquiry come to nothing. It was a good idea; your suggestion certainly saved us a great deal of time, and a possible stand-off with some angry taxi drivers. A couple of my mates drive cabs, and have said the same to me about not being supported by the police.

"Hopefully, Debbie may be able to help as far as the forensics are concerned. When she's able to tell us what she thinks happened, I can almost guarantee it will be as good as if the whole scene was filmed. So often in the past, when a case has been solved, her description of events often proves to be remarkably accurate."

Gary still secretly hoped that Neil Hughes was not the intended victim, but understood that no more time would be wasted on that line of enquiry. He was, however, grateful to Tinny for telling him it was a good idea. It was near the end of the day when Tinny received a call from Debbie. She explained that, after speaking to the fire forensics team and studying her own findings, coupled with the details of the victim's injuries which she received from the hospitals, something did not make sense.

"We're stopping off at the ambulance station and fire station to try and clear something up," said Tinny, as he and Gary were going back to headquarters. "Debbie had a theory on what happened, but it looks like your photographs have thrown a spanner in the works." Tinny glanced mischievously at Gary. "That'll teach you to keep accepting bribes."

They went into the ambulance station first, where Tinny spoke briefly to the ambulance driver who was first on the scene, then went next door to the fire station, and asked to speak to the station officer. As they walked into his office, Mike Campbell, the station officer, got up and shook hands with Tinny, saying "All right Tinny, long time no see." Gary was in no way surprised at this greeting, as throughout the day, wherever they went and whoever they spoke to, everyone seemed to know, or know of, Tinny Smith. What had impressed Gary was that they had spoken to quite a cross-section of the community.

"Nice to see you, Mike; I thought you'd have been retired by now."

"I was going to say the same to you."

"Not long now mate, not long."

"I take it this is to do with the taxi fire?"

"Indeed it is. Any chance we could speak to the firefighter who found the victim?"

Mike pursed his lips. "Is it absolutely necessary?"

"Why, is there a problem?"

"She's not long been with us, but has the makings of a first class firefighter. Unfortunately, this business has really knocked the stuffing out of her. You and I both know she may never witness something like that again for the rest of her career, but she doesn't know that. Is it very important that you speak to her now?"

"I'm afraid so, it's a particular piece of information Debbie Price needs."

Mike nodded. "Fair enough. I'll go and get her, but do us a favour and go easy."

"Cheers, Mike."

As firefighter Jane Tunstall entered the room, Tinny and Gary immediately stood up and smiled.

"I believe I may be able to help with your enquiries?"

"I hope so," replied Tinny. "When you stumbled over the victim's body, can you remember if he was on his back or on his side?"

Jane thought for a moment, then said "He was on his side, facing the front of the cab. As I stumbled over him, I think I knocked him onto his back."

"Thanks very much for that information, it's a great help, and I can only apologise for reminding you of what must have been a very upsetting sight."

"At least you weren't sick," said Gary, before he could stop himself.

Jane looked at Gary knowingly. "I certainly wanted to be, but managed to concentrate on putting the fire out."

As Jane walked out of the office, Mike Campbell came back in.

"She's a tough girl, Mike, I can see why you want to keep her in the service," remarked Tinny.

"Good ones like Jane don't appear often enough; it will be a shame if we lose her because of this incident. I hope she was of some help."

"She was, Mike, thanks; Debbie will be overjoyed when I give her this information."

As Tinny and Gary walked away from the fire station, Tinny rang Debbie to give her the information he had just received.

"This may not be as valuable as yours, but I am able to make and receive calls from it," said Tinny when he saw Gary, with one eyebrow raised, glance at the phone.

Gary endeavoured to look innocent. "I was just thinking it may be worth more than mine as a collector's item," he offered.

He now knew that he could make a joke like that with Tinny, something he had not expected to be able to do at the start of the previous day.

....

Caroline was on her own when the doctor entered the room.

"How's Neil?"

"We've just taken him out of the coma and he's still with us."

"Oh, thank God," breathed Caroline. "When can I see him?"

"Hopefully soon." The doctor sat down, as he considered how best to prepare Caroline for what she would have to face; it would not be easy.

"Firstly, Mrs Hughes, I need you to understand a number of things concerning your husband before you go in and see him."

Caroline's heart sank. "Is he going to live?"

"Well, your husband's still not out of the woods yet, and I'm always reluctant to give family members false hope; however, the fact that he's still with us is remarkable. I can only say that I believe he'll survive, and the information I'm going to give you is based on that belief." The doctor paused for a moment, then continued. "Mrs Hughes......"

"I'd much prefer Caz, Mrs Hughes always makes me feel old."

"Of course," the doctor smiled. "Well, Caz, I should explain that the induced coma undoubtedly saved Neil's life. Unfortunately, however, there are some after effects of being in an induced coma; when Neil is able to speak it will sound like he's drunk, as his speech will be slurred."

Caroline laughed nervously. "That'll be a first, Neil's never been drunk in his life!"

"Yes, I gather your husband doesn't drink or smoke; that, and his being in excellent physical shape, have played a big part in his survival. However, I believe what has really pulled him through is his strong will to live.”

“Yes, that sounds like Neil.” Caroline hesitated, as she was afraid of the answer to her next question. “Doctor……….we were told by other members of your staff, and the police, that Neil’s head injuries were severe. Is there likely to be brain damage?”

The doctor shook his head. “I can say now, categorically, there’s definitely no damage to his brain; but there is, I’m afraid, a great deal of damage to his face.” The doctor paused, as he allowed Caroline to take this in. “I know you’ve been asking to see Neil, but the room he was in needed to be absolutely sterile. When you go in to see him you’ll find his head and face are completely bandaged.” Caroline nodded silently.

“There are some other things I need to make you aware of. I’ve informed the police they cannot, under any circumstances, question Neil. Naturally, I understand their desire to catch the people who did this to your husband. We all hope these people are caught, but any form of questioning would presently be too stressful for him. The priority for the police is to catch your husband’s attackers; my priority is not only to have saved his life, but to keep him alive.

“I also need you to understand that Neil may, temporarily, have no memory at all. With regard to the night of the attack specifically, however, he may never remember that for the rest of his life. We know a great deal of how the brain works, but there’s still an awful lot we don’t know; the brain will sometimes block the memory of a traumatic experience permanently.”

“I see,” said Caroline slowly; “how long will his normal memory loss last for?”

“Well, it can vary from patient to patient, but at some point Neil will regain his memory.” The doctor paused again. “I know this is a lot to have to take in, but I do need to prepare you for when you go in to see him. It won’t look or sound like Neil because of the bandages and the effect on his speech and, quite probably, he won’t know who you are. It’s best to avoid asking him anything, or even telling him anything, as he will simply get confused. ”

The doctor looked sympathetically at Caroline’s stricken expression.

“I understand how upsetting this will be for you, but we all need to remind ourselves that he’s still with us. Please be patient; as every hour goes by, he’ll be getting stronger.”

“Yes, I know, doctor,” nodded Caroline, sadly. “I was just thinking...when my sons are here, they’ll want to go and see their dad as well; would it be better if we were only in there one at a time?”

“Yes, at the moment, it would; hopefully, as he gets stronger, he’ll be able to cope with more people in the room.”

The doctor stood up and smiled. “If I was a betting man (which actually I am, much to my wife’s annoyance!), when Neil was brought in yesterday morning, I would definitely have not put a bet on him surviving. While I must stress again that what I’ve told you is my belief, not a fact, I’d certainly have a few bob on him now.”

Caroline managed the ghost of a smile.

“That’s good to know………well, doctor, thanks for being so straight with me. I’ll tell my sons everything you’ve said, and I know we all want to thank you for everything you’ve done for Neil.”

…………………………………………………………

After the doctor left, it occurred to Caroline she had completely lost track of time. She suddenly realised that Neil had actually been brought in during the early hours of yesterday morning, and she was uncertain what time it was now. She was just about to go out for a cigarette, when Michael and Paul arrived.

Caroline explained the situation to the boys. “Hopefully, we may be able to go in and see your dad soon, but we can only go in one at a time.” She pushed the hair back from her face, and stood up wearily. “I’m just popping out for a smoke; I’ll only be five minutes.”

“Mum, can I just borrow your phone for a few minutes? The battery’s run out on mine,” said Michael.

Caroline handed her phone to Michael, then she and Paul went outside while Michael stayed in the family room, hoping it would not be too long before he could see his father.

....

As Caroline and Paul re-entered the room, Michael appeared to be confused.

"That was strange. I just rang that Graham Benton fella, and he said "Hi, Caz"; I mean, do I look like a Caz?"

Paul smirked. "You would if you grew your hair long and wore a frilly skirt."

"Oh," said Caroline "he rang just before you arrived, so he probably thought it was me ringing back. I'd given the police all our mobile numbers the night your dad was brought in; although I don't know why I bothered to give them yours," she continued, glancing at Paul, "you've never got your phone with you."

"I have sometimes."

"Yes - usually about three o'clock in the morning when you're stuck somewhere, and you need your dad to pick you up because you've got no money for a taxi," said Caroline, drily.

Paul looked over at Michael, shrugging, and said "It's only the truth!"

"That Superintendent sounded like a right slimeball," remarked Michael.

"You can't say that, you don't even know the man." Caroline folded her arms as she looked at Michael. "The Superintendent rang me because the doctor won't allow the police to question your dad under any circumstances, so he asked that, if your dad says anything to us concerning the attack, we should let him know straight away. That's why he gave me his mobile number, so even if he's not at the police headquarters, we could pass on any information immediately."

Michael looked chastened. "Sorry, mum; I just feel the police don't seem to be doing anything."

As Caroline looked away, Michael looked at Paul and mouthed "Slimeball!", which caused Paul to snort with laughter. Caroline fixed him with a glare.

"What are you laughing at?"

"I was just picturing our Mike with long hair and a frilly skirt."

Caroline's mouth started to twitch, then they all collapsed into laughter. It occurred to Caroline that this was the first time they had laughed since the night Neil had been attacked.

When they had all got themselves under control again, Caroline said "Anyway, Michael, what did you ring the police for?"

"I forgot to tell you, we bumped into Burnsy today, and told him what had happened to dad. He then mentioned to us that, when dad sold the taxi business, the bloke who bought it said that he'd been stitched up and would get even; mind you, Burnsy did say it was a bit of a long shot."

Caroline frowned. "That was about ten years ago when your dad sold the taxi business. It seems unlikely someone would hold a grudge for that long; anyway, that fella wasn't stitched up at all, he just made a mess of it."

"That's exactly what Burnsy said; so, I asked him if I could pass his mobile phone number to the police, and he said that was fine."

Caroline raised her eyebrows. "That does surprise me. Years ago, Burnsy used to do quite a bit of ducking and diving, and was never quite fond of the police. What did Superintendent Benton say when you rang him?"

"He said he'd pass the information to one of his team, and it would be acted on immediately. Maybe Burnsy's right, and it is a bit of a long shot, but at least it's something."

"Exactly – you did the right thing by passing it on, and obviously the Superintendent thinks so as well."

They heard footsteps coming down the corridor. The door opened, and in walked a smiling doctor.

"Mrs.......sorry, Caz, you can go in and see Neil now. Unfortunately, as he's still very weak, you will not be able to spend much time with him."

Caroline nodded. "I realise Neil may or may not be able to speak to me, and that I shouldn't say too much to him; but am I at least able to hold his hand?"

"Of course, absolutely," said the doctor.

....

While Caroline was sitting with Neil, he mumbled something, but she could not make out what it was he said. At one point, Neil appeared to squeeze her hand gently; she was elated, but then the tears came.

After all three had been in to sit with Neil, they went back to the family room to find Jill Rathbone and Mark waiting for them. Caroline and Jill instinctively hugged each other.

"So Jill, how come you're not in uniform?"

"We're actually off duty at the moment, so we thought we'd come over to see how you were doing."

Caroline smiled. "That's really nice of you, I'm a lot happier now than I was the night before last."

"Well, it was actually Mark's idea, he's just a big softy." As Jill said this, Mark smiled and looked slightly embarrassed. Paul glanced at Mark; looks pretty hard to me, he thought.

"You should go home mum, and get some sleep," said Michael. "Paul and I will be here through the night in case anything changes."

"I'm okay, I've had the chance to have a doze from time to time."

"Michael's right, you've been here nearly forty-eight hours," said Jill firmly. "Mark and I can run you home. You get some rest, then tomorrow you can drive back over in your own car."

Caroline nodded wearily. "Yes, I suppose you're right." She turned to Michael and Paul. "But you must ring me if anything changes, no matter what time it is." She hugged both of the boys and smiled.

"Don't worry mum, dad's going to be okay," said Michael.

As she was leaving, Caroline suddenly stopped.

"Mike, how can you ring me if your battery's flat?"

Michael smiled. "Chill out mum, I left it in the van charging up, so it'll be fully charged now."

…………………………………………………………

Superintendent Benton entered the briefing room.

"The most up to date reports we have from the hospital are that the victim will probably survive. Unfortunately, he's still too weak for us to interview him but, as he's completely lost his memory, it would be a pointless exercise anyway. Obviously, although this is still a major incident, the size of this team will be scaled down, as we're now looking at an attempted murder enquiry rather than murder."

Benton turned to D.S. Lloyd. "Dave, where are you up to with the financial investigations?"

"Nothing so far, sir, regarding recent activity, but there was a large sum paid into the victim's bank account ten years ago, so I'm still digging."

Benton nodded, and looked around at everyone in the room. "Anything from your informants as far as drug supply is concerned?" This question was met with silence.

He then turned to Tinny. "D.S. Smith, what about the mistaken identity line of enquiry?"

"Nothing, sir; we've been around a number of nearby authorities as well, but….."

Benton cut straight across Tinny while he was still speaking, and said "Paula, any more information regarding the CCTV footage?"

"The images we have are slightly better, but we can only say that the two people who got into the victim's cab were probably male, judging from their height. Unfortunately, they both had hoods up and their backs to the camera, so we're unable to see their faces."

"Right," said Benton. He glanced again around all the other officers. "D.I. Eriksson will discuss any further lines of enquiry, and will inform you who is staying on the investigation." He then left the briefing room.

…………………………………………………………

Michael and Paul had decided to take it in turns to sit with their father while the other had a sleep in the family room. Despite the fact that, when Neil spoke, it was difficult to understand what he was saying, they both felt his speech was certainly becoming clearer; however, it was obvious he was confused as to where he was, who he was, and who they were.

While they were both in the corridor outside the family room, they heard a voice behind them.

"Alright, Mike?"

Michael turned; it was an old school friend of his.

"Alright Rob, I'd forgotten you worked here."

"I'd heard there was a Neil Hughes in here, but hadn't realised it was your dad. How's he doing?"

Michael explained the situation to Rob. He was surprised when Rob began to say "He's lucky to be here now," but before Rob could finish his sentence, Michael sensed the movement from Paul.

"I'd re-word that quickly if I were you Rob; our Paul tends to punch first and ask questions later."

Rob held up his hand.

"Sorry lads, that didn't come out the way I meant it. What I meant was that, currently, we have the best plastic surgeon in the world working at this hospital. The reason I said that your dad is lucky to be here now, is because this surgeon is going to America soon. I'm going outside for a ciggy, so if you come with us, I'll explain the situation more clearly; and hopefully, not get a smack in the mouth from a lad I used to look down on."

At this point, Paul just smiled sheepishly. "Sorry Rob, I can be a bit of a nark sometimes."

Michael raised his eyebrows as he looked at his brother.

"Sometimes?" He shook his head.

…………………………………………………………………..

While they were outside, Rob continued to tell them more.

"This plastic surgeon has more letters after his name than in his name; he's world famous in the specific field of maxillofacial surgery……..."

"Hold on Rob, you're forgetting I'm a joiner, and know nothing about any type of plastic surgery," said Michael quickly.

"Of course, sorry. I mean, his field is specifically head and facial injuries, such as your dad received. During the time I've been working here, I've seen some horrendous facial injuries that this particular plastic surgeon had done an incredible job to correct. Tell you what, at some point today, I'll drop the latest medical journal into the family room; the journal contains all the information you'll need about Dr. James Braithwaite. One thing you can be sure of, whatever he's able to do regarding your dad's injuries, there's no-one in the world who could do a better job."

Rob glanced at his watch.

"Right, I've got to get back; I'll see you around."

………………………………………………………………

As Rob walked back in through the main door, something else caught Michael's attention.

"Clock these two fellas walking across the car park."

Paul looked over in the direction Michael indicated. "Wouldn't fancy meeting them on a dark night," he remarked.

The brothers started to feel uneasy, as the two men appeared to be walking directly towards them. As they got nearer, Michael took a step forward to put himself between Paul and these two very dangerous looking men; they were both bigger than Michael, and were extremely muscular. As they came nearer, one of the two men spoke.

"It's Michael and Paul, isn't it?"

"Who's asking?" said Paul, sharply.

The slightly smaller, but much broader, of the two men smiled.

"I'm Dean, and this is Jonjo; we're mates of your dad's," he said, as he offered his hand. Both men shook hands with Michael and Paul; curiously, it was obvious that the men knew which brother was which.

Dean continued. "How's your dad doing?"

"He's still drifting in and out of consciousness, but he's certainly stronger now, and it looks like he's going to survive," replied Michael.

"Has he got any idea who attacked him?" asked Jonjo.

Michael turned to Jonjo. "He's completely lost his memory at the moment, but we hope he'll regain it as he gets stronger." He went on to explain what their father's injuries were, and what the hospital had done to keep him alive.

Dean nodded. "We don't want to give him any mither, so we'll come back and see him when he's up and about."

Michael then realised these men were from Manchester; he had worked there recently and had often heard the expression "mither" used.

The two men shook hands again with Michael and Paul.

"Just tell your dad Dean the Manc and Jonjo were asking after him, and we'll see him again," said Dean.

Michael studied him. "I could, but he won't know who I'm talking about. He's lost his memory of everything, not just the night of the attack."

"That's possibly caused by the induced coma but, in the circumstances, maybe it's not a bad thing," replied Dean.

As Dean and Jonjo walked away, when Michael was sure they were out of earshot, he turned to Paul.

"'Who's asking?' What the hell was that about?"

"I know, I know, I could have bitten my own tongue off as soon as I'd said it."

Michael sighed, exasperated. "I've got a couple of calls to make, so do you want to check on dad and I'll meet you in the family room?"

....

As Michael was ringing Burnsy, Paul went back into the hospital, and went straight to see how his father was doing. Paul spent some time with him, then went back to the family room. He was surprised to find that Michael was not there. He was just about to go out and see where Michael was when the door opened, and in walked his brother.

"I was just about to come and find you, I wasn't expecting you to be this long."

"At teatime yesterday, that slimeball said they would be acting immediately on the information I gave them. That was obviously nonsense; Burnsy hasn't heard anything from them at all."

"So what's happening now?"

"I gave Burnsy the incident room number, and he rang them directly. He spoke to a woman there, and has arranged to call in to the police headquarters tomorrow afternoon to tell them what he knows."

"Maybe Burnsy's like me, and never has his phone on him."

"I asked him that; he said he's had his phone with him all the time, and there are no missed calls on it. The trouble is, I was so annoyed, I rang mum to tell her about the police not doing anything. Unfortunately she was still asleep so, when my call woke her up, she panicked when she saw it was from me."

Paul shook his head mockingly. "I just love it when you get something wrong, it gives me a break."

"Yes, well," said Michael ruefully, "it took me ages to calm her down. Eventually, I told her that me, you and dad were playing football in the corridor, which made her laugh, luckily. Needless to say, when I told her about the police not contacting Burnsy, she made excuses for them."

Michael looked at his watch. "I rang the police at about five o'clock yesterday afternoon, it's now nine in the morning, so they've had sixteen hours to contact Burnsy, and haven't bothered."

"Did you tell her what Rob said about the plastic surgeon?"

"She already knew about him from what the doctor had told her. I also asked her if dad had ever mentioned Dean the Manc or Jonjo, but she wasn't sure. As she said, dad's got mates everywhere, so it didn't surprise her that he has mates in Manchester."

Paul scratched his chin. "I had an idea about that. There's a nightclub dad does a lot of pick-ups from, and all the bouncers are from Manchester."

Michael nodded. "My first thought was that they were bouncers, but did you notice how they walked?"

"Yes; now you mention it, it looked more like they were marching rather than walking."

"That's what I thought. Another thing was that the broad fella, Dean, seemed to know something about induced comas, and they definitely weren't doctors."

"Hm. Well, when dad gets his memory back, he'll be able to tell us himself."

....

It was nearly midday when Caroline arrived at the hospital. She went to the family room first, but neither Michael or Paul were there, so she went to see if they were with Neil. Paul was in the room sitting by his father, while Michael was standing outside.

"How's your dad doing?"

"I think he's still a bit shattered from the football."

Caroline smiled. "I'm sorry I got in such a panic. I hadn't realised how tired I was, so I was still fast asleep when you rang."

"No, it should be me who's apologising. I should've waited till you came over before I moaned about the police."

"Well, as it happens, I stopped off at the police headquarters on my way over to see where they were up to with the investigation, but it proved to be a waste of time. I spoke to a Chief Superintendent, but he was no help at all. Apart from being a particularly unpleasant man, he didn't seem to be in any way sympathetic with what's happened to your dad."

Paul stepped out of the intensive care room, and gently closed the door behind him.

"Dad's asleep now, and from what Michael and I have discovered during the night, will probably be asleep for at least a couple of hours."

They stopped off at the coffee machine, then went into the family room.

"So," said Caroline, "other than the football, which must have taken a certain amount out of your dad, how's he doing?"

Michael and Paul took it in turns to tell Caroline how things had developed during the night. Both stressed they had not asked their father anything, and had only given him answers to any questions he asked.

Michael looked at his mother carefully. "I'm going to tell you something, but you've got to promise not to cry."

Caroline sighed. "I don't think I've any tears left in me now."

"Well........dad asked who the beautiful woman with the blonde hair was."

Caroline hung her head, and her shoulders began to shake.

Paul put his arm round her, and said "I think he was still a bit delirious at the time, but I'm sure that will pass."

Caroline nodded, both laughing and crying at once. The boys waited silently until her emotion subsided, then Michael spoke.

"I think I've come up with a plan, with regards to one of us always being here."

Caroline waved her hand dismissively. "I can spend most of the time here, and just go home occasionally."

"Hold on mum, just hear me out," said Michael. "Paul and I have worked out a shift system. You can spend all day at the hospital, but you won't have to drive in the dark, which we all know you hate doing."

"Do I get a say in this shift system plan?"

"No," said both her sons at once.

"This is how it'll work," continued Michael. " I'll be over late afternoon into early evening to take over from you, then Paul will come over about midnight, and will be here till you come over in the morning."

"Of course, we'll be having a clocking-in machine fitted, and you'll be issued with a card;

there'll be no slacking," said Paul.

As they were all laughing, Rob came in to the room.

"Hello, Mrs Hughes."

Caroline smiled. "I think you're old enough to call me Caz now."

"Okay," said Rob, returning the smile. "Anyway, Caz, have a look at this – it's the medical journal which tells you all about Dr. Braithwaite."

As Caroline was reading it, Rob turned to Michael and Paul.

"Everybody's buzzin' over your dad."

"How do you mean?" asked Michael.

"Well," continued Rob, "in far too many cases, people who are brought in here don't survive. Then someone has the unenviable task of telling their family. When your dad was brought in his chances looked pretty slim; to see him sitting up in bed and talking to you has lifted the spirits of everyone working here."

"Yes," remarked Paul, "I was talking to Dr. Hargraves before, and he mentioned he liked a little flutter from time to time. He said when dad was first brought in, he wouldn't have put a red cent on him living, but he'd put his shirt on him now."

Rob nodded enthusiastically. "He's a top man, not just as a surgeon, but as a sound bloke. Whether you're a nurse, porter, cleaner or whatever he doesn't look down his nose at anyone, and has the total respect of everyone who works here." He paused reflectively. "It really annoys me when I read or hear that the NHS is all about saving money. That might be true of these pen pushers at the top, but certainly isn't where the medical staff are concerned, those people really care."

"I can see that," said Michael. "When we were at school and you said you wanted to be a nurse, I thought it was a strange choice, but I understand now why it's such a passion to you."

Rob grinned. "I don't run the risk of hitting my thumb with a hammer either, which is a definite plus. Well, I'm off my break now, so I'll speak to you soon."

As Rob left the room, Michael glanced at his mother, who was still poring over the article in the medical journal.

"Does it say much about that plastic surgeon then, mum?" he asked.

"It's almost all about him; from reading this, it's obvious that what Dr. Hargraves told me, and what Rob told you, is no exaggeration."

"I believe he's off to California soon, though," said Paul. "Is he still going to be here to do anything with dad's injuries?"

"From what I can gather, he's actually already started treating your dad, and won't leave this hospital until he's completely satisfied with the work he's done. Dr. Hargraves said to me that when the plastic surgeon has finished, your dad's face will look quite different from the way it did before the attack. But as I said to him, I don't care what he looks like, I'm just glad he's still with us." She looked fondly at the two boys. "You two should get home now and get some rest. Needless to say, I'll ring you if anything changes."

Michael nodded, and stood up. "I'll be back later this afternoon to take over, and I'll make sure that, when I drop Paul off, he puts his mobile phone in his pocket before he comes over later." He smiled at Paul. "Or I can staple it to his ear."

"Call me picky, but I think I prefer the phone in the pocket idea," said Paul.

…………………………………………………………

After the boys left, Caroline went down to see if Neil was awake and, as she entered the room, was pleased to see him sitting up and talking to Dr. Hargraves.

"Ah, here's Caz now, so I'll leave you two alone." As he passed Caroline, the doctor said quietly, "he's still very confused, so avoid anything that may cause any form of stress."

As Caroline sat down and held Neil's hand, she was determined to keep smiling, and not get emotional, for fear of upsetting him.

"I believe I'm Neil and you're Caz."

"That's absolutely right."

Caroline tried to convince herself that Neil calling her Caz did not matter, but in her heart she knew it did. She certainly was not going to correct him, but hoped that, when he got his memory back, he would call her Caroline again.

Throughout the day, Caroline would sit with Neil until he fell asleep; then she either got a cup of tea, or went outside for a cigarette. She realised Michael's idea of a shift system actually made sense. She also discovered that, either sitting alone in the family room, or sitting quietly with Neil, was actually far more tiring than she would have imagined.

....

Caroline was outside having a cigarette when Michael arrived.

"How's dad?"

"He's still very weak, but his speech is much clearer now; unfortunately, he still has no memory at all. During the day, there are times I can't go in to see him because the plastic surgeon's with him."

"Well, I'll be here now till Paul arrives; he'll probably get here about midnight."

Caroline and Michael went back to the family room. She explained to him that, as well as having no memory of the attack or anything before the attack, Neil was obviously struggling with his short term memory, as he had asked her the same thing several times during the day. She mentioned this to Dr. Hargraves, who again told her that this was quite common, and would soon pass.

"So don't be too concerned if your dad asks you the same question, or if he forgets who he is, or who you are. Although his speech is better now, he's still very weak and is still easily confused. Make sure you pass this information on to Paul when he arrives."

Caroline got home just before it started to go dark. She was glad of this, because Michael was right, she hated driving in the dark. After she had tidied up the house, she had a shower, then lay on the bed and was soon asleep.

....

Michael was determined that, unless it was an absolute emergency, he would not ring his mother. When Paul arrived, Michael explained everything their mother had told him, and stressed that, if there was a problem, to ring him first.

Paul spent most of the night sitting with his father, even though Neil was asleep for a great deal of the time. When Caroline arrived the next morning, they both went into the family room, where Paul explained that his father had had a peaceful night, and there had been no problems at all.

....

At the same time that Paul and Caroline were having this conversation at the hospital, in Cheshire, the morning's briefing was just about to start.

Gary had expected to see that the major incident team would be reduced in numbers; however, he was surprised to observe that, when the door opened, it was not Detective Superintendent Benton entering the room.

"Morning; for those who don't know me, I'm Detective Chief Inspector Fred Davies, and I'll be the senior investigating officer from now on.

"Debbie's coming in soon, as she's now completed the forensic investigation and, hopefully, will be able to shed some light on what happened the night of the attack. I think most of us are aware when Debbie says she 'thinks' something, she knows it, and when she says 'possibly', she really means 'probably'. When Debbie's finished, I'll see where we are as far as our investigation is going. After speaking to D.S.I. Benton, it doesn't seem to be going very far."

Shortly afterwards, Debbie entered the briefing room, and immediately had the full attention of everyone, particularly Gary. She cleared her throat and began.

"After speaking to and working with the fire forensics team, as well as the paramedics and the hospital staff, this is what I believe happened.

"Neil Hughes was initially attacked elsewhere, and was then taken to the site where he was found. Unfortunately, I can only say that the first attack was within a two mile radius of the industrial site.

"I believe he was struck on the back of the head, probably from behind and, judging from the fragments in the wound and the shape of the wound, I would say the weapon was possibly a baseball bat. The severity of the blow would certainly have knocked him unconscious; I'm surprised it didn't kill him.

"He definitely wasn't transported in his cab, so someone else will have driven the taxi to the industrial site. I think the victim will have been taken there in another vehicle, possibly the back of a van, which will have had cement dust and brick fragments on its floor.

"At the site where he was found, he was obviously dragged out of the van, and beaten savagely by at least three assailants, all using baseball bats. I can also say for certain one of the assailants repeatedly stamped on the victim's head and face."

Tinny noticed a slight hint of emotion in Debbie's voice; this surprised him, as he had worked with her on numerous occasions, and had always been impressed with her scientific detachment. As Debbie carried on, he began to understand why this particular case had obviously upset her.

"The victim was then put into the driver's seat of the taxi, where he was tied in using the seatbelt, so he would not have been able to move. I think most of us have at some point travelled in a black cab and, as you probably know, there are five seats in the back of the cab: three at the back facing forward, and two drop down seats, one of which is immediately behind the driver.

"The seatbelt from that particular seat was fed through the perspex partition, and placed round the victim's neck. At this point, petrol was poured on the cab, and it was set on fire. The assailants must have been aware that Neil Hughes was still alive at that moment, but obviously assumed he couldn't possibly escape, so left the scene for him to burn to death.

"With the help of the fire forensics team, the following is guesswork, but it's the only way we think the victim could have escaped from the burning vehicle. He must have been conscious, or had regained consciousness, in order for this to work. I must say, at this point, he would have been in incredible pain, and the terror of finding yourself trapped in a burning vehicle doesn't bear thinking about.

"Fortunately, the ground on which the taxi was parked was slightly sloped, and the taxi was facing downhill. I did some tests on the driver's door, and found that it took very little effort to open the door from inside. As the door is so heavy, I believe the victim managed to open the door and, as he did so, the door will have flown open wide.

"What we think happened then, is that both seat belts burnt through, which effectively released the victim. He was then able (although how he found the strength to do this is incredible) to launch himself out of the cab and on to the floor, where he would have landed on his side, facing the front of the cab. Fortunately, the burns he received were superficial, but by escaping when he did, it certainly saved his life.

"This was a brutal, evil, cowardly attack by at least three men armed with baseball bats on a defenceless man. Whoever did this will certainly have been covered in blood, as will the vehicle they travelled in."

Debbie paused, her expression grim.

"I must say one last thing. We know the victim has completely lost his memory, which is probably a result of the induced coma. If I'm right on the sequence of events from that night, and I believe I am, I sincerely hope that when he does get his memory back, he never remembers the night of the attack for the rest of his life, even though it does hamper the investigation."

There was a subdued air in the room as she paused, and nods of agreement from some of the officers.

"I will now hand you back to D.C.I. Davies."

"Thanks Deb," said Davies. "I'm in full agreement with you, and hope Neil Hughes never remembers that night."

The D.C.I. then turned to Dave Lloyd. "Dave, I believe you've been looking into the victim's finances."

"Yes, boss. It was suggested that there may be a connection with drugs or the supply of drugs; we've all spoken to our informants, and found there's no connection whatsoever."

It seemed to Gary that Dave's tone of voice was almost defiant, although Gary did not feel it was aimed at the D.C.I. Dave Lloyd continued.

"As far as the villa in Spain is concerned, Neil Hughes acquired that through hard graft. Twelve years ago, he took over a small taxi company, and built it in to a very successful one. He then sold it two years later for a substantial amount. He used the money from the sale of the taxi business to improve his home.

"Two years ago, because his house is worth a lot more than what he owes on his mortgage, he was able to remortgage his house, and buy the villa in Spain. He bought the villa off-plan and, therefore, now has a villa worth considerably more than what he paid for it.

"Not only is Neil Hughes a good worker, he's obviously a good businessman as well. To put things into perspective, this fella doesn't drink, doesn't smoke, and doesn't gamble; what he does do is work all the hours God sends, in order to make a better future for himself and his family."

D.C.I. Davies simply nodded, and said "Good".

Gary wondered whether the D.C.I.'s response was for Dave's work, or the fact that Neil Hughes had acquired the villa through perfectly legitimate means; he suspected it was the latter. Gary also noticed, out of the corner of his eye, that Tinny was nodding; this made Gary realise that, once again, Tinny's instincts were correct.

D.C.I. Davies continued. "Paula, I believe the CCTV images don't give us much on the identity of Neil Hughes' last fare. Leave that with me, I've got an idea how we may be able to get round that." He then turned to Tinny. "Tinny, at the end of this briefing, if you and I can have a quick word." Tinny nodded.

The D.C.I. then prepared to address all the officers in the room; Gary noticed that he commanded their full attention, as soon as he began to speak.

"Yesterday afternoon, I spoke to all the emergency services involved in this case, and it struck me that a mixture of good fortune and good judgement proved to be vital.

"In the first instance, it was lucky that a passing motorist dialled 999 and reported the fire, and from what the crew tell me, the taxi had not been on fire long. On that particular site, there have been a number of vehicles burnt out that have not been reported at all. It was good judgement on the part of the fire crew to go directly to the correct place, even though the report was vague.

"One of the crew literally stumbled over Neil Hughes, so the paramedics were alerted quickly and, fortunately, were quite close to the scene when they got the call. The ambulance driver made what proved to be a life saving decision by taking the victim to the hospital he could get to quickest, which, in turn, was a lot nearer to the Liverpool hospital, the place where the victim needed to be.

"Luckily, Mike Bates was on duty that night. For those of you who don't know Mike, to give you an idea of his driving ability, the best pursuit officer we have in our traffic division would be the first to admit that Mike Bates is a different league. Mike was able to get the victim to Liverpool quicker than anyone else could.

"It strikes me, therefore, that when you consider this sequence of events, somebody up there did not want Neil Hughes to die."

D.C.I. Davies paused for a moment.

"Let's get the scum who did!"

Chapter 3

Gary looked round the briefing room, and could feel the difference in the attitude of his colleagues; there was no laughing or fooling around. The D.C.I. had made his impression.

"Are there any comments before we press on with this investigation?"

Gary was about to raise his arm, then glanced at Tinny first; he proceeded when Tinny nodded.

D.C.I. Davies looked over at Gary. "D.C. Ward, the floor is yours."

Gary's mind was racing, and that introduction made him feel even more nervous.

"Sir," he began, "from the evidence we have, the last sighting of Neil Hughes picking up on the town rank suggests that that must have been his last job."

D.C.I. Davies nodded. "Carry on."

"Judging from the time he left the town rank and the time the Fire Brigade got the call, that job he did must have stayed local, and he wouldn't have had time to do another one."

The D.C.I. smiled encouragingly. "Keep going Gary, I'm still with you."

"Although we can't pinpoint where the first attack took place, surely we can say where it definitely didn't. Obviously, we can discount any areas which have CCTV in place." Gary paused. "Debbie, as the first head wound was so severe, is it likely that the assailants would have taken a large detour in order to get to the industrial site?"

"Definitely not," replied Debbie. "From the blood loss at the scene where the victim was found, whoever did this must have taken the most direct route."

Gary nodded. "In that case, we can also discount any areas which don't have CCTV; but, by taking the most direct route, in order to get from those places to the industrial site, the assailants would have to drive through areas that are covered by CCTV." Out of the corner of his eye, he noticed Tinny smiling and nodding slightly. "In that case, by using a map of the area covering a two mile radius from where the victim was found, we'll be able to blank out a substantial amount and, hopefully, subject to any further leads or information, may be able to pinpoint where the first attack took place."

D.C.I. Davies looked at Gary appraisingly.

"I believe you picked up the nickname 'Morse?'"

Gary's heart sank; "Sir," he acknowledged, in a subdued tone.

D.C.I. Davies smiled. "Well, I can see why. Well done, Gary." He turned to Paula. "We can do what D.C. Ward suggests, can't we?"

"Absolutely, boss," replied Paula, beaming at Gary.

"Excellent," said the D.C.I. "Now, Tinny, could we have that quick word I mentioned before?"

....

When the D.C.I. and Tinny went into a side office, D.C.I. Davies closed the door behind them.

"Right then, Ron," began the D.C.I., "there's a Stephen Burns coming in this afternoon with some information regarding the case. It could be something and nothing but, as we have very little to go on so far, if you could have a chat with him and see what you think?"

"No problem, boss."

"First of all this morning, though, you could do me a big favour. I know you've got a couple of mates on the cabs; any chance you can speak to them?"

"Absolutely. I haven't seen Jacko for some time."

"Cheers, Ron; we desperately need these fellas on our side. The CCTV images of those two hoodies are useless, unless any of the taxi drivers can give us either names, or a destination, for what could prove to be Neil Hughes' attackers. Ask Paula to print up some pictures, and take them with you."

Tinny smiled. "I'll take Gary with me as well; Jacko will frighten the living daylights out of him."

"Indeed," nodded the D.C.I. thoughtfully. "Look, Ron, I know you must've felt you were stitched up but, realistically, Gary Ward will learn more from you than anyone else. I'm of a similar opinion to you as far as this fast track business is concerned; but then, you and I are old school and, whether we like it or not, this is the future."

Tinny shrugged. "To be fair, the lad's keen; he thinks, and is certainly heading in the right direction. As you saw in the briefing before, he's not lacking in confidence either, which is no bad thing. I know what he suggested you would have done anyway, but it shows he's intelligent. Naturally, he's making mistakes, but he's learning from them."

Fred Davies smiled ruefully. "Well, let's just hope that we've both retired before we have to start calling him 'sir'."

As Tinny got up to leave, the D.C.I. said "By the way, it's not important, but did D.S.I. Benton pass a mobile phone number to you a couple of days ago?"

Tinny frowned. "Definitely not, boss."

"That's okay, it doesn't matter anyway. Try your best with the taxi drivers, and let's get this investigation moving."

....

Tinny walked into the briefing room and gave Gary the thumbs up.

As they stepped out of the building and were walking across the car park, Gary turned enquiringly to Tinny.

"Sarge, is it usual to change the senior investigating officer during a case?"

"It's unusual, but not unheard of."

"Is it because the investigation has been scaled down from murder to attempted murder?"

"It's possible; at the end of the day, it's down to Chief Superintendent Turnbull. However, it wouldn't surprise me if D.S.I. Benton has come up with some feeble excuse to be taken off the case. You must have heard the disappointment in his voice when he announced the victim will probably survive."

Gary had to admit to himself that he had; but he began to feel slightly uncomfortable, and to regret asking the question, as Tinny continued.

"Realistically, this was looking like a high profile murder investigation which you and I may have solved but, undoubtedly, Benton would have claimed credit for. It's now moved to a low profile attempted murder investigation which you and I may still solve; the difference is that, where Fred Davies is concerned, I can guarantee we would get the credit."

Gary was now feeling even more uncomfortable, as he knew which way the conversation was going.

"Anyway, you're well aware of my opinions regarding D.S.I. Benton, I believe." Tinny glanced at Gary, a sly expression on his face. "You don't need years of experience as a detective to know that, when someone goes into a toilet before you, and doesn't come out, that they are still in there."

Gary was now almost squirming, and was trying to look everywhere other than at Tinny.

"As Dave and I were walking out, I was tempted to shout "you can come out now, Morse"; but I felt you'd suffered enough from the bucket incident, so I resisted the temptation."

Gary took a deep breath.

"Look, Sarge, I have to say this. I haven't particularly enjoyed the last two years. The fact that I'm well spoken, and from a wealthy background, seems to make some people feel that I don't deserve to be a policeman; but I tolerated the jokes and snide comments, in the knowledge I would get the opportunity to work as a detective." Gary paused, shaking his head. "Then on my first morning as a detective, it couldn't have been any worse; so I'm glad you didn't say anything, because that would have been the last straw - you would now be looking at a printer in a Porsche."

"Well then, I'm so glad I kept quiet," smiled Tinny. "Anyway," he continued, bringing his hand down on Gary's shoulder, "have you got your riot gear handy?"

Gary raised his eyebrows. "It's in my locker, Sarge."

"There's no time to get it now, we'll just have to take a chance."

"A chance on what, Sarge?"

"We're going to speak to some taxi drivers."

…………………………………………………………

Tinny and Gary were sitting by the taxi rank for some time as taxi drivers were coming and going; then, as one taxi pulled up, Tinny said "Let's talk to this one here; I bet he was probably one of the drivers who was unpleasant to Dave the other day."

As they walked towards the taxi, the driver stepped out of his cab, but did not observe Tinny and Gary approaching him. He was well over six feet tall, had a shaved head and was covered in tattoos on both arms. His biceps are probably bigger than my thighs, thought Gary.

As they got nearer, Tinny called "Jacko!"

The big man turned and, much to Gary's amazement, his expression changed from a tough, angry expression to a large beaming smile.

"Tinny! Where've you been hiding? We haven't seen you down the club for ages."

Tinny shook hands with the driver; in response to Gary's quizzical look, he explained "Jacko and I used to play rugby together, and had the occasional glass of beer after the game." Jacko chuckled at this.

"Jacko, this is my mate, Detective Constable Gary Ward."

"Nice to meet you, Gary."

Gary was relieved that this frightening looking man felt it was nice to meet him, and that he still had all his fingers after shaking hands.

"I'm looking for a favour, Jacko," began Tinny. "We're not getting anywhere on the Neil Hughes case, and could do with any help you or any of the other drivers could give us."

"Yeah, how's Neil doing? I heard he nearly died."

"As far as I know, he's off the critical list now; but you're right, when he was taken into hospital, they thought there was very little chance of him surviving."

"Well, if I'd known you were involved in it, I would've made sure the lads had been more helpful the other day. The trouble was, they were all a bit wound up over Yosser getting attacked. He's a popular lad with all the drivers. When he had a radio in his cab, whenever there was any trouble, he'd always be there to back the driver up."

"I believe he didn't have a radio in his cab on the night of the attack?"

"That's right, he hasn't had one for some time. He just works the ranks - sometimes days, sometimes nights, sometimes both."

Tinny produced the CCTV pictures, and showed them to Jacko.

"Any idea who these two could be? We're pretty sure this was the last job Neil Hughes did before he was attacked."

Jacko scratched his head as he looked at the images.

"Was it Tuesday night when Yosser was attacked?"

"I think it was actually early hours Wednesday morning."

"Alright," said Jacko, "I'll find out who was working that night, and see if I can catch up with them so they can have a look at these pictures. I don't know who these two are, but I'll pass these round the drivers. If they're regular taxi users, someone will know who they are, or at least where they go."

"Great," said Tinny. "As far as you know, has Yosser got any enemies, or has he fallen out with anyone recently?"

"Not as far as I know; but what I'll do, I'll stay on later tonight, and speak to as many drivers as I can. By tomorrow night, I'll have definitely spoken to all the drivers, day drivers and night drivers." He tapped the CCTV picture with his finger. "You need to get these people before Yosser's sons do. Don't get me wrong - Michael and Paul are good lads, polite, well-mannered, they've been brought up properly by Neil and Caz, but you wouldn't want to cross them. *I* wouldn't want to cross them."

Jacko then smiled. "I've got to tell you this, because it was so funny.

"Michael and Paul were on the rank the other day, telling us about what had happened to their dad when a new cab driver, who nobody likes, poked his nose in. This fella has been in the job five minutes and thinks he knows it all, he's a bit of a bully - not with me or any of the other big lads obviously, but very full of his own opinion.

"As he walked over towards Michael and Paul, he was spouting how he thought Yosser was stupid not having a radio in, and was asking for trouble. But, he didn't get to finish the sentence, because Paul just stepped forward and sparked him straight out." Jacko paused. "Anyway," he continued, rubbing his chin, "the reason I'm telling you this is I wouldn't like to see Michael and Paul getting into trouble, even though we can both understand how they feel."

"Yeah," said Tinny, "if I was in hospital after being attacked, and someone called me stupid, I dread to think what my sons would do to them. Well, thanks for your time, Jacko; let me know if you find out anything which may help."

As they were walking back to the car, Tinny turned to Gary.

"By the way, we have a Stephen Burns coming into the headquarters this afternoon. It appears he may have some useful information."

"Is he a suspect, Sarge?"

"No, he's a friend of Neil Hughes from when Neil had his own taxi company. Apparently, when it was sold, the person who bought it felt Neil Hughes had in some way stitched him up; he made threats that he was going to get even."

Gary frowned. "But didn't Dave say it was sold ten years ago?"

"I know, it seems unlikely that this individual would wait ten years; but, realistically, we haven't got much else to go on at the moment. So it's definitely worth having a chat to Mr Burns, and then we can decide if it's a lead worth following up." Tinny grinned. "As it's Saturday, and I would very much like to watch the rugby on television this afternoon, hopefully it won't take too long."

....

Shortly after Tinny and Gary arrived back at the headquarters, Stephen Burns walked in, and spoke to the Sergeant on the front desk to tell him who he was and why he was there. He was taken to an interview room, where he was joined by Tinny and Gary.

As Tinny sat down, he introduced himself as Detective Sergeant Smith, and Gary as Detective Constable Ward.

"Mr Burns, may I call you Stephen, and do you mind if we record this conversation?"

Burnsy shifted uncomfortably in his chair. Here we go, he thought; all coppers are bastards.

"Just call me Burnsy. Only my mother calls me Stephen, and that's just to annoy me. As far as recording the conversation is concerned, I'd rather you didn't."

"That's fine. Amongst his many skills, my young colleague here is able to write shorthand, so he'll take notes, if that's okay with you."

Burnsy smiled warily. "Sounds good to me."

"Now," continued Tinny, "I believe you have some information regarding threats made to Neil Hughes when he sold his taxi business."

"First up, the threats were made behind Yosser's back, certainly not to him. If the bloke who bought the taxi office had made the threats to Yosser's face, he would have ended up on his back."

"Can you remember the name of the man who bought the taxi office from Neil Hughes?"

"Gareth Davies. He made a right mess of the business, then he tried to say he'd been stitched up by Yosser, and that at some point he'd get even. He was talking nonsense, that was a good taxi firm when he took it over, but he ruined it."

"Well," said Tinny, "I must be honest, Burnsy, and say I don't know much about the taxi business, as far as how it works with the money the drivers make, and how the taxi companies make their profit."

"Okay - do you use taxis yourself?"

"Yes, certainly. If the wife and I are going somewhere where we are both likely to have a drink, then I ring for a taxi. I get picked up, and at some point ask the driver if he's been busy." Burnsy smiled. "Then get dropped off, and pay the driver."

"No doubt with a substantial tip?"

Tinny raised his eyebrows, with a mischievous look in his eye. "Steady, you're talking to a Scotsman now."

Burnsy laughed, and relaxed a little. Maybe not all coppers are bastards after all, he thought.

"Well," he continued, "as drivers, our money comes from the amount of people we pick up. If we're sitting round doing nothing, we're not making any money. Drivers are self-employed, not on any sort of wage. The taxi company makes its money by charging the drivers for the use of the radio. It's usually a set figure, so the more vehicles a taxi company has, the more profitable it is."

"I see," said Tinny. "And what was Neil Hughes' taxi company called?"

Burnsy looked embarrassed. "It was called Cumfycars. Even Yosser didn't like the name, but that's what it was called when he took it over, so he stuck with it."

"So, at the point when Neil Hughes sold Cumfycars, was it profitable?"

"It was well profitable. We were absolutely bouncing, particularly on a Friday and Saturday night. There was even a time when a couple of lads didn't even have badges, but we had so much work to cover."

As Burnsy said this, Gary looked up and frowned slightly; me and my big mouth, thought Burnsy.

"Oh……don't get me wrong, they weren't driving illegally, they had the proper insurance, and the cars were plated and everything. It's just that, sometimes, the council could be a bit slow with the badge application."

Tinny immediately put his hand up in a defensive gesture.

"Burnsy, we are in no way concerned about a slight oversight concerning local government rules ten years ago." As he said this he glanced at Gary, who quickly looked back down at his shorthand notes.

"Well, anyway," continued Burnsy, "it was doing really well, and if I'd have been Neil, I would've asked for more."

"Then," mused Tinny, "it begs the question: why did Neil Hughes sell it if it was doing so well?"

"It was doing so well because Yosser was there practically night and day. If he wasn't driving, he was answering phones, or he was on the radio giving out work, as well as training operators for when he couldn't be there. Caz, Yosser's wife, used to come in sometimes with the boys and say 'here's your dad, you probably forgot what he looks like.' She was only joking, she hasn't got a nasty bone in her body, but to be fair it was taking a lot out of him and so, looking back, I don't blame him selling it." Burnsy paused for a moment. "It was funny the other day when Michael and Paul approached me, because I didn't recognise them; I hadn't seen them since they were little lads at primary school. They're not little lads now. Michael must be six foot tall, and Paul's not far behind him. As I'm only about five foot six, overweight, and the wrong side of fifty, when they said "it's Burnsy isn't it?", I said "it depends whether you're friends or enemies." He chuckled.

"So what went wrong after Gareth Davies took over the company?"

Burnsy sighed. "In a word, everything. That Davies fella thought he knew everything about taxiing when, in actual fact, he knew nothing. I've been at this game a long time, and could see what was happening as soon as he took it over. We'd built up a good reputation for being very reliable. Straight away, good regular customers were being let down because he was taking work on that we couldn't do. On top of that, he was creaming off the good jobs for himself, and the drivers were only getting the short, round the corner jobs. I was probably the first driver to leave, but I know shortly after me, a few other drivers left as well. So in a relatively short time, Cumfycars went from making a good profit to making a loss. That's when Davies was trying to tell people he'd been stitched up."

"So how long did Gareth Davies carry on trading for?"

"I'm not sure, but I think the firm folded within six months of him buying it."

"Have you any idea where Gareth Davies is now?"

"Haven't got a clue. The lads asked me that the other day, but I didn't know, so I went to the solicitor Neil used, and got one of his business cards to pass on to you. The solicitor may have an idea where you can track Davies down." Burnsy produced a card from his pocket, and handed it to Tinny.

"Cheers for that, Burnsy, that could save us some time." Tinny took the card. "Well, unless there's anything else that you can tell us, I think that's about it."

Burnsy made a supplicating gesture. "Do us a favour, don't tell Yosser about the badge business. He was dead strict on that sort of thing, and even after this long, he'd still be annoyed if he found out."

Tinny affected a vacant look. "I don't remember badges being mentioned in this conversation. Gary, is there anything in your notes there about badges?"

Gary glanced down at this notebook. "There's nothing about badges in these notes, Sarge." Burnsy stood up, looking relieved.

"You're a gent. If I hear anything at all that's of any use, I'll let you know straight away. Who do I ask for?"

"Just ask for Tinny Smith."

....

It was now early afternoon on the Saturday, when D.C.I. Davies announced to everyone in the briefing room that they did not need to come in on Sunday. Tinny was pleased at this announcement, as he would be able to spend some time with his grandchildren; some of the younger officers, however, were disappointed at missing out on the overtime.

....

Caroline had spent the day similar to the previous one, sitting with Neil while he was awake, then taking a short break when he fell asleep. As it was Saturday, some other family and friends had visited, but were not allowed in to see him, as it was felt that he was still too frail; the problem with his short-term memory seemed to be improving, but he still remembered nothing from before the attack.

When Michael arrived, Caroline was sitting with Neil just holding his hand, although Neil was asleep. When she saw Michael, she gently released Neil's hand, and came out of the room, closing the door quietly behind her.

"Alright, mum," said Michael. "Any change from yesterday?"

"Not really; he still can't remember anything from before the attack. Still, the plastic surgeon seems very pleased with the work he's been able to do, so far, in reconstructing your dad's face."

Michael grimaced slightly. "Have you been there when they take the bandages off?"

"No; Dr. Braithwaite said 'never let a fool or a woman see a job before it's finished!' A bit sexist, maybe - although he was smiling when he said it."

"Well, if plastic surgery is anything like joinery work, I totally agree with him."

"You're not too big for me to turn you over my knee," remarked Caroline.

Michael smiled. "Yes I am."

....

They went for a cup of tea in the family room before she went home; as she was leaving, Caroline again reminded Michael to make sure he and Paul would ring her if anything happened. Michael spent the evening, either sitting with his father or sitting alone in the family room; when Paul arrived, Michael updated him on the situation, and said he would see him tomorrow night. As Michael left, Paul went down and sat with Neil.

....

Caroline set off for the hospital on the Sunday morning feeling quite relaxed, as she did not have to contend with the peak hour traffic. As well as not particularly enjoying driving in the dark, she also hated driving when the roads were very busy. When she arrived at the hospital, she was pleased to see the car park had plenty of spaces available.

She went straight to see Neil, and was surprised that Paul was not with him. She could see Neil was asleep, and he looked so peaceful that she did not want to disturb him. As she walked into the family room, she was shocked to see Paul had clearly been crying.

"Paul, what's happened?"

"It's okay, Dad's fine; but something happened last night. I'll explain, if you let me tell you the whole story."

"What do you mean, something happened?"

"I'll say again, it's important that you listen to everything I'm about to say, and not panic when you hear what the problem was."

Caroline smiled to herself, because this was exactly how Neil would handle something if ever there was any sort of emergency. She sat down next to Paul.

"Okay, I promise not to panic." She waited expectantly.

Paul paused to collect himself, and then turned to face his mother.

"The first thing I need to say is that dad is absolutely fine, and is probably stronger now than when you left at teatime yesterday." He paused again as he studied Caroline's face, then continued. "When this happened, I'm not sure what time it was, because I tend to sit with dad all night and I lose track of time; but at some point, in the early hours, dad's heart stopped."

Caroline gasped as she jumped up, and was about to say something when Paul said "Please, let me finish, please."

She stood there for a moment looking at him, visibly shaking; then she slowly sat down again, trying not to cry by holding her hand over her mouth. Paul waited for a moment, then continued.

"I called for a crash team, who got there immediately, and they got dad's heart beating again straight away. I was able to explain to Dr. Hargraves what had happened leading up to dad's heart stopping, so they've changed his medication, and it can't possibly happen again. I promise," he stressed, "it will not happen again."

Caroline's own heart was thumping, as she tried to take this in. "How long ago did this happen?"

"I'm not sure, but I think about five hours ago."

Caroline closed her eyes, taking deep breaths, and eventually the feeling of panic began to subside; but then the panic turned to anger.

"*Why* didn't you ring me? Don't tell me you forgot your phone again?"

"I'm sorry, mum. I did remember my phone, but I forgot to put it on charge when I got home yesterday, so the battery was flat."

"Then why didn't you use one of the pay-phones in the hospital?"

"I haven't got a clue what your mobile number is, and I'm not even sure what our home number is because, remember, the other week, dad changed the home number because he was fed up with people ringing and trying to sell him something."

Paul looked so crestfallen, that Caroline's anger evaporated.

"So," she said, "you've been sitting on your own since it happened, and you look like you've only just stopped crying."

"Not exactly," said Paul; "I only started crying about ten minutes ago."

"Oh," said Caroline, "I see." She looked at Paul affectionately. "Want to talk about it?"

Paul shrugged awkwardly, as if uncertain how to put his feelings into words.

"Well, I sat and thought about what had happened, and I got upset. I love dad; it was only when his heart stopped I realised how much I loved him. This is difficult to describe, but the only thing I could think was that I was willing him to live. At that point, I would have gladly changed places with him. If there was a way where he would live and I would die, I would have done that in a split second. I know that sounds daft, but it's the only way I can describe how I felt."

Caroline smiled, put her arm around his shoulders and hugged him.

"It doesn't sound daft at all. I don't know how it must feel, because I've never been in a situation like that; but your dad has. I'm going to tell you something now which I always knew I would when the time was right. I've always felt guilty over what I'm about to tell you, because you almost died as a result of my selfishness and stupidity."

Paul looked at his mother wonderingly, as she explained.

"When Michael was born, there were a lot of problems with the birth. I was strongly advised then that it would be dangerous to me, and to the unborn baby, if I were to get pregnant again. The trouble was, I was desperate to have a daughter. It was something I had dreamed of from when I was a young girl.

"I hadn't told your dad what the hospital had told me about the risks, so when I became pregnant with you, he was really pleased, and hoped for my sake it was going to be a little girl. Throughout the pregnancy I had no problems at all and so, stupidly, I thought I'd made the right decision.

"Your dad was with me in the hospital when I was about to have you. It was early hours of the morning when I arrived; I was in a great deal of pain, and it was getting worse. They had injected me with something which eased the pain, and I was being given gas and air which has a similar effect to being drunk, so at the moment you were born, I wasn't really aware of what was going on; your dad told me afterwards what happened.

"When you were born you weren't breathing, and when they picked you up and smacked your bottom, it had no effect. I remember saying to your dad that I couldn't hear you crying, but he convinced me you were, and that there was no problem. Apparently, one of the midwives left the room quickly and returned with a doctor, who she'd obviously just got out of bed. Your dad explained later that he was wearing jeans and a jumper, and nothing on his feet.

"Your dad told me the first thing the doctor did was to put two tubes down your throat: one for putting oxygen into your lungs, the other for removing anything that could be hampering your breathing. Next, the doctor put you on a small metal plate, which your dad always assumed sent a mild electric shock through your body. This worked because, when the doctor lifted you up and smacked your bottom, you let out a loud cry.

"I heard that cry, and it put my mind at rest. Your dad just smiled and said 'see, I told you everything was okay.' Later, when I was stronger, your dad explained everything that had really happened. He told me it seemed like a lifetime between the midwife leaving the room, and coming back with the doctor; and it was then your dad said he was willing you to live, and would gladly have swapped places with you."

Mother and son were silent for a short while. It was Paul who spoke first.

"Well, I'm glad you decided to have another baby, otherwise I wouldn't be here now." He thought about the events of a few hours ago. "You know," he said, "maybe, dad willing *me* to live helped with my survival and me willing *him* to live helped with his."

"Yes," said Caroline, reflectively; "funny how things work out in life."

Paul glanced sideways at his mother.

"I'm also glad that you didn't put me in frilly white dresses – you didn't, did you?"

Caroline laughed. "No, I didn't; they were frilly *pink* dresses, but you did look very pretty in them."

"Naturally," agreed Paul, grinning.

He stood up and stretched.

"Anyway," he asked, "what time is it now?"

"Just after nine o'clock - why?"

"Dr. Hargraves should be down with dad at the moment; he said he'd be checking every hour on the hour."

"I'll go down and speak to him. Are you coming as well?"

"Definitely not; it's bad enough you seeing I'd been crying, I certainly don't want anyone else to see me like this. I have a certain reputation to uphold."

....

As Caroline was walking down the corridor, Dr. Hargraves was just coming out of the room after checking on Neil; he immediately smiled when he saw her approaching.

"Ah, hello Caz," he greeted. "Neil's fine, but he's fast asleep at the moment, so it would be better not to disturb him."

Caroline decided to come straight to the point.

"Dr. Hargraves, what caused Neil's heart to stop?"

"Of course, I'll explain everything; but first, if I may, I would like to ask you a question. How old is Paul?"

"He's seventeen; why?"

"Because, in my opinion, he's a very remarkable young man. Paul was in the room alone when Neil's heart stopped. There was a member of staff nearby who later described to me Paul's actions. Paul stood up, opened the door, shouted "crash team", then stood back out of the way as the crash team came through.

"When I arrived, he was able to describe to me precisely what led up to Neil's heart stopping; as a result, I was able to decide which medication to use in order to stop it happening again. I've been checking on Neil each hour for the last five hours, and now know it was the correct medication to use. For Paul to be able to stay so calm in such a situation is, in my opinion, truly remarkable.

"But now, to answer your question: I believe Neil had a dream, or rather a nightmare, relating to the events from the night of his attack. Although the brain frequently blanks out traumatic experiences, unfortunately, there's no guarantee that the memories won't resurface. At the point when I believe Neil had a flashback, his body was too weak to take the shock, and so his heart stopped. I regret that there's no way to control such flashbacks, so it may happen again but, if it does, Neil's heart won't be affected by it."

Caroline looked subdued. "So, if the nightmares persist, will Neil have to stay on this medication for ever?"

"Definitely not," replied the doctor. "He will be off this medication within the next forty-eight hours, because by that time, his own constitution will be strong enough to withstand the shock. Neil's powers of recovery for a man of his age have been incredible. In the early stages, I didn't think he would survive; after forty-eight hours I felt there was a chance he would survive. I can now say, absolutely, at some point you will be taking Neil home."

Caroline related the story of Paul's birth, and Paul's belief that he had willed his father to live, in the same way as Neil had willed him to live when was born.

"Yes, it makes you think," said the doctor. "Naturally, I'm a man of science; but I also believe that we know very little about the strength of the human spirit. From what I've observed, though, one thing is for sure; Paul is very much his father's son."

....

Caroline walked back into the family room and, instinctively, hugged Paul again.

"The doctor was just telling me how calm you remained; if it was me or Michael, we would have panicked."

Paul kept a straight face. "Well, I did think about running up and down the corridor and jawing a few people, but didn't think it would be much help. I decided that staying calm may be the better option."

"You know, I was just thinking about your phone battery going flat; in some respects, that may have been a good thing after all."

"I know, I thought the same. Funny how something that can seem to be a disaster can prove to be a Godsend. Well, I'll shoot off now; I'll see you in the morning."

....

When Paul was well away from the main entrance to the hospital, he took his phone out of his pocket, and rang Michael.

"Mum will probably ring you soon. Act surprised when she tells you what happened."

....

Shortly after Paul had left, Caroline rang Michael and explained what had happened during the night.

"God Almighty – look, I'll come straight over................."

"No, no, there's no need, everything's fine now."

"So why didn't our Paul ring?"

"It wasn't his fault – he had his phone, but the battery had run out. It was just as well in a way, because he handled it much better than I would've done; your brother's got hidden depths, that's for sure."

"Well…………..as long as you're absolutely sure you're okay."

"Yes, I'm fine now, don't worry – I'll see you at teatime, as normal."

…………………………………………………………

Caroline went and sat with Neil, and waited for him to wake up. She decided not to tell him what happened during the night, after discussing it with the doctor; he considered that the stress on Neil would be too great. As Neil woke up, Caroline squeezed his hand gently.

"Morning, Caz. I know it's morning, because Paul explained the shift system to me."

Paul's right, he does seem stronger today, thought Caroline; she smiled, and nodded.

"You're right, it is morning, and you seem a lot better than when I left yesterday."

"I feel a lot better, and get the impression the doctor seems to be pleased with my progress."

"Definitely; he also said that, at some point, you'll be able to come home. Obviously, the plastic surgeon still has a lot of work to do, but I imagine it will be nice for you when they remove those bandages."

Neil was silent for a few moments, as if in thought.

"Caz," he said eventually, "this may seem like a strange question but, as I don't remember anything, I feel I have to ask. Before the attack…….would you describe me as handsome?"

"*I* would, definitely; I always thought you were handsome, from the night we met."

"Okay," said Neil uncertainly, "but perhaps I ought to put it another way. Would anyone *else* think I was handsome?"

Caroline blushed slightly. "Well…….not really, but you were never concerned about your looks."

"The reason I'm asking…………well, it's a reasonable assumption that I may be scarred or disfigured in some way. Would that bother you?"

"Absolutely not," said Caroline emphatically. "I love you as a person; it wouldn't matter to me what you looked like."

Neil appeared to ponder over this for a moment.

"You mentioned the night we met," he said. "I'd love to hear how we met, where we got married, and everything about our life." He hesitated again. "I know this may seem very strange to you, explaining to me our history together, but it may help me to regain my memory."

"I would love to tell you about our life together."

Caroline was overjoyed to get this opportunity of telling Neil all about their life. She told him everything, except the part about his always calling her 'Caroline'; she felt it might now embarrass him, as he had called her Caz so often. She asked him several times to stop her if he felt tired; although she was pleased to note that, whenever she did ask, Neil said that he was really enjoying the story, and hoped that, soon, he may be able to remember some of it himself.

Eventually, however, it was clear that he needed a rest; so, as he dozed off, Caroline left the room quietly, carefully closing the door behind her.

…………………………………………………………………

She went straight out of the hospital to have a cigarette, and was surprised to see Michael walking across from the car park.

"Michael! You're early."

"No I'm not; it's nearly five o'clock."

Caroline glanced at her watch.

"Well I never!" she declared, "I didn't realise it was that late; I've been talking to your dad all day, and lost track of time."

"Dad must be a lot stronger if you've been able to talk to him all day."

"Oh yes," said Caroline, "since the night your dad was brought in here, today has been the best day by a mile."

She explained about Neil being able to come home as soon as the plastic surgeon had finished, and how she had told Neil all about their life together. Although Neil still had no memory, Michael agreed with his mother that today represented a major step forward.

....

The day's events had obviously tired Neil out a great deal as, whenever Michael checked on him, he was fast asleep. When Paul arrived for the night shift, Michael was standing outside the main door to get a breath of fresh air.

"Everything okay?" asked Paul.

"Yes; dad's great, he's sleeping really well, but was strong enough today to talk to mum for most of the day." Michael shook his head. "I'm so glad you were here when his heart stopped and not me. I'd have panicked, rang mum, and instantly regretted it."

"I just felt it was the right thing to do in that situation. Mum driving over at that time of night, when she would obviously be upset, could've been dangerous. We could have ended up working a two shift system, visiting them both in here."

"You know, even though you'd already warned me what to expect before mum rang me, I still didn't have to try too hard to sound 'surprised', as you suggested, when she phoned. It knocked me for six, I can tell you," asserted Michael. "Good move, by the way, saying the battery had run out," he remarked.

"I know," grinned Paul. "If I'd said that I'd forgotten my phone, I may have been in a worse state than dad by the time mum would've finished with me. Anyway, realistically, even if mum had got here in one piece, there was nothing she could've done; so I thought it better for her to come over as normal, and explain the situation to her then."

Michael looked at his brother curiously.

"How do you do it? You go up like a bottle of pop over the most trivial thing, but when it's really important, you can stay so controlled."

Paul shrugged. "I don't know mate, I don't know."

"Anyway," said Michael, "I'll dive off now, and I'll see you tomorrow night. You might find dad will sleep right through, tonight."

As Michael left, Paul went straight down to his father and sat by his side, which was where he remained throughout the night.

....

Monday morning's briefing started with Paula displaying a map of the area showing the possible sites where the first attack may have taken place. Gary noticed something straight away, had a quick word with Tinny, then raised his arm.

"Paula, I notice that you have the Rockford estate as an area with CCTV coverage."

"Yes, there are cameras all over the estate."

"The cameras are there, but none of them work, as far as I know." Gary smiled ruefully. "When I was still in uniform, we were constantly on that estate trying to catch the people who were vandalising the CCTV cameras. First, it was youths on mountain bikes with their hoods up and faces masked, using catapults and ball bearings; the local authority had to keep sending out people to repair the glass, but the actual cameras weren't damaged. Next, someone started going round in a large van, and standing on the roof in order to spray the cameras with paint, but again, this problem was easily cured. Finally, however, someone drilled in to the cameras and destroyed the wiring. The local authority then said that they couldn't afford to repair this damage; in any case it would be wasting money, as no doubt the cameras would be damaged again."

Gary took out his mobile phone.

"To make absolutely sure, I'll just make a phone call to someone who can confirm that I'm right about them not working anymore."

As Gary started speaking on the phone, he smiled and winked at Tinny.

"Can you put me through to the department responsible for CCTV cameras in the area? This is Detective Constable Gary Ward." There was a slight pause. "Is that Miss Taylor? Sorry, *Mrs* Taylor, I should've remembered."

Gary turned to Tinny, and mouthed "She's older than Debbie." Tinny quickly put his hand over his mouth and turned away from Gary, so that his snort of laughter could not be heard by Mrs Taylor.

"That's right, Detective Constable now………….well let's hope so, I'll try my best. I'm currently involved in an investigation, and hope you may be able to help. It's regarding the CCTV cameras on the Rockford estate…..I thought so; I assume that was the case Tuesday night, early hours of Wednesday morning?...........Great, thanks very much, Mrs Taylor……thanks very much, Rachel. I hope to see you soon, bye."

Gary smiled as he looked over at Paula. "The cameras aren't working on any part of the estate, so we'll have to add it to the list of possible sites."

"Good work, Gary," said D.C.I. Davies. "Tinny, how did it go with Stephen Burns?"

"The man who made the threats concerning Neil Hughes has been found in the system, so we're going along to speak to him today."

"What sort of offences has he committed - do any of them involve violence?"

"No, boss; they're just motoring convictions, and he's currently banned for drink driving."

"Okay; I'll leave it with you, Ron, I've got plenty for the others to do. We'll meet up later, and you can tell me how you got on."

……………………………………………………………

The Monday morning traffic was very heavy. This would normally have bothered Caroline, but she was so excited after yesterday's visit, it did not matter to her as much; she was just keen to get to the hospital. When she arrived, she glanced in the family room first, and was glad to see that Paul was not there.

However, when she reached Neil's room, and looked through the glass panel in the door, her stomach turned to see Paul sitting on his own; Neil was not in bed. She almost burst through the door.

"Where's your dad?"

"Well, he took a shine to one of the nurses; when he told the nurse about the villa in Spain, that was it, you didn't see them for dust," said Paul, adopting a serious expression; "or, he may have gone to the toilet, I can't remember which now."

Caroline raised her eyes to the ceiling, and sighed with relief. Then she smiled, and said "I'll swing for you one of these days. How's your dad been during the night?"

"He slept through most of it; but when he's been awake, his short term memory is obviously spot on now, as he was talking about what you told him yesterday."

"Did you get the impression he was happy with what I told him?" asked Caroline, as she sat down. "It was still at the back of my mind what the doctor had said about saying too much, and possibly confusing him."

"Oh no, dad thought it was great, and is hoping you'll tell him more today." Paul looked at his mother with a slightly amused expression. "I didn't know dad asked you to marry him only three weeks after you met."

"Well, I've always thought it was a bit of a girly story, and didn't think you or Michael would have been interested."

"I thought it was brilliant," declared Paul. "I've never considered dad to be in any way romantic."

"Ah well, the reason for that, really, is that, as you and Michael have been growing up, your dad works such long hours, none of us see him as much as we'd like."

Just then, Neil walked through the door.

"Hiya, Caz."

"Paul was just telling me that you'd run off with one of the nurses to the villa."

"I changed my mind," said Neil. "I only got half way down the corridor, and realised he wasn't my type. I think it was the beard that put me off."

Paul sniggered, but Caroline beamed with delight; Neil might have lost his memory but, clearly, not his sense of humour. She could not wait to tell him more about their life.

"Anyway," said Paul, "on that bizarre note, I'll leave you both to it. I'll see you later on."

....

As they heard Paul walking away down the corridor, Neil said "Did Paul tell you what Dr. Hargraves said earlier about the therapist?"

Caroline shook her head. "No, he didn't mention it."

"Starting today, there's someone coming in to speak to me regarding the memory loss. I'm not sure exactly what they are, but I'm guessing maybe a psychiatrist or something like that. Hopefully, with whatever they're able to achieve, coupled with all the stuff you can tell me, it may not be long before I get my memory back."

"Brilliant!" said Caroline; but then something occurred to her. "The only problem I can see is that you could be confused between actual memory, and what I've told you."

"I know, I thought of that as well; so, try and think of something that's either important or personal to you and I, and make sure you don't tell me what it is. Then when I mention it, we'll know that my memory has either come back, or is beginning to come back. Does that make sense?"

"Absolutely; I'll have to think of something, and make sure I don't let it slip." She was now glad she had not told Neil that only he called her 'Caroline'; if he did, that could be the hoped-for sign of his memory returning. She would have to explain the situation to the boys and everyone else so no-one corrected Neil if they heard him call her Caz.

"Paul told me that you smoke, so any time you want a cigarette, just go out and have one. I don't mind, don't feel you have to stay in here all the time I'm awake."

"That's alright," said Caroline dismissively. "I don't smoke much anyway, but I'll get the opportunity to go out for a smoke when you're with the plastic surgeon, or the psychiatrist. I should stop really; I don't know what possessed me to start in the first place."

"Have you always smoked in the time you've know me?"

"When we met I smoked, but I've never been a heavy smoker," she told him. "When I discovered I was pregnant with Michael, I stopped immediately, and stayed off them till after I had Paul. I think it wasn't long after I was told that I could never have any more children that I started smoking again." Caroline looked sad for a moment.

"Anyway," said Neil, "feel free to go out if you fancy one; just be careful who you speak to outside, Paul said you can get some weirdos hanging round outside hospitals."

Caroline looked slightly uncomfortable when Neil said this; he noticed the expression on her face, and immediately said "Sorry Caz, I didn't mean to sound like I was telling you what to do. Paul was probably talking about the night rather than the day."

"That's okay," she replied. "I think I might try to give them up again. I can't think of a better time than now, as everything is looking really good; and anyway," she smiled, "you never really liked me smoking, although you never said so."

....

Neil's session with the plastic surgeon was followed immediately by the visit from the therapist. To Neil's disappointment, no progress was made as far as his memory loss was concerned; but the therapist assured him that he would definitely regain his memory at some point.

Once Neil's sessions were finished, Caroline walked in, smiling.

"So, how did it go?"

"Basically," replied Neil, "it seems that, either my memory will come back slowly and progressively, or it could come back all at once. Apparently, it could be triggered by a number of things: for example, the name of a place, a person's name, a song, a film, or anything at all for that matter. She'll be coming in each day to try various methods and hopefully, sooner or later, she'll be successful."

He thought Caroline looked a little disappointed.

"There was something else," he continued; "she did also say to take no notice of the nutty blonde woman who keeps escaping from the psychiatric ward, and goes round telling vulnerable patients that she's married to them. She told me that my real wife is fat and ugly, and can't be bothered to visit me. So I said, 'tell the fat ugly one I died - I'll settle for the nutty blonde one every time.'"

Caroline laughed. "I can't wait for those bandages to be removed, so I can give you a big kiss."

"Which reminds me," said Neil, "the therapist is going to check with Dr. Hargraves first, but thinks it may help if they allow me home for a couple of hours each day, even though I'll still have the bandages on. I think the idea is that, if I'm back in familiar surroundings, it could help, and I'm sure she's right."

Caroline's face lit up. "I agree, that would be fantastic if we could do that."

"And another thing," continued Neil, "both Michael and Paul have told me that you don't like driving through the Mersey tunnel at peak times, so I think I have a cunning plan. If this business of going home for a couple of hours comes off, you could be here in the day as normal, but just leave a couple of hours earlier with me, then Michael could bring me back over."

That having been settled, Caroline then carried on chatting to Neil about their life, the places they visited, and their family and friends. She was so excited at the thought of being able to bring Neil home, if only for a short time; she had thought yesterday was the best day so far, but was thrilled to discover that today was even better.

As Caroline was speaking, she failed to notice that Neil had fallen asleep; it was still difficult to see his eyes, as he was so heavily bandaged. Neil was holding Caroline's hand while she was talking, when he suddenly gripped it tightly, and appeared to gasp for air.

Caroline panicked. "Neil, what's wrong?"

"It's.......it's okay, it was just one of those nightmares. I'll be all right now."

"Should I get a doctor?"

"No, I'll be fine, honestly. I must have been dozing, because that's when they usually happen. From what Paul tells me, when I'm in a deep sleep, there's never a problem."

"Can you remember anything about them?"

"Not really............the only thing I can remember is flames, and not being able to breathe properly." He squeezed her hand reassuringly. "I'll be okay now, I promise; they don't happen very often."

....

Shortly afterwards, Neil fell asleep again; but as he appeared to be in a deep sleep, Caroline took the opportunity to speak to Dr. Hargraves.

Neil was still asleep when Michael arrived. As Caroline was not with Neil, Michael checked in the family room, and was surprised to find she was not there either. He checked outside the hospital in case he had somehow missed her on the way in, but again drew a blank. When he got back to the family room this time, he was relieved to see his mother there.

"I've just been searching for you."

"I went to see Dr. Hargraves, about your dad coming home."

Caroline went on to explain everything that had happened that day, and said they would know by tomorrow if she was able to bring Neil home each afternoon; she had been told that, once the plastic surgeon had finished with him, Neil would be home for good.

As Caroline was walking across the car park, she automatically took out her cigarettes; then she smiled to herself, and put them straight back into her handbag.

....

When Tinny and Gary arrived back at the headquarters, they went straight to speak to D.C.I. Davies.

"Any joy?" asked the D.C.I.

"I don't think so, boss," replied Tinny. "Although Davies has no alibi, I'd be very surprised if he had anything to do with this. He lives on his own, has no immediate family, and doesn't appear to have any friends either."

"Did he admit to making threats regarding Neil Hughes?"

"No; he did say he thought he'd been conned, but he's had two failed business ventures since the taxi office, and felt he'd been conned with those two as well. He's currently in a bedsit and living on benefits, most of which are spent in a nearby pub. We spoke to the staff in the pub; they told us that he was there Tuesday night until about eleven-thirty, but by the time he left, he was so drunk he could barely walk."

"Hm," said the D.C.I. "We're not having much luck so far with this case, Tinny. We've even had a close look at the two sons to see if either of them are involved with the wrong people. No joy there; they're tough lads, but not bad lads."

"Well, you'll be pleased to hear that I do have some good news, boss. My mate Jacko rang before to say one of the drivers is going to meet us on the rank tomorrow morning, because he thinks he may know where Neil Hughes took that last fare."

"That is good news."

"There's more. The driver told Jacko that if the two hoodies Neil Hughes picked up are who he thinks they are, he described them as trouble, and said most of the drivers won't take them. On top of that, guess where they go?" Tinny paused for effect. "The towers on the Rockford Estate."

"That's more like it," said the D.C.I. "Let's keep our fingers crossed Tinny; this sounds very promising."

……………………………………………………………

Caroline was up early on the Tuesday morning, she was so excited at the possibility of bringing Neil home that afternoon. She set off earlier than normal; as a result there was less traffic, and she got through the tunnel quite quickly.

When she looked into Neil's room, Paul was sitting next to his father holding his hand, although Neil was clearly fast asleep. When Paul saw his mother, he quietly stood up and stepped out into the corridor, gently closing the door behind him. He smiled reassuringly.

"No problems; dad's had a good night's sleep."

They made their way to the family room, and sat down.

"I believe dad had one of his nightmares when you were with him yesterday," said Paul. "Was he holding your hand at the time?"

"He was, yes."

"Doesn't half hurt." Paul grinned, flexing his fingers. "I'd forgotten how strong dad is."

"Does it happen very often during the night?"

"No, luckily; it tends to happen when he first starts to doze, so I make sure he's holding my hand till he gets into a deep sleep."

"Is that because you like having your hand crushed?" asked his mother, mystified.

"No," replied Paul, "it's another one of my daft theories. You've got to assume that dad is re-living the night of the attack. He was on his own when that happened; by being able to grab my hand, at least he can feel I'm with him now, or at least someone is with him. I don't know if that's actually what he feels, but it makes me feel I'm helping him in some way."

Caroline looked visibly moved. "In future," she said, "whenever I get annoyed with you, just say to me "hospital visits", and you'll be instantly forgiven."

"I will," he agreed. "Anyway, who decides whether dad can come home this afternoon or not?"

"It's Dr Hargraves who makes the decision; I think he just needs to check with the plastic surgeon first that the arrangement doesn't affect his plans." She got up from her chair. "Right, I'll go and sit with your dad now. Hopefully, if all goes to plan, I'll see you later this afternoon."

……………………………………………………………

Neil was awake as Caroline walked in.

"I see you've managed to escape from the psychiatric ward again; the security there must be very lax."

"I tell them I've just been visiting someone, and they fall for it every time."

"Any news on the possible trip home?"

"Yes; just as I was walking down the corridor, I met the plastic surgeon, and he said he was quite happy with the arrangement. He will arrange to see you either in the mornings, or early afternoon; if not, he can come in the evening to do what needs to be done."

"Brilliant," said Neil. "I'm really looking forward to seeing our house. From your description it sounds great, and I can't wait to see the garden; I gather it's been my passion for quite a few years."

"Yes, that's true," said Caroline. "So, do you know what time the therapist is coming in to see you?"

"I'm not sure; but if you want to go out for a cigarette, that's fine. I don't think the nurse with the beard is on duty today anyway."

"Actually," said Caroline proudly, "you'll be pleased to know, I haven't smoked since yesterday afternoon."

"That's not because of what I said yesterday about talking to strangers, is it?"

"No, not at all. I can't think of a better time to stop smoking."

Neil's session with the plastic surgeon followed. When it was over, and Caroline came back to sit with him, Neil explained that sometimes Dr. Braithwaite appeared to do very little; it took longer to remove the bandages, and to put them back on again, than to do the actual work on his face. Neil told Caroline that he had asked one of the nurses about Dr. Braithwaite's methods; the nurse had explained that the surgeon was an absolute perfectionist, and would not be satisfied with himself if he rushed any part of the process.

A further session with the therapist followed; then, shortly after her departure, Neil got dressed, and was sitting in the chair next to the bed, when Caroline came back in. Neil told her that, once again, there had been no progress in regaining his memory, but that the therapist was hopeful.

"She's really pleased about my going home this afternoon. She's firmly of the opinion that my memory will return; it's just a matter of time."

…………………………………………………………………

Tinny and Gary waited patiently on the taxi rank, both hoping this could be the lead they were looking for. Jacko pulled on to the rank, and smiled when he saw Tinny and Gary walking towards him.

Jacko glanced at his watch. "Danny should be here soon. I'll show him the picture of the two hoodies, and hopefully, he'll know where Yosser took them."

"Oh," said Tinny. "I thought he'd actually seen the picture."

"No; after I'd spoken to most of the other drivers, and was getting nowhere, I remembered Danny always works late during the week. He's got a caravan in North Wales, which is where he's been this weekend. So when I rang him, and described the two fellas Neil picked up that night, Danny's pretty sure he knows who they are."

Tinny was somewhat disappointed; he hoped that this would not, after all, turn out to be a dead end.

"Here comes Danny now," said Jacko; "let's hope he recognises these scumbags."

Danny approached the three men. "Alright, Jacko," he greeted.

"Alright, Danny; this is Tinny, who I've told you about, and this is Gary."

Danny shook hands with them both. "Sorry to keep you gents; that last job was a bit of a runaround."

"No need to apologise," said Tinny, "we really appreciate you giving up your time to help us with this."

Jacko produced the CCTV picture, and showed it to Danny; Danny looked at the images, and nodded.

"I thought so – they're the two that most of the lads won't pick up any more."

Tinny was relieved. "Jacko told me you said they were trouble; are they aggressive?"

"Not as such," replied Danny, "although they probably could be, if they thought they could get away with it. No - the problem with those two is either they haven't got any money, or haven't got the full fare. The trouble is, you don't find that out till you've got them home."

"Do you think they could have pulled that stroke the night Neil Hughes took them home?"

Danny smiled knowingly. "You don't know Yosser, do you?" He glanced at Jacko, and when Jacko nodded, he continued. "Neil Hughes is a hard man; he's not a bully, and avoids trouble if he can, but certainly wouldn't take any lip from scum like these."

"Dan's right," agreed Jacko. "A few weeks ago, one of the lads was having trouble outside the kebab house. I pulled up at about the same time as Yosser, and by the time I'd got out of my cab, Yosser had put two of them on their back."

"Where exactly on the estate would Neil Hughes have dropped these two?" asked Tinny.

"Jump in your car, and follow me," offered Danny. "I'll show you exactly where they get dropped off."

....

As Gary and Tinny arrived, Danny showed them the spot where Neil would have dropped the two hoodies, then immediately left to go to a job. Tinny took one look at the scene, then turned to Gary.

"Get on to headquarters. We need this area taped off, and Debbie here as soon as possible."

Gary looked confused, until he looked down and saw the large stain on the ground; it was clearly blood.

Chapter 4

"I'm just popping along to see Dr. Hargraves to check what time they want you back, and then we can set off," said Caroline. "I'm so excited, I feel like a child."

"You and me both," said Neil.

………………………………………………………………

As Caroline walked in to the doctor's office, Dr. Hargraves stood up and smiled.

"No later than six o'clock, before you ask." The doctor paused, and appeared to be slightly embarrassed. "There is one delicate matter I need to discuss with you, however. Please, take a seat."

Caroline sat down, and looked at him expectantly.

"I'm pleased to be able to tell you that Neil's heart is much stronger now, and he's no longer on the medication; however, he must avoid any excitement."

"To be fair, he is quite excited at being able to go home; we both are."

"I'm sorry Caz, but I'm not very comfortable in these situations," said Dr. Hargraves. "I'm not talking of excitement about going home; I'm talking more of, well, a physical excitement."

"Oh, I see," smiled Caroline, "you mean no sex."

Dr. Hargraves seemed relieved not to have to spell it out. "Yes, that's exactly what I mean. I have informed Neil as well, but did say this situation won't last forever; in due course, I'll only be too pleased to tell you otherwise."

………………………………………………………………

The journey from the hospital back to Cheshire went smoothly, although Neil did get some strange looks from passing motorists. As Caroline drove down the lane and into the driveway, she hoped in her heart Neil would say something like "Caroline, our house is fantastic"; in the event, however, he simply said "Caz, this is even better than you described it."

Caroline took Neil on a full tour of the house, hoping that at some point he would recognise something, but he showed no sign that anything was familiar. She saved going into the back garden until last because, when Neil was not working, he would often spend more time in the garden than indoors.

"This is absolutely beautiful."

"Yes," agreed Caroline. "This garden has been your passion since we bought this house. There's nothing you like more than sitting out here on a nice day, just relaxing and being away from the taxi."

"I can see why; it's so peaceful out here."

"Have a sit down here. I'll go and make a cup of tea - or would you rather have a cold drink of orange or lemonade? On a warm day like this, you often liked a pint glass of orange with lots of ice in it."

"A cold glass of orange sounds great."

Caroline watched Neil from the kitchen window strolling round the garden, inspecting all the various features he had put there over the years. She desperately hoped that something out there might kick start the process of his regaining some memory.

As she stepped back into the garden, Neil said "Isn't that water feature fantastic?"

"Funny you should say that, because it's always been your most favourite thing in the whole garden."

"My therapist did say that my memory may come back slowly, so something as simple as looking at the water feature could start the process off. I think that's why she was so keen for me to come home as soon as possible, even though the plastic surgeon still has a lot of work to do."

"When you say a lot of work, do you know how many more sessions you'll have with Dr. Braithwaite?"

"No idea; from what I can gather this work he's doing on me is experimental."

Caroline looked concerned, so Neil patted her hand.

"Don't worry; judging from his explanation of how the process works, he's confident that when he's finished, my face will be perfect. He has tried to explain to me the difference between the usual method of reconstructing a face and the new method he's using but, to be honest, I don't quite understand what he means."

"Dr. Hargraves told me that he's, probably, the best in the world. Reading that medical journal about him, that seems to be the opinion of many more in his profession."

"Yes," said Neil thoughtfully. "This sounds a bit ungrateful, and I don't mean it to, but I don't think he's doing this work for my benefit. I suspect he's using me to prove he *is* the best in the world. Because there was so much damage to my face, I can't help feeling that he was almost pleased, given that he was able to use his new method, effectively, on a blank canvas."

"So you're a guinea pig, really."

"Well, there's no need for that attitude; I know you said I was ugly, but I think that's going a bit far," said Neil, shrugging in mock resignation.

Caroline laughed. "I *didn't* say you were ugly."

"I know, I was only kidding. So anyway, are there any features in this garden with a wheel I could run round for a bit of exercise?"

"I'll get Mike to put one up for you tomorrow. Anyway, isn't it hamsters that run round wheels?"

"Oh, so I look like a hamster now? Make your mind up!"

"Thinking about it," mused Caroline, "you did have more of a hamster look than a guinea pig. By the way, I believe Dr. Hargraves explained the position as far as no physical excitement was concerned?"

"He did; but to be honest, I thought he was talking about sex. If he was actually talking about running round giant hamster wheels, then I must have really embarrassed him."

Although Caroline had been disappointed that bringing Neil home did not seem to have jogged his memory, she was so grateful to be sitting in the garden and laughing at the things Neil was saying; something which, a week ago, she thought may never happen again. Consequently, when Michael duly arrived to take Neil back to the hospital, she began to get upset.

"Don't worry," assured Neil. "I'll see you in the morning, assuming you can get past security on the psychiatric ward. Don't tell them you're married to a gerbil, though; if you do, you'll have no chance."

....

Not long after Michael and Neil set off for the hospital, Neil asked:

"Have your mum and I ever won money on anything?"

"Not to my knowledge; why do you ask?"

"It's just that I'm a bit confused as to how I've managed to own a house like that, particularly in that area, as well as a villa in Spain."

"Working long hours, and hardly ever having any time off. Usually, you're only off when the cab's in the garage and getting some work done to it." By the time they got back to the hospital, Michael had explained everything to his father, relating to the house and villa.

It was obvious that the trip home had tired Neil out more than he had expected as, back in his hospital bed, he was soon fast asleep. When Paul arrived, Michael warned him not to be surprised if their father slept for most of the night; sure enough, he was right.

....

As Jill and Mark were taping off the area and keeping people well away from it, Tinny and Gary stood nearby, and waited for Debbie to arrive.

"This is an ideal place to attack someone and not be seen," remarked Gary.

"Indeed," said Tinny. "Even if they were seen, the chances of anyone coming forward as a witness are pretty slim on this estate, and particularly this part of it."

At this point, Mark walked over to them. "Is this where you think Neil Hughes was first attacked?" he asked Gary.

"Naturally, it depends on confirmation that the blood is a match to Neil Hughes, but it certainly looks very promising," replied Gary. "After speaking to one of the other taxi drivers, he was sure that the two hoodies from the CCTV footage at the town rank live in the towers, and would've been dropped here."

Just then, the two suspects appeared from the gap between the garages, saw the police, and ran off in different directions. Mark immediately sprinted after one of them and soon caught up with him; Mark was a regular in the police rugby team, and was one of the fastest and strongest players. The smack in the face the hoody received as Mark tackled him certainly looked like an accident.

Gary had shot after the other suspect, who had run back down the passage between the garages, and was therefore, temporarily, out of sight; Tinny was about to go after Gary, when Jill stopped him. "No need Sarge; Gary'll catch him," she said, smiling.

Tinny was impressed to see Gary appear with the suspect in handcuffs. As Gary walked past Tinny, he said "I may be posh, but I'm not soft."

....

When the suspects were taken into the police headquarters, one was saying nothing at all, while the other was shouting for a solicitor, and something about 'police brutality'; however, after he was examined, the doctor said he was fit to be interviewed.

Paula and Dave were given the job of interviewing each suspect, while D.C.I. Davies, Tinny and Gary watched the interviews on a monitor in an adjoining office. Paula and Dave were getting nowhere, as the answer to any of their questions was always the same.

"The trouble with these sort of people is that, as soon as they enter a police station, they only know two words," remarked the D.C.I. "We'll keep them in overnight, and have another go in the morning."

"Has Debbie come up with any results from the blood stain?" asked Gary.

D.C.I. Davies nodded. "It's definitely the victim's blood."

"I assume these two are known to the police?"

"They certainly are," interjected Tinny. "They've been arrested countless times for a number of different offences, some of which have involved violence."

"Debbie said there were at least three assailants; so, if these two are involved, we should assume they had at least one accomplice, possibly more," said Gary, thoughtfully.

"From what we've been told about Neil Hughes," said Tinny, "I'd be very surprised if Matty Grant and Degsy Jones would have got the better of him on their own."

....

Paul looked up, and saw his mother walking along the corridor, so he quietly stood up and carefully left his father, who was sleeping soundly. Paul smiled and gave a thumbs up to Caroline, as he stepped outside the room.

"Dad's slept for most of the night, but when he was awake, he couldn't stop talking about our house."

"I was only thinking, after Mike and your dad left; for him to see the house, and especially the garden for the first time, must have been really enjoyable for him; and, hopefully, to discover that it was his hard work that achieved it all, it will have lifted his spirits even more."

"Let's hope so," said Paul. "Anyway," he continued, as he gave his mother a hug, "I'll see you later this afternoon." She noticed, as he walked away down the corridor, that there was certainly more of a spring in his step.

....

Caroline was sitting quietly next to Neil as he woke up.

"It's me again," she said, smiling. "I just can't stay away."

"Have you got your phone on you?"

"Yes, why?"

"I need to phone the fancy dress shop, and cancel the gerbil suit."

Caroline just giggled, and squeezed Neil's hand.

"As he was driving me back here," said Neil, "Michael was explaining to me about how we managed to acquire such a lovely house, and a Spanish villa. It did occur to me that I've been a bit selfish by working all the time, and spending very little time with you, particularly in the last couple of years."

Caroline appeared to be about to say something; but she stopped herself, and looked slightly upset.

"Sorry," said Neil hurriedly. "I've obviously said the wrong thing again; I should just stick to the jokes."

Caroline smiled, and squeezed Neil's hand again.

"No, not at all; and let me tell you, you have never been selfish. Since we got married, I've had everything I always dreamed of.

"When we met, I was working in a hairdressers shop, but all I ever wanted to be was a housewife and mother. When I became pregnant with Michael, you said it was up to me whether I wanted to go back to work after having the baby, or stay at home. I liked being at home with Michael, and was even happier when Paul was born. I loved being with the children all the time. Then, not long after Paul was born, you taught me to drive, and bought a lovely car for me to go visiting family and friends in; that car was considerably better than the one you had."

Neil nodded in understanding. "I believe I'm quite handy with cars, so it would make sense for me to drive the one that was more likely to have problems. Mind you," he continued, "I'm assuming that you're *not* handy with cars?"

Caroline laughed. "I ring you when I've got a flat tyre! I know nothing about cars."

"I also gather," continued Neil, "that although I'm handy with cars, I'm useless as far as do-it-yourself is concerned."

"Well, I wouldn't say 'useless.'"

"Michael did. He said all I was good for is labouring."

Caroline looked at him affectionately.

"It is true that, whenever you attempt something, you end up getting Michael to finish the job, and to repair the damage you've done. In the early days, you'd just work longer hours, and pay someone else to do any work of that kind on the house. You have mates who are brickies, plasterers, roofers and electricians, and they never charged you as much as they'd charge someone else." Caroline looked wistful. "I wish now, we'd taken photographs of the house when we first bought it."

"Why do you say that?" asked Neil.

"Well, it was really run down, because it had been empty for some time, and the former owners had been elderly; when the house was put up for sale, the price was too high, so there wasn't much interest. Anyway, when you first took me to see it, I didn't like the look of it at all; but you contacted the estate agents and made (you told me later) a ridiculously low offer, so you were pleasantly surprised when it was accepted. Later, when you sold the taxi office, I said we should use some of the money and go on a cruise; but you convinced me it would be better to spend all the money on the house."

"That's the sort of thing I meant about me being selfish."

"No, *I* was being selfish, wanting to waste the money on a cruise; you were absolutely right. We were able to have a new kitchen, exactly as I wanted it, as well as a new bathroom and separate shower room, and all new windows throughout the house; what was left over we saved, then within twelve months, thanks to your working all the hours God sends, we were able to have the conservatory built. I love having friends and family visiting our house, because I'm really proud of it."

Caroline warmed to her subject, as she continued.

"As well as having a lovely house, from when the boys were little and starting school, I was able to be a proper mother by giving them a good breakfast before I took them to school, and cook proper meals after I'd brought them home. This was what I always wanted, and would never have got if I'd married someone who spends all their time in the pub or the betting shop. Even after the boys had grown up, you made sure I always had a good car to run around in, so I could still do what I wanted. You are *not* the selfish one."

Neil seemed to ponder over what she had said.

"So, all in all, I'm a bit of a saint, really," he said eventually. Caroline smiled wryly.

"I wouldn't go that far," she commented, "but I think you're quite nice."

....

After an unproductive session with the therapist, and a longer than normal time with the plastic surgeon, Neil was given the all clear for another home visit, to return to the hospital by six o'clock.

....

As Matthew Grant was led into the interview room with his solicitor, D.C.I. Davies turned to Tinny.

"Do you fancy having a go this morning? Paula and Dave weren't getting anywhere yesterday."

"I'll be glad to, boss."

"Who would you prefer in there with you, Paula or Dave?"

"If it's all the same to you, boss, I'd prefer to have Gary in there with me."

Fred Davies looked gratified. "By all means, Ron, absolutely."

....

When everyone was seated, and Gary had gone through the formalities of introducing who was present for the benefit of the tape, Tinny smiled at Matty.

"Morning, Matthew. Did you get a good night's rest?"

"No comment."

"Would you rather I called you Matthew, or would you prefer Matty?"

"No comment."

"Matty it is, then. Now," continued Tinny, "can you explain why you appeared to wait until Neil Hughes arrived on the town rank, before you and Degsy got into his cab?"

"No comment."

"On the CCTV footage, it can clearly be seen that you made no effort to get into either of the two cabs which had pulled onto the rank before Neil Hughes; so, obviously, you were waiting for him."

"No comment."

"At the exact point where Neil Hughes dropped you off, do you know how a large amount of his blood got there?"

"No comment."

Tinny then turned to Gary.

"You know," Tinny mused, "after speaking to the taxi drivers, it struck me that Neil Hughes is a very popular man."

"Me too, Sarge." Gary paused slightly; then he continued. "There's some big lads working on those taxis; I certainly wouldn't want to fall out with any of them."

"Nor me; still," said Tinny, "they'll understand when we let this young gentleman go that he must have had nothing to do with this, otherwise we would've charged him."

"Not necessarily, Sarge; sometimes, people jump to the conclusion that if someone is arrested they must be guilty, and may have got off on a technicality, or lack of evidence."

"Surely not." Tinny raised his eyebrows.

"I'm afraid so," said Gary seriously; "for example, there was that tragic case..................."

"Hold on, hold on," blurted Matty, "we had nothing to do with this."

His solicitor immediately spoke up. "I must advise you, Mr Grant, to make no comment at the moment."

Matty turned to the solicitor. "You can keep your advice, girl, it's not you who's going to get ripped apart by a gang of headcase taxi drivers."

He then turned back to Tinny. "Yosser picked us up off the rank, took us home, we paid him, got out of the cab and went down the entry to the towers. End of story."

"Why did you wait for him to pull onto the rank?" asked Tinny. "Why didn't you get into either of the other two cabs?"

"We weren't waiting for Yosser particularly, those first two cabs wouldn't take us, but we knew Yosser would."

"Why wouldn't the first two take you and Degsy?"

"We can be a bit stupid sometimes, we're usually off our heads by the time we get to the taxi rank, and what we do is tell the driver when he gets us home that we've got no money, or we haven't got enough."

"So, why was Neil Hughes willing to take you?"

At this point, Matty paused, as if he was considering whether to carry on.

"Okay," he began. "It was a while ago. We didn't know Yosser then, because we used to go home from a different rank. That first time he took us, when we got to the towers, we just jumped out of the cab and said we'll pay him tomorrow.

"He got out of the cab as well, and stood between us and the entry to the towers. He just stood there and said 'it's four pounds.' Yosser doesn't look hard and we're both bigger than him, so Degsy said something stupid like 'you can take it out of my face if you like.' The next thing was, we were both on the floor. He took Degsy out with a straight left, and me with a right hook, I've never been hit so hard in all my life. We were on the floor and had no intentions of getting back up again, d'you know what I'm saying?"

"That sounds very much to me like a motive for revenge."

"No, no, you don't understand, Tinny, he could've stamped all over us if he'd have wanted to, he could've kicked hell out of us. He didn't, what he'd done is put us in our place. The funny thing was, he spotted a fiver in my top shirt pocket. I'd forgotten it was there."

I bet you did, thought Tinny, cynically; but he did not interrupt.

"He took the fiver, went to his cab, took a quid out of his cash bag, and put the change back in my pocket, then just drove off. It was only when he was well clear that we got up. We had a laugh the next day, as much as we could 'cause we had very sore faces, about him giving us the pound change.

"He's picked us up loads of times since then, and there's been no problem. But we know better than to push our luck with him." Tinny looked at him questioningly. "What it was, a few weeks ago, it was lashing down, and my stomach turned to see the only cab on the rank was Yosser's. We really didn't have any money that night, so I asked him if there was any chance he'd take us home, and I would definitely bring the cash up to the rank in the morning. He just told us to get in, he put the meter on, took us home, and when we got there, he said 'bring four pound to the rank in the morning, or I'll come and collect it.' We couldn't get out of the cab quick enough and legged it down the entry, in case he changed his mind.

"The next morning, I've never been up that early in all my life, I went straight to the town rank and waited for Yosser. The weather was worse than the night before so I was like a drowned rat by the time he pulled onto the rank. I shot over and gave him a bluey, he went to give me a pound change, and I said 'keep the fiver.' Any time he's picked us up since, we always give him a fiver."

"It's not that far from the town rank to where you get dropped off. Why didn't you walk home?"

"Would you walk through our estate early hours of the morning?"

Tinny just nodded. "Fair comment."

Tinny then indicated to Gary that the interview was terminated. As they both stood up, Tinny turned to Matty, and said "What's this about police brutality?"

"Take no notice, Tinny, I was just mouthing off, it was an accident."

The solicitor was about to say something, when Matty snapped "I said, it was an accident!"

He then smiled at Tinny. "I don't know why I tried to out run the big lad, I've never managed it in the past."

....

As Tinny and Gary walked in to the room where the D.C.I. had been watching the interview,

Fred Davies explained that Paula and Dave were next door with Derek Jones, but were still getting no comment from him.

"Leave it with us, boss," volunteered Tinny.

Gary and Tinny took over the interview, used the same routine as with Matty, and got the same result; the only difference being that Degsy blamed Matty for saying "take it out of my face."

Tinny and Gary re-entered the room where the D.C.I. had been watching their progress.

"What do you think, Ron?"

"As far as I'm concerned, they are certainly still in the frame. But my gut reaction is that it wasn't them."

The D.C.I. nodded. "Gary, what's your opinion?"

"They're obviously frightened of Neil Hughes, which may go back to the incident over not paying the fare," replied Gary; "it's also possible that they were responsible and are dreading the repercussions; however, personally, I don't think so."

"We've spoken to some of the taxi drivers who know these two, and the general consensus is that they are not likely to be responsible for this," explained Tinny. "We spoke to one of the drivers who was on the rank that night, and he said they were both very drunk, and certainly weren't capable of attacking anyone, certainly not Neil Hughes."

The D.C.I. smiled. "So there isn't going to be a lynch mob waiting for them?"

Tinny affected a look of confusion. "No boss, what gave you that idea?" He then turned away, and winked at Gary.

As D.S. Smith and D.C. Ward left the room, Fred Davies continued smiling to himself, and nodded his head.

....

Tinny and Gary were standing in the car park, near to the entrance to the police headquarters, when Matty and Degsy walked out of the building. Matty immediately walked up to Tinny.

"God's honest, we know nothing about this."

"Well," replied Tinny, "if forensics tell us otherwise, I know where I can find you."

"We're certainly not going back to the towers, we're going to stay at our Colette's till you catch who really did this." Matty scratched his head. "I don't know if this is any use, but me and Degsy have just been talking about it, and we think that night Yosser dropped us off, we saw a van driving into the yard by the garages."

"Can you remember what sort of van, or even the colour?"

"It was too far away, and we're not even sure if it was that night, but Degsy thinks Yosser said something about checking one of his tyres, because he thought he had a slow puncture."

Degsy nodded, and said "We're not dead sure about this, so it may not be any good."

Tinny nodded; then, as Matty and Degsy walked away, he turned to Gary.

"If these two scumbags are right, it would explain why Neil Hughes was out of his cab; and, if he was crouching down checking a tyre, he may not have seen his attacker."

....

Neil's second trip home was just as exciting as the first one. The night before, Caroline had dug out lots of photograph albums ready for Neil to look at; she also found some old videos from when the boys were small, but had more difficulty finding the old video player.

When Neil had finished looking at their wedding album, he turned to Caroline.

"After looking at these photographs, and comparing them to a more recent photograph of me, I think it's fair to say you've aged slightly better than I have."

"Well," smiled Caroline, "you've had the worry of being married to me, whereas I've had the pleasure of being married to you."

"You smooth talker," remarked Neil; "so, this is how you chatted me up on our first night?"

"It worked, didn't it?"

Neil seemed to reflect for a moment.

"When we met," he mused, "you were a hairdresser; was I a taxi driver then?"

"No; you worked in a factory, and you hated it."

"So when did I become a taxi driver?"

"I think, after we'd been married for about three years."

Neil nodded. "In that case, I assume I enjoy what I do?"

"Well, no - you hate it more than working in the factory."

"Oh?" He sounded surprised. "Then what possessed me to become a taxi driver in the first place?"

"Well," replied Caroline, "the factory job was quite well paid, but you felt that you were never able to earn any extra money; whereas you believed that, as a taxi driver, you could work as much as you liked."

"I see," said Neil thoughtfully. "In that case, from what Michael has said and what you've told me, would you describe me as a workaholic?"

Caroline shook her head. "Strangely enough, no; it's simply that you've always set goals for yourself, and the only way of achieving them, in your opinion, is to work hard."

"What sort of goals?"

"The best example is this house, I'd say. We actually bought it while you were still working in the factory, but you felt that the only way of getting it how we wanted it was to find a way of earning more money."

Neil nodded again. "I must admit, I think this house is absolutely stunning. Why did we buy the villa in Spain?"

"Because," smiled Caroline, "at some point in the future, we're going to live there."

Neil seemed nonplussed. "Why on earth would I want to live in Spain and give this house up?"

"Living in Spain, and particularly the part of Spain where we have the villa, has been your dream for some time. However, we won't be giving this house up."

"How are we going to manage that?"

"I have to be honest, and admit that I'm not sure."

There was a short pause. "You're not sure?"

Caroline seemed ill at ease for a moment.

"Well, the fact is, you've always sorted things out, which I've been more than happy to let you do; it's only with recent events that I've realised how selfish I've been. You've tried, a number of times over the years, to involve me more in our plans for the future; the trouble is, because you're so good at sorting things out, I've left you to it."

Neil appeared to ponder over this.

"This idea of living in Spain," he said eventually, "you say it's always been my dream; is it your dream as well?"

"Totally and absolutely," said Caroline emphatically. "I can't wait to move there, because we'll be able to spend a great deal more time together. This is what you've been working so hard for, and said only recently we'll get there sooner than you'd hoped. You've spoken of very little else for the last two years."

"Well," said Neil, "I can't wait to get my memory back to see how I'm going to pull this trick off."

"Talking of which, do you think these sessions you're having with the therapist are helping in any way?"

"To be perfectly honest, no." Neil sounded disappointed. "She's told me, basically, the same thing on a number of occasions. I hope that, being here with you, there's a much greater chance of re-gaining my memory. The sooner the plastic surgeon is finished with me, the better."

"Has he still given you no idea when that will be?"

"He hinted, today, that it won't be much longer," said Neil more brightly. "Today's session was certainly longer than previous ones; apparently, tomorrow's will be longer again, and soon there will be one final session. From what I can gather, that final session will take most of the day. So far, he appears to be happy with the work he's done."

"You said yesterday, you felt that he was doing this more for his benefit rather than yours?"

"Oh, yes indeed," replied Neil, caustically; "after today's session, I'm convinced of it. I've noticed the difference between the way the staff are with Dr. Hargraves, as compared to Dr. Braithwaite. Dr. Hargraves has obviously got the total respect of everyone who works there, whereas Braithwaite is an arrogant man and is, I think, quite unpopular. There appears to be a fear of him; not in the physical sense of course, rather the way in which he appears to use his position to bully people."

Caroline raised her eyebrows. "I've only spoken to him twice - the second time was about your being able to come home for short spells, and he seemed very pleasant."

"I imagine he is, quite possibly, in certain circumstances; but when he's working, he expects absolute perfection from everyone around him, including himself. He uses the word 'perfect' regularly and, so far, every time he's finished with me, he appears to be totally satisfied with the work that's been done."

"Well," said Caroline, "as I've said before, it'll make no difference to me what you look like."

"I'm glad about that; you see, he gave me the choice of hamster or guinea pig, but I said I preferred gerbil. I also said that if possible, I would prefer handsome gerbil rather than pig-ugly gerbil." Caroline chuckled. "Seriously, though," Neil continued, "in some respects I'm dreading having the bandages removed in case I look awful."

"Neil, I can't stress this enough - it won't matter to me what you look like."

"So, handsome gerbil would do?"

"Well, now you mention it," said Caroline archly, "I must admit I would have preferred hamster."

"Damn," said Neil. "So anyway, do our conversations often deteriorate into silliness?"

"They have for the last twenty years!"

"Do we ever fall out or have rows?"

"Honestly, no. We don't always agree, but we don't fall out over disagreeing."

"Okay," said Neil slowly, "so, when I get my memory back, it'll be a shock to discover that for the last twenty years, you've been beating me about the head and body with a frying pan on a regular basis?"

"Brilliant!" exclaimed Caroline. "*That* was the secret piece of information I was keeping from you! This may be the start of the process - but you've got to hope you don't remember what I did with the nutcrackers........."

"Caz, I can't wait to get these bandages off so I can laugh properly!"

....

As with the previous day, Michael seemed to arrive far too quickly in order to take Neil back to the hospital. When Caroline and Neil were hugging each other, neither wanted to let go. Neil eventually left with Michael, and said he would see Caroline in the morning.

When Neil was back at the hospital, after speaking to some of his friends from the taxi rank who had come over to visit him, Neil slept soundly for the rest of the night.

....

Thursday morning's briefing was quite subdued. Everyone involved in the case had hoped the arrests made on Tuesday would prove to be crucial; however, this proved fruitless, as forensics were not able to connect the two suspects with the victim.

"The bad news," announced D.C.I. Davies "is that we'll need to go door to door in the immediate vicinity of where the victim's blood was found. We know that's where the first attack took place but, let's face it, as we all know, the chances of anyone giving us any information are pretty slim.

"Sadly, on that estate in general, and certainly round the area of the towers, drug dealers and ram raiders are top of the tree; anyone talking to the police are thought of as scum, equivalent to paedophile status. Needless to say, make sure you're all wearing your anti-stab vests, and don't enter any property on your own.

"Fortunately, the Chief Super has given us some uniformed officers as backup; just make sure that, when you are at any door, you can been seen by at least one other officer. All I can say is that you try your best."

………………………………...

Caroline spoke to Neil only briefly before his session with the plastic surgeon began. It was certainly the longest as far as Caroline was aware, which she hoped was a good sign regarding Neil being able to come home permanently. Unusually, Neil had been sedated, but it was not too long before Caroline could speak to him.

"Are you all right to talk, or should I leave you a bit longer?"

"No, I'm fine; I don't remember what went on, so I assume they must have put me out for this one."

"So, you didn't get to put the hamster request in?"

"Nope, it's handsome gerbil I'm afraid."

"Damn," said Caroline, impishly. Neil squeezed her hand.

"Completely going off the subject," continued Caroline seriously, "are you still having the nightmares?"

"I am, but I think I'm beginning to control them."

"Control them? In what way?"

"Sometimes, not every time, I can sense them coming, and am able to wake myself up."

"When you do have one, are they any less terrifying?"

"No, I'm afraid not; although, by being able to spot when they're coming, at least they're not as frequent as they were. The strange thing is that, although I still only remember the same thing, I feel that, if I tried, I could remember more; the problem is, I suspect that they'd be even more terrifying."

"So it's possible you could remember who attacked you?"

"Maybe, assuming I actually saw them; but, to be perfectly honest, I think I'd rather let my attackers get away with it, than try to deliberately extend the nightmares."

"Paul has a theory that, when you have someone with you, they're not as bad."

"He's absolutely right. If I'm holding someone's hand, I feel that I'm not on my own and am going to live; but, if they happen when I'm on my own, I think I'm going to die."

Caroline visibly shuddered. "Caz," said Neil hurriedly, "it's okay; now I've started controlling the frequency of them, hopefully, I may be able to stop them altogether."

Caroline smiled ruefully. "I'm sorry I asked now; I should have stuck to the handsome gerbil conversation."

"Anyway, when we get home today, I'm going to inspect the frying pan for dents."

"You shouldn't have told me that," said Caroline, "while you're having your session with the therapist, I'll sneak out and buy a new one. I'd best get a new nutcracker as well, not to mention the curling tongs and the wire brush."

Neil squeezed Caroline's hand again, and said "Enough! Any chance we can get back to the nightmares?"

……………………………………………………………………

Neil's time with the therapist seemed shorter than the previous sessions, so they were able to set off home a little earlier than expected. Once again, Caroline watched Neil inspecting everything in the house; she thought it was like watching a child at a Christmas grotto.

The phone rang while Neil was in the garden. Caroline answered it, and immediately recognised Dr. Braithwaite's voice, asking if he could speak to Neil. Caroline took the phone outside and handed it to Neil, mouthing "Dr. Braithwaite"; Neil just held the phone to his ear for a while as Braithwaite was speaking, then ended the call with a simple "Okay, I'll see you tomorrow."

As he handed the phone back to Caroline, he said "Do you want the good news first, or the bad news?"

"Bad news first, as long as it's not too bad."

"Alright," said Neil, "here goes, then. There's no point in you coming over early in the morning, as you won't get to see me till later in the afternoon."

"Does that mean..........."

"It certainly does."

They held each other tightly for some time, before Neil said quietly "I know you've said it loads of times, but please don't be disappointed."

………………………………...

Everyone had gathered back in the briefing room.

"Any luck at all?" D.C.I. Davies looked around the room, but could see only people shaking their heads.

"Chin up everybody, tomorrow's another day. Get your thinking caps on tonight, and let's see if we can come up with any ideas for tomorrow morning's briefing. Look on the bright side; you've just done a door to door on the Rockford, and lived to tell the tale."

………………………………...

When Paul arrived home on Friday morning, he was surprised to see Michael's van parked outside. As he walked into the living room, he could immediately see his mother had been crying.

"What's wrong? What's happened?"

Michael was holding some papers in his hand. He held them up.

"Mum's had a letter from the mortgage people to say that the mortgage hasn't been paid, and a letter from the bank to say that there were insufficient funds in the bank account to pay a direct debit, which has therefore incurred bank charges."

"I don't understand this at all," said Caroline distractedly, "your dad always made sure there was plenty of money in the account to cover everything. Even if he didn't work for a few days because the cab was off the road, it was never a problem. It just doesn't make sense, I can't think what could've gone wrong."

Paul put his hand to his head. "I think I can," he said, his tone subdued.

Caroline and Michael looked at Paul, with quizzical expressions.

"Remember the other week, when my car was having some work done to it? Well……the bill was quite big, so dad paid it, and I arranged with him to pay him back over a period of time."

Caroline looked exasperated. "You're already paying off debts! How did you think you were ever going to pay your dad?"

Paul shrugged. "I was going to do it over two years."

"Two years!" Caroline's voice was outraged. "How much was the garage bill?"

"Just over……. Two thousand, four hundred pounds."

"You're joking!" exclaimed Michael. "The car isn't worth much more than that!"

"It had to have a new engine and all the front-end rebuilt." The expressions on the faces of Caroline and Michael prompted him to explain hurriedly, "What happened was, I was driving back to Jenny's late one night, after dropping a couple of friends home who'd been with us that evening; they couldn't get a taxi, so I volunteered to give them a lift. After I'd dropped them off, I was coming along a country road which I didn't know very well, when something just shot out in front of me. I swerved and went straight into a tree."

"Had you been drinking?" snapped Caroline.

"Definitely not mum, and when dad gets his memory back, I can prove it. Obviously, after hitting the tree and seeing the damage to the car, I rang dad; when he arrived he had a look, and rang his mate who does the twenty-four hour breakdown service. While we were waiting for dad's mate, the police turned up; I can only guess that a passing motorist must have seen me wrapped round the tree, and rang the police. They immediately breathalysed me, and discovered I was stone cold sober. I wouldn't have gone out in the car if I'd been drinking." Paul paused. "I'm sorry mum; I didn't realise dad was using everything you had in the bank to pay for the repairs. When he said to me he hoped the cab didn't go down after paying the bill, I thought he was joking."

Caroline's expression was grim. "Why didn't you or your dad tell me about this?"

"Dad said there was no point in worrying you unnecessarily, he could sort everything out so I could get back on the road as soon as possible. I need the car for all the running round I do because public transport is useless." Paul smiled, and continued, "anyway, I needed it for "hospital visits" as things turned out."

Caroline's stern expression did not flicker. Paul was disappointed that she had clearly forgotten what she had said to him in the hospital; however, he did not show it.

"Sorry," he muttered.

Michael glanced down at the paperwork. "I've been looking at the bank statements, and can now see why dad worked so hard," he remarked to his mother. "Do you know how much you have going out of the bank each month on direct debits and standing orders?"

Caroline looked sheepish. "I've got no idea. I know your dad made sure everything was always paid, but I really don't know any of the details of what's being paid, or when."

"When dad gets home later, we'll have to show him, and hope he can come up with a solution," suggested Paul.

"How can he," said Caroline patiently, "when he's lost his memory?"

Michael smiled wryly. "He's lost his memory; he hasn't lost his mind."

Caroline gave a wintry smile in return. "Good point," she acknowledged.

Michael put his hand on his mother's arm reassuringly. "Don't worry, we'll get something sorted out."

Caroline nodded; I must pull myself together, she thought.

"Anyway," she said to Paul, "when you left this morning, did your dad know when the plastic surgeon would be finished, and when they'd be removing the bandages?"

"Dad said to tell you there's no point in getting there any earlier than mid afternoon. From what he's been told, it will probably be late afternoon before they're finished."

"Right," said Caroline. "I'll make sure I leave in good time in case the traffic's heavy. I've got to be there before they remove the bandages."

Michael and Paul looked confused. "Why?" they both asked at once.

"When they remove the bandages, your dad will still be sedated; so, no matter how awful he looks by the time he regains consciousness, the first thing he'll see is me, and I'll be all smiles. Depending on how bad his face is, I can ring you and warn you before we get home, so that you can do the same."

Michael waved his hand dismissively. "We're like you mum, we don't care what he may look like; it's just great that he's coming home. Anyway, while you're over there, I'll make a list of all the various payments that are made through the bank; with a bit of luck, dad may well have some ideas on how to sort out the problem."

…………………………………...

Friday morning's briefing was even more subdued than the previous day.

"Right," began D.C.I. Davies, "has anyone come up with any new ideas as to where we go from here?"

"Yes, boss," offered Tinny. "When I was talking to my mate Jacko the other day, he mentioned that there'd been some trouble, in which Neil Hughes was involved, outside the kebab house. I'll speak to Jacko again, and see if we can establish exactly when it happened. Hopefully, if we can get an approximate date and time, we may be able to find the incident on the CCTV footage."

"What sort of trouble, Ron?"

"Another one of the taxi drivers was having a problem with a gang outside the kebab house; then Neil Hughes and Jacko showed up - end of problem. My thinking is: could this be a revenge attack by the thugs who Neil Hughes dealt with that night?"

"Excellent, I'll leave that with you. Anyone else have any ideas?"

Gary raised his arm. "Would it be worth contacting the D.V.L.A. to find any vans whose registered keepers live on or near the Rockford estate? Once we have a list, although it would be time consuming, the vehicles could be checked forensically. Debbie thought that a van was used, and the two suspects we had in the other day thought they may have seen a van the night Neil

Hughes dropped them off."

"Good idea, Gary. Time is one thing we do have at the moment, as we don't have any other leads to follow up; so, Tinny and Gary, if you can track down Jacko and speak to him, while the rest can follow up on Gary's idea concerning the vans. For the sake of Neil Hughes and his family, I desperately want to catch these people, and bring them to justice."

……………………………….....................................

Caroline set off in good time and knew that, even if the traffic was heavy, she would still be able to get to the hospital well before the plastic surgeon had finished. As she got nearer to the Mersey tunnel, however, she was surprised to see a long line of traffic ahead. She started to get more concerned when the line of traffic did not appear to be moving at all.

Eventually, it started to move, but very slowly; by now, Caroline was getting more concerned, so she rang Michael to see if he could find out what the problem may be. When Michael rang back, it was to tell her there had been either a breakdown or accident in one of the tunnels, so everything was being diverted to the other one.

Although the traffic was still moving slowly, Caroline was constantly looking at her watch, and starting to panic. She rang Michael again to tell him she was only just reaching the tunnel entrance, and to ring the hospital to explain the situation to them. As she finally entered the tunnel she hoped that, even if she missed Neil having his bandages removed, he would still be sedated before she got to the hospital.

……………………………………………………

"I'm ringing mum but I'm getting no reply, it's just going to voicemail." Michael was walking up and down, agitation in his voice.

Paul smiled. "Chill out, she's probably in the tunnel and won't be able to get a signal in there. Just give it ten minutes then try again."

Michael waited about five minutes, then tried again, but still only got the voicemail. He kept looking at his watch, then after another three minutes tried again, and was relieved when his mother answered.

"Finally! I rang the hospital and told them you've been delayed; they said dad's been moved to a different ward and he's in room twenty, on the first floor."

……………………………………………………

Caroline was now frantic; as she was trying to get through the Liverpool traffic, everything seemed to be moving slowly, and every traffic light was on red. By the time she got to the hospital, it was late afternoon and the car park was packed. She drove round several times, desperately looking for a space, but to no avail. Finally, she just parked on yellow lines, got out, forgot to lock the car, and ran into the hospital; she ran up the stairs to the first floor and along the corridor, following the signs to room twenty.

As she ran into the room, she immediately stopped.

"Oh, sorry," she said breathlessly, "I'm in the wrong room – sorry to disturb you," she said to the man in the hospital bed, as she turned to walk out.

"Caz - it's me!"

Caroline froze; she turned again to look at this complete stranger, and was totally confused. The nurse sitting at the side of the patient's bed smiled at Caroline, and said "Caz, isn't this fantastic?"

Caroline's head was spinning. She had prepared herself to see Neil with what may have been a badly disfigured face; she was now looking at a face that was completely free of disfigurement, that looked as if it had never been damaged. But the face she saw was not Neil's.

Neil turned to the nurse. "You'd better pass me that mirror again; I didn't think I looked *that* bad."

Caroline simply stared. "Neil?"

Neil had been smiling when Caroline first entered the room; now, he looked quite despondent. "I'm afraid so."

Caroline immediately felt guilty. "I'm…….I'm so sorry, you look fine - it was just the initial shock of seeing this very different man, it's……..it's just not what I was expecting."

"It was a surprise to me as well, when I first looked in the mirror. Even though Dr. Braithwaite had repeatedly told me that my face would be perfect, I couldn't understand how that could be possible. Needless to say, it was a very pleasant surprise."

"Well, now you're here, I'll leave you two alone," said the nurse, getting up. "I can't wait to tell the rest of the staff about the job Dr. Braithwaite has done; the man is an absolute magician."

As the nurse left the room, Caroline walked to Neil's bedside.

"Just lean forward a little bit, you're gown appears to have come undone at the back."

Caroline felt awful doing this, but she thought there was some kind of cruel trick being played on her. As Neil leaned forward, she untied his gown so that she could see the top of his left shoulder. Neil had a scar there from when he was young and, although it was not very big, it was a peculiar shape. The scar was there; this *was* Neil. She re-tied the gown. "There, that's better; you'll be more comfortable now."

When Caroline looked at Neil again, that sparkle he had in his eyes when she first entered the room had gone. If only she had set off earlier, and missed the traffic jam; she would have been able to see Neil's new face before he did, and would therefore have been better prepared for the shock.

"I think Dr. Braithwaite would like to speak to you before we leave; apparently, he was a bit disappointed you weren't here when he removed the bandages."

Caroline could tell by Neil's voice that he was also disappointed. She was trying to think of anything she could say that, hopefully, would lift Neil's spirits; however, she could not, so she just held his hand and smiled.

After what seemed an uncomfortable silence between them, Caroline said "I'll go and see him now, and then we can go home."

……………………………………………………………

As Caroline entered Dr. Braithwaite's office, he stood up and smiled.

"Ah, Mrs Hughes; I take it you have now seen your husband. Well, what do you think of my work?" He continued to smile, even though Caroline did not, but was quite taken aback when she started speaking.

"Because of your work, I've just been looking at, and talking to, a complete stranger. You must be aware that Neil has no memory, and now doesn't even look like he did before. Surely you could have reconstructed his face so it looked a bit like his own?"

Dr. Braithwaite looked at her steadily for a few moments.

"You're right," he replied, "I could have made him look a bit like he was before. However, had I done so, this would have been the result. One side of his face would have had a large dip in it, giving the impression that his face had collapsed through being hit with a baseball bat, which apparently it was; on the other side, there would have been a number of unsightly scars, looking as if someone had repeatedly stamped on him, which apparently they did. Dr. Hargraves saved your husband's life; I have now given him a future where he will be able to go into public places without people staring at him, and he won't need to be uncomfortable round little children who shy away from the monster."

He paused.

"I apologise if my work was not what you were hoping for, but my priority is to do the best possible job for my patient who, I believe, is very happy with the work I've done. I would have expected that you would have been too; I was obviously wrong. So, if there is nothing further," concluded Braithwaite, "I am a busy man."

……………………………………………………………

Caroline turned angrily and stormed out of Braithwaite's office. However, as she was heading back to the new ward Neil was in, as much as she was still angry with him, she began to think that possibly he was right, and she was just being selfish.

When she got back to the ward, she was surprised to find that Neil was still in bed.

"I thought you'd be dressed and ready to go."

"They've just got to change the dressing on the back of my head, and then we can make a move. Apparently, the blow to the back of my head was far worse than any to my face, so I'll still have to come over here from time to time, until everything is sorted out. Is everything alright? You look a bit upset."

"I'm fine," said Caroline. She looked at him searchingly. "I can see what you mean about Braithwaite being a bit arrogant, but it has to be said, he has done an incredible job."

As Caroline said this, she realised that she should have said so earlier, because Neil's eyes lit up and he smiled.

"Do you really think so? When I saw that look of horror on your face before, I felt awful."

Caroline began to get upset. "It wasn't horror," she said, struggling to get command of her voice, "it was just shock. I'm not sure what I was expecting, but I had mentally prepared myself to see a badly disfigured face. As Dr. Braithwaite has just said, he's given you a future without people staring at you."

"I think getting my memory back will be a big help." He took Caroline's hand. "I understand you are now about to take a complete stranger home with you; and that can't be easy; when I do get my memory back, hopefully, in time you'll get used to the new Neil Hughes."

Just then, as the nurse came in to change Neil's dressing, she was immediately followed by Dr. Braithwaite.

"Mr Hughes," he said, "this is a formality, but I obviously need your permission. When you are over on Monday to see the therapist, I have arranged a press conference for the afternoon."

Neil's facial expression immediately changed.

"A press conference? Regarding what, exactly?"

Braithwaite looked slightly confused. "The incredible success of my new method of facial reconstruction, of course. I could not have hoped for a better example than yourself."

"And at this press conference, I assume there would be photographers and television crews?"

When Neil said this, it seemed to lift Dr. Braithwaite's spirits. "Absolutely," he said enthusiastically, "it will be national press as well as local, and I expect international media coverage."

There was a moment's silence; then, as Neil began to speak, Caroline immediately recognised the tone of voice he was using. Neil very rarely got angry with anyone, but would speak to someone who had annoyed him as though he was speaking to a child.

"Dr. Braithwaite," he began, "why exactly was I brought in to this particular hospital?"

"You had severe head and facial injuries, which is what we specialise in."

"And how did I come about those injuries?"

"You were attacked by a group of people armed with weapons."

"Do I remember anything about the attack?"

"No, which I believe could be a good thing."

"Has anyone been arrested or charged regarding this attack?"

"Not to my knowledge; we did ask the police to keep us informed."

"So," concluded Neil, "at some point in the future, I could be walking along the street, pass my attackers, and not recognise them. As a result of the incredible job you've done they wouldn't recognise me; unless some fool were to plaster my picture all over the national press, or to have me sit in a press conference where I could be seen on television."

Braithwaite appeared to be struggling for words, just as Dr. Hargraves entered.

"Dr. Hargraves," he said, "I'm glad you're here. Mr Hughes appears reluctant to take part in the press conference on Monday. This is international news, and will really put this hospital on the map."

"Indeed," replied Dr. Hargraves. "Why not use billboards? We could use 'before and after' photographs of Mr Hughes, along with the caption 'Is this the man you tried to kill? If so, this is what he looks like now.' He looked at Braithwaite with contempt. "Don't be ridiculous."

Caroline looked down at the floor, and smiled to herself as Braithwaite left the room. Although she now thought he was probably right, in respect of the things he had said to her earlier, nevertheless she was pleased that both Neil, and Dr. Hargraves, had taken him down a peg or two.

Dr. Hargraves turned to Neil. "Apologies for my colleague. It's said that there is a fine line between brilliance and insanity; I sometimes think there's a fine line between brilliance and stupidity."

"To be fair, I think it's more a case of brilliant people often have no common sense."

"Neil, you are, as always, a gracious man; it's been a pleasure to have saved your life, and to have got to know you and your family. I know you'll be back over to see the therapist and to have the dressings changed but, if we don't bump into each other again, I wish you all the luck for the future."

As he was about to leave, the doctor turned, and added "By the way, you're still not quite ready for running round the wheel yet." He turned and smiled at Caroline. "He told me." He then turned back to Neil. "I will inform you when you can."

After the doctor had left, Caroline stood up. "While you're getting dressed, I'll go and ring the boys, and tell them we'll be on our way home soon. Let's hope the problem in the tunnel's been sorted out."

"What problem in the tunnel?"

"Didn't you get the message as to why I was delayed? There'd been a problem in one of the tunnels, so it created huge tailbacks; that's why I was late."

"I just thought you weren't bothered."

"Oh Neil, I really wanted to be here when they removed the bandages...."

"Caz, it was a joke."

Caroline smiled and thought, of course it was; for the last few days, she and Neil had been joking a great deal. It now occurred to her that she had pictured the man in the bandages with Neil's face, whereas now things were different. She would have to come to terms with this as soon as possible.

When Caroline was outside, she rang Michael, and explained the situation to him as best she could. She stressed that both Michael and Paul should make a big show of being pleased to see their father, even though he would look like a stranger. When she got back to the ward, Neil was ready to go.

....

As they walked out of the main door of the hospital, Neil noticed two very muscular men walking towards them. He instinctively stood between them and Caroline, and watched them as they approached. As they came nearer, for a split second, Neil thought one was taking his photograph on his mobile phone; he then realised that he was just holding it out of the sunlight. As they walked past, they merely smiled and nodded to Neil, so he nodded back.

He had not consciously noted his protective behaviour towards Caroline, but she did. From the night they met, Neil had not only loved her, but had always felt it was his duty to keep her safe. She saw then that, even though Neil had no memory at all, his first instinct was to stand between her and any possible danger. She felt annoyed with herself for doubting that this was Neil when she first entered the hospital ward.

Just as they got to the car, Caroline groaned. "That just about puts the top hat on my luck today."

Neil looked down; the car had been clamped. "Leave it to me," he said, "I'll go back in to reception, and find out how we sort this out."

As Neil walked back towards the main entrance, he saw the two men who had passed him previously talking to one of the security staff. As he got nearer, the security man walked towards Neil and spoke. "Sorry mate, didn't realise whose car it was, I'll get it sorted straight away."

Neil walked back to Caroline. "The security fella's getting it sorted out so, hopefully, we'll be able to get home soon. Have you got any cash on you, as I expect there'll be a release fee?"

"Not much, but I've got the credit card, if that can be used; if not, I've got the debit card, but we'll have to find a cash machine."

As Caroline said this, she suddenly felt sick, as she realised there was no money in the bank;

also, she was not sure how to draw cash out using a credit card, because she had never done it before. She therefore decided that, if the people who were coming to remove the clamp would not accept the credit card, she would ring Michael, and ask him what to do.

They did not wait for long before a van pulled up behind them, and a young man started removing the clamp.

"How much is this costing?" asked Neil.

The young man looked up at him. "It's costing nothing, we didn't realise whose car it was. I'm sorry if this has held you up." Neil turned to Caroline and raised his eyebrows, but said nothing.

After the clamp had been removed, Neil watched the departing van curiously.

"I wonder if, because I've become a bit of a celebrity here, someone's decided that it would be bad publicity if they'd clamped the car? Mind you, now I come to think of it," Neil reflected, "only we know that I won't be here for the press conference on Monday; maybe the hospital thought clamping our car might be mentioned." He looked bemused.

"I don't know; I thought he looked a bit frightened," remarked Caroline.

"He didn't need to be," shrugged Neil. "I wasn't in any way aggressive with him; I just asked him how much it would cost."

"No, I meant he looked frightened as he got out of the van, before you even spoke to him; anyway, let's go before they change their minds."

"Shall I drive, assuming I can remember how it's done?"

"I'd rather you did," smiled Caroline. "I'd imagine we'll know before you get out of the car park whether or not you can do it."

Once Neil had sat in the driver's seat, and adjusted both the interior mirror and the door mirrors, Caroline knew straight away that he remembered how to drive; as it turned out, the trip home was a pleasure to her as, for some reason, it reminded her of the night they first met.

………………………………………………………

As they pulled into the driveway, Neil said "I still can't believe this is our house. Did I do those hanging baskets, as well as the garden?"

"You really take pride in the hanging baskets; it's one of the first things people notice when they come to our house."

As they stepped out of the car, Michael and Paul came out of the house to greet them.

"Handsome dude," remarked Paul.

"Mum, are you doing Sunday lunch this weekend?" asked Michael. "Because Paul and I will have to keep an eye on Jenny and Cathy when they see dad; it looks like we've got some serious competition here."

Chapter 5

"Any luck with Jacko?" the D.C.I. asked Tinny, as the team gathered in the briefing room.

"He's not sure, boss. Jacko said that the problem, nowadays, is that these sort of things are on the increase. He's going to ask some of the other drivers if they can remember that particular incident, and will contact me if he comes up with an approximate date. We also went to the kebab house itself, but the staff said that there are regular fights outside, so the particular one we're interested in could have happened at any time."

D.C.I. Davies turned to the rest of the room. "How are we getting on with the list of vans registered in that area?"

"I'm afraid there's a lot more than we expected," replied Dave, "so this is going to take some time."

The D.C.I. shrugged. "As I said this morning, that's one thing we've got plenty of. We may need to get our traffic division involved, because there's probably a few vans knocking round that estate that aren't even registered to anyone. I'll speak to the Chief Superintendent, and see if he can help us out on that score. Stay positive, and keep thinking; above all, if you have any ideas, please, run them past me."

……………………………...

As Neil walked in to the dining room, he turned to Caroline and remarked "See what happens when your back's turned? These two have made a right mess!"

Michael smiled. "Putting documents all over the dining table is a trick Paul and I just can't resist. We've been doing it since we were kids."

Caroline looked at Neil apprehensively. "I wish we could have left this for a few days, but Michael said this needs sorting out straight away."

"Why, what's the problem?" enquired Neil.

Caroline explained the situation with regard to the mortgage not being paid, and her understanding that nothing else could be paid, because there was no money in the bank. In response, Neil smiled ruefully.

"I'll have to start by apologising for the fact that, sometimes, I think of Neil Hughes as being me; however, because of the memory loss, sometimes I also think of him as a different person. So bear with me if I say things like, 'I would imagine Neil would do this' instead of just saying what I would do."

Michael nodded. "Either way dad, we're hoping you can come up with some ideas."

"Well," said Neil, "judging from what you've told me about myself, I'm surprised I didn't have surplus money in the bank to cover the bills, in case of emergency."

Paul looked guilty. "That was my fault. I had a crash in the car, and you paid for all the repairs."

Neil immediately looked concerned. "Were you all right?"

"Sure. The airbag stopped me from butting the steering wheel."

"They're like that, airbags; they just get in the way when you're trying to have a bit of fun."

As Michael and Paul started laughing, Caroline said "I'd hoped that, when you came out of hospital, you'd be stress free; I'm sorry to burden you with this, but I'm really concerned."

Neil shook his head, as he took her hand. "Caz, I thought that I was going to die, then that I was probably going to look like some sort of monster even if I survived; those things were stressful. Sorting out a financial problem doesn't compare – in fact, I'll probably enjoy trying to find a solution."

Caroline looked relieved. "Well, in that case, who wants a cup of tea?"

As she walked into the kitchen, Michael grinned at his father.

"Mum's answer to everything is to put the kettle on."

"Does it suit her?"

"Not really; it makes her look a bit silly, to be honest."

Neil shook his head. "Women!"

Caroline could hear the laughter coming from the dining room, and was so grateful to the boys for doing exactly what she had asked them when she rang from the hospital. She just wished she could turn the clock back to this morning.

As Caroline brought in a pot of tea, Neil said "I'll take this stuff into the conservatory, and see what I can come up with. Mike, while I'm doing this, have a look on the internet for male model jobs. Your mum tells me I hate being a taxi driver, but couldn't think of anything else to do. I think I'd look quite good on a catwalk." Neil stood up, winked at Paul, then strolled out of the dining room holding all the documents under one arm, with his other hand on his hip.

When Neil went into the conservatory and closed the door behind him, Caroline knew he would not be able to hear what was being said in the dining room. She turned to Michael and Paul.

"Thanks for that."

Paul looked confused. "Thanks for what?"

"Making a big fuss of your dad, and pretending it didn't matter that he looks so different."

Paul raised his eyebrows. "I don't know about our Mike, but I think dad looks brilliant. I wasn't pretending that it didn't matter, because it doesn't matter."

"Paul's right," agreed Michael. "Dad must have been dreading having those bandages removed, so for him to be able to see himself like this must be great. That's dad in the conservatory in one piece, looking fantastic. None of us, particularly dad himself, thought that could possibly happen."

Caroline lowered her voice, even though she knew Neil could not hear them. "Did either of you think there was something different about your dad's eyes?"

Both boys shook their heads. "Mum," said Michael, "that's definitely dad in there."

"I know, I know, it's just going to take some getting used to."

Neil was in the conservatory for some time before he came back in to the dining room. Although he was smiling when he entered the room, he looked slightly uncomfortable before he spoke.

"Well," he remarked, "after looking at all the figures, I now understand why I worked so much. What happened to me must have been about the only thing I wasn't insured against! Anyway," he continued, "I think I may have found a solution to the problem; however, I wouldn't exactly describe it as good news." He paused, as the others looked at him expectantly.

"Okay," he said briskly, "looking at everything we are paying now, there's very little that can be ignored for any length of time. Mike was right, this situation does need to be sorted out as soon as possible otherwise we could lose this house. Realistically, from what I can see, the only way out of this is to sell the villa."

Caroline looked shocked. "We can't do that!"

"Sorry, I must have misunderstood - I thought you owned it outright?"

"*We* own it outright."

"Sorry, I meant 'we.'"

"When I say we *can't* sell it," explained Caroline, "I mean that we could if we wanted to, but the villa has been your dream for so long. When you get your memory back, you will be devastated, almost suicidal to know that the villa has been sold."

"That may be true," considered Neil, "but, as I can't remember how strong my desire was to move over there, I don't know how I would feel. What I can say for certain, is that one payment has been missed on the mortgage; if the next two payments aren't made, the mortgage company can sell our house, and there would be nothing we could do about it."

"Yes; however," argued Caroline, "you've said in the past that this house is worth considerably more than what we owe on the mortgage, so we'd have a lot of money left over."

"Caz, they wouldn't sell it for its market value; they'd simply sell it for what we owe them. In other words, miss two more payments, and you'd have no house, and no money."

Caroline looked stricken. "They can't do that."

"I'm afraid they can," said Neil seriously; "and, after reading the letter we received from them, I can guarantee that they would."

"But what if we can't sell the villa quick enough?"

Neil patted Caroline on the hand. "This sounds rude, and I certainly don't mean it to be; but, if you let me explain the whole plan, hopefully, you'll understand what I mean. Even if I say so myself," he said smiling, "I do think it's a particularly cunning plan."

Caroline smiled for the first time since Neil had come back into the room; he was pleased by this, and noted "Clearly, I've just said something that has cheered you up a little bit."

She laughed. "You always describe ideas you have as being a 'cunning plan.'"

"It's good to know I have a lot of ideas," he grinned. "Okay, this is how it'll work. The first thing is to contact the solicitor in Spain. I believe you said that it was a young woman who speaks excellent English?"

"Yes, remember when........... sorry," said Caroline, annoyed with herself, "that was a stupid thing to say."

"Caz, don't apologise," Neil said emphatically. "It's an expression everyone uses, you're bound to say it again at some point; it's not stupid, and it doesn't bother me at all. So, to get back to the fiendishly cunning plan - did I mention before that it was fiendish? Because if I didn't, I should have." Caroline smiled wryly at the two boys, as he continued. "The solicitor in Spain can arrange for the villa to be put up for sale. If she then confirms in writing the fact that it's up for sale, together with the asking price, then that needs to be taken to our bank. Needless to say, you'll have to go to the bank, not me."

"Do I have to go on my own? Can't you come with me?"

"Do the staff in the bank know you?"

"Yes; you and I have been there a number of times over the years."

"So, obviously, they know me as well."

"They know you very well, as you regularly pay cash in to our account."

Neil smiled. "Well, they certainly wouldn't know me now. If you and I turned up there, they'd probably think you'd bumped off Neil and traded him in for a more handsome model, who's very good at forging his signature."

Neil turned to the boys. "That's me, by the way." As Michael and Paul laughed, Neil continued. "The bank will take notice of a solicitor's letter, albeit a Spanish solicitor; hopefully, they'll either arrange some form of bridging loan or, at least, cover the standing orders and direct debits for a certain period. This will buy us time.

"If the villa were to be sold quickly, so be it; from what you've told me, if I could acquire a villa once, then I could do it again. Alternatively, if it didn't sell, but all the payments are being made, then when I regain my memory I could sort things out anyway. Either way, the priority must be to keep this house."

Caroline still looked unconvinced; then Michael said "I could go to the bank with mum. They know me from when I took out the business loan, for which you were guarantor." This suggestion made Caroline look slightly happier, although still somewhat doubtful.

"So," concluded Neil, "what do you think? It's not a question of wanting to sell the villa, it's more a question of finding a way of keeping the house which, I believe, has got to be the priority. Have a think about it tonight; I'll have another look at the paperwork tomorrow, and see if there's anything else I can come up with."

Caroline pursed her lips. "I'm really not happy about this; not for me, more for you."

"Believe me, you don't need to dwell on that. You've often said that the villa was my dream, but I have to say, losing this house would be an absolute nightmare. Talking of which," said Neil, stifling a yawn, "do you mind if I go to bed? I'm absolutely shattered."

"Of course," said Caroline, "you must be. I'm so sorry you had to sort all this out on your first day home."

"It's no problem," smiled Neil. "I'll see you in the morning, and I'll take another look at the figures; but don't worry - one way or another, we'll get through this."

....

Neil went upstairs, and went straight into Michael's room. He took off his shirt, and was looking at some school photographs of Michael and Paul, when Caroline walked in behind him.

"Oh my God!"

Neil quickly turned round, looked round the room, and said "Caz, what's wrong?"

"I didn't realise there was so much damage to the rest of your body."

"Oh, this," Neil said dismissively, "it's okay, it's only bruising. Nothing was broken, luckily; this will all fade soon."

Caroline looked rueful. "The last few days I've been hugging and squeezing you; it must have been really hurting."

"Honestly, it looks a lot worse than it actually is; anyway, it was worth it."

"Is your whole body like that?"

"More or less. You can hug the back of my left leg, though; they managed to miss that bit."

"No," said Caroline firmly, "I'm not going to hug you while you're like this; I'd feel guilty putting you through so much pain. I'll see you in the morning."

As Caroline left the room, Neil's smile faded. He sat on the edge of the bed, a feeling of sadness beginning to wash over him. Days ago, when he had made a joke about the fat ugly wife, Caroline had said that she would give him a big kiss when the bandages were removed; but that had not happened. Today he had realised that, each time he touched Caroline's hand, she had tensed up slightly; now, being hugged was out of the question.

When the bandages were removed and he saw his new face for the first time, he thought things could not be any better. He was now beginning to have his doubts.

....

As Caroline walked back in to the dining room, both Michael and Paul could see that she was upset.

"What's up, mum?" asked Michael.

"You should see the bruises on your dad's body – they're huge, and he's covered in them." Both boys looked uncomfortable; she looked at them suspiciously. "You've seen them, haven't you?"

"They don't look as bad now as they did last week," said Paul hurriedly.

Caroline folded her arms. "Why didn't you tell me about them?"

"Dad told us not to," Michael said, guiltily.

"Why?"

"He said it would just upset you if you saw them."

"It does upset me seeing them," said Caroline hotly, "but it upsets me more, knowing that I've been hugging your dad without realising that I must have been really hurting him."

"I think it would hurt him more, if you didn't hug him," said Paul, trying to placate her.

Michael looked grim. "When we saw, for the first time, what these people had done to him, we weren't upset; we were just angry. I know you said that we should leave the police to do their job, but I just wanted to kill them. I still do now."

Caroline dropped into a chair; she hung her head, so that the boys could not see the tears in her eyes, and said "So do I."

....

Caroline was up early on the Saturday morning, but was not surprised to see Neil in the dining room with all the paperwork laid out in front of him, and a calculator in his hand. As she walked in, she said "Did you sleep alright last night?"

"I slept really well; it just seemed strange that Paul wasn't there, when I occasionally woke up."

"You didn't have any nightmares, did you?"

"No; I had the starting of one, but I was able to wake myself up."

"Were you comfortable? It must be very painful, lying down covered in all those bruises."

"Caz, honestly, they are nowhere near as bad as they look." Neil's tone was almost pleading.

Caroline looked unconvinced. "Well, I'm making a cup of tea, would you like one?"

"No, thanks," he replied quietly.

While Caroline was still in the kitchen, Neil called to her "Danny's coming round today to help me sort out the insurance on the taxi."

"Well, if he brings Jacko with him, I'd better get the bacon ready," Caroline shouted back. "Did you pick up a new frying pan?"

"No, but I managed to get most of the dents out of this one."

Neil carried on with what he was doing, but was glad that they were able to share a joke for the first time since Caroline had seen him without the bandages on his face. The banter carried on while Caroline was still in the kitchen, but soon stopped when she came back into the dining room; at once, the realisation dawned on him - Caroline had been laughing and joking with the old Neil Hughes, because she could not see the new one.

Just then, Michael and Paul arrived. "Any chance of breakfast?" they demanded, without ceremony.

Caroline looked relieved at their arrival. "Sit down, I'll make it now. I assume you both want the full English?"

"It can be the full Welsh if you like, as long as there's plenty of it," said Paul, sitting down and rubbing his hands together.

Caroline then turned to Neil. "Would you like some breakfast?"

"Oh, well…..did Neil...... sorry, did *I* normally eat breakfast?"

"Not usually," replied Caroline; "you normally went out so early to work, I was often still in bed."

"I'll give it a miss, then." Neil had been thinking that, if he could find out what his habits and routines were, it might help in the present situation, until he got his memory back. I must try not to think of Neil Hughes as a different person, he thought.

Just as the boys finished their breakfast, there was a knock on the door. Michael immediately stood up, saying "I'll get it."

Neil could hear a conversation and laughter coming from Michael, and whoever he was speaking to; then Michael shouted "It's Danny and Jacko."

As they all came into the dining room, Jacko turned to Michael.

"I thought you said he was dead handsome?" Jacko then winked at Neil. "Well, it looks like my title as best looking taxi driver has been taken from me - you can't get into any more fights now, looking like that. You never had much to lose before, you have now."

Danny looked at Neil, amazed. "Yosser, you look brilliant!"

When Caroline heard Jacko and Danny, she came out of the kitchen, and hugged them both; Neil continued to smile, but felt extremely envious of his two friends.

"Caz," said Jacko, his tone wheedling, "have I ever told you this before? You are beautiful, and completely wasted on this Liverpool scoundrel."

"Every time you see me," said Caroline, rolling her eyes upwards.

"It must be the truth then, if I've said it that many times." Jacko hugged Caroline again. "By the way, be careful you don't put too much butter on the bread, otherwise the bacon might slide off."

Caroline laughed. "I can take a hint! Bacon butties, coming up."

Meanwhile, Michael and Paul had finished eating, and got up from the table.

"Right, we're off now," announced Michael; "some of us have got work to do."

"Are you coming round later?" asked Neil.

"Too right," declared Paul, "the girls can't wait to see you."

As Michael and Paul left, Jacko stared openly at Neil. "Any chance I can have a close look at your face?"

"Sure," laughed Neil, "why not?"

Jacko studied Neil's face in detail; he was clearly astounded. "This is absolutely incredible," he said finally. "As you know, I've picked up a few scars over the years – oh, hang on, no you don't; sorry, I'd forgotten about the memory loss. I hope *you* haven't forgotten about the thousand pound you owe me."

Neil's face dropped slightly before Jacko said, hurriedly, "I'm only kidding! We're going to have some laughs while you've got no memory."

Caroline brought in the bacon sandwiches at that point, to the beaming smiles of Jacko and Danny.

"Right," said Danny, as he helped himself to a sandwich, "we need to get the insurance sorted out on the cab as soon as possible. The problem, is the plate."

"I don't follow," said Neil.

Danny went on to explain that the plate on the back of the taxi was actually worth considerably more than the vehicle itself; the local authority rules were that, if a vehicle was off the road beyond a certain period, they could take the plate back, and Neil would lose it.

"I see," said Neil. "So, what's the plate worth, and how long have I got?"

"One changed hands recently for twenty-five thousand pounds," replied Danny. "I'm not sure how long you can be off the road, but I'll check the taxi rules and regulations."

After getting through a mountain of bacon sandwiches, Danny and Jacko stood up to leave, advising Neil to contact his insurance company first thing Monday morning to get a claim form from them; they shook hands with him, and Caroline came out of the kitchen and followed them into the hall.

As they were all standing by the front door, Danny remarked "It's great to see Neil like this. After what happened, you must be so happy." Caroline managed to smile, but felt guilty; she was far from happy.

As Danny walked down the driveway to his cab, Jacko put his arm around Caroline. "I know how difficult this must be for you. It's going to take some time to get used to this, but Neil needs you now more than ever."

…………………………………………………………

When Caroline walked back into the dining room, she said "Everything all right as far as the taxi's concerned?"

"No problem; Danny's told me everything I need to do but, if there's anything I'm not sure of, he can help me sort it out. There is one thing: as far as you know, have we got any savings?"

Caroline frowned. "I don't think so, but I'm not sure; why?"

"It was just something Danny said – something about if necessary, my having to dip into my savings." Caroline simply looked mystified. "Well," continued Neil, "I didn't say anything about our present problem, but I got the impression that both Danny and Jacko felt I had some extra money somewhere."

Caroline shrugged. "I hope they're right, but I'm not aware of anything. The trouble is, you may well have told me at some point in the past about savings, and I haven't been listening properly." She sighed, looking somewhat ashamed. "When you get your memory back, probably one of the first things you'll remember is that you have to tell me something several times before it sinks in."

"I'm sure that not true."

"Oh, but it is. You would often tell me something, and be really enthusiastic over it, but I'd be thinking of something completely different; usually, worrying about something Paul's done."

"Does Paul often do things that worry you?" Neil's voice was concerned.

"It's not so much what he does, it's more the company he keeps. I just wish he was more like Michael."

Neil looked thoughtful for a few moments.

"This'll sound strange," he said eventually, "but it's the only way I can explain it from where I stand." He paused, as if choosing his words carefully. "When I was brought out of the coma, from my point of view, I was meeting you, Michael and Paul for the first time; however, although I have no memory of you all, I still understand that we all have strengths and weaknesses. I've come to admire Michael for what he's achieved, so far, for someone so young; I've no doubt he'll be very successful, but I hope he doesn't make the same mistakes that I think I did with regard to getting his priorities right."

Caroline was about to say something, but Neil held up his hand.

"Please, let me finish. Having Paul with me," he continued, "particularly when I was having the nightmares, was a great help; and, I believe he helped me get through this. As to his mixing with the wrong people, well, I've no doubt he'll grow out of that. His strengths may be different from Michael's; but, in the end, we are what we are."

Caroline nodded thoughtfully; "Oh, damn!" she then exclaimed suddenly, putting her hand to her head.

"What's wrong?" said Neil, startled. "Have I said the wrong thing again?"

"No," she replied, "I've just remembered a promise I made to Paul in the hospital, and I let him down." She looked angry with herself. "And another thing - when he told you about the accident, your first thought was to ask him if he was alright. That should have been my first thought as well, and it wasn't."

Neil looked confused. "But you'd have known whether or not he was alright; I didn't, because I've no memory of what happened."

"That's not the point," said Caroline; "I was too busy thinking about things that affected me, and not other people."

"You're being too hard on yourself, I think," said Neil. "Paul probably didn't even notice, and I'm sure he wouldn't expect any sort of apology."

"Exactly! *That's* why he's so much like you. Since we met, you've felt it's your job to look after me, and protect me. Paul is exactly the same, and wouldn't expect an apology - but he deserves one."

"Caz, be honest," said Neil teasingly, "you love Michael more than Paul."

"No I don't! I love Paul just as much......."

Neil raised both hands in a placatory gesture. "Caz, it was a joke. I know you love Paul as much as Michael; sorry, it was obviously a very poor joke." He made a mental note that, in future, he would restrict his jokes to times when they were in separate rooms, when Caroline could not see him.

………………………………...

D.C.I. Davies entered the briefing room.

"Listen up everybody; there's overtime for anyone who wants it this weekend," he announced. "As we still don't have an approximate date for the trouble outside the kebab house, I'm looking for volunteers to trawl through the CCTV footage, until we can find the incident involving Neil Hughes.

"So far, we've had no luck with the vans that have been checked in connection with our case; however, the Chief Super is well pleased with what's been found relating to a number of other cases. This has included a great deal of stolen property; drugs; and, in one of the vans that was stopped, they found a sawn-off shotgun hidden in the back.

"The problem is, now that the word has gone round the Rockford that we're stopping vans and checking them, it's fair to say that, whoever has the van in which Neil Hughes was probably transported, they'll keep a low profile for the foreseeable future. So, overtime for anyone who wants it; weekend off for anyone who doesn't."

………………………………...

While Neil was still in the dining room checking all the figures again, Caroline shouted from the kitchen "Do you fancy a brew? I'm just putting the kettle on."

"Mike said it doesn't really suit you," called Neil back to her.

"What does he know? I think I look quite fetching with the kettle on. Admittedly, I do get some funny looks at the supermarket, but some people just don't understand fashion."

As Neil heard Caroline putting the teapot on the tray, he stood up and walked to the window, and kept looking out, with his back to Caroline, when she came into the room. He heard her put down the tray. "I've just had a thought," she declared.

"Didn't you have one of those a few days ago?"

"I think I did; I hope this isn't going to become some sort of habit."

Neil started to laugh, when Caroline suddenly said "Oh, no!"

Neil was about to turn around, in case she had spilt the tea and burned herself; however, he stopped himself, and kept looking out of the window.

"What's up?"

"I've just had a *second* thought. My brain can't handle that, we may have to get the doctor out."

Neil took a sharp intake of breath. "*Two* thoughts in the one day? Might need a specialist."

"We might at that," said Caroline. "So before he gets here, come and have your cup of tea, and I'll tell you my *two* thoughts."

Neil smiled to himself, reluctantly turned away from the window, and sat down by Caroline; he was still smiling as he asked "Go on then; tell me quickly, before you forget them."

"It's to do with the possibility of having savings somewhere," said Caroline. "Your dad used to hide money in the house in case of emergency, which used to really annoy your mum. So, possibly, you may have done the same."

"Surely I wouldn't have hidden money from *you*?"

Caroline smiled knowingly. "If you did, it would've been a very wise move. If I knew there was a secret stash of money, I'd have certainly dipped into it; and now I think about it, there has been the odd occasion when there's been a bit of a problem, and you've produced the money we've needed from somewhere."

"This is sounding very promising," said Neil, brightening up. "The only trouble is that there are so many places in the house, as well as the garage and the garden shed. Have we got a torch? I'll try the loft first."

"Don't you want to hear my second thought?"

"If it's as exciting as this one, I may have to have a lie down. Go on, hit me with it."

"We don't need to wait until Monday to contact the solicitor in Spain," said Caroline.

"Do solicitors work on Saturdays over there?"

"I don't think so; but I've got her mobile phone number, so I could ring her now."

Caroline looked forlorn as she said this; Neil was about to take her hand, but then stopped himself. He simply said "I've looked at the figures over and over again, and I just can't see any other way out."

Caroline nodded. "I know," she said sadly, "I've been thinking about it all night and you're right, we can't risk losing this house; you've worked too hard to get it like this. The trouble with me, is that I've just taken it for granted; whereas, effectively, you saw it for the first time a few days ago, and made me realise how much I love it as well."

"Right," said Neil, "think positive. You ring the solicitor and get that started, while I search the premises. All being well, I'll find the pot of gold, and then you can ring her back and tell her it's not for sale after all." Neil grinned. "I feel like I'm going on a treasure hunt - keep your fingers crossed."

....

Caroline rang the solicitor, explained the situation, and asked if she could get the ball rolling as soon as possible; the solicitor sympathised with Caroline's position, and said she would treat it as a matter of urgency.

A short time later, as Caroline was doing her housework, she could hear Neil up in the loft on his treasure hunt.

"Do you fancy a cup of tea?" she shouted up to him.

"Yes please," he called from above. "There's some really interesting stuff up here, but there's an awful lot of junk as well."

"That's your fault, you won't throw anything away. You always keep hold of things and say they may come in handy in the future. If I hadn't made a few sly trips to the re-cycling place, you wouldn't have been able to move up there. I take it you haven't found any treasure yet?"

"I found a big stash of used notes, but they were creased and dirty, so I threw them out the window. I'm only interested in nice crisp twenty pound notes; the ones I threw out were only grubby fivers." Caroline smiled to herself, shook her head, and went to make the tea.

For the rest of the afternoon, Neil searched the loft thoroughly, but without success; he therefore climbed back down the ladder disconsolately, and slowly walked downstairs. As he came into the kitchen, Caroline observed how despondent he looked.

"No luck there," he said with a sigh, collapsing into a chair; "mind you, when I get my memory back, it'll be interesting to see why I've kept so much junk. I'll have a look in the garage next; is that full of junk as well?"

"No, it's quite tidy in there, but you'll probably have to drive your car out in order to get at everything."

"I've got a car?"

"Yes; it's very old, but you like it because it's so reliable. You don't use it very often - only if the cab's away, having work done on it that you can't do yourself; that's when you use the car to do any running around."

Neil did not spend as much time in the garage as he had in the loft, but still found nothing; by now, he was feeling very disappointed. When he came back into the house, he told Caroline he was going to have a shower and a short sleep before the boys arrived. Caroline had seen the enthusiasm and excitement in his eyes disappear over the day, and felt very sorry for him.

……………………………………………………………

Neil was woken by the sound of voices downstairs; he realised, as he looked at the clock, that Michael, Paul, Jenny and Cathy must have arrived.

As he walked downstairs, he could hear the chattering and laughter coming from the living room. He felt slightly uneasy before going in; Jacko, Danny and his sons had seemed to accept his new look without any problem, whereas Caroline obviously had not. He wondered what the girls' reaction would be.

He took a deep breath, and walked in, smiling. "Evening, ladies."

There was a slight pause, which made Neil feel even more uncomfortable; then Cathy said "Neil! Tell you what, I'll ditch Mike, you can ditch Caz, and we'll run off together."

Everyone in the room was laughing, particularly Neil himself, as he could not have thought of a better welcome; the comment had immediately put him at ease and, as he sat down next to Caroline, she took his hand, and said to Cathy "Too late - I saw him first!"

Neil smiled; but he could not forget that Caroline's reaction, when she saw him first, was in stark contrast to Cathy's. As the evening progressed, he even felt that the girls were almost flirting with him; this embarrassed him slightly, as his confidence with the opposite sex did not match his looks. He noted that, other than him, everyone was drinking, and seemed to be really enjoying themselves.

"Have I never drunk alcohol?" he asked Caroline.

"You must have tried it when you were younger; but, when you met me, you didn't drink. You told me that, not only did you not like the taste of it, but it actually made you feel quite ill."

"That must be a bit awkward for you, if we go out anywhere."

"Far from it - it's great, because we don't have to worry about taxis, as you always drive."

"Yes," said Michael, "just imagine if you'd got a taxi to and from your cousin's wedding last month, it would've cost you a fortune."

As Michael said this, Caroline seemed slightly uncomfortable, which no-one else noticed, apart from Neil; he turned to her, and said "What's wrong, Caz?"

Caroline just smiled, and shook her head. "Nothing; it was quite a hike, and I don't think either of us enjoyed it very much. You always say that when you wear a suit, you look like a bouncer."

"I didn't do anything silly, did I?"

"No, not at all; as always, you were on your best behaviour, but I think I drank a bit more than I should have."

"Talking about that," mentioned Neil," my brother obviously likes the odd glass, judging from the state he was in, sometimes, when he visited me."

"Well," said Caroline, "the truth is, he's an alcoholic, and you've never really had much to do with him for some time now. I used to go and see him regularly with the boys, and he always made a big fuss of them but, as they've got older, they don't see him much either. I feel quite sorry for him; but, unfortunately, you don't."

Paul had overhead Caroline say this, and commented "Dad stopped feeling sorry for him after constantly lending him money, and never getting it back."

"As he's my brother, though," pondered Neil, "maybe I should have had more time for him."

"Paul's right," said Caroline firmly, "you were a soft touch for too long; not just with your Ian and Sally, but *my* brother, who let us down as well. We went guarantor on a loan he took out, and it nearly cost us this house. It was after that happened that your attitude changed, as far as helping either of the families was concerned."

"Even so," persisted Neil, "I'd have thought you should help your family when you can. I'm sure Michael would help Paul, and vice versa, if either were struggling."

"I wouldn't work extra hours in order to give Paul money, so that he could go out drinking more," remarked Michael.

"And I wouldn't expect him to," agreed Paul. "To be honest, as we've got older, we haven't got much time for people like uncle Ian or uncle Pete."

Neil felt that he needed to change the conversation; so he asked Michael "Did you have a look on the internet for male model vacancies?"

Michael laughed. "You're just too handsome, dad, you'd show the others up."

"Actually," said Neil more seriously, "you could do me a favour, and show me how to use the computer to access information; it could be a help in getting my memory back. How long would it take you to show me what I need to do?"

"I'll show you now, if you want," said Michael. "It won't take long, it's dead easy."

They left the others talking in the living room, and went into the study; Michael spent about thirty minutes showing his father about accessing the internet, sending and receiving emails, typing and printing documents, and all the basics he needed to know.

Once they had finished, and went back to the living room to join the others, Neil sat down next to Caroline, and was elated when she kissed him on the cheek.

"We should have a big party, to celebrate you coming home."

Neil smiled broadly. "That's a great idea; once we've got all the finances sorted out, I'm all for it."

After that, Neil thoroughly enjoyed the rest of the evening; but the effort of being sociable had exhausted him, and he felt he had to apologise for being so tired, and having to go to bed. Nevertheless, as he walked up the stairs, all he could think about was Caroline kissing him on the cheek.

....

Neil was up early on the Sunday morning, and went straight out to the garden shed to resume his treasure hunt; unfortunately, there was even more junk in there than in the loft, so his only option was to take everything out, which took quite some time.

At one point he went back into the house to get a cold drink, and was surprised that Caroline had still not got up. Well, he thought, she did tell me that I was the early riser in the house.

He went back outside and continued with his task. Eventually, he cleared the shed, and started searching through all the drawers and boxes that were left in there. He saw a long wooden box at the back of the shed, which he thought would be an ideal hiding place. At first, he was disappointed to find that it was full of old tools which, judging from the amount of rust they were covered in, had obviously not been used for some years; however, as he looked at the box, something did not seem right about it. He examined it more closely, and noticed that, when he moved some of the tools, the box appeared to have a false bottom.

He could not get the tools out quickly enough, in order to see if there was anything underneath. When he removed the false bottom, he was surprised to see a baseball bat underneath, which had obviously been hidden; what concerned him more, was the fact that the bat had brown stains on it which may have been old blood stains.

After Neil had put everything back in to the shed, he went into the house and just sat in the dining room, feeling really dejected; then, as he heard Caroline coming downstairs, his spirits lifted, as the kiss on the cheek was still fresh in his mind. She came into the dining room, walking slowly and carefully, and sank into a chair, putting her head in her hands.

"Caz, are you all right? You don't look well."

Caroline groaned. "I shouldn't have drunk so much last night; I've got a terrible hangover."

"Is there anything you can take for it? Can I get you anything?"

"A nice cup of tea wouldn't go amiss, and can you bring the headache tablets in as well, please."

Neil went and made the tea. "Milk and sugar?" he called from the kitchen.

"Milk, no sugar, thanks."

"Where do you keep the headache tablets?"

"The cupboard above the sink."

Neil brought the cup of tea into the dining room, and placed it carefully on the table, also handing the headache tablets to Caroline. She gave him a watery smile of gratitude.

"I was watching you all last night," said Neil, "and was a bit envious, thinking it was a pity I don't drink; but looking at how you're suffering now, maybe my not drinking isn't such a bad thing."

"I'll be okay, are you going to have a search of the shed today?"

"I already have; but I'm afraid I found nothing, and I was quite thorough."

"So," said Caroline, sipping her tea, "what are your plans for the rest of the day?"

"Well, Michael left a list of places we've been to over the years, so I'm going to go on the internet and see if anywhere, in any way, looks familiar. It's worth a shot, you never know."

As Neil stood up, he squeezed Caroline's hand; but was disappointed to discover that the slight feeling of tension had returned.

………………………………………………………………

As he sat staring at the computer screen, he was not even looking at the image in front of him; he was confused, wondering why Caroline was, clearly, uncomfortable with him again. He had been so sure that the evening before was a step forward; now, it seemed that he had misread the situation.

He heard Caroline's mobile phone ring, and she appeared to be speaking on it for some time. When she came into the study, Neil was still staring at the computer screen; as he looked up, he could see that she had been crying.

"What's happened?"

"It looks like the solicitor has a buyer for the villa."

Neil was taken aback. "That's not possible; you only told her yesterday that you wanted to sell it………I mean, that *we* wanted to sell it."

Caroline sighed heavily, and sat down.

"About six months ago, we all went over there – you and I, Mike and Cathy, Paul and Jenny. We threw a bit of a party, and invited the builder and his family, the solicitor, and her husband; we also suggested she bring some of her own friends. It turned out that the couple she brought along were English, but live over there permanently. Anyway, at the end of the party, one of these friends of hers said to you that, if we ever wanted to sell the villa, he'd like first option."

"What was my reaction to that?"

Caroline hesitated; Neil could see that she was trying to get command of her emotions before she spoke.

"You said you would never sell it," she said, sadly.

Neil suddenly felt overwhelmed with remorse, as he saw her unhappiness.

"Caz……… I'm so sorry; I've obviously got something terribly wrong in my life, but I don't know what it is. That attack on me was deliberate and planned – it wasn't a robbery that went wrong, or a fight with some drunks. Someone wanted me dead, but I don't know what I could have done to merit that; all I know is that it has ruined your life, and you are totally innocent." He looked at her, misery etched on his face. "When I was looking at the various insurance policies the other day, I thought then it would have been better for you if I had died. Seeing how unhappy you are now, I feel so guilty, and don't know how I can make things better. I'm sorry." At this, he got up from his chair, walked out of the study, and went through the house into the back garden.

Caroline remained where she was for a short while, staring into space; then she went into the kitchen, stood at the window, and just watched Neil sitting on his own, holding his head in his hands. There had been times in their life when Caroline had felt sorry for Neil, particularly when his father died. She could never have imagined she would ever feel pity for him.

Chapter 6

Caroline knew that she needed to do something, and quickly; but, as she was unsure what to do, she rang Michael, and asked him if he could come round straight away.

Michael and Paul arrived together, as they had been working nearby. They found their mother just sitting in the kitchen, looking out into the garden.

"What's happened?" asked Michael.

Caroline explained to the boys about the phone call from the Spanish solicitor, and what their father had said. She looked angry with herself.

"I should've waited a while before going in and telling him about the sale. That way, it would have given me time to come to terms with the situation, and appear more cheerful when I told him."

"None of this is his fault," declared Paul, shaking his head. "We wouldn't have this house, or a villa in Spain, if it wasn't for dad."

"Right," said Michael briskly, "Paul, you go and sit with dad, and see if you can cheer him up a bit." Paul nodded, and went out into the garden. "Now, mum," continued Michael, "the solicitor told you she had emailed the documents through, as well as the letter for the bank. What email address has she sent them to?"

"Your dad's, I think."

Michael pulled a face. "That's awkward; when I was showing him how to open emails, I had to use my email address because, obviously, he didn't know the password to his."

"I do; it's 'scouseneil.'"

"'Scouseneil?'" Michael frowned. "I've never heard anyone call him that."

Caroline shrugged. "Nor have I. Maybe that's what he was called when he first moved over here from Liverpool."

"Anyway, I'll fire up the laptop, connect the printer, and we'll get things sorted."

As she looked at Michael walking towards the study, Caroline realised that, as he was getting older, he was becoming more like Neil when it came to thinking positively, and getting things done. "I'm putting the kettle on," she called after him; "I assume you want one."

He gave her the thumbs up without turning around, and continued into the study.

Caroline then stood at the kitchen door, and called "I'm making a cup of tea if anyone wants one."

She saw Paul speak to Neil. "No thanks," he called back; then, she saw the two of them stand up, and walk towards the house. She took a deep breath; she was determined to smile, and look as happy as possible, as they came into the kitchen.

Neil kept his head down and did not look at her; but it was obvious to her that he had been crying, and she realised that he probably felt embarrassed.

"We're just going to the training room," said Paul.

"Oh – but……." began Caroline; however, they had left the kitchen before she could raise any objection.

As Paul and Neil approached the study, Paul put his head round the door.

"Dad and I are going to give the heavy bag a good pasting."

"Brilliant," murmured Michael, without looking up; "as soon as I've done this, I'll join you."

Paul led the way upstairs to the training room. As they walked in, Neil glanced around; there were various pieces of equipment, including a very heavy punch-bag, a speedball, and a floor to ceiling punch-ball.

"You'll feel a lot better after a workout here," said Paul.

Neil had noticed the concern in Caroline's voice when Paul had told her where they were going; however, he knew something that she did not. While she had been speaking to the solicitor earlier, he had received a call from the hospital; his most recent test results had shown that his heart was fine, and they anticipated no further problems. He had planned to give her the good news when she came off the phone, but decided against it when he saw how upset she was; and now, he was uncertain as to when, or even if, he would tell her.

....

Caroline could hear the noise of the punch-bag being hit even in the kitchen, and hoped that it might help Neil get rid of some of the anger he must be feeling.

Shortly afterwards, Michael came back into the kitchen.

"I've downloaded everything, and printed it up; there are a number of documents you both need to sign, then I can scan them, and email them back to the solicitor. When dad sees the letter for the bank from the solicitor, hopefully, that might cheer him up a bit." Caroline nodded silently; Michael put his hand on her shoulder. "I know you don't want to sell the villa, but there doesn't seem to be much of a choice; getting upset in front of dad will only make things worse."

When Michael went upstairs to join his father and brother, Caroline went through to the dining room, and spread out all the papers on the dining table. As she looked at them, she was concerned that all the documents she needed to sign were in Spanish; however, the letter for the bank was in perfect English. She was uncertain whether to point out to Neil that, when they bought the villa, the documents they signed at the time were in English, together with an additional set in Spanish.

Later, when Michael and Paul came into the dining room, Neil was not with them.

"Where's your dad?"

"In the shower," replied Paul.

"By the time I got up there," said Michael, "dad was just in a pair of shorts, and the sweat was pouring out of him."

Caroline looked worried. "He needs to be careful, because the hospital haven't given him the all clear yet on his heart."

"Well," said Paul, "the way he just trained then, if there was still a problem with his heart, we'd soon know about it."

"Does all that bruising still look bad?"

Paul was about to say something, when Michael interjected "Yes, it'll take some time for that to clear up." Paul fired an angry glance at his brother. "I mean," continued Michael, hurriedly, "it's not too bad, and it doesn't seem to be bothering him."

"I'm glad I wasn't the heavy bag or the punch-ball, after watching dad attack them," remarked Paul. "He was hitting the bag with such power, I was sweating as much as him just holding on to it. It's a relief that Michael Hughes is my brother and Neil Hughes is my father - I wouldn't like them as enemies."

All three fell silent for a few moments; then Caroline spoke.

"I should tell you - remember when we had a party at the villa, and there was an English couple there who were friends of the solicitor?"

Both boys nodded; then realisation dawned on Michael's face. "Don't tell me *he's* the one who's going to buy the villa?"

"I'm afraid so."

"Whatever you do, don't tell dad it's him," said Michael emphatically. "I know at the moment he wouldn't remember him anyway but, when he gets his memory back, dad would be gutted to know that sleazebag had bought the villa."

"I thought he was quite nice," mused Caroline; "I'm not sure why your dad didn't like him."

"Because he was full of crap - anyone who keeps telling you how wealthy and successful they are, I'm always very wary of."

"Mum," said Paul "you only liked him because he was so charming and flattering when he was talking to you, and you fell for it. He didn't do it when dad was anywhere near, or when his wife was in earshot. Dad saw straight through him, and said he was trying to be something he's not."

"I'm a woman," pointed out Caroline. "We *like* being charmed and flattered, particularly as we get older."

"Surely, not from a toe rag like that?"

"Anyway," said Caroline, changing the subject, "when your dad comes down, we'll show him the letter for the bank and, hopefully, that might lift him a bit. Mind you, I'm a bit concerned that the things we have to sign are all in Spanish."

"By the way, has dad had any more nightmares since he's been home?" asked Paul.

"I'm not sure; he's still sleeping in Michael's room, but I don't think so. Which reminds me - I owe you two apologies."

Paul winked at Michael. "You don't mean for not asking me if I was all right after the accident, or not remembering the promise about forgiving me anything?"

"Yes I do."

"You apologised last night, you drunken woman – and, as I said to you then, it really doesn't matter, I know you love Michael more than me." He heaved a theatrical sigh.

Caroline laughed. "You've caught me out again! Come here, Mike."

As she hugged Michael, she stuck out her tongue at Paul, at which they all started laughing.

They all heard Neil coming downstairs. As he came into the dining room, they were surprised to see he was still wearing shorts and a T-shirt.

"Have a look at this dad," said Michael, handing the solicitor's letter to his father. "I think it really fits the bill, as far as the bank's concerned."

Neil studied it silently; he then simply nodded, and handed it back to Michael.

"We both need to sign these documents so that Mike can scan them, and send them back to the solicitor," said Caroline. "I'm just a bit concerned, though, that they're in Spanish, so we can't be sure exactly what we're signing."

"Did……" Neil paused slightly, before continuing. "Did I trust the solicitor in Spain?"

"Definitely; you liked her, and got on really well with her."

"In that case, just show me where to sign."

He signed all the forms without further comment. When Caroline added her signature, although she felt emotional, she was careful to show no visible sign.

"Well," she said, with forced brightness, "now that's sorted, I'll go and put the kettle on. Who wants one?"

"Yes please," said both boys at once; Neil just shook his head.

While Caroline was in the kitchen, Paul looked at his father. "Why've you left your shorts and training shoes on?"

"I'm going out for a run later."

"We'd come with you, but we still have to finish that job off today," said Michael regretfully. "Incidentally, you normally take your mp3 player to listen to music while you're running."

"What sort of music do I like?"

"Well, when you're at home, you listen to all sorts of different stuff; but, when you're training or running, you like dance music - rave music, really. You hated it years ago, but you've developed a liking for it in the last few years."

"Not jazz music, though," chuckled Paul; "mum loves jazz, but you really hate it."

"How long have I had that training room upstairs?"

"Strangely enough, round about the same time you started to like the dance music - probably about four years ago. Remember the time……. damn, sorry," said Michael, striking himself on the forehead.

"Try me," encouraged Neil. "You never know; I might remember."

"Fair enough. Well," continued Michael, "a few months ago, I had a big job on, so you and Paul were labouring for me; anyway, we had a competition carrying bags of cement across the site."

"That's not the time when I tripped over the spade, is it?" enquired Neil.

"Do you remember that happening?"

"Did it really? I just made that up."

Michael smiled. "No it didn't, but I had you going for a minute there!"

Just then, Caroline came in from the kitchen with the tea, and caught the three of them laughing; after seeing Neil so sad earlier in the day, this was something of a relief to her.

"Talking about music that you like," Michael went on to say, "didn't the therapist mention something about a favourite film being able to jog your memory?"

"To be honest, the list of things she mentioned was almost endless," said Neil. "It included films, music, place names, people's names, in fact almost anything. Why do you ask?"

"There's a particular film you love," explained Michael, "called 'Zulu'; you probably knew it word for word, the amount of times you've watched it. It's about a small group of British soldiers fighting the Zulu warriors in South Africa, sometime in the late nineteenth century."

Paul nodded. "I think the reason you like it so much is that those soldiers wouldn't back down, and wouldn't give up."

"Enough, or you'll spoil the plot," said Michael, grinning. "I'll dig out the video," he said to his father, "so you'll be able to watch it."

The boys finished their tea, and then got up to leave; at the same time, Neil also rose from his chair. "I'm just going out for a run, clear my head a bit," he explained, in response to Caroline's questioning look.

"Okay," she said uneasily; "and what about you two? Are you round later, seeing as how I didn't do Sunday lunch after all?"

"Yes, we will be, but not with the girls," replied Michael, "they're going out somewhere with their friends tonight."

"Alright then," said Caroline. "Well, I'll see you all later."
…………………………………………………………………

As Neil was running, he had the music turned up very loud, in the hope that it would stop him thinking about the day's events; that proved to be futile, however, so he simply ran until he was almost exhausted. He stopped for a while, in order to get his breath back; then, reluctantly, he headed home.

As he was making his way back, Neil was thinking that he would have liked to sit and talk to Caroline, to see if there was a way of improving the present situation; yet, in truth, he was afraid that to attempt this might make things worse, so felt that his only option was to hope things may improve. He felt that he was stumbling around in the dark; was it just his memory loss, and his new face, that was causing the problem, or could there be something else? He reflected that Caroline had told him they had been really happy for the last twenty years – but was that really the truth?

When he arrived back home, as he walked through the front door, Caroline happened to be standing in the hall immediately in front of him; and, for a split second, he thought he saw a look of fear.

"Caz," he said, "I must know the truth. Have I ever hit you, or even raised my hand to you?"

Caroline, taken aback, was about to laugh; but when she observed the sadness in his eyes, she knew that would be unwise.

"Neil," she said seriously, "since the night we met, I don't ever remember you even raising your voice to me, let alone your hand."

Neil's expression of sadness did not change.

"When I was hitting the heavy bag upstairs," he mused, "at one point, I told Paul to let go of it, and then I really attacked it, kicking and punching. I was shocked with the ferocity of my attack, and thought that, if that were another person, they'd have been lucky to survive."

"Neil, I can only tell you that all you've ever done since we met is loved me, and looked after me; I realise, now, that I just took that for granted. I know you've only got my word for that, but when you get your memory back, you'll know it's true."

Neil simply nodded. "I believe you," he said. There was a slightly awkward silence; then he continued "Anyway, I'd better go and get a shower, and I'll have a bit of a sleep as well; just give me a shake if I'm still asleep when the lads arrive later."

"Don't worry, I will – you go and get your head down, and have a rest."

As he walked up the stairs, he reflected on what she had said. Her tone of voice had been so emphatic, it convinced him that he had not, in any way, been violent towards her; yet he still felt that there was something she was not telling him.

She had assured him how much Neil Hughes loved her; but the problem was that he, the new Neil, knew that he did not have those feelings for her, and he was overwhelmed with guilt. He desperately wanted his memory back, so that he could love her again. Could it be that she knew this? If so, it would explain her reluctance to touch him, the tenseness when he touched her, and her obvious discomfort when they were alone together. Looking at the situation logically, how could any woman let a complete stranger into her home and act normally? The trouble was, he could not think of anything that could possibly remedy the situation, other than regaining his memory.

He had a shower, and then lay down on the bed; but sleep would not come. After a short while, he got up, and slowly walked back downstairs. He hoped that, when Caroline saw him, there would not be another expression of fear on her face.

....

Caroline sat in the living room, looking at the picture of herself, Neil, and the boys; her mind was a jumble of emotions. She was annoyed with herself for not being able to accept Neil the way everyone else had; at the same time, she was ashamed to feel that she was cheating on Neil, for trying to love the man upstairs. She knew that she must come to terms with the fact that it *was* Neil and, if she did not love him soon, she could lose him forever.

She was disturbed from her reverie by the sound of Neil coming downstairs; she sighed, got up, and went into the kitchen. Neil joined her a few moments later, to find her making tea.

"Just making a brew, as usual," she smiled. "Fancy one?"

"Please," he replied. "Did the lads say when they were coming round?"

"They're going to be later than they expected. Michael wants to finish the job tonight, because he's on another one first thing in the morning."

"In that case, I'll watch that film Michael suggested."

"Good idea," said Caroline. "I'll set the video player up for you in the living room, and while you're watching that, I'll do a bit of tidying up."

....

While the vacuum cleaner droned upstairs, Neil put the video into the player, settled down, and watched the film from start to finish.

Shortly after the film was over, he heard Michael and Paul come in; he practically leapt into the hall, giving them something of a start. "Is that really based on a true story?"

Michael smiled. "It certainly is. I assume from your reaction, then, that you enjoyed it?"

"It was absolutely brilliant," enthused Neil. "I can honestly say it's the best film I've seen; admittedly, as things stand, it's the *only* film I've ever seen, but I can't imagine watching something better than that."

"Yes," said Paul, "it must be quite strange, really; it'd be like seeing Michael Jackson's 'Thriller' video for the first time."

Michael nodded, and Neil just smiled; he had no idea who Michael Jackson was, or what a thriller video meant. When he first started watching the film, he had hoped it might jolt his memory; but, as he became engrossed in the story, he ceased to care.

"What impressed you most about the story?" asked Paul.

"The bravery," replied Neil seriously; "not just of the British soldiers, but of the Zulu warriors as well. It takes some guts to run at someone with a gun when you're only armed with a spear. The fact that the British were so outnumbered, and yet stood their ground and fought, really impressed me."

"Great," said Michael. "I don't suppose it helped in any way as far as the memory's concerned?"

"I'm afraid not," said Neil, shaking his head. "There again, I would've been a bit miffed if I'd remembered the end while I was still watching it."

As they went into the dining room, Caroline had a pot of tea and a large plate of sandwiches waiting for them. She was glad to see Neil's smiling face, and was proud of her sons for lifting their father's spirits again; it was something she herself needed to learn how to do, and quickly.

After he had eaten, and stayed talking to the others for a while, Neil found that he felt tired enough to sleep, and went up to bed. As he was drifting off to sleep, he realised that his spirits had improved; although watching the film had not helped with his memory, it seemed to lift him. It was a strange feeling; there was something about it that really made him happy.

....

Monday morning's briefing had a different feel about it, which the D.C.I. could sense straight away; as he looked around the room, he could see an enthusiasm from his team which had been lost over the last few days.

"Dave," he began, "how's it gone as far as the vans are concerned?"

"You were right, boss - the only vans we've been pulling now are all above board, taxed, insured, and owned by legitimate people. I don't think we're going to get much further with that, as things stand."

"Paula," commented the D.C.I., "you're looking very pleased with yourself."

"I've found it, boss; wait till you see this."

D.C.I. Davies walked over to view the CCTV footage. "We have clear images of the people involved," continued Paula. "Although none of us who've watched it know these people, when the Sarge comes in, he's bound to know one or two of them."

"Paula, just show the boss the whole event start to finish," advised Dave.

Fred Davies watched the entire footage, and nodded with satisfaction.

"Great," he said. "As soon as Tinny comes in, we need him to watch this, because I believe you're right; he'll know those two bullies. Neil Hughes dealt with them pretty successfully," he remarked; "and, I have to say, almost terrifyingly."

The D.C.I. turned to Dave. "You're into martial arts aren't you? Is that some form of karate Neil Hughes was using? It was clearly very effective."

Dave considered for a while. "It could be, but I don't think so, boss; I'm more inclined towards a mixture of kickboxing and cage fighting. That was a perfect round house kick he used to drop the big man, and although it all happens very quickly, we've been able to slow things down in order to see the type of blow he used to drop the second fella."

"At first glance, I thought it was just simply a punch," said the D.C.I.

"So did I, boss, but when you slow it right down, you'll see that Neil Hughes actually hits him with the palm of his hand. I'll re-run the footage more slowly, so you can see what I mean."

He did so, and the D.C.I. saw it for himself. He shook his head. "Remarkable," he murmured.

"We've been on to the local accident and emergency departments to check their records for that particular evening....."; as Dave was speaking, Tinny and Gary entered the briefing room.

"Hold on a minute, Dave," interrupted the D.C.I. "Tinny, come and have a look at this; we're all hoping you'll know this crew that your mate Jacko and Neil Hughes sorted out."

Tinny viewed the still shot of the footage, and smiled. "Yes, I know them all, and they're all in the system. Let's have another look at the whole event from start to finish."

While Tinny and Gary were viewing the footage, the D.C.I. said "Sorry to have interrupted you before Dave - you were saying about the A. and E. department records?"

"All five of them show up on the hospital's CCTV cameras for that night but, apparently, when the hospital staff asked them if the police should be informed about their injuries, they all declined. That 'punch', or whatever you want to call it, from Neil Hughes broke that thug's jaw."

"Well," interjected Tinny, "after watching the whole footage, and seeing what they did leading up to this incident, as far as I'm concerned they got what they deserved."

Fred Davies nodded. "I agree completely. Had Jacko and Neil Hughes not got there in time, that little taxi driver they were attacking wouldn't have stood a chance."

Tinny laughed. "I bet those other three regretted running away in the direction of Jacko."

"Alright, Tinny", said the D.C.I., "let's bring them all in, and check their alibis for the night Neil Hughes was attacked."

"The one I'm most interested in is the first one Neil Hughes put down. His name is Carl McCabe, and he's connected to the infamous McCabe family. He sometimes collects debts for them, and is a nasty piece of work."

"Why him particularly, Tinny?"

"He has the reputation of being a hard man; being put down with one blow by a man almost twice his age, and about four inches smaller than him, will have humiliated him in front of all those low-life spectators. That's a serious motive for revenge."

Fred Davies rubbed his chin thoughtfully. "I know we've checked both Neil Hughes and his sons' background, and nothing has showed up; but watching him in action makes me wonder if we've missed something."

There was a short pause; then Gary spoke.

"A few days ago, when we were on the taxi rank, I had a good conversation with Neil's best mate Danny; Jacko was also nearby, nodding in agreement with everything Danny said.

"It seems that Neil Hughes is a real family man, desperately loves his wife and is not embarrassed to say so; whenever they all go out together, Neil's friends are forever pulling his leg, because Neil and his wife are like teenagers on their first date, and yet they've been married for nearly twenty years. He's a good father, and, as we already know, a good worker.

"One significant thing Danny pointed out, is that Neil Hughes does have a strong sense of right and wrong, good and bad. It appears that he's a very good friend but, if you're an enemy, then look out; and, as we've just seen from the footage, he's very effective in dealing with his enemies."

Tinny nodded solemnly. "Debbie described the attack on Neil Hughes as cowardly; I would describe the attack by those five thugs on the taxi driver in the same way. I find it easy to believe that one or more of them could have carried out both."

……………………………………..

Caroline got up, and came down to make breakfast. She felt very uncomfortable; she was dreading going to the bank, even though she would have Michael with her. Neil was already downstairs, and could tell there was a problem; however, he wrongly assumed it may have had something to do with him, and decided to go out into the garden to sit on his own.

While Neil was still outside, he heard Michael's voice coming from the kitchen. He went back indoors, to see Caroline and Michael preparing to leave for the bank.

"Alright, Mike," he greeted, "so the two of you are all set to go. You know what needs to be done, don't you?"

"No problem, dad; I'll get it sorted, one way or another."

"What if they just won't help?" said Caroline fretfully. "What do we do then?"

"Let's cross that bridge when we come to it - if we come to it at all." Neil's voice was reassuring. "Think positive, and keep smiling; I'm sure the bank will help if they can."

As Caroline and Michael left, Neil stood at the front door, and gave them a thumbs up sign. He hoped that his plan would work, but was nowhere near as confident in it as he would have them believe.

He went back into the garden, taking with him the family photograph; as he examined it, he really envied the man in the picture, whose face was so different from his own. Just sitting by himself, trying to think positively for the future, was far more difficult than he had expected it to be. His mind was churning, as he tried to think of anything that could improve the situation; not only the finances but, more importantly, his relationship with Caroline. Exasperated, he realised that it was no use; until he regained his memory, he could not see a way forward.

Neil sat in the living room facing the window, waiting for Caroline and Michael to get home. When the car pulled up, he felt a great sense of relief, as they were both smiling.

He went out into the hall as they came through the front door. "I'm hoping, with the smiles, that things went well?"

Michael raised his thumb. "Sorted," he declared.

"It was brilliant," said Caroline, relief in her voice. "I get really intimidated in places like that. I've been dreading going there since you first suggested it."

"What's going to happen is, for the next three months, the bank will cover all the standing orders and direct debits you have," explained Michael. "They'll also pay the recent mortgage payment which was missed, so there are no worries about the house."

"We spoke to someone called Sam, and she was really helpful," mentioned Caroline.

"Sam is a 'she?'"

"Yes - short for Samantha, I assume; it was like talking to a friend. She was really sympathetic to our situation, and said that, if there was any delay on the sale of the villa, that she could review the situation in three months' time. In other words, she would make sure there was no risk of us losing this house."

"Good," said Neil. "I'm really sorry this was forced on you, though. I understand how much you were dreading having to do it, but I couldn't see any other way round it; I couldn't have turned up at the bank trying to convince them that I was Neil Hughes."

Caroline beamed. "In a way, I'm glad you couldn't; I feel really pleased with myself today, and have made a new friend into the bargain. So, anybody want tea?"

"Not for me, thanks," said Michael, "I've got to get back to the job. Dad, when you get back from the hospital, could you do me a favour, and help me out later?"

Neil clicked his fingers. "It's just as well you reminded me about going over to the hospital; in all the excitement, I'd completely forgotten."

"Shall I come with you?" asked Caroline.

"No, it's okay; I shouldn't be there that long anyway, I'm only going in to see the therapist, and to have the dressings changed on the back of my head. I'll see you later – and yes, Mike, I will come and give you a hand."

……………………………………...

Although Neil arrived at the hospital in high spirits, after the session with the therapist had gone the way of all the previous ones, he felt somewhat despondent. Walking along the corridor on his way out, he saw Michael's friend Rob.

Neil walked towards him, smiling. "You're Rob aren't you, our Mike's mate?"

Rob looked at him for a moment. "Mr Hughes?"

"I know," said Neil wryly, "I look a bit different from when you first started changing the bandages - and Neil will do fine."

"I'm going for a coffee Mr........ sorry, Neil. Any chance you could join me? I've got loads of questions for you."

"Certainly, as long as they have nothing to do with my life before the attack because, unfortunately, I still have no memory."

As they sat down in the cafe, Rob said "Would you think me very rude, if I inspected your face?"

"Not at all, Rob," smiled Neil. "I'm quite proud of it, even if I do say so myself."

When Rob finished looking, in detail, at Neil's face, he sat down again.

"You have got to hand it to Braithwaite," he enthused, "that is an incredible job. The scarring can only be seen on very close inspection; no wonder he wanted to parade you in front of the television cameras."

Neil looked slightly guilty. "I hope my not doing the press conference didn't disappoint the staff too much; Dr. Braithwaite said it would really put your hospital on the map."

"Ah, take no notice," said Rob dismissively. "We don't need to be put on any maps, we're already on them. Braithwaite just wanted to do that for personal glory; he doesn't care about this hospital, or any other hospital, for that matter."

"So, I assume he's on his way to America now?"

"No, as a matter of fact, he's still with us. The day after you left, a woman was brought in with terrible facial injuries from a car crash. The poor soul not only went through the windscreen of the car she was a passenger in, but went face first into the vehicle it crashed into. Incredibly, she survived, but her facial injuries are nearly as bad as yours."

"I take it Braithwaite is confident he can do a similar job on her as he did on me?"

"He's certain of it. This new compound he's developed worked perfectly on you, as well as the synthetic skin he used to hide the scarring. They are his own personal inventions, and a closely guarded secret. One thing I do know, any blow you receive to your face in the future will have little or no effect; the compound he's developed is much stronger than bone, and is almost indestructible."

"Interesting," commented Neil. "So, I take it that he'll be arranging the media circus for her, like the one he'd planned for me; if she's agreeable to it, of course."

"Huh," said Rob contemptuously, "Braithwaite made sure that she can't disagree."

"How did he manage that?"

"Basically, by blackmailing her family into signing a consent form on her behalf, while she was still on the operating table. One of my colleagues was present while Braithwaite was talking to the family, and she said she felt ashamed to be on the same staff as him."

"He's probably sorry he didn't do that with my family," remarked Neil. "Not that it would've made much difference; had he produced some type of consent form to try and make me attend the press conference, he'd have found himself eating it."

Rob laughed. "The nurse who was in the room at the time told us all about that. I believe you made a right fool of him, and then Dr. Hargraves finished the job. Braithwaite always had the respect of the staff for his ability, but never as a man. With recent events, we'll all be glad to see the back of him."

"Well," said Neil, getting up, "I'd better get back home now, I'm doing some labouring for our Mike this afternoon. It's been nice talking to you, Rob – you'll have to call round and see us some time."

....

By the time Neil got home, it was quite late and he was very tired, although he did really enjoy helping Michael on the building site. As he walked into the dining room, he found Caroline sitting at the table, with some documents in front of her. She looked up at Neil, and smiled.

"Ah, there you are - I forgot to tell you this morning, there are some forms for you to sign. I've already signed them, so if you do the same, I'll take them back to the bank tomorrow."

"You looked very pleased with yourself, when you got back this morning with Mike."

"I was, and I still am now. I'm really pleased you forced me to sort it out myself."

Neil's expression changed. "Oh, Caz, I'm really sorry you felt I forced you to do this; I just couldn't see any other way round it."

"No, no," she said hurriedly, "I didn't mean to say it like that. What I meant, was that the situation was forced upon us, and I'm glad you encouraged me to do something about it. It's high time I started getting more involved – and, before you say it, it's not your fault I'm like this, it's mine."

"So, are you taking Michael with you tomorrow?"

"No - I'm going to do it myself; I'm really looking forward to it."

"As I suspected," he said soberly, "Sam isn't really a woman; it's a man, and you've taken a fancy to him."

Caroline was stung. "No, honestly, it's a woman - ask Michael, he'll tell you......."; then she saw the hurt in Neil's eyes, and fell silent.

"It was a joke, I didn't mean to upset you," said Neil wearily; he appeared to be about to say something else, but then he just sighed. He got up from his chair. "I'll see you in the morning," he said quietly.

As she heard him walking along the hall and up the stairs, she sat there for a few moments; then she went into the kitchen. While she was waiting for the kettle to boil, she reflected sadly on what had just happened. Once again, just as Neil was trying to be Neil, she had treated him like a different person; of course it was a joke, she thought, reproaching herself. She had to think before saying anything in future; otherwise, the new Neil would start to believe that she did not even like him, let alone love him.

....

Meanwhile, as he went into Michael's bedroom, Neil was cursing himself. Caroline had been really happy, and then he spoiled it with a stupid joke. He had made a mental note days ago, to try not to joke with Caroline when they were face to face; he was determined not to make the same mistake again.

He sat on the bed, and wondered whether he should have offered to accompany Caroline to the bank tomorrow; but then it occurred to him that, had he done so, she might think he was checking up on her, and that he had not been joking after all. He knew that the strain on Caroline was beginning to show, and he was not helping at all; he needed to know when to keep his big mouth shut.

....

Three of the thugs had been picked up and interviewed, but without success; all had alibis for the night Neil Hughes was attacked, although these were being checked thoroughly. The police had still not been able to find Carl McCabe or Tony Walters, the latter being the man who had his jaw broken.

"Right," said D.C.I. Davies to his officers, "fresh start in the morning. Speak to all your informants, and let's see if we can track down Carl McCabe and Tony Walters; they were the two that Neil Hughes dealt with and, from what Tinny has told me, Carl McCabe in particular is definitely in the frame for this.

"Naturally, check out all known associates of these two, and see what we can turn up there. As I'm sure you're all aware, the McCabes are involved in drug dealing, money laundering, extortion, controlling prostitutes and, we've discovered recently, even people trafficking.

"Carl McCabe is certainly not one of the main men of the family - it's his uncles who are the gangsters. Carl's father has never had anything to do with the rest of his family, and is a law abiding citizen; his son, however, has tried his best to be part of the family business, and is willing to do anything they tell him.

"This incident outside the kebab house will have lost him credibility with the family itself; that will have meant a great deal to him, so a revenge attack on Neil Hughes, in his eyes, would re-establish him with the family. We need to find this man and, hopefully, find some connection to the attack."

....

As Neil came downstairs, he was surprised to find Caroline had got up before him, and was in the kitchen making breakfast. He deliberately coughed before entering the kitchen, so that he did not startle her; it had occurred to him that, when he came in after his run, the look in Caroline's eyes was not fear, just simply fright.

Caroline turned around, and smiled. "Morning," she said brightly. "Would you like some breakfast?"

Neil was tempted to say yes; however, as Caroline had told him that he did not normally bother with breakfast, he shook his head. "No thanks; but I'll have a cup of tea, if there's one going."

"Well, you're in luck, because I've just made a fresh pot."

Neil sat down, considering carefully, before he spoke, how to open the conversation.

"I may still have no memory," he said eventually, "but I've certainly noticed, you do like the odd cup of tea."

Caroline was similarly conscious of trying not to say the wrong thing, so she paused slightly before replying "You should have been a detective; I don't think anyone has spotted that before."

They were both pleased with themselves that they were in the same room, facing each other, and had shared a joke; it broke the ice slightly.

"So," said Caroline, sipping her tea, "any plans for today?"

"If Michael needs me, I just told him to give me a ring," replied Neil; "but, if he doesn't, I was thinking of going on the internet, and seeing if I can find anything that might jog my memory; I might even watch another film or a television programme that I used to like."

"Good idea - you've got box sets of programmes you like that the boys have bought you for Christmas and birthdays. One of your favourite things is crime and the detection of crime, whether it's real or fictitious; something you particularly find interesting is crime scene forensics."

"Sounds great. I assume these are DVDs? Michael explained about the change from video to DVD."

"That's right." Caroline hesitated slightly. "The funny thing is, it will actually be the first time you've watched some of them."

"Do you mean that I've never seen them?"

Caroline beamed with relief, because Neil had not misunderstood what she had meant.

"Exactly; whereas, when you watched 'Zulu', you've watched that loads of times before. You've never had the time to watch most of the DVDs, because you work so much."

"In that case, the lads will be pleased to find out I'm finally enjoying their gifts to me."

"They certainly will! Let's go in to the living room, and I'll show you how to work the DVD player."

Caroline left Neil in the living room, after showing him how to work the DVD, and picking out a box set which she hoped he would like; as she walked back into the kitchen, she felt more upbeat, given that they had had a proper conversation without either of them getting upset.

Sometime later, Neil walked in to the kitchen, to find her cleaning the cooker.

"I've just been watching programmes involving serial killers - you're just a serial cleaner, aren't you?"

"I have to hold my hands up, and admit that I am," laughed Caroline. "I can't settle for half a job; no matter how long it takes me, if I'm cleaning something, it has to be perfect."

"Anyway," said Neil, sitting down, "I meant to tell you before, Mike's printed up some stuff for me and some maps because I was thinking of going to see the people who helped save my life."

"How do you mean, exactly?"

"To begin with, the fire station, then the paramedic and the ambulance driver who got me to the Liverpool hospital so quickly - they all played a part in my survival. Michael printed a map, showing the locations of the fire and ambulance stations, and the first hospital I was taken to; I'm going to go and see these people, and thank them."

"When are you going to do that?"

"Well, as much as I'm enjoying watching those DVDs, I feel I should be doing something more constructive. Mike definitely doesn't need any help this afternoon, so I thought I'd do it now."

"Would you like me to come with you?"

"I'll be fine. You carry on with your cleaning, and I'll see you later."

Neil went upstairs and got changed; then, giving Caroline a thumbs up as he was leaving, he set off. Caroline was relieved; she could now go to the bank with the signed documents, without it reminding either of them of the upset from the night before.

As Neil was driving to the fire station, and at the same time, Caroline was driving to the bank, they could not know that they were both having much the same thought – that is, how today had been an important step in the right direction.

Chapter 7

Not only had Michael printed a map of where Neil needed to go, but also a list of names of the people who were involved in saving his life. Fortunately, the fire station and ambulance station were next door to each other; Neil went to the fire station first, and asked for the chief fire officer.

"Good afternoon Mr Hughes; I am Mike Campbell, and I'm the officer in charge."

Neil introduced himself, explained who he was, and why he was there.

Mike Campbell smiled. "I appreciate your giving up your time to come and thank us, but there's really no need - it's our job."

"I understand that," said Neil; "but, from what I've been told, the fact that the fire crew got to the scene so quickly, and also that the paramedics were alerted almost immediately, played a big part in my survival. If possible, I'd very much like to speak to the firefighter involved who, I believe, literally stumbled over me."

"That would be Jane Tunstall." Mike Campbell hesitated for a moment. "The truth is, Mr Hughes, I'm not sure whether it would be advisable." In response to Neil's questioning look, he continued. "You see, witnessing the extent of your facial injuries turned out to be a traumatic experience for her. She's got the makings of a good firefighter; however, as a result of that incident, I suspect we may be about to lose her."

"That would be a pity," remarked Neil; "on the other hand, perhaps if she sees me as I appear now, and realises that she helped save my life, it could change her mind."

Mike Campbell considered this, then nodded. "You may have a point. Alright," he smiled, "we'll give it a try – give me a moment while I fetch her."

As Mike Campbell and Jane re-entered the room, Neil immediately stood up and put his hand out to her.

"You won't recognise me now; but you helped save my life."

Jane looked confused. "I'm sorry; I don't recognise you, but I'm pleased I was obviously of some help," she offered.

"Jane - this is the taxi driver you found by his cab on the industrial estate," explained Mike.

Jane looked again at Neil, this time with disbelief. "Remarkable," she declared. "May I say that, whoever the plastic surgeon was, they have done an amazing job."

Neil smiled in acknowledgement. "You know, it's interesting," he reflected; "in the short time I've been out of hospital, I can already see the difference in reaction from those people who knew me before the attack, compared to those who had the unfortunate experience of seeing my face that night, and seeing the damage which had been done to it."

"Well, anyway," said Jane diffidently, "as far as saving your life is concerned, all I did was trip over you."

"But that's exactly why I'm here," assured Neil. "The fact that I was moved from my side to my back, apparently, helped to keep me alive; had there been a paramedic or doctor there at the moment you found me, the first thing they'd have done is turn me onto my back." He spread out his hands. "I don't entirely understand why; but, from what I've been told, it has something to do with the blood loss. All I know for sure is that, if I'd got to the hospital any later than I did, I would certainly have died." He smiled. "I gather you've not been in the fire service for long; but, let me tell you, your enthusiasm for your job played a major part in my being able to speak to you now. All I can say is, I'm very grateful – and, if I ever find myself in danger from fire in the future, I sincerely hope you're on duty."

At this, Jane beamed at both Neil and her commanding officer; she subsequently left the office with far more of a spring in her step than when she had entered.

"Thanks for that – that's certainly lifted her spirits," said Mike gratefully; "although, I must admit, it's news to me that your body position made a difference."

Neil grinned sheepishly. "It may not have - I made that up! I just thought that, after what you said, it might convince Jane to stay in the fire service, and that's obviously what you would prefer. Having good firefighters benefits everyone; and your crew's professionalism that night certainly benefited me."

Mike Campbell stood up, and held out his hand. "You are a gentleman, Mr. Hughes, and I very much appreciate what you've done today."

As Neil was walking from the fire station to the ambulance station, Mike Campbell, Jane, and another firefighter named Ray, watched him walk across the yard.

"He seems like a decent bloke," commented Ray; "let's hope the police catch whoever attacked him."

Mike was not a man who normally shared his thoughts with anyone, and never swore in front of the crew; hence, his curt response surprised the other two officers.

"I wouldn't mind five minutes with the bastards first."

....

Neil was only in the ambulance station for a short time; the paramedic he was talking to had to hurry out to a job, but Neil was glad that, at least, he had the opportunity to thank him. His next port of call was the hospital to which he had first been taken on the night of the attack, to thank the staff there; then, his final destination was the ambulance station, where he hoped to meet the driver who took him to the Liverpool hospital.

Neil was directed to the canteen where the ambulance crews went for their break, and was told that Mike Bates could be found there. As Neil walked in, he said "I'm looking for Mike Bates?"

Neil had pictured in his mind what Mike Bates would look like; he was, therefore, quite surprised when a small, greying, middle-aged man stood up.

"That's me - what can I do for you?"

Neil introduced himself and, as they both sat down, explained what he had been doing that afternoon, and his wish to thank everyone concerned.

"Actually, it should be me thanking you," declared Mike. Neil looked somewhat nonplussed. "Well, you see, I knocked one minute, forty-two seconds off my record that night," his companion went on to explain; he paused, grinning. "I can't see me ever beating that!"

Neil immediately took a liking to this straight-talking man, and returned the grin.

"You're the second Mike I've been speaking to today," Neil informed him, "and my eldest son is called Mike as well."

"Why did you call your son Mike?"

Neil smiled apologetically. "As a matter of fact, I've got no idea."

He went on to explain the memory loss, and the change to his facial features from the plastic surgery; he had a photo of himself from before the attack, which he showed to Mike.

Mike shook his head. "My God; this must be a nightmare for your missus."

"I know; it's putting a real strain on her, and I seem to be making matters worse."

"I'm not surprised; we are what we are because of things we know, things we do, and our memories. Until you get your memory back, you can't possibly be Neil Hughes; so, effectively, your missus is trying to live normally with a complete stranger."

Neil nodded. "What I've been trying to do, is to try to be *like* Neil Hughes, with regard to his likes, dislikes, and any sort of routines or habits he had. The trouble is, though, I can't stop thinking of him as a different person."

"Well, in a sense, he *is* a different person to you at the moment; that must be a nightmare for you, as well as your wife." Mike looked at Neil sympathetically. "I don't envy you, mate - you've just got to hope you get your memory back soon."

Just then, the door to the canteen swung open, and another ambulance driver appeared. "Mike?" he called, raising his thumb.

"Gotta go!" barked Mike, without ceremony; he jumped up, and was gone in seconds. Neil smiled; he was impressed that this man was clearly just as fast on the ground as he was behind the wheel.

As he made his way back to his car, Neil realised that the conversation with Mike had given him a great sense of relief; the reason being that, as Mike Bates did not know him, Neil was able to be completely honest about his feelings.

....

Neil duly arrived home. "Anyone in?" he called out.

"I'm in the kitchen," replied Caroline.

"Making a cup of tea, no doubt."

"I might be; or, I might be seeing how tough this new frying pan is by testing it on this bowling ball."

"Any chance we can keep the bowling ball?"

"No, I've only borrowed it; when I take it back, I'll have to think of something else, or some*one* else, to test this pan on."

Neil laughed. "Any chance of a brew first?"

Shortly afterwards, Caroline walked in to the dining room with a pot of tea. "So, did you get to see everyone you wanted?"

"I did, yes; it occurred to me today how we all take the emergency services for granted, and don't appreciate what a great job they do."

Caroline pondered for a moment. "I know; I think we all take things for granted from time to time."

Neil was about to say something; but then he changed his mind, and confined himself to smiling and nodding in agreement.

"Well," sighed Caroline, leaning back in her chair with a self-satisfied air, "I now have the cleanest cooker in Cheshire, and my plates are so clean, you could eat your dinner off them."

"Oh, very droll," laughed Neil.

"I'm wasted in this place," said Caroline, affecting a look of superiority as she sipped her tea.

"Anyway," said Neil, after a short pause, "I had a really good conversation today with one of the ambulance drivers; he was quite sympathetic regarding the situation we've found ourselves in."

"So did I - I was talking to Sam, and............." Caroline stopped abruptly in mid-sentence, and simply looked down at the table.

Neil was puzzled for a moment; then it dawned on him.

"Caz, is this about that stupid joke I made yesterday?" From the look on her face, he realised that he was right. "I'm really sorry - I didn't think for a split second that Sam was a man, or mean to suggest you were seeing someone else behind my back. From everything you've told me about us, I wouldn't dream of making a joke like that if I'd known that you would take me seriously."

As Neil was saying this, he could see that Caroline appeared to be getting more upset; he felt as if his brain was screaming at him to shut up, so he did. He just looked at this sad woman who, a minute ago, had been so happy. He desperately wanted just to hold her, but felt that he could not take the risk. "I really, really didn't think it was a man," he said, in a subdued tone.

"I know you didn't, Neil," Caroline almost whispered; "I know you didn't, it was just me being stupid again."

Neil was about to say something, but Caroline held up her hand. "None of this is your fault," she said vehemently. "It's the bastards who did this to you."

Neil looked up, taken aback by her tone; then he smiled.

"That surprised me! I haven't heard you swear before. What about me - do I swear?"

Caroline also smiled faintly; her outburst seemed to have released some of the tension in the air. "Never in the house; of course, I don't know whether you swear or not on the taxi rank with your mates but, if you do, you certainly never swear in front of me."

Neil nodded. "Well," he said, getting up, "I think I'll have a session in the training room, and try and picture the heavy bag as one of my attackers."

"Good idea! If you start flagging, give me a shout, and I'll set about it with the frying pan."

....

After Neil had finished training, he had a shower, got changed and came back downstairs. "Are you in the kitchen?" he called from the hallway.

"I am - just take a seat in the dining room, I'm about to bring in one of your favourite meals."

Neil thoroughly enjoyed the meal that Caroline had cooked for him. "That was superb!" he said in admiration. "I take it you really enjoy cooking?"

"I do; my cooking is a bit like my cleaning, in so far as I like to take my time over it, and get it perfect."

Neil smiled. "Well, that *was* absolutely perfect; the best meal I can ever remember having." He immediately laughed.

Caroline also laughed; this gave Neil the idea that, perhaps, he should always laugh whenever he made jokes in future; it could help reduce any possible misunderstandings.

The rest of the evening went well, from the point of view of them both; as usual, however, Neil began to feel exhausted. He stifled a yawn.

"I'll go to bed now, as I'm tired once again," he announced. "Have I always slept this much?"

"Strangely enough, it was the other extreme; I was always concerned you weren't getting enough sleep, because you were working so much."

"Maybe my body's catching up for the last few years, and grabbing as much sleep as it can while I'm not working," suggested Neil. "Anyway, I'll see you in the morning."

………………………………….....................................

In the briefing room, D.C.I. Davies and his team were taking stock of their progress.

"Well, we can take Tony Walters off the list," declared the D.C.I., "because he was in Turkey the night of the attack. I don't want to sound bitter here, but this man has never worked since leaving school, yet has just had a three week holiday in Turkey."

"We're in the wrong job, boss," commented Dave.

"Indeed," said Fred Davies, ruefully. "How are we doing tracking Carl McCabe down?"

Everyone in the room simply shook their heads, and looked despondent.

"McCabe keeping out of the way makes me feel he has some connection with this," asserted Tinny. "He'll know we're looking for him, so he's making himself scarce."

The D.C.I. nodded. "I think you're right, Ron; we really need to find McCabe."

Gary looked thoughtful. "Would it be worth our while hounding Carl McCabe's uncles?" he suggested.

Fred Davies looked slightly confused. "What's your train of thought, Gary? These people wouldn't give up one of their own."

"Well, boss," explained Gary, "the Sarge has told me that he isn't really one of their own, but he'd like to be. If the McCabe family are behind this attack, then we'll get nothing from them, so we'd be no worse off than we are now; on the other hand, if Carl McCabe has taken this upon himself, the family won't be pleased to be getting, in their estimation, all this unnecessary attention from us."

The D.C.I. gave Gary an approving look. "Carry on, Gary, I'm starting to see where you're coming from."

Gary considered for a moment. "I still wouldn't expect them to tell us anything directly; however, I'm sure they could arrange for one of their low-life associates to point us in the right direction."

Fred Davies turned to Tinny. "What do you think, Ron?"

Tinny had been looking thoughtful, and now he nodded decidedly. "It's an excellent idea. I love going after people like the McCabes, and wish we could afford to do it twenty-four hours a day."

"Okay," concluded Davies, "I'll run it past the Chief Super, and see how much manpower he can spare us to really rattle their cage."

As the D.C.I. left the briefing room, Gary glanced at Tinny, his eyebrows raised; in reply, Tinny merely smiled and nodded.

…………………………………...

Caroline was up early again the following morning, and was in the dining room when she heard Neil coming down stairs.

"I'm in the dining room."

"I quite enjoyed that lay-in," said Neil, as he joined her. "Would you like a cup of tea?"

"It's okay, I'll make it," she offered; "I was going in to the kitchen to make breakfast anyway. Would you like some breakfast?"

Neil hesitated. "It's okay, I'll just have a cup of tea, thanks."

Caroline was smiling. "Neil used to eat breakfast sometimes........" she put her hand to her mouth. "Oh Neil, I'm so sorry."

"It's okay - I'm always doing it, it's an easy mistake to make. Don't worry about it, no harm done."

As she looked at him, she could see that his words did not match what he felt. By those few words that she had spoken, she knew that she had hurt him more than by anything else she had said or done since he came home from the hospital; she was mortified. "I'm so, so sorry."

"Honestly, I constantly think of Neil Hughes as being someone else; don't get upset over it."

"You have every right to - you can't possibly be someone that you have no memory of."

"I tell you what," said Neil, "I'll nip up and do a bit of training, which will work up an appetite for breakfast. Just give me a shout when it's ready." He walked quickly out of the room, and she heard him going upstairs even more quickly.

Caroline sat down, and held her head in her hands. She kept playing over and over in her mind what she had just said, cursing herself; she could not think of anything that could possibly undo the damage. She continued to sit, listening to the sound of him hitting the heavy bag; when the sound stopped, she went into the kitchen to make a pot of tea. She poured out a cup for Neil, then carried it upstairs.

As she entered the training room, Neil had his back to her while he was training on the speedball.

"I've made a nice cup of tea, if you fancy it."

Neil immediately grabbed a towel from the floor, and held it against his face.

"Is the central heating on?" His voice was muffled by the towel. "I seem to be sweating an awful lot, and my eyes are really stinging."

Caroline put the cup on the window ledge. "I don't think so, but I'll go and check."

Once Caroline had left the room, Neil wiped the sweat from his face, then went into the shower, where he remained for some time. Eventually, he dried himself off, got dressed, and went back downstairs.

"Well," he called out, as he reached the foot of the staircase, "I've certainly worked up a good appetite!"

As they were eating their breakfast, very little was spoken. Each of them was carefully considering everything they said, for fear of upsetting the other; it was a relief, therefore, when Michael and Paul arrived, and asked Neil if he wanted to help them on the site that day. Neil jumped at the opportunity, and said he would see Caroline later.

....

As the three of them arrived, Michael glanced over to one section of the site. "Oh, no – that's all we need," he said, wearily.

"What's the problem?" asked Neil.

"See the big fella over there? He's a real bully, and creates a bad atmosphere, whenever he's working."

Neil looked curiously in the direction Michael was pointing. "He doesn't bully either of you, does he?"

Paul snorted. "He doesn't come anywhere near us, because he knows what he'd get. No, he's your typical bully - he only picks on the old or the little fellas, or anyone who he thinks wouldn't fight back."

"So, why does this outfit employ him, if he just causes trouble?"

"A lot of the people on these sites are like me, and are just sub-contracting the work," explained Michael. "The main building firm use people like him as labourers, and just pay them cash in hand on a daily basis. I think the foreman is frightened of him, so he turns a blind eye to whatever's going on."

It was getting near to the end of the day, and Neil was walking past this loud-mouth labourer, when he heard a taunting voice aimed in his direction.

"Who's the pretty boy pushing that wheel barrow?"

Michael and Paul both heard this; however, as Paul went to move, Michael grabbed the back of his belt, and simply shook his head at his brother. Meanwhile, Neil ignored the comment, and carried on walking; he tipped the contents of the wheelbarrow into the skip, and headed back to where Michael and Paul were working.

As Neil was walking past him again, the bully pushed him in the back.

"I'm talking to you, pretty boy, don't turn your back on me!"

Neil put the wheel barrow down carefully, then calmly turned and smiled. "I'll give you one chance to apologise, or you'll be very sorry."

At this the labourer, who was a good three or four inches taller than Neil, took a swing at him, but missed completely; Neil appeared to have only moved his head slightly to avoid the punch, so was still close enough to deliver a powerful blow, which knocked the other man over.

Neil looked down on his opponent; he was no longer smiling.

"You've got two choices," he informed his adversary. "Get up and walk away, or get up and have another go; but, if you take the second choice, I'll put you down again, after hurting you a great deal. It's up to you."

The labourer slowly got to his feet, but just kept looking down at the ground. Neil turned away and walked towards the wheelbarrow; his opponent took this opportunity to pick up a piece of wood, with the intention of hitting Neil from behind.

Without looking, Neil kicked backwards straight in to the man's stomach, then followed it up with an elbow into his face, before he had even turned round to look his attacker in the eye. Neil then gripped the man tightly by the throat, and hit him, rapidly, three times in the face with the palm of his hand; one of these blows certainly broke his nose, one possibly broke his jaw and the other badly damaged his eye. Neil continued to hold his opponent by the throat, just for a few seconds; then released him, to let him drop to the ground.

Neil looked down on him. "You made the wrong choice," he observed; then, almost casually, he walked away.

When Neil was a reasonable distance away, the labourer turned to the other workers.

"Did you see that?" he spluttered. "I'm getting the police - he just attacked me for nothing!"

The foreman walked over to him, and threw some money on him with a contemptuous gesture.

"That's it - there's your money for today, and don't come on this site again. If the police are involved, we'll all tell them that Mike's dad was defending himself; and, if you turn up here again, I'll get Mike to ring his dad." The foreman smirked. "We've just really enjoyed that, and would love to see it again."

Michael and Paul were grinning as their father approached them. "Well," said Neil, "I'd imagine that's got to be a first."

"You've put bigger and tougher than him down in the past," asserted Paul.

"Not that; I meant, being called a pretty boy."

All three were laughing as they headed back to Mike's van; but before he got in, Neil stopped.

"Seriously," he said to his sons, "don't tell your mum about this; she might think it had something to do with a misunderstanding this morning. It didn't - I just don't like bullies."

Michael and Paul knew full well that their father could not tolerate bullying; but they were unaware that, in spite of what he said, what had just occurred on the site had everything to do with what had happened between Neil and Caroline that morning.

As they were driving home in the van, Paul asked "Dad, how do you do that? Dodge a punch by just moving your head slightly, as though you know exactly where it's going?"

"Another thing," joined in Michael, "that fool grabbed the wood so quickly before we had chance to shout, and yet it was as though you knew he was there without even looking; and why do you hit with the palm of your hand, rather than your fist?"

Neil kept a straight face. "It's actually the same answer to all three questions;" at this, both young men looked confused. "Haven't got a clue!" he told them cheerfully.

As they arrived back home, Caroline observed them from the bedroom window, and she noticed that they were all laughing; this should have cheered her up, but it almost made her feel worse, given the upset she had caused that morning.

Neil spent the rest of the evening watching DVDs in the living room; on the odd occasion that Caroline came in to ask him if he wanted a cup of tea or a sandwich, he smiled, and said 'yes, please' every time. She noticed that the programmes he was watching related to forensics and crime scene investigation; and, after a while, it occurred to her that he appeared to be almost studying them, rather than just watching them.

Caroline woke up with a start the next morning, and realised she had overslept. She glanced in to Michael's room, and saw that Neil had already got up; as she was walking downstairs, she told herself that she was not going to say or do the wrong thing today, if that was possible.

She found Neil in the dining room, with a number of documents spread out on the dining table; she could see straight away that there was a problem, but was reluctant to ask what it was. Neil glanced up at her; the expression in his eyes was one of sadness.

"The taxi authority have taken my plate back."

Caroline was confused. "I'm sorry Neil, but I don't quite know what you mean."

"Danny explained to me the other day that if a taxi is off the road for a certain amount of time, the authority can take the plate, and give it to whoever's next on the waiting list."

"I still don't understand – why does it matter?"

"It's because the taxi plate is what contains all the value," explained Neil. "Although my taxi is only worth about five thousand pounds as a vehicle, with the plate I would get about thirty thousand pounds for it if I were to sell it. Even if I get the insurance sorted out soon, there would be no point in buying another cab, as I no longer have the plate to go on it."

"Can't you ring them, and explain the situation to them?"

"I did this morning," sighed Neil. "Their attitude was that, had I informed them as soon as I left hospital, they may have been able to grant me an extension. When I pointed out to them that I'd completely lost my memory, and therefore wasn't aware of the rules, they didn't appear to be overly interested."

"But that's not fair! Did Danny not warn you that they could do this so quickly?"

"It's not his fault," said Neil, shaking his head. "Danny believed that the time period allowed for being off the road was longer. That's why I've been looking through all these documents relating to the cab; about a week before I was attacked, it appears that I received this letter, stating the new rules and regulations." He held up one of the pieces of paper from amongst those on the table top. "Danny mustn't have read them thoroughly himself, as there are so many changes. However," he observed wearily, dropping the letter back onto the table, "I've no doubt Nell Hughes would have read them thoroughly."

Caroline noted with concern that, this time, he made no attempt to correct himself. She began to wonder how many times this lovely, sad man could be knocked down before he gave up. She did not know what to say to him; all she could think of was to resort to something mundane.

"Tell you what," she said, "I'll go and make a brew, and then we'll think of something."

Michael and Paul arrived a short time later, and walked in to the dining room.

"What's up dad?" asked Michael, glancing at the documents on the table. "Something else to sort out?"

"I'm afraid so," replied Neil; "I'm going to have a bit of a job sorting this one out. My taxi plate has been taken off me which, effectively, has cost me twenty-five thousand pounds." He smiled ruefully. "I said the other day that, if I could buy a villa in Spain once, I could do it again; I must admit, though, not having my own cab to drive would make that very difficult."

Caroline was returning from the kitchen with the tea and some toast for the boys, and caught what Neil said.

"Twenty-five thousand pounds?" she said, outraged. "That's just not fair on you - it's not your fault you're in this position!"

Neil shrugged his shoulders. "That's their rules, and there's not a lot I can do about it."

Caroline looked at the resignation in Neil's eyes, and had to turn away; she found an excuse to tidy up some things by the dining room window, and had her back to the others while they continued talking.

"So," said Paul, munching on his toast, "what are you going to do, dad?"

There was a long pause. "Sod them!" declared Neil eventually. "I'll just drive someone else's cab. Danny explained to me the other day that some of the taxi owners have drivers on their cabs, which they call jockeys."

Caroline, pottering about by the window, began to smile; she could hear the change of tone in Neil's speech and realised, once again, that he never gave up. She felt guilty for doubting that this man was anyone other than Neil Hughes.

"I could find an owner who's looking for a day driver, and one who's looking for a night driver; if I put the hours in, although I wouldn't be making as much as when I owned my own cab, at least I'd be earning something."

Caroline was really beaming by now, as she heard the enthusiasm in Neil's voice; she was, however, still facing away from everyone when she said, in a light-hearted tone, "What are you going to do when someone gets in your taxi and says 'John Street please'?"

There was a short pause. "Of course," said Neil, his tone suddenly dull; "stupid of me. How can I drive a taxi when I don't know where anywhere is?"

Caroline turned quickly, to see the sadness back in Neil's eyes. "I'm sorry," she faltered, "I was only joking - I didn't mean you were being stupid."

Neil held up his hand. "No, you're right – who'd want to get in a taxi when the driver didn't know where he was going?"

An awkward silence followed. Michael and Paul looked at each other, and shrugged; Caroline, however, felt her heart sink - she could not believe she had been so tactless.

"Anyway," said Neil, glancing at his watch, "I'm off over to Liverpool, for another pointless session with the therapist."

He stood up, forced a smile, and walked quickly out into the hall; they all listened as he closed the front door behind him.

Paul looked at his mother. "What did you say that for? You just made dad feel really stupid."

"I didn't mean to - it was a joke, I was smiling when I said it."

"Smiling, when you say something to someone, tends to work only when you're facing them," said Michael wryly. "What you said just came across as being sarcastic."

Caroline sat down and sighed. "Honestly, it *was* meant as a joke. I just hope your dad realises that as he's driving to the hospital."

"Well, anyway," said Michael, "is your car still available for me to borrow, or do you need it at all today?"

Caroline just handed the car keys to him, without saying anything; Michael then put his arm around her shoulders.

"*I* know it was a joke," he said reassuringly, "it just didn't come across that way. No doubt dad will understand that, and is probably laughing about it now."

....

Neil arrived at the hospital, knowing that this would be his last session with the therapist. Apart from the fact that he felt it to be a waste of time, he had noticed that, since his bandages had been removed, the therapist had started flirting with him, which was making him feel uncomfortable; as well as some of the things she had said to him, he was aware of how she had started to dress differently. Although he still had no memory, as far as he was concerned, he had no interest in anyone other than Caroline; he could only hope that, one day, Caroline would come to feel the same way about him.

When the session was over, Neil explained to the therapist that this would be his last, as he felt that they were making no progress in retrieving his memory.

"Anyway, I'd like to thank you for your time," he said, as he stood up. He held out his hand to shake; she took it, and held it for a little too long.

"Caz is a very lucky woman." Her smile was disarming.

Neil surveyed her critically; almost, with disgust.

"Caz has had all her dreams and plans for the future destroyed, through no fault of her own," he pointed out. "She's tried her best to cope with an impossible situation, and is totally innocent of any wrongdoings. She's now trying to share her home and her life with a total stranger. I don't think that's very lucky at all."

The therapist's smile vanished. Neil left the room without another word, and closed the door behind him.

....

As Neil was walking along the corridor, he saw Dr. Hargraves heading towards him; as soon as the doctor recognised him, he smiled broadly, and offered to shake Neil's hand.

"Is Braithwaite still here?" asked Neil.

"You're in luck – today's his last day, he's in his office clearing out all his belongings."

Neil just nodded, and started to walk away; Dr. Hargraves looked concerned.

"Is everything all right?"

Neil glanced back at him. "No," he said abruptly; then he carried on walking.

....

As Neil entered Dr. Braithwaite's office, the doctor stood up, smiling.

"Mr Hughes, my finest creation!" he boomed. "May I take this opportunity to apologise for my insensitivity concerning your attendance at the press conference."

Neil did not return his smile. "I'd like to see the pictures of my face when I was brought in here."

Braithwaite shook his head. "You really don't want to see them. To the untrained eye, they are very unpleasant to view; it would serve no purpose."

Neil fixed Braithwaite with a cold look. "That was not a request."

The expression on Neil's face, and the tone of his voice, sent an icy shiver down the doctor's spine; but he composed himself, extracted a large folder from a filing cabinet, handed it to Neil, and then sat down behind his desk.

As Neil was studying the photographs, Braithwaite continued to talk nervously, but he was not certain whether Neil was even listening; what surprised him was that Neil appeared to show no emotion at all, although some of the images were gruesome, to say the least.

When he had finished, Neil carefully replaced the photographs inside the folder, and stood up to leave. "Thank you," he said shortly, and walked out of the office.

When Neil had gone, Braithwaite felt a sense of relief. He exhaled deeply; for the first time in his life, he had a feeling of self-doubt, and wondered whether Caroline was right and he was wrong. He also felt suddenly fearful; perhaps his 'finest creation' might prove to be his worst.

....

Dr. Hargraves observed Neil leaving Dr. Braithwaite's office, but thought better than to approach him. He was bewildered; he thought he had come to know this man, someone with such a strong will to live, and an enthusiasm for the future – so what could make him look so unhappy? He knew the induced coma had saved Neil's life; but had it, somehow, just succeeded in condemning him to a living hell?

....

Long after Neil and the boys had left, Caroline was still sitting in the dining room, feeling guilty for what she had said, and racking her brain for some way to make amends.

Suddenly, it came to her; she was annoyed she had not thought of it before. When Neil came home, she was going to suggest they go to the restaurant by the church, the scene of their first date. Why not? It was certainly her fondest memory, and she knew it had also been Neil's; in any event, although he would not now remember, she felt sure that he would love the restaurant, and enjoy going in the church where he proposed to her. This idea really lifted her spirits, and she began to get excited.

She also made another resolution - when Neil got home, she intended to hug him, kiss him, and tell him how much she loved him. She had let him down, badly, since he came out of hospital; but she would make up for it now. She went upstairs quickly; she took out her favourite dress from the wardrobe, laid it out on the bed, and went into the shower.

………………………………………….................

When Neil arrived home, he assumed Caroline must have gone out, as her car was not in the drive. He called out as he entered the hall but, hearing no reply, he thought he was alone in the house; he began to walk up the stairs.

Caroline had no idea that Neil was in the house; she had not heard him while she was in the shower and, as she had drawn the bedroom curtains before getting undressed, she did not see Neil's car parked in the driveway when she went back into the bedroom.

As Caroline was drying herself, Neil walked into the bedroom, and was startled to see her standing there naked; Caroline instinctively grabbed the bath-towel, and covered herself with it.

"I'm so sorry," blurted Neil; "I didn't realise you were in." He quickly turned, and headed back to the staircase.

Caroline called after him. "It's okay Neil, I didn't hear you come in - you just caught me by surprise, it's okay." But by the time she had said this, Neil was already back downstairs.

……………………………………………………

Caroline quickly got dressed, and rushed downstairs to find Neil sitting in the living room, looking down at the floor.

"I'm sorry about that, I thought you were out." His tone was subdued.

"There's no need to apologise - I was just taken by surprise, I hadn't realised you'd got home."

There was an uncomfortable silence; then Caroline spoke. "How did it go with the therapist?"

As Neil spoke, he kept his head bowed, looking at the floor.

"I won't be bothering anymore; it's a waste of time. The therapist's description of the chance of my memory returning has changed from "definitely", to "almost certainly", to "probably". I wonder how many more sessions I'd have to go to, before it's described as an outside chance?

"Caz, I don't remember our meeting, getting married, Michael and Paul being born, or anything of our life together. The friends and family who visited me in hospital, and called here since I've been home, have all meant well by talking about my past, in the hope it may help; but all it's actually done is remind me, constantly, of what I've lost." He paused "We've had to sell the villa, which you tell me was my dream – but all I know for sure is that I don't have dreams any more, only nightmares; in any case, as I've lost the taxi plate, it seems unlikely I'll ever be in a position to buy a villa again.

"You know, when I first looked in a mirror, and saw this new face, I was ecstatic; I know you always said it didn't matter what I looked like but, as you're so beautiful, I would have felt uncomfortable going anywhere with you if I'd had a badly disfigured face. Now, I hate this face – more than anything, I want to look like Neil Hughes again, even if I was disfigured. Braithwaite said you weren't happy with my new face, and would have preferred it if I was disfigured."

Caroline flinched; that was not exactly what she had said, but it was not far enough away from the truth for her to argue the point, so she remained silent as Neil continued.

"Looking at what's happened since leaving the hospital, I think you're right. The problem is, even if I do get my memory back, my face isn't going to change. What would you do if a stranger walked in to your bedroom while you're getting dressed?" Before Caroline could say anything, he carried on. "You don't need to answer that, because we both now know what you'd do."

He heaved a heavy sigh.

"The police tell me that whoever did this wanted Neil Hughes to die. I think they succeeded, don't you?"

Caroline looked down at Neil, and could see his tears falling on to the floor as he kept his head bowed. She desperately wanted to hold him; but she knew he would probably think her action was due to her feeling sorry for him, or worse still, pitying him – and that would be the final insult. She also knew that any words would be useless. Neil did not raise his head as she left the room, and walked slowly back upstairs.

....

Caroline went into the bedroom, and sat on the edge of the bed; as she looked at the pretty dress she had laid out earlier, she broke down, sobbing uncontrollably.

From the night she met Neil, he had loved her with an intensity and passion that you only read about in stories; he had not just loved her, he had looked after her and did everything he could to make her happy. For the last twenty years, Neil had done everything in his power to protect her and keep her safe. He had never cried in front of her; even when his father died, he controlled his emotions, and even comforted *her*.

And now, she thought bitterly, this is how I have repaid him: in the short time since he was attacked, she had somehow managed to make him feel guilty for doing the right thing where the house was concerned; she had really hurt him, by referring to Neil as if he were a different person; and then capped it all by hiding herself from the man she was supposed to love, as if he were some kind of intruder. She had only been taken by surprise, and reacted instinctively – the old Neil would have known that; but the new Neil could not.

Neil had said that the people who did this had killed him, but he was wrong - they *almost* killed him. *She* had finished the job for them with the things she had said and done, the way she had behaved and, more importantly, with what she had failed to say and do. She could see no way back now, even if Neil regained his memory. He would remember everything that he had done for her; and then he would realise, when he had been vulnerable, how dreadfully she had treated him.

....

Neil was still staring at the floor, but had stopped crying. He had cried like a child three times in a matter of days; there would not be a fourth.

If he could get to the people who attacked him before the police found them, then the authorities would not have to worry about a long and expensive trial.

Whoever did this had chosen to leave him to die, instead of making sure he was dead. They made the wrong choice.

....

Caroline heard the front door close; she looked out of the bedroom window, and watched Neil get into his car and drive off.

She feared she may never see him again; but what terrified her more, was the thought that, perhaps, no-one would ever see him again.

....

Neil just sat in the car considering what had happened and what he felt he had to do. He must have hurt Caroline by what he had said, then driving off and leaving her alone; but the time for regrets and recriminations was over. The longer he thought about it, his resolve hardened. There was only one solution: to take revenge on the people who had ruined their lives.

People had told him that he was a good planner and organiser; well, he would need those skills, if he was to be successful. With detachment, he went through it in his mind: how he would identify his attackers, track them down, discover why they had left him for dead, and then deal with them, but leave no trace of his presence; to that end, he had already been carefully studying the subject of crime scene forensic investigation. He had no intention of being caught. With regard to identifying his assailants, he knew how he would go about accessing the memory of that night; he did not relish the thought, but there was no other way.

The police report suggested that there were either three or four people involved in the attack;

ideally, he would go after them one at a time but, if necessary, he would face all of them at once. He needed to be stronger and fitter in order to do this, and would take the appropriate action to ensure that he was prepared.

It would be necessary to distance himself, from both Caroline and his sons, until he had achieved his aim; it was vital that they knew nothing of his intentions. He certainly did not want the boys involved, as this was something he had to do alone; as for Caroline, she had already been through the agony of almost losing him – given the risks he would be taking with his life, she must be shielded from any knowledge of his activities.

He desperately wanted to regain his memory, so that he could love her again; but he could not move forward until he had completed his task. From this point on, therefore, he was determined that nothing would upset or hurt him, and he would be sure to avoid any such situations.

His attackers were the ones who would get hurt.

Chapter 8

Shortly after Neil had driven off, Michael arrived in Caroline's car, followed by Paul in his own vehicle, and they both walked into the hall; finding no-one about, Michael went to the foot of the stairs.

"Mum!" he called, "I'm just dropping the car off - Paul's taking me back to the garage to get the van."

The speed with which Caroline came down the stairs surprised both the boys, and they could see that she had been crying.

"What's wrong?" asked Michael, alarmed. "Where's dad?"

Caroline explained to them what had happened, and told them everything that Neil had said.

"Hell," said Michael vehemently. "Where did he go? What did he say as he left?"

Caroline shrugged helplessly. "I don't know - I was upstairs. He just went out, got in the car, and drove off. I've no idea where he went, but I'm really worried."

Paul realised that his mother and brother were beginning to panic, and saw that he needed to intervene.

"Let's all calm down," he said evenly. "Dad's not going to do anything stupid; he's evidently just upset and angry."

"We can't just wait here, and hope he comes home," protested Michael.

"You're right, we can't," smiled Paul; "but I've got an idea where we might find him. We'll go in my car. While I'm driving, you need to make some calls, so you'll need your mobile and mine."

Michael looked vacant. "Calls to who?"

"I'll explain while I'm driving; the sooner we set off, the better. Mum," said Paul, putting his arm around her shoulder reassuringly, "don't worry - I'll find him."

…………………………………………………

As Paul set off down the lane, he turned to Michael.

"Ring Jacko and Danny, and tell them to put the word round all the other taxi lads to keep an eye out for dad's car," he instructed. "Just tell them dad's gone out without his mobile phone, and we need to contact him; after you've done that, use your phone to ring all your mates who've got transport, and then use mine to ring my mates. Give everybody the details on dad's car, but stress it's not an emergency – tell them they just need to let us know if they've seen him anywhere."

Michael nodded. "And where are we going?"

"The hospital where grandad died."

Michael looked at his brother in surprise. "It's not there anymore," he pointed out. "It was demolished a few months ago; it's just a large area of waste ground."

"I know - but I think that's where dad may be."

"But, without his memory, how could he possibly know of the connection?"

Paul smiled knowingly. "Just make the calls, mate; just make the calls, in case I'm wrong."

Michael, puzzled, just shook his head, convinced that it would be a waste of time; however, as he had no ideas of his own to offer, he felt unable to argue the point further, so he got on with making the phone calls.

A short time later, Paul turned on to the road leading to the site of the old hospital.

"Look," said Michael, pointing, "you can see from here - there's fencing all around the site and, as far as I know, there's no way in."

"Hold on," replied Paul, patiently, "just humour me."

As they pulled up alongside the wire mesh fencing, they could see their father's car parked, roughly, in the middle of the site; as Paul drove slowly along the road, he saw a gap in the fence, large enough to drive a car through. He drove in, but stopped about one hundred yards away from their father's car. Michael turned to his brother, his eyebrows raised questioningly; however, Paul did not explain himself. He got out of the car.

"Wait here, while I see if he's okay."

Michael was somewhat relieved at his brother's suggestion. Although he could see his father sitting in the car, he did not appear to be moving; he felt his stomach churning as he watched Paul approaching the stationary vehicle.

As he reached the car, Paul could see that the driver's window was down; he looked inside, to see his father gazing, unseeingly, straight ahead.

"Dad?" he said gently. "What are you doing here?"

Neil seemed to awake from his reverie, and looked up at his son.

"To be honest," he said slowly, "I don't know. This is the third time I've been here since getting out of hospital, but I've no idea why."

"Okay," said Paul. "Do you just sit in the car?"

"No; I was just about to get out, and stand over there." Neil pointed to an area, behind where Paul was standing.

"Interesting," commented Paul; "show me exactly where you mean."

Neil got out of the car, much to the onlooking Michael's relief, and walked over to the part of the site he had indicated, followed by Paul; once there, he stood still.

"It's strange," mused Neil; "each time I've been here, this is where I stand - but I haven't got a clue why."

Paul gave a satisfied nod. "I have. The place where you're now standing is where your dad died."

"I don't understand," said Neil. "Your mum said my dad died in hospital."

Paul smiled. "He did. This was where the ward used to be – and grandad's hospital bed was on that exact spot where you're standing."

Neil was silent for a moment, as he took this in.

"Was I with him when he died?" he asked eventually.

"Yes; and so was mum."

At the mention of Caroline, Neil looked worried.

"Is your mum okay?" he asked, concern in his voice. "I must have frightened the living daylights out of her when I walked into the bedroom, because she didn't realise I'd come back in to the house."

"Mum's fine," assured Paul; "but, admittedly, she does keep blaming herself for everything that's going wrong."

"It's not in any way your mum's fault," said Neil emphatically. "Somehow, I'm to blame - but I intend on putting it right."

"So, can I ring mum and tell her to put the kettle on?"

Neil smiled wearily, and nodded. "Tell your mum that I'll definitely come home later; but I think I'll stay here for a while. I've got a lot of things to think about."

"Fair enough," said Paul, "I'll let her know."

As he walked back over to his car, Paul could see that his brother was on the phone; when he got into the car, Michael proffered the phone to him.

"It's mum," explained Michael. "Everything okay?"

Paul nodded silently, and took the handset to speak to his mother.

"Hello, mum..........it's okay, dad's sound; he just wanted a bit of time on his own.......there's no need to worry, he told me he'll definitely be home later.........yes, that's right, so I'll drop Mike off at the garage, then he can pick up his van. Anyway, how do you fancy a take away instead of you cooking something?...good idea, Indian it is. Needless to say, I'm skint, but our Mike will have money.....yeah, same old story! Alright, we'll see you later."

Paul rang off, and handed the phone back to Michael, grinning.

"Let's hope the garage bill isn't too big – you'll need enough money for the Indian takeaway which I just volunteered you to pay for."

Mike gave a smile of resignation; then he turned, and looked at his brother wonderingly.

"How did you know dad would be here?"

Paul simply shrugged, as he started the car; he could not give Michael an answer, because he did not know himself.

....

Although it was much later when Neil arrived home, Michael and Paul had only just turned up with the Indian takeaway.

"You timed that nicely," remarked Caroline brightly; "Michael has treated us to a takeaway."

As soon as she spoke, however, she noticed a difference in his demeanour, and this troubled her. Since the day his bandages had been removed, she had observed a range of emotions on his face, and in his eyes: the happiness and excitement he showed while he was still in the hospital bed which, in an instant, Caroline managed to kill with her shocked expression; the sparkle and enthusiasm he had for his plan to save the house, about which, again, Caroline had made him feel guilty; and the hurt and sadness she had created, simply by not showing her love for him as she should have done. Now there was only a dullness, even a blankness; in his expression; in all the years she had known him, she had never seen him like this.

I warned myself that if I did not love him soon, I could lose him, she thought miserably; I was right.

Michael and Paul could usually lift his spirits; she desperately hoped they could do it again this time, because if they could, she would grab the opportunity of holding him, and assuring him of her love. However, Neil barely spoke and, after a short time, announced he was tired, and was going to bed; she could see the disappointment in the boys' faces as they watched him climb the stairs.

"Dad will be okay by tomorrow," said Paul, forcing a smile, "and he'll be back to looking to the future again."

Privately, however, he was not convinced of that.

....

After the boys had left, Caroline tidied up, washed, dried and put away the dishes, then went to bed herself. She glanced into Michael's room, and saw Neil asleep on top of the bed; she found herself wishing, sadly, that she had found him asleep in her bed.

Caroline was unable to sleep; she lay, staring up at the ceiling, going over everything that had happened, and realised it had started to go wrong from the moment she first saw Neil's new face. If only she could turn the clock back to that day – if she had left home earlier, taken a different route, got to the hospital in time to be with him before his bandages were removed – things might have been different…

Suddenly, she was jerked back to reality; from Michael's room, she heard the chilling sound of Neil crying out, as though he was in terrible pain. She jumped out of bed, naked; instead of grabbing her dressing gown to cover herself, she rushed into Michael's room as she was, to see what was wrong.

The first thing she saw was the look of absolute terror in Neil's eyes. She had seen that look once before in her life; in the eyes of Neil's father, immediately before he died of a massive heart attack. She had hoped she would never see that look again.

As soon as Caroline came into the room, Neil looked down at the floor and, clearly, was not going raise his eyes while she was there.

"What's happened? Was it another nightmare?"

"It's okay, I'm fine." Neil's tone was dull, unemotional.

Caroline could see that he was covered in sweat, and went to the bathroom to get a towel. As she handed it to him, she hoped he may look up at her – she wanted him to see that she had no intention or desire to hide herself from him; however, Neil kept his eyes lowered, as he wiped the sweat from his face.

"I'm sorry about today," he muttered, "for saying that you thought I was a stranger. I realised later that I only caught you by surprise when I walked into the bedroom; I apologise for saying such a cruel thing to you."

"There's no need……….."

"Yes there is," he interrupted, "and I'm sorry."

Caroline did not know what else to say to reassure him; she was also worried by his apparent calmness, remembering the terror in his voice when he cried out.

"When you were still in hospital, didn't you say you thought that you could control the nightmares?"

"I'm okay, I'll be fine; trust me it isn't a problem." He decided not to tell her the truth: that he *was* controlling them.

Caroline remained standing, looking down at him, and hoping that he might raise his head, if only to glance at her; but she soon realised that he would not.

She sighed. "Well, then - is there anything I can do?"

"Honestly, I'm okay - go back to bed, I'll be fine."

As Caroline turned away, Neil could not stop himself from looking at this beautiful woman; he smiled to himself at the thought that women half her age would probably sell their souls for a figure such as hers.

Caroline, reluctantly, went back to her bedroom, and lay wide awake in the darkness. She was very much afraid; Neil had been a fighter all of his life and, no matter what the setbacks were, he had always been positive, with a determination to look to the future. She wondered now if her strong, brave, lovely man had finally given up.

....

As Tinny and Gary walked into the briefing room, the D.C.I. beckoned them over, smiling broadly.

"Guess who we've got downstairs in the cells?"

"Carl McCabe?" ventured Tinny.

"Correct," replied the D.C.I., still smiling. "We had an anonymous tipoff, and found him in a squat on the Rockford."

"Excellent," declared Tinny. "It'd be interesting to know who the tipoff came from, and if the McCabe family were behind it."

"Have a listen to the tape," suggested the D.C.I.; "whoever it was tried to disguise their voice, but I've got an idea who it is."

Tinny and Gary listened to the recording, then nodded to each other.

"That's Matty Grant," said Tinny.

Fred Davies nodded. "I agree; although, I wonder whether the information was fed to him, or he's just taking the opportunity to redirect our attention away from himself."

"Either way, it will be interesting to find out what McCabe was doing the night of the attack."

"Well," said the D.C.I., "Dave and Paula are just about to start the interview, so let's see how they get on."

As Tinny, Gary, and D.C.I. Davies were examining the monitor in the room next door to the interview room, Fred Davies remarked "He's a nasty looking piece of work."

Tinny nodded grimly. "He's a thug and a bully - and I have to say (in the confines of this room) that I was delighted when I saw how Neil Hughes dealt with him. This piece of scum should be kicked in the head on a regular basis."

The interview was running its usual course, the response to every question being 'no comment.' Carl McCabe seemed to be very relaxed, almost smug, as he smiled at his interrogators; Tinny noticed that he appeared to be regularly looking at the clock on the wall. Eventually, he became more forthcoming.

"Right," he said, in a business-like fashion, "the snooker club will be open in half an hour, and I've just remembered where I was that night."

Dave looked expectant. "Alright - where exactly where you, and can anyone else confirm it?"

McCabe's expression became particularly smug. "I was in a police cell in Warrington, and I expect the nice policeman will confirm that."

Dave, suppressing his irritation, turned to Paula. "Interview terminated."

....

As Tinny was on the phone to the Warrington police, Dave and Paula came into the room, shaking their heads.

"Warrington have just confirmed it, I'm afraid," said Tinny. "McCabe was arrested shortly before midnight, and wasn't let out until seven o'clock in the morning."

"Blast," sighed D.C.I. Davies. "Even so, I still feel he's connected to this in some way; but knowing and proving are two different things."

"I agree, boss," nodded Tinny. "From what Warrington tell me, McCabe made sure he was arrested that night."

"How do you mean, Sarge?" asked Paula.

"There was a bit of a skirmish outside a pub involving McCabe, but the officers who attended were just going to move him on. Anyway, it seems that he took a swing at one of the officers, and was therefore arrested; but, when he took the swing, he made sure he didn't make any contact, and was released without charge in the morning."

"Interesting," remarked the D.C.I. "In that case, from the sounds of it, although he definitely didn't take part in the attack on Neil Hughes, there's a fair chance he arranged it."

Gary had been listening intently. "I've got an idea, Sarge," he now offered, "but it could be a bit risky."

Tinny and the D.C.I. listened intently as Gary explained his idea; when he had finished, they both decided it was worth a try.

"At the very least, it may wipe that smirk off his face," commented D.C.I. Davies.

....

Tinny and Gary entered the interview room, and duly went through the usual procedure before speaking to McCabe.

"Alright," began Tinny, "we've checked with Warrington; they have confirmed you were arrested that night, and so couldn't possibly have attacked Neil Hughes."

McCabe sneered. "I don't know any Neil Hughes, so it couldn't have anything to do with me."

"Actually, you may know him better as Yosser Hughes - the one who put you on your back outside the kebab house."

"That was a lucky shot, I could take Yosser Hughes on any time," said McCabe, dismissively.

"Well, you could get your chance - he's out of hospital now and has, I believe, been training solidly, and is back in shape."

As Tinny said this, the smile disappeared from McCabe's face.

"But I heard he almost died, and has brain damage?"

"No, no, far from it - he's in excellent physical condition. I would imagine, therefore, that whoever did this, or whoever was *behind* it, will now be very concerned."

Tinny could see the look of fear on McCabe's face; he affected a genial manner.

"Anyway, as this has nothing to do with you, you are free to go. Did you say you were going for a game of snooker? Enjoy yourself, won't you?"

....

Tinny and Gary went back into the room next door, to find a smiling Fred Davies, and a confused Dave and Paula.

"What was that all about?" asked Dave, scratching his head. "What's your train of thought, Sarge?"

Tinny smiled self-effacingly. "It's not my train of thought, it's Gary's; he can explain it to you."

Gary took his cue. "If McCabe has no connection to this at all, he has nothing to concern him; if, on the other hand, he did arrange this, then he'll feel he has a lot to worry about. If Neil Hughes tracks down his assailants, they would happily give up Carl McCabe, if they thought it would save them from a severe beating; McCabe will know that and, hopefully, may flush them out for us."

Dave still looked confused. "But Neil Hughes has no memory of the attack; and, from what Debbie said, may not have seen his attackers anyway."

Gary smiled. "True; but McCabe doesn't know that."

Paula's puzzled expression began to clear. "So effectively, McCabe will feel he needs to get to these people first - before Neil Hughes does."

"Exactly," said Gary. "Judging from his change in demeanour in the interview room, he was not best pleased to discover Neil Hughes is out of hospital, and fighting fit."

Dave frowned. "By telling McCabe that Neil Hughes survived, and may remember his attackers, aren't we putting Mr Hughes in a dangerous position?"

"That was my thought," agreed Gary; "but, as the Sarge pointed out, whoever attacked him will already be aware that they failed; so that situation is already in place, regardless of what we do."

"Neil Hughes now looks completely different, so he could walk past his attackers in the street, and they wouldn't recognise him," interjected the D.C.I. "What we need to do now is go through all of McCabe's known associates, and start bringing them in. Carl McCabe is being followed as we speak; it will be interesting to see who he goes to first."

Tinny grinned. "I bet he's not going to the snooker hall!"

………………………………..

Caroline had been up early and, after having checked Michael's room and found that Neil had also already risen, was surprised that he was not anywhere in the house, despite his car being outside. She had just made a pot of tea when Neil came in through the back garden, carrying a haversack on his back; he was gasping for air.

Caroline was aghast. "What have you been doing to sweat that much, and get so winded?"

Neil paused a moment before replying, in order to catch his breath.

"I've just been on a run, carrying this weight in the haversack. Mike said I used to do this whenever I got the opportunity, so I thought I'd give it a try."

"You look absolutely shattered! You need to sit down, and get your breath back. Would you like a cup of tea and some breakfast?"

"No, thanks; I'm just going to have a shower, then have a lie down for half an hour."

Caroline had hoped that, while having breakfast with him, she could take the opportunity to tell him how she felt; however, she did not let him see her disappointment, and smiled.

"Okay," she said. "Just give us a shout if you change your mind."

Neil went upstairs, feeling guilty for the way he had just behaved; but he could not risk getting into any sort of conversation.

……………………………………………………………

Neil spent the rest of the day between the training room, and watching DVDs in the living room; Caroline tried several times to engage him in conversation, but now, she sensed that an invisible barrier had somehow formed between them. He was always polite when he spoke, and was in no way unpleasant in his behaviour towards her; but to Caroline, it seemed more like having a guest in her house, rather than the man she loved.

Later that evening, when they arrived, Caroline was relieved to see that Michael and Paul had brought Cathy and Jenny with them, as she hoped Neil would be more like himself in the company of the girls. He was pleasant and polite, but could not be drawn into conversation, generally restricting his answers to monosyllables; it was only when Caroline, Michael and Paul were not in the room that Neil visibly relaxed. The girls glanced at one another, noticing the reduction in tension; Cathy decided to take the opportunity to try and draw him out.

"So, Neil," she said, "until you get your memory back, and you can start driving the taxi again, what are you planning to do?"

Neil shrugged. "From all accounts, I'm not much use for anything else, so I thought I might see if I can get any labouring jobs in the day and, maybe, get a job as a bouncer for some of the evenings. I'm stepping up the training; so, I'm fit to do both, if I get the opportunity."

"I think you have to have some sort of badge or something to work as a bouncer now," said Jenny, "but I'm not sure."

"I think I might have an old milk monitor's badge from school - would that do?"

The girls laughed.

"You could give it a try! Has it got your photograph on it?" asked Jenny.

"You're just trying to make things difficult for me now, aren't you? I could always use my taxi badge, although it is a bit burnt round the edges."

"Ah, but the trouble with that, is that the picture on your taxi badge looks nothing like you now," pointed out Cathy.

Neil laughed. "I was thinking about that the other day; it occurred to me that you should really have a picture of the back of your head on the taxi badge, because that's what the customers are looking at."

Jenny giggled. "You should go into one of those photo booths and get some "back of head" shots, to stick on to your taxi badge."

"Hm; or, I could wear a wig, and stick one on my monitor's badge - that would really confuse people."

"You could even get a false pony tail," suggested Cathy.

"I don't even know where I'd *find* a false pony, let alone try to get the tail off one," said Neil in mock seriousness, which sent both girls into peals of laughter.

Once the laughter had subsided, Neil said "Changing the subject completely, I was watching a DVD today, and heard a strange accent; what country are these people from?"

He used the remote control to turn on the DVD player, at the exact point in the film he had prepared.

"That's not an accent from another country," said Cathy; "it's a traveller accent."

At Neil's prompting, she went on to explain what travellers were, and how their accent was quite distinctive, but very difficult for outsiders to understand; just then, Michael and Paul came back into the room.

"We were just telling your dad about travellers, and the unusual accent they have," explained Cathy.

"It wasn't important, we were just having a laugh." Neil made his voice sound casual, but he felt uneasy, as Michael was looking at him searchingly.

"It's strange you should be interested in the traveller accent," he observed.

"I wouldn't say I was interested; I just thought it was a strange way of speaking."

"What I mean," elaborated Michael, "is that you can speak in a traveller accent."

Neil was not expecting this, so was slightly off guard. "That's news to me."

"Here," said Michael, holding out his hand, "pass us the remote control, and I'll show you what I'm talking about."

Michael chose a particular point in the film, played a short portion, and then paused it.

"Now, what did he just say then?" he asked his father.

Neil repeated what was said in the film, and was confused when all four of his companions laughed. He looked at them questioningly.

"None of us understood what was just said - but you obviously could," explained Paul.

"See if you can repeat it, using the traveller accent," suggested Michael.

Neil repeated precisely what the actor in the film had said, complete with accent, much to the amusement of everyone else.

"Brilliant!" exclaimed Paul. "You would swear you were a traveller, when you speak like that."

Neil smiled. He had got the information he needed; but to discover, also, that he could speak like a traveller, was an unexpected advantage.

"Well, if you'll excuse me, I think I'll go and do some training, and then I'm off to bed," declared Neil. "See you all tomorrow."

Shortly after he had gone upstairs, Caroline came into the room, and was disappointed to find that he was not there. "Where's your dad? I heard you all laughing before, when I was in the kitchen."

Cathy and Jenny recounted the bizarre conversation about badges, which made the boys laugh, but Caroline just smiled weakly; she was annoyed with herself for missing the opportunity to see Neil enjoying himself. Soon afterwards, she also went to bed, hoping that Neil would still be in the training room; but by then, he was already in bed, asleep.

As had occurred the previous night, Caroline heard Neil cry out; she sprang up and rushed into his bedroom, to find him sitting on the edge of the bed, with the same look of terror in his eyes.

"I'm okay, it's fine, I'll be all right now." He fixed his gaze firmly on the floor.

Caroline could see that he was shaking uncontrollably and, once again, drenched in perspiration. Carefully, she sat down next to him.

"Is there nothing I can do to help?"

"I'll be fine, really; these nightmares won't last forever, don't worry."

Caroline took his hand, holding it in her own until he stopped shaking. "Please, let me do something to help you."

Neil continued looking at the floor, and did not answer her; so, reluctantly, Caroline eventually released his hand, and went back to her own bedroom.

After she had left, Neil sighed deeply. He felt badly about shutting her out in this way; but he was determined to make sure that she could have no suspicion of his plans. He needed to avoid having the nightmares during the night, when she could hear him; in future, where possible, he would try to develop them during the day, when she was not in the house.

He had known for some time that he could control the nightmares; and now, traumatic as it was, he found that he was able develop them to a point where he could remember more about his ordeal. In last night's dream, he had heard a voice; in tonight's, he had seen a face. He still had no memory from before the attack, but he was certain of one thing: he had seen that face since coming out of hospital.

…………………………………....................................

"Unfortunately, Carl McCabe managed to lose the officer who was following him," said D.C.I. Davies, ruefully. "We know he went straight to his uncle's club, but didn't come out again; so, we assume he left by another door."

"Are we having any luck with the known associates, as far as alibis are concerned?" asked Tinny.

The D.C.I. shook his head. "Nothing yet; however, we're looking closely at those individuals who are giving each other alibis."

"Do any of these people connected to McCabe own a van, or are any of them involved in the building industry?" enquired Gary.

"Most of these people have never done a legitimate day's work in their life," said D.C.I. Davies, tartly. "They're making a good living out of drug dealing, selling stolen goods, or forcing protection on small businesses."

"Is it possible McCabe could have hired people who are not connected to him?" suggested Gary.

D.C.I. Davies nodded wearily. "I'm afraid so. There are people out there whose own lives are worthless and, therefore, have no qualms about taking someone else's. There are also people who are prepared to do anything for a price."

"I think I'll have a word with Matty Grant," said Tinny. "I'd like to know if he took it upon himself to give us the information, or whether it came from the McCabe family."

"Just an idea, Sarge," said Gary; "if Grant is made aware that you – *almost* - let slip at the interview that it was he who told us where to find Carl McCabe, he might be able to point us in the right direction again."

Fred Davies laughed. "Gary, you're a cunning man - I'm glad you're on our side!"

…………………………………....................................

It had taken some time for her to get to sleep, so it was quite late when Caroline finally woke up in the morning. While she was getting dressed, she could hear Neil in the training room; she looked in, and could see that he had been training for some time, judging by how much he was sweating.

"Still at it, I see," she observed. "Do you fancy a cup of tea or anything to eat?"

"I'm okay; I made a bit of toast when I came back from the run, but I'll have a cup of tea, thanks."

"Do you want me to bring it up here?"

"There's no need - I was just about to have a shower, so I'll be down soon; thanks anyway."

"Alright then, I'll have it ready when you come down."

As she went downstairs, Caroline was glad that, at least, they were going to share a pot of tea together; she hoped it would give her the opportunity to tell Neil how she felt, without it sounding as if she was just being kind, or that she felt sorry for him.

A short time later, as she was sitting at the kitchen table, waiting, she heard Neil coming downstairs; she finished making the tea, and took it over to the table, as he came in and sat down.

"I'll have this brew," he said, "then I'm going to call at a few building sites to see if there are any labouring jobs going, even if it's only part time, or odd days cash in hand."

"Jenny said you were thinking of working as a bouncer as well?"

"Yes," he replied. "While I was still in hospital, Paul said a couple of Manchester lads were asking how I was doing, and he thought they may have been bouncers; apparently, I'd got to know quite a few of the doormen in the area, through driving the taxi."

"Michael and Paul mentioned that, to work as a bouncer, you need to be licensed by the local authority."

"Well, in that case, I'll find out how you get a licence."

Caroline hesitated for a moment, but then decided to say what was on her mind.

"Don't misunderstand me when I say this," she said carefully, "but, so far, you haven't once referred to Neil Hughes as being someone else."

"Because I *am* Neil Hughes," he said with emphasis. "I don't have my memories from before the attack, but I am still Neil Hughes." He paused. "When I came home from the hospital the other day, and frightened the living daylights out of you upstairs, the speech I made afterwards was just me feeling sorry for myself. In spite of what I said, those people *didn't* kill me - I am very much alive."

"Yes you are – and I love you," said Caroline, before she could stop herself.

Neil simply patted her on the hand.

"I know you do," he said; "it's just going to take some time before either of us can properly come to terms with such a terrible upheaval in our lives. Don't worry about me; and, please, don't feel sorry for me, either."

He had almost said "feel sorry for the people who did this", but stopped himself, just in time; Caroline suspected nothing about his plans, and that was how it must remain.

"Well," he said, quickly draining his teacup, "I'd better get going; I'll see you later."

As she heard him closing the front door behind him, Caroline felt an overwhelming sense of release. She knew that there was still a barrier between them; however, his warm response, when she told him that she loved him, had almost brought her to tears. Neil was right, she just needed to be patient; she had told him she loved him and, one day, she hoped, he would say the same words to her.

....

Neil headed for the building site where he had helped Michael, in the hope of finding some part time work there; even if there was none, he hoped that the site foreman would be able to suggest other sites which might be looking for labourers.

He was driving past a petrol station, when it suddenly triggered a recent memory. After his final trip to the hospital, he had stopped there for petrol on his way home; while he was filling his tank, there had been an argument between a van driver and another motorist. He had not paid much attention to it at the time - but he now had a strong feeling that the face in his nightmare was that of the van driver.

Neil pulled into a nearby car park and sat, his eyes closed, trying to replay in his mind what he had seen that day; but the more he tried to remember, the more uncertain he became. Eventually, he realised that he had no choice but to find a way of remembering more from his nightmare; he did not relish the prospect. Frustrated, he resumed his journey.

The foreman that Neil had hoped to speak to at the building site was not there, so he headed home; on the way, however, he called in at the petrol station, and deliberately took his time filling up the car, in order to glance around, and see where the CCTV cameras were situated. When paying for his fuel, he examined the images on the monitor inside the shop; this enabled him to ascertain which areas were, and were not, covered.

Satisfied, he continued his journey home.

……………………………………………………

Just as Neil arrived, he saw that Caroline was about to leave.

"Oh," she said, surprised, "I didn't realise you'd be back so soon; I was just popping round to see Alice." Neil looked vacant, so Caroline went on to explain. "She was a regular customer at the hairdressers where I worked before we got married, so we've known each other for over twenty years; she's old now, and housebound, so I go round pretty regularly – she likes the company." Caroline smiled with affection. "She may be frail, but she's still as sharp as a knife, and she always tells me how much she looks forward to our chats; truth to tell, she treats me like the daughter she never had."

"Okay, fine," said Neil; "that works out well, because I was going to go on another run, carrying the weight in the haversack. Mike said that, when I used to do it, I recorded the time it took me, and always aimed to reduce it."

Caroline looked concerned. "Yes, but you don't want to overdo it - don't push yourself too hard."

"Don't worry," he assured her, "each day I'm getting fitter and stronger, which I'm really enjoying. I feel all this training is helping in some way, although I'm not sure how."

Caroline smiled. "Alice keeps asking when you're going to come round and see her."

"I definitely will," he said, "I'm just not sure when. I assume you've told her I look slightly different?"

"Of course, and she can't wait to see you; when I tell her you'll definitely be coming to visit, she'll be so excited."

"I hope I'm not a disappointment to her," remarked Neil.

"I doubt that," laughed Caroline. "She met you only two weeks after you and I first met, when you picked me up from the hairdressers were I used to work. The following week, when I told her you'd asked me to marry you, she said to me 'I hope you said yes!' and she was delighted when I said I had."

"Well, let her know that I will definitely visit her, sometime in the near future."

"I will," smiled Caroline. "Anyway, I must go – I'll see you later."

As he watched Caroline drive away down the lane, Neil decided that this was an ideal opportunity to try and doze off on the bed; hopefully, he would experience another nightmare, while he was alone in the house.

………………………………………………………

In his mind, while he was running, Neil went over the details revealed in the nightmare he had experienced earlier. The face had been clearer, and he was now certain that it was the same man he had seen at the petrol station; in addition, he now knew that there were at least two other people involved, although in the nightmare, their faces were obscured. He was also certain that all three spoke with a traveller accent.

When he reached home, Caroline had already returned; as he staggered into the kitchen gasping for air, she rushed to him.

"Neil! Are you all right?"

"I'm great," he panted, "I've just knocked three minutes off my time." He dropped his haversack on to the floor, and quickly sat down, leaning on the table.

"Please, please be careful; you can do yourself a lot of harm by trying to do too much too soon."

"I'm fine really, I just need to get my breath back, and then I'll be okay." Caroline hovered anxiously, but after a minute or two, his breathing returned to normal; then he leaned back in his chair. "Cup of tea wouldn't go amiss, if you know how to make one."

Caroline smiled. "Go and sit down in the living room then; I'll bring a pot through, if I can find the recipe in one of my cookery books."

A short time later, as Caroline was pouring out the tea, she said "I meant to ask before - how did you get on at the building site?"

"The foreman wasn't there, so I'll probably go again tomorrow, and see what I can find out. Tonight, I'm going into town to speak to some of the doormen at the clubs, to see if there's any work; or, at least, to ask how I can get a badge to work on the doors."

Caroline could still detect a slight reserve in Neil's attitude towards her; and yet, she herself felt more relaxed speaking to him now, than at any time since he came out of hospital. It occurred to her that it was due to her acceptance, finally, that this really was Neil; why, she asked herself guiltily, could she not have accepted it from the day his bandages were removed?

"Did you have a good gossip with Alice?"

"I certainly did; this sounds awful, but I'm more comfortable with Alice than I am with my own mum."

"How did that come about?"

"Ever since that business when we went guarantor for my brother, and he let us down; my mum and dad took his side at the time, and there were some hurtful things said. They know now what he's really like; but, to a degree, the damage was done then, as far as I was concerned."

"So, you bear a grudge? I'd better make sure I don't fall out with you at any time in the future."

"Don't worry; with that new compound Dr. Braithwaite used on your face, the frying pan would probably have little or no effect. It won't save you from the nutcrackers, though."

"Well, on that note, I think I'll go down and speak to some nice gentle bouncers; I'll just go for a shower first." As Neil stood up, he leaned down and gently kissed Caroline on the cheek, then left the room.

Caroline smiled to herself. She had told herself earlier that she would have to be patient, and let things develop; she was now certain that she was right.

……………………………………………………

Neil came back downstairs, having changed into another pair of tracksuit bottoms and a running vest.

"I thought you were going into town to speak to the bouncers?" said Caroline.

"I am; but I thought I'd run there and back, rather than take the car."

"Are you sure you're not trying to do too much?"

"I won't be carrying the haversack this time, so without that, it'll be like floating along."

"One thing is for sure - by just wearing that vest, the doormen will see you are certainly built for the job," commented Caroline.

"That's what I thought. This new face doesn't make me look particularly menacing, and I assume that looking tough is quite important in that line of work."

"Do you want something to eat before you go?"

"I'm okay at the moment; I'll probably have something when I get back."

…………………………………..

"Well, Carl McCabe has certainly gone to ground this time," remarked the D.C.I. "He appears to have disappeared completely."

"We've spoken to all our informants, but with no luck at all," said Tinny. "He could be frightened of us bringing him in again because, for all he knows, we may have some new evidence; or, it may be that he's scared of Neil Hughes catching up with him – which, again, makes me think he's connected to the attack in some way."

"Yes," said Davies, pensively; "well, we've been looking very closely at the alibis of his associates, but are getting nowhere."

"Right," said Tinny decisively, "in that case, tomorrow, I'm going round to see Matty Grant, and see what he knows."

"Unfortunately, as things stand, we have no other leads concerning this case," said the D.C.I., looking despondent. "Even if we find Carl McCabe again, we still have nothing on him and, so far, nothing on anyone who's connected to him. Gary may be right; McCabe may have hired someone else to do this, knowing that it would be more or less impossible to trace them."

"I assume Neil Hughes still has no memory of the attack?" asked Gary.

"The poor sod has no memory at all," said Tinny, shaking his head. "Those people have ruined his life."

"And, so far, we've been no help to him at all," added Davies, his expression grim. "Alright - fresh start tomorrow, and we're looking for a break; otherwise, whoever did this is going to get away with it."

Privately, Gary was determined that the attackers of Neil Hughes would not escape justice; to that end, and unbeknown to the rest of the team, including Tinny, Gary was following his own line of enquiry, in his own time. So far, he was without success; however, he was convinced that his theory was right – and, at some point, he would be able to prove it.

Chapter 9

As Neil arrived back at the house, Caroline said "Jacko's here, he's in the garden having a beer."

"Great!" said Neil. "Those poetry classes weren't a waste of money after all."

Caroline chuckled; meanwhile, Neil carried on into the garden.

"Alright, Jacko," he greeted, pulling up a chair. "What are you doing, sitting out here in the dark?"

"It's a nice night, so I thought I'd just sit here and chill out."

"What's the taxi work been like tonight?"

"No idea," shrugged Jacko. "I hardly do nights any more - it's too much hassle."

"Where's your cab? I didn't notice it when I came in."

"There's a night driver on it now, I just basically work days. The only time I take it out in the evening, is when the night man has some time off."

"Fair enough," said Neil; after a short pause, he continued "did Caz tell you I'm thinking of working the doors till I get my memory back, and can get back driving a taxi?"

"She did," said Jacko, glancing at Neil astutely; "she was also telling me how you've been training."

"The training seems to help with keeping my mind off the things that have gone wrong since I was attacked," said Neil, carefully.

Jacko was quiet for a moment, as though he was considering the next thing he was going to say; then he looked steadily at Neil, and his expression was serious.

"You're going after them, aren't you?"

Neil hesitated, considering how much he should reveal. He knew that there would be no point in lying to this man; everyone had told Neil that Danny was his best friend, but he had discovered that Jacko seemed to have a greater understanding of the situation. He therefore concluded that, in the circumstances, Jacko was probably the only person in whom he could truly confide. Neil turned to face his companion, and nodded slowly.

"For my own peace of mind, I've got to know who did this, and why," he explained. "Everyone tells me how close Caz and I were, and how happy we'd been for the last twenty years; and now, both of us have to be so careful in what we do or say, for fear of upsetting the other." Neil paused, "I've lost the villa in Spain, the taxi plate and, most importantly, my past; so, I can't see any way of looking to the future, until I've dealt with the people who've ruined my life."

Jacko nodded in understanding, and remained silent for a while, drinking his beer.

"Don't take offence at this," he said eventually, "but don't let the boys get involved. I know they're your sons, but until you get your memory back, I actually know them better than you."

Neil shook his head. "There's no chance of them being involved and, needless to say, Caz must know nothing of this either," he said firmly. "I've only known Michael and Paul since coming out of the coma in hospital, so I can only rely on instinct; but I reckon that, even if there'd been a dozen people who attacked me, our Paul would go against all of them, without fear or concern for what might happen to him – and Mike would kill them without a moment's hesitation, and without an ounce of remorse."

Jacko smiled. "You obviously do know your sons as well as I do." His expression became serious again. "Let *me* back you up. I'm like Mike, I'd gladly kill these people - my concern is, you wouldn't."

Neil put his hand on Jacko's shoulder. "I appreciate the offer, Jacko, but this is something I've got to do myself. As much as I don't want our Mike spending the next fifteen years in prison, I wouldn't like it to happen to you either."

Jacko snorted. "It wouldn't be my first time behind bars."

"You surprise me," said Neil, in mock seriousness; "I'd imagined you'd spent your youth in Bible classes, or just being a bit of a Jessie."

"You've caught me out again, Yosser - you see through me every time!"

Just then, Caroline walked out into the garden, carrying another beer for Jacko.

"Any chance I can join you, or is this man's talk?"

"Well actually, we've just been discussing knitting patterns, and talking about maybe joining a flower arranging class," said Jacko, accepting the beer gratefully.

Caroline raised her eyebrows. "And how are you going to find the time?" she demanded. "It means you'll both have to cut back on the ballet lessons."

Before Neil or Jacko could formulate a riposte, Caroline got a fit of the giggles. "I've just had a mental image of you two in leotards," she spluttered.

Jacko also laughed. "Do you mind? There's men drinking here, we don't want any of that smutty talk."

Caroline noticed that, during this exchange, Neil had barely cracked a smile. She was disappointed to see that, to a certain extent, he remained aloof; she wished that she knew how to break through his guard.

"Is anyone hungry? I could make a snack, if anyone's feeling a bit peckish."

Neil shook his head. "I'm alright."

"I'll have his," piped up Jacko, "I'm starving!"

Caroline put her hands on her hips. "I'd rather feed you for a week than a fortnight," she remarked drily, as she turned to go back to the kitchen.

As soon as she was out of earshot, Jacko turned to Neil. "So, what went on in town tonight?"

Neil frowned. "I was just talking to the bouncers about getting a badge."

"That wasn't the only thing you did." Jacko paused. "One of the lads rang me, and told me what went on."

Neil shrugged. "It was nothing; I'll tell you about it another time."

"Yosser, be careful," advised Jacko; "otherwise, there may not *be* another time."

Jacko placed a ten pound note on the table. "I believe this is yours."

Neil simply smiled, and put the note in his pocket.

As Caroline came back in to the garden with a small mountain of sandwiches, she was amused to hear Jacko say, in a serious voice, "No - I think it's knit one, pearl one, for that *particular* garment."

Jacko stayed for another hour, by which time he had devoured all the sandwiches. Caroline could not remember the last time she had laughed so much listening to Neil and Jacko, who were like a double act when they got together; she could never understand how two people could keep such a straight face, and yet be so funny.

When Jacko was leaving, and as they were all standing by the front door, he turned to Neil. "Don't forget what I said earlier."

Neil nodded solemnly. "Knit one, pearl one; I'll remember that."

………………………………………………………

As Neil closed the door, he turned to Caroline.

"I hadn't noticed before," he said, "but when I was looking in that trophy cabinet we've got, I noticed you have a few for swimming, and cross country running."

"Yes," said Caroline. "When I was at school, I ran for the county, and I've always loved swimming."

"Do you still go swimming now?"

"Until recently, I used to go swimming about three times a week."

"Can I swim?"

"Yes, you're a good swimmer; if we had a race, you can beat me over one length, but I can beat you over fifty lengths."

"Impressive," he commented. "Have we ever had a race over fifty lengths?"

Caroline grinned. "No, because you can't swim fifty lengths - that's how I know I'd beat you. I can swim for miles, and can spend hours in the pool, just swimming up and down."

Neil also smiled. "You should start going again; then, when I've got a few things sorted out, I'll start coming with you."

When he said this, Caroline had the urge to throw her arms around him; however, she stopped herself, and confined herself to saying "Good idea – and, when you're ready, we should also go out running together."

"Are you going to tell me, now, that you could beat me at running as well?"

"Over a mile, you're much faster than me; over ten miles, I'd leave you for dead."

Neil smiled broadly. "Now I'm *really* impressed! I take it, then, that if you and I get into a scrap, I'd need to finish you off in the first minute - otherwise, if it went on for half an hour, you'd knock seven bells out of me."

"Hang on while I get the frying pan, and we'll find out," offered Caroline mischievously.

Neil laughed out loud at this. "That's it, I'm going to bed to hide under the covers!" He then hugged Caroline, and said "See you in the morning."

Caroline watched Neil walk down the hallway and up the stairs, and she was elated; Neil had hugged her because he wanted to.

She spent some time tidying the kitchen, working with a much lighter heart as she reflected on what had been, from her perspective, a fantastic day. Neil telling her he knew that she loved him, kissing her on the cheek later in the day, and then hugging her before he went to bed, was more than she could possibly have hoped for. Of one thing she was certain; if Neil had another nightmare, she would not just hold his hand - she would hold him tightly.

……………………………………………………

Neil lay in bed, feeling slightly guilty; although he knew that, if Caroline took up swimming again, it would be of benefit for her to do something she really enjoyed, it was also an ideal opportunity for him to carry out his plans. His next course of action was to watch the petrol station as often as he could; his aim, to find the man whose face he had seen in his nightmares – because that face, he was convinced, belonged to one of his attackers.

……………………………………………………

"We've got a warrant for the McCabes' nightclub," announced D.C.I. Davies; "so, if it was them who made sure that we found Carl McCabe last time, having us ransack their "private members club" may have the desired effect again."

"And I'm going to pay Matty Grant a visit, and see what I can find out from him," put in Tinny.

Davies acknowledged this with a nod.

"Fortunately, once again, Chief Superintendent Turnbull has given us plenty of uniformed support. Mind you," he added ruefully, "so far, we've managed to get a great deal of success as far as other people's cases are concerned, but not with the one that matters most to me. Hopefully, we'll get a breakthrough soon."

"Amen to that, boss," said Tinny. "We'll head over to see Matty Grant right now."

As they left the D.C.I.'s office, and were walking along the corridor, Gary asked "Are we still treating Matty Grant as a suspect, or as a possible informant?"

"To a degree, neither," replied Tinny. "I may inform him that it's safe for him to go back to the towers, and see if we can just get him talking; if we can, we'll see what information he's got, and try and find out how he knew where McCabe was last time."

……………………………………………………

Tinny and Gary arrived at Matty's sister's house, and could hear shouting coming from inside. Tinny knocked loudly on the door.

"Police!" he called through the letterbox.

The door was opened almost immediately; the woman who stood before them was clearly the source of the shouting, judging by the ill-tempered expression on her face.

"Hello Colette," began Tinny pleasantly. "Is your Matty in?"

"What's he done now? I'm just trying to get the lazy bastard out of bed."

"He's not in trouble, honestly - we just need a quick word with him."

"You'd better come in, Tinny, and bring this nice young man in with you," she said, eyeing Gary; "and what's your name?"

Before Gary had time to answer, Tinny smiled. "You're wasting your time, Colette - he's gay."

"That's typical, that is," she said, rolling her eyes upwards; "all the best ones nowadays seem to be gay. Ah well, go into the living room you two, and I'll go and drag that idle sod down here."

As Colette went back upstairs, the two men sat down in the living room, and waited.

"Thanks for that, Sarge; I didn't know I was gay."

"I've just saved you from a fate worse than death," pointed out Tinny. "The last Constable Colette took a shine to has never been seen since; I keep meaning to get a warrant to search the cellar. Listen carefully while we're talking to Matty – should you hear chains rattling and a moaning sound, you'll know why."

"Fair enough, I'm gay," smiled Gary. "When she comes back down, I'd better get into the part. I might start rearranging the cushions – God knows, they *so* don't match the wallpaper."

When Matty and his sister came into the room a short time later, they were surprised to find Tinny and Gary sniggering like a couple of schoolboys who had done something naughty.

Tinny composed himself, and looked up.

"Good news, Matty," he said brightly; "I've had a word with some of my mates on the taxis, and it's now safe for you to go home."

"Thank God for that!" said Colette, as she looked at her brother with disgust. "I'll start sorting your stuff out now," she declared, and promptly left the room.

Matty sat down. "Cheers for that, Tinny, you're a diamond. Me and Degsy have only been going out in the dark, and walking everywhere, to dodge the cab lads."

Tinny nodded. "So, what's the story on Carl McCabe? We know it was you who rang in the information."

Matty laughed. "So the Scottish accent didn't fool you, then?"

Tinny affected a shocked expression. "Don't ever go to Scotland and speak like that because, if you do, you'll never be seen again."

"I'll have to try the Irish one next time," said Matty, still chuckling.

"Will there be a next time?" asked Gary, pointedly. "Do you know where McCabe is now?"

"I wish I did, mate. I'd be only too happy to tell you, but I've got no idea."

"So, would I be right in saying that Carl McCabe is no friend of yours?" enquired Tinny.

Matty's expression was grim as he replied.

"A few months ago," he explained, "me and Degsy were coming out of the McCabes' club, and by accident, Degsy knocked into Carl McCabe. Straight away, Degsy said 'sorry Carl mate, I didn't see you there', but that scumbag just laid into Degsy, while his mates held me up against the wall."

Tinny was surprised to note that Matty was beginning to get upset, as he was telling the story.

"He didn't just hit Degsy," he continued, "he battered him, and when Degsy was on the floor, he kicked and stamped all over him."

"Why didn't you report it to the police?" asked Gary.

Matty snorted. "No disrespect mate, but you can't protect us from people like the McCabes. If they couldn't get to us, they'd get to our families. And even if something like that got to court, McCabe would have ten witnesses to say he was defending himself."

Tinny gave a confirmatory nod to Gary; he knew full well that what Matty had said was true.

"I hope McCabe is behind the attack on Yosser, and that Yosser gets to that scumbag before you do," said Matty fervently; then a new thought seemed to occur to him. "Here's a question for you," he continued; "is Yosser out of hospital now, and does he look completely different?"

Tinny frowned warily. "Why do you ask?"

"Haven't you heard what happened in town last night?"

Tinny and Gary both shook their heads.

"I'm not telling tales here," said Matty, with emphasis; "I got this story second-hand, and I'm definitely not trying to get anyone in trouble."

Tinny nodded. "I understand. This conversation we're having is completely off the record as far as I'm concerned, so feel free to tell me what you heard."

Matty looked satisfied, and continued.

"Okay, the trouble started in the afternoon. Three big lads from out of town had been throwing their weight round in all the pubs they went into. A couple of the local hard cases crossed these three, and were well beaten." He paused briefly. "Do you know the club where all the bouncers are from Manchester?" Tinny nodded. "Well, it was still early evening as the club had just opened its doors, when these three turned up, and tried to get in. The bouncers were having none of it, because they'd obviously heard what had gone on that day. The three Scousers or Mancs, or whatever they were, tried to get the doormen out into the street to fight them." Matty paused again. "You know the script as far as that's concerned - bouncers will sort out any fights inside the club or at the door, but won't be drawn out into the street. Remember that lad a couple of years ago, who went out to stop that fella hitting his girlfriend, but it was a set up, and he got shot?"

Tinny nodded grimly. "We did catch the people who did that, and they'll be behind bars for a very long time."

"Maybe," said Matty, clearly unimpressed, "but that bouncer's in a wheelchair for the rest of his life, so you can't blame the doormen last night for not getting involved with those three thugs."

"Okay," said Tinny, "but what's the connection with Neil Hughes?"

"I'm getting to that," said Matty. "It was still early on, when my mate saw some fella talking to the bouncers on the door. The way my mate described this man, was that he had muscles in his snot. He was wearing tracksuit bottoms and a running vest, but he was no 'roid-head.' He wasn't covered in tattoos, didn't have any ear rings, and had a normal haircut, not a shaved head. That sounded to me like Yosser Hughes – but what threw me was, my mate's girlfriend said this fella was dead handsome. That's why I was asking if Yosser looks completely different." He paused, and grinned. "Let's be honest, you could never describe Yosser as handsome. I'm not talking behind his back here - after that trouble we had with him, we got on well, and could have a laugh and joke with him. He said once that his missus had a photo of him on the mantelpiece, to keep the kids away from the fire when they were little."

Tinny smiled inwardly; he used to say the same about his wife, whenever they were out with other couples. She always took it as a joke, luckily - because if she had not, he would soon have known about it; Tinny was brave, but certainly not stupid.

"Anyway," continued Matty, "the three bullies had moved away from the door, and were picking on people and pushing them around, when a young couple came along. They were just kids, teenagers, no harm in them at all. Well, one of these bastards pinned the young lad up against the wall, while the other two were grabbing his girlfriend, I mean feeling her tits and trying to put their hand up her skirt." Matty appeared upset, and showed signs of anger as he recounted the incident. "This little girl was crying and telling them to stop. I tell you one thing, Tinny, if I'd have been there, I'd have done some damage to at least one of them."

He paused for a while to collect himself. Tinny was amazed; Matty was clearly appalled at what had happened to the unfortunate teenagers. He began to reconsider his opinion of Matty Grant; it seemed that this man, whom Tinny had always thought of as a low-life, did have standards after all.

"Listen to this," resumed Matty, as his face lit up. "This man – I say 'this man', but I reckon it was Yosser Hughes - walked over to these three, was dead calm, wasn't shouting or swearing, and just said 'leave the youngsters alone, and walk away while you still can.'

"This is how my mate described what happened next. They let go of the young lad and his girlfriend, and all went for this man in the tracky bottoms. You know yourself, Tinny, most street fights are just brawls – well, this was no brawl. My mate said it was something like a scene from a martial arts movie. As this man was elbowing one of them, he was kicking another one, and even when one of them was behind him, he was still taking them out. Because these thugs had been snorting coke all day, each time they went down, the fools were getting back up, only to be put down again. By the time this man had finished with them, they weren't capable of getting back up.

He then put his arm round the young girl, nodded to her boyfriend, and asked them where they lived. He walked them down to the taxi rank, put them in a cab, bunged the driver a tenner, and told him to take them home. And that," said Matty, now smiling from ear to ear, "that's Yosser Hughes!"

He fell silent for a few moments, as if pausing for effect; then he continued.

"As Yosser was walking to the taxi rank, the head bouncer came out and said to everyone to tell the police, when they arrived, that these three had been fighting amongst themselves, and that no-one else was involved. Everyone there was more than happy to do that, I just wish I'd seen it myself."

Tinny and Gary said nothing, reflecting on what they had been told; they also wished that they had seen it.

"Well," said Gary, "I'm just going out to the car, Sarge; I think I may have left the lights on."

"Just as a matter of interest," said Tinny to Matty, after Gary had gone outside, "how did you find out where Carl McCabe was when we were first looking for him?"

Matty shrugged. "One of the lads overheard someone in McCabe's club shouting his mouth off about where Carl was, and how the police would never find him."

"Is it possible that, whoever this was, they *wanted* the police to find him?"

"Hadn't really given it much thought," replied Matty, frowning; "but now you mention it, this fella who was telling everybody where Carl was holed up, apparently, wasn't bothered who heard what he was saying."

"Hm," said Tinny. "Alright, well I think that's about it," he continued, getting up. "Thanks for the information."

As Tinny came out of the house, Gary was still outside on the phone; he finished his call just as Tinny reached the car. Neither of them said anything until they had both got in.

"Well, Sarge," said Gary, "Merseyside police are ecstatic, there are arrest warrants on all three, and the Merseyside boys have been after them for some time. From all accounts, each of them will be in hospital for a while but, when they're fit to be moved, it will be straight to prison. The officer I spoke to said that, if we could find out who did this to them, he'd like to come over, and pin a medal on him."

Tinny smiled. "What was your response to that?"

"I simply said that, from what I can gather, they were fighting amongst themselves, and no-one else was involved." Gary looked sideways at Tinny, a wry smile on his face. "After he told me what the arrest warrants were for, I'd be inclined to pin a medal on Neil Hughes myself."

"So," said Tinny, looking thoughtful, "what conclusions did you draw from the story of what happened?"

"I would say," said Gary slowly, "that Neil Hughes is, effectively, practising his fighting skills; he can either remember who attacked him, or he's preparing himself for any future attack, and he wants to be ready to take them on."

Tinny nodded approvingly. "Yes; he may not remember now, but is possibly hoping that, at some point, he will."

Gary hesitated for a moment; then decided to say what was on his mind.

"Sarge," he said, "to be candid, there's a small part of me that would like to see Neil Hughes get to his attackers first. I'm not condoning vigilante justice, or people taking the law into their own hands; however, after what I've seen in the last two years, I wonder if we really are making any difference."

Tinny nodded sagely. "The first thing I'd have to say," he cautioned, "is that it would be very much in your own interests not to voice those opinions to anyone else. Having said that, believe me when I say that I totally agree with you – there's a large part of me that would love to see Neil Hughes deal with his attackers." He sighed. "Unfortunately, years ago, I blighted my career prospects by being a bit outspoken and, as a result, was looked upon as being a bit of a loose cannon; but, over the last twenty-five years, I believe I've been proved right. We are now surrounded by scum and riffraff, who are not in any way bothered by the police or the courts.

"Listening to the story Matty told us, it did occur to me that, if the police had been called earlier and had arrested those three thugs, it's almost certain that the young couple would not have pressed charges, simply because they'd be too frightened to pursue it; so, were it not for the current arrest warrants, that scum would now be walking free. Whereas, in view of what actually happened, I like to think that, when they do get out of prison, they may think twice before bullying anyone else; not for fear of being arrested, but because there may be another Neil Hughes around the corner, prepared to intervene. I sometimes think it's the only thing those kind of people really understand."

Gary nodded mutely; Tinny's words had given him much to think about.

"So," said Gary eventually, "without Carl McCabe, and no other leads, what's the next step, Sarge?"

"I would say that, at some point, we should go and have a word with Neil Hughes," replied Tinny. "He may get to his attackers first, and that concerns me; not because I'm in any way bothered about their welfare, but because he could end up behind bars. You and I, and the majority of law abiding citizens, may feel that he has every right to deal with these people himself, for what they did to him; however, the courts wouldn't take the same view."

....

As Tinny and Gary arrived back at the police headquarters, they saw Sergeant Pete Jones and Constable Mark Walker walking across the car park; Tinny got out of the car, and called over to attract their attention.

"So, Pete, I imagine you turned up a few interesting things in the McCabes' club?" Tinny commented, as the two officers approached the car; but the response came as a surprise.

"Absolutely nothing, Ron," stated Pete Jones; "not even so much as a dodgy packet of cigarettes - which seemed strange, when you consider we would have expected to find drugs, weapons, and who knows what else."

"They knew we were coming, Sarge."

Tinny seemed taken aback by Mark's forthright statement; but before he had a chance to speak, Pete Jones continued.

"He's right - there's no question in my mind. Uniform only found out about this raid half an hour before we left, but when we arrived, one of the McCabe brothers was there with his accountant." He paused, as if considering what he should say next. "It didn't come from us, and we don't believe it came from you or Gary either - so let's keep this conversation to ourselves for the moment."

Pete and Mark then walked away, leaving Tinny dumbstruck. Gary, however, did not appear to be particularly surprised, let alone shocked, by what had been said; but he kept his thoughts to himself, as he and Tinny walked into the police headquarters in silence.

....

Caroline was late getting up; she had stayed awake as long as she could the night before, in case Neil had another nightmare, so it was very late when she finally dropped off. When she checked Michael's room, it was no surprise to find that Neil had already risen; however, he was also not to be found in the training room. She went downstairs and, noticing that the weighted haversack was missing, concluded that he was already out on his run.

She had only just switched on the kettle when Neil came in, smiling broadly; although, as usual, he was gasping for breath.

"I take it, from that smile, you've broken your record again?"

"Certainly have!" he gasped. "Another two minutes off it this morning. I'm building myself up to take *you* on, over ten miles."

"I see," said Caroline. "In that case, I'd better start training as well! I was thinking of going swimming today, unless you need me for anything?"

"No, not at all," he said, shaking his head, and still panting. "Great idea. How long do you normally spend at the swimming baths?"

"Between two and three hours, depending on how busy it is."

"Fair enough," he said, dropping into a chair. "I may go out again later, to see if the foreman is at the building site, and then on to the local council offices to find out how I can get a form to apply for a doorman's license. I'll have my phone with me, so if you get home and I'm not here, just give me a ring."

"Shall we have a brew first, before we do anything?"

"I thought you'd never ask; I've got a thirst you could photograph."

As they sat at the kitchen table drinking tea, Caroline said "I need to get into training soon, to get back into shape."

"Get back into shape? You're a perfect shape."

Caroline gave a girlish laugh. "I know; I was just fishing for compliments."

"Then again, you do seem a bit bulky in some areas."

"Where's that bloody frying pan?"

The laughing and joking, which they both enjoyed, continued as they finished their tea; then, draining his cup, Neil said "Right, I'm going to have a quick session in the training room, and then I'll have a shower."

"I've just got some tidying up to do, then I'll dig out my swimming stuff, but I'll give you a shout before I leave."

Even before Caroline had driven off, Neil had quickly got dressed, so that he could get to the petrol station as soon as possible.

....

It had been weeks since Caroline had last been swimming, and she was really enjoying herself.

In her mind, as she swam length after length, she replayed everything that had happened since the night of Neil's attack. She had thought, days before, that she would like to turn back time to the moment before Neil's bandages were removed; she now realised that was selfish. If she could, she would turn the clock back even further – not just to the point before his attack, but to weeks before it happened. She had done a stupid thing, which she bitterly regretted; she hoped that, when Neil got his memory back, that he could forgive her; in truth, however, she was unsure whether she should tell him at all.

....

Meanwhile. Neil was parked near to the petrol station, and had positioned himself where he had a clear view of the forecourt, but could not be seen by any of the CCTV cameras. He was still somewhat uncertain as to exactly what he was going to do, should he see his attacker; however, he hoped he could stay calm, and think clearly.

From time to time, he found that he was drowsy - not through tiredness, but boredom. He therefore got out of the car and walked around periodically, but made sure that he did not venture too far from his vehicle, in case his attacker appeared. After a while, he began to wonder if he was wasting his time; but, as things stood, he could not think of any better course of action.

....

"Well timed, Ron," commented D.C.I. Davies, as Tinny and Gary walked back into the briefing room. "There's a call just come in for you, on line three."

Tinny lifted the receiver. "This is D.S.Smith........alright, Burnsy.....good man........... and they're both coming in tomorrow............any idea what information they've got?"

As they watched Tinny listening to the caller's reply, everyone in the room could see the stunned expression on his face; he whistled, long and low. "I see!..............thanks, Burnsy," he said, and put the phone down.

"What's up, Tinny?" asked Davies. "You look like you've seen a ghost."

Tinny moved towards a chair, sat down, and puffed out both cheeks.

"Well," he said, "there are two taxi drivers coming in tomorrow with some information. This goes back to when Neil Hughes had his own taxi company. To cut a long story short, he had a run-in with a drug dealer, and a week later he was paid a visit by a man that you and I remember well, boss."

Davies looked at him, questioningly. "Well, go on then, Ron, put us out of our misery!"

Tinny paused, as if for dramatic effect. "His visitor," he announced, "was none other than............William Raymond Cooder."

"What?" It was the D.C.I.'s turn to look shocked; he appeared to take time to compose himself. "Not 'Tex' Cooder, surely?" he said finally, in a voice of studied calmness.

"I think so. I won't know for sure until these drivers come in tomorrow; but, from what Burnsy has just told me, it certainly sounds like 'Tex' Cooder."

The other officers in the room were looking at each other blankly.

"So, who or what is 'Tex' Cooder, boss?" asked Dave.

"'What' is probably more appropriate," answered the D.C.I.; his expression was sober. "The answer is one word: murderer."

"Who did he murder, boss?" asked Paula.

"Several people, over a period of time; although we only caught him for one, we were pretty sure that was his fifth victim, possibly his sixth."

Paula looked confused. "So, was he some sort of serial killer?"

"No, not a serial killer," interjected Tinny; "Cooder was a hit-man, for whoever could afford him."

"A hired assassin," clarified Gary, absently, as he opened up his laptop.

"Exactly," said the D.C.I.; "and, he made a very good living out of it, because Billy Ray Cooder did not come cheap."

Dave looked intrigued. "How did he acquire the nickname 'Tex'?"

"Simply because it was obvious, from his accent, that he was American," explained Tinny. "I don't think he is actually Texan, but I'm not sure exactly where he came from."

Gary had been paying attention to the conversation while, at the same time, searching the police archives on the laptop.

"Here it is - I've found it!"

"Found what, Gary?" enquired Davies.

"All the info. on 'Tex' Cooder, including what he was suspected of, but never charged with."

"Does it mention there who conducted the final interview with 'Tex' before he was charged and convicted?" asked Tinny, innocently.

Gary scrolled down through the information, and nodded, glancing at his senior officer with a wry smile. "Detective Sergeant Frederick Davies, and Detective Constable Ronald Smith."

Dave grinned. "So, boss, you and the Sarge cracked the case, when all the previous people had failed?"

Davies and Tinny exchanged a knowing smile.

"If only that were true," was the D.C.I.'s rueful reply.

"We were both convinced he didn't do it," Tinny elaborated. "'Tex' was old school, none of this "no comment" business; he could chat to you for hours, but his mind was razor sharp."

"Billy Ray Cooder was the most accomplished liar I've ever encountered in all the years I've been doing this job," declared Davies. "What caught him out was DNA evidence."

"That's right," said Tinny. "Forensics, and particularly the collection of DNA from crime scenes, were in their infancy then; but that's what we were able to use to prove the case."

"Assuming, then, that he was guilty of all the murders - did he always use the same method?" asked Paula.

"I can answer that," offered Gary. "Reading this information about him, he despatched each victim in a different way, as follows; he shot one (a hand gun to the head, at point blank range); he garrotted one; stabbed one; drowned one in his own bath; injected one with a massive dose of heroin; and the final one, he killed with an axe." Gary ticked them off on his fingers as he spoke.

"So all in all, not a particularly nice man," remarked Paula, smiling.

"Quite," agreed Fred Davies. "He was a very frightening man; when he entered a room, a pub, a club, or anywhere for that matter, people were scared of him, and would steer well clear."

Dave shrugged. "Well, if he was guilty of all those murders, it's hardly surprising people gave him a wide berth, boss."

Davies shook his head. "No; what I'm saying is that, even before he committed any of the murders, there was something about him that was very menacing. All these cases, with the exception of the last one, were before my time; but he had, from an early age, already acquired the reputation of a man not to be crossed."

Tinny took up the tale. "He made a very good living by allowing various crime families and gangsters to simply use his name, in order to collect a debt."

Dave looked blank. "Sorry Sarge, you've lost me there."

Tinny smiled. "When money was owed – and, in many cases, we are talking about considerable sums - if those who owed it were led to believe that 'Tex' Cooder was coming to collect, they would quickly pay up."

Dave was frowning. "But what was to stop these gangsters just saying that, without asking for Cooder's permission?"

"That would be tantamount to committing suicide," the D.C.I. pointed out. "No-one dared use Billy Ray's name, without paying him a commission on what was collected."

Gary, meanwhile, had continued to examine the police records. "From studying the histories of the victims here, boss, it seems that they weren't particularly nice men either," he remarked.

Fred Davies nodded. "Make no mistake, Gary, there were no tears shed by the various police authorities over any of his victims. In a strange way, 'Tex' Cooder destroyed some of the biggest crime families, merely by taking out the top man."

Paula regarded the D.C.I. curiously. "I may be out of order here, boss," she ventured, "but I get the impression that, in a way, you and the Sarge *liked* Mr. Cooder."

Davies hesitated before he answered; then he shrugged.

"I was frightened of him," he confessed, "and I'm not ashamed to admit it; that's why I insisted I had Tinny in the interview room with me. Even so, it has to be said that Cooder was a well-educated, polite, and well-mannered man."

Dave immediately looked at Tinny. "So, I take it you *weren't* frightened of him, Sarge?"

Tinny simply folded his arms, leaned back in his chair, and looked smug; everyone in the room knew that he had no need to answer that question.

"So," said the D.C.I., rubbing his hands together, "as we're having no luck with McCabe, and have no other leads, it will be fascinating to hear what these taxi drivers have to say tomorrow. Class dismissed, everyone - see you in the morning."

………………………………...

After some time, and with no sign of the van driver, Neil decided to go to the building site and speak to the foreman, just to give himself a break from sitting doing nothing. As he was driving away, he wondered if, perhaps, he had been wasting his time, staking out the petrol station; his attacker may only have used it on that one occasion and, therefore, it was unlikely that he would be seen there again.

The conversation with the site foreman, also, did not go as well as Neil had hoped. Apart from the fact that there was no work available, it became obvious to the foreman, and to Neil himself, that all he was good for was the heavy work; Neil had no knowledge or experience of the other tasks labourers were expected to do.

On his way home, Neil called in to the council offices, to collect the forms he needed in order to apply for a doorman's license. While he was there, he thought that he might as well call in at the taxi department; however, this proved to be a mistake, as it simply added to his day of disappointments. He had assumed that it would be a simple matter to replace the photograph on his taxi badge; instead, he found that he would have to apply for a new badge, which would require him to complete a knowledge test relating to the local area. With no memory, it was impossible for him to pass such a test, but there was also the question of the cost; although the bank were covering all the direct debits and standing orders, as far as day-to-day living costs were concerned, he and Caroline were only just scraping by. There was certainly no extra money to pay for badge applications, medicals, and compulsory police checks. Crestfallen, Neil made his way back to the petrol station, and parked; he sat in his car, watching the forecourt, and reflected on what had happened that day.

Since the attack, he had been in a peculiar situation where, due to his memory loss, he could stand back, and look at himself from another's point of view. From what Caroline, his sons, and everyone else had told him, Neil had done everything in his power to shield Caroline from any upset or bad news, and he realised that this had been because of his love for her; but now, he was beginning to wonder if he had done the right thing. Caroline may have been better able to cope with the present situation if, during the ups and downs of their twenty years together, he had involved her more in dealing with the harsh realities.

He nodded to himself, started up the car, and headed towards home. While he was en route, Caroline called to say that she was already there; as he was driving along, he resolved that he would tell her exactly what had happened at the building site, and give her the bad news regarding the taxi badge.

…………………………………………………………

As he expected, he found her in the kitchen, making a pot of tea; she turned, and he noted that she looked extremely happy.

"Well," she said brightly, "I've had a great day; the pool was almost empty, so I was able to spend hours there, just swimming up and down, without anyone getting in the way."

"How many lengths are you able to swim, before you have to stop?"

"I don't know, to be honest. Years ago, I used to try and keep count; then at some point, I'd forget where I was up to, so I gave up trying."

"What do you think about while you're swimming?"

"It's funny you should say that," she remarked, "because, while I was swimming today, I came up with a great idea."

"Go on then," smiled Neil, "I'm all ears."

Caroline giggled. "I know; you've been like that since you were a little boy, but with you being so ugly, people never really noticed the ears."

Neil laughed. "Where's that bloody frying pan?"

"I'm only kidding - they did notice the ears as well."

Neil was still laughing. "I'm crying inside, you do know that, don't you?"

"Don't be trying to get any sympathy from me, big ears!"

"Stop," he protested, almost crying with laughter, "my ribs are beginning to ache now! Do us a favour - tell me about your great idea instead."

"Hold on, then – let's take the tea through, and I'll tell all."

They went through to the living room; Caroline poured out the tea for both of them, then sat down, folded her hands, and gave Neil a huge smile.

"I'm going to start up my own mobile hairdressing business," she announced.

"Brilliant! What made you think of that?"

"Well," she explained, "I first thought of just going back to work in a hairdressers' shop; the trouble is, of course, that fashions have changed over the last twenty years, and I wouldn't know where to start with the new styles. That's when I thought of getting in touch with some of my old customers, to see if they would like me to come to their house, instead of them having to go out to have their hair done."

"So, you've actually been to see some of them?"

"I certainly have," she replied enthusiastically; Neil observed how excited she was. "The ladies I've spoken to are really keen on the idea. I also have a list of names and addresses of some of their friends – who, they're sure, would jump at the chance of having me do their hair in their own homes."

Neil nodded thoughtfully. "Yes; I would imagine it would be ideal for some of them, particularly if they're elderly, and don't drive."

"Exactly," beamed Caroline. "It just means that, for the next few days, you won't see much of me during the day; I'll be going round to see these people and, hopefully, have plenty of customers to keep me busy."

"I think that's absolutely perfect!" said Neil, rubbing his hands together. "I won't have to tolerate the constant abuse, day in and day out."

"Don't get lippy, big ears! I'll still be here in the evenings, to keep you in place."

"I knew there'd be a catch!" laughed Neil. "Even so, it's still a great idea – besides the fact that it will be great for you to see some of your old customers again, having an extra few bob coming in isn't going to hurt at the moment."

"I know," said Caroline. "It's our twentieth wedding anniversary in three weeks - we were going to have a big party to celebrate the anniversary, and.............." She suddenly stopped smiling, and looked wistful.

"What's wrong?"

"Well……. it was also going to be a leaving celebration. When we were at Michael's birthday party, you said that everything had gone according to plan; so, not long after our anniversary, we would be moving to Spain."

Neil shook his head. "I've gone through the figures over and over again, and I just can't see how we were going to manage that."

"There was something else I remembered, when I was swimming," added Caroline. "It doesn't matter now, as we won't be going to Spain; but I remembered what your plans were for keeping this house, after we'd moved abroad."

"This I *have* got to hear," said Neil, "because I really can't see how I could have done that."

"Well, this is what you told me at the time," she explained. "It seems that you got talking to one of your taxi passengers about the possibility of buying a place to live in Spain, but also keeping ownership of this house. It turned out that he was some sort of agent, who acted on behalf of some of the large companies in this area; apparently, they sometimes have people from other countries working over here, who also bring their families with them. His job was to find suitable properties for rent – intended, mostly, for executives; they'd be prepared to pay far in excess of the going rate for the right property, in the right area. Anyway," continued Caroline, "you looked into it, and found that, if we rented out our house, the amount we would receive in rent was much greater than what we pay out in mortgage, and all the other things. So, you checked this man out, talking to several of the senior people you knew in some of the bigger local companies; the upshot was, you discovered that he was absolutely genuine."

Neil nodded thoughtfully. "I see; well, that solves one mystery. Even though we're not moving to Spain after all, it's handy to know that such an option exists."

"Yes; but the trouble is, I've no idea how you'd contact him, even if things were to change. You probably had his number stored on your old phone, but that was destroyed the night you were attacked. I think you had a business card of his, but that was probably in the cab as well."

"Right," nodded Neil. "I know it doesn't really matter now but, out of curiosity, was it a good phone that I had?"

"It was useless," grinned Caroline; "because it was so old, and the battery kept running out; but you really liked it, and wouldn't part with it."

"Something else occurred to me," said Neil, "when I was going over the calculations; although the police say that the attack wasn't a robbery gone wrong, I'm pretty sure now that, whoever my attackers were, they may have come away with a substantial sum of money."

"Oh? What makes you think that?"

"Well, I noticed from the bank statements that, for the last few years, I've regularly paid a large sum into the bank account every week, usually on a Wednesday. I was attacked on the Tuesday night; however, no money was found on me – and, I take it that there was no money in the house?"

"No," replied Caroline, shaking her head and frowning; "there was nothing here. How much do you think you may have had on you that night?"

"Possibly, about a thousand pounds; obviously, I can't be certain, and I never will be, but that was the average amount I paid into the bank each week. So," he said regretfully, "whoever did this made a few bob as well - unless it was in the cab, and went up in flames."

"Let's hope whoever did this rots in hell forever," said Caroline, bitterly; "even though you don't believe in heaven and hell, I do."

Neil was tempted to say that his attackers may be going to hell sooner than they expected; however, he felt that he needed to change the conversation, before he slipped up.

"Well, never mind," he said, smiling, "what's gone is gone. Let's look to the future - you mentioned our wedding anniversary?"

Caroline's mood visibly brightened. "Yes; although we wouldn't be able to afford a big party, we could have a small one here, if this mobile hairdressing business goes well."

"Well I think it's a great idea; it'll give both of us something to look forward to, which is what we really need."

"I know," agreed Caroline. "From when I first thought of it, I've been really excited all day; and, after talking to some of my old customers, I couldn't wait to tell you about it. So anyway, how did your day go?"

Despite the intention that Neil had formed on the way home, when he looked at this beautiful woman who was so happy and excited, he decided that he could not bring himself to tell her any bad news. It was true that he still had no feelings of love for her; however, he desperately wanted his memory to return, so that he could be in love with her again. Instinctively, his first thought was to shield her, and keep her happy, as much as he was able.

"It was okay," he lied; "although there's no work on the site at the moment, the foreman has taken my mobile number in case anything comes up. I also nipped into the council offices, and picked up a form to apply for a doorman's badge." Neil sounded enthusiastic for her benefit. "I tell you what - in between drumming up business for your mobile hairdressing, you certainly need to get swimming again, and see what else you can remember."

"Definitely," she asserted. "Michael and Paul are coming round later with the girls, so I can't wait to tell them."

"Er - any chance of leaving my big ears, and being ugly when I was younger, *out* of the conversation?"

Caroline affected a concerned expression. " I promise, I would never mention that in front of the girls.........because they already know." This set them both laughing again.

"There's a thing," said Neil, once he had composed himself, "our twentieth wedding anniversary is in three weeks, correct?" Caroline nodded. "And Michael's nineteenth birthday party was just over two months ago?" he asked.

"Right again," she smiled, looking at him coyly. "It was the standing joke, with the families and our friends, that there were no prizes for guessing what you and I were doing on our wedding night."

Neil started to go slightly pink. "The beauty of marrying a man who doesn't drink, and is stone cold sober on his wedding night," remarked Caroline mischievously.

Neil was, by now, very red in the face. "I knew that would embarrass you," said Caroline, "it always has. The trouble is, you look so sweet when you're embarrassed, I can't resist it."

Neil started to laugh; then, to his surprise, Caroline leaned forward, and stared curiously at his face.

"Oh, isn't that strange..........I can see where Braithwaite used the synthetic skin. Don't be offended," she said hurriedly, "but, at the moment, one side of your face looks like a jigsaw puzzle."

This made him laugh even more. "Offended? After the comments about big ears and being ugly, I'm almost flattered!"

Just then, Michael, Paul, Cathy and Jenny came through the front door, and immediately overheard Neil and Caroline giggling in the living room; Cathy grinned at her companions, put her finger to her lips, then silently poked her head round the living room door.

"What are you two laughing so much about?" she demanded.

Caroline and Neil both nearly jumped out of their skin, much to the amusement of everyone else.

"Oh, hello you lot," said Neil, as they all came into the room. "Well, apparently, when I go red, I look like a jigsaw puzzle."

"Oh?" said Cathy. "What made you go red?"

Neil put on a serious expression. "I asked Caz where I could find false ponies, but she said they didn't exist, so I felt a bit silly; but then, I looked on the internet for false pony sanctuaries, and there are loads of them."

"Are there really sites for false pony sanctuaries?" asked Jenny, uncertainly.

"Absolutely," replied Neil, as the others started sniggering; "you just have to speak to the fairies to get directions."

"Okay," said Jenny, noticing the mischief in his eyes, and laughing self-consciously. "It's my turn to get embarrassed now!"

"Look on the bright side – at least you don't look like a jigsaw puzzle when you blush," said Neil plaintively. "Which reminds me - I found an old jigsaw in Paul's room the other day, so I thought I'd have a go at it; on the box it said four to five years, but it only took me three days to do it."

"No, when it says four to five years........" Jenny did not reach the end of the sentence, as her voice was drowned out by everyone's laughter.

"Alright, I give up!" she said, holding up her hands, and laughing as much as the others. "I'm not going to say another word!"

Neil shook his head, and put his arm around her. "You can't stop now," he admonished; "I've got loads more lined up for you!"

"Anyone fancy a cup of tea?" said Caroline. "There's no beer left, I'm afraid - Jacko drank it all last night."

"I bet you had the odd laugh last night, if Jacko was here," commented Paul.

"Jacko and I were trying to have a serious conversation, but your mum just kept laughing all the time," complained Neil. "We were trying to discuss world politics, the strength of the pound against foreign currencies and, obviously, the fluctuating price of banana splits."

Michael grinned. "Naturally - it's a crucial issue."

"Seriously, do banana splits fluctuate in price?" asked Cathy.

Neil smiled. "You're spending far too much time with Jenny," he said, wagging his finger at her.

"Listening to those two last night," said Caroline, "at one point, I was laughing so much, I nearly wet myself."

Neil looked at Caroline, with an almost hurt expression on his face. "Actually, you did - Jacko and I didn't have the heart to tell you, but you definitely shouldn't have worn that white skirt."

"Take no notice," laughed Caroline, "I didn't really."

Neil mouthed "She did, really," to the others, which set them all off again.

"That's it - I'm getting the frying pan!" declared Caroline.

"That's just reminded me," said Neil. "When you said, the other day, that it would have little or no effect on my new face, I meant to tell you about what happened on the building site. No-one noticed this, which is just as well; but, as I was pushing the wheelbarrow, I tripped over, and went face first into a scaffolding pole."

Caroline's hand shot to her mouth; but before she could say anything, Neil raised his hand.

"Don't worry," he assured her, "I didn't even feel it - the scaffolding pole definitely came off worse. My only concern, when it happened, was whether anyone saw it; luckily, they didn't."

Michael and Paul looked at each other, then they both laughed.

"Oh, but *we* did," Paul informed his father; "we were killing ourselves laughing, but when you looked up, we hid behind the cement mixer."

"We were concerned initially, because the scaffolding actually shook," added Michael; "but when you got up straight away, and quickly looked round, it just creased us up."

The rest of the evening flew past. Caroline explained her plans for the mobile hairdressing, which was met with enthusiasm by everyone; and the banter also continued so that, by the time the cheerful party broke up, everyone was practically aching from having laughed so much.

"Well," said Neil, as he and Caroline stood by the front door, waving to their visitors as they drove away, "everyone's really excited about your mobile hairdressing idea."

"I know," said Caroline, as they came in and closed the door. "I reckoned that it was a good idea, but it's great when everyone else agrees with you."

Neil stretched, and yawned. "I feel absolutely shattered after all that laughing; so, I think I'll go to bed - I'll see you in the morning."

"Yes, I'm going to bed myself, after I've tidied up - I can't wait for tomorrow."

…………………………………………………………………

Neil lay on his bed, staring into the darkness, his mind going over the events of the last few days.

He had been so convinced that he was unable to look to the future, until he had dealt with his attackers; now, he realised that he was not as certain of that as he had been, several days ago.

It occurred to him that, as much as he would like to discover why he was attacked, and to punish the people involved, there was a danger that it might become an obsession – and that, in itself, could destroy his future anyway.

Chapter 10

"Tinny, what time are the taxi drivers coming in this morning?" asked D.C.I. Davies.

"They should be here soon, boss. As soon as I get a shout from the front desk, I'll take them into one of the interview rooms." Tinny grinned. "I have to admit, if it turns out not to be 'Tex' Cooder who visited Neil Hughes, I'll be bitterly disappointed."

"I've been checking the time line, Sarge," volunteered Gary. "Cooder was sent down just over twenty-five years ago, and he did fifteen years. He'd only been out of prison about two months when Neil Hughes sold the taxi business."

"Okay," said Tinny; "now, I was thinking about this last night. Let's assume that the taxi drivers confirm that it was 'Tex', and that there is some connection with the drug dealer with whom Neil Hughes had a problem; as we already know, it's more than ten years since Mr Hughes sold the taxi business – why wait all this time to take revenge on him?"

The D.C.I. nodded. "I know; I was trying to look at the various possibilities, but couldn't come up with anything either."

Just then, the door to the briefing room opened; it was the desk Sergeant. "There's a Terry Hawkins and a Phil McNab downstairs, asking to speak to you, Tinny."

"Cheers, Jeff - I'll be straight down now."

……………………………………………………………

As Tinny and Gary walked into the interview room, Tinny smiled at the two men who were waiting there.

"I'm Tinny Smith, and this is my mate Gary," he announced.

The older of the two men stood up. "I'm Terry Hawkins, and this is Phil McNab."

"How do you do," said Tinny. "Burnsy tells me you've got some information which may be of some help to us?"

"Yes," replied Terry. "There's two separate parts to the story - so I'll tell you what I can remember, then Phil can tell you his bit."

"Fair enough," said Tinny, as they all sat down at the table. "Do either of you two gents mind if we record this conversation?"

Terry shook his head. "Not a problem as far as I'm concerned."

"Okay by me," added Phil.

Tinny nodded. "We'll all be on film as well, by the way; it's so the boss next door can see I'm doing my job properly."

Terry laughed. "Burnsy said you were the only copper he'd ever trusted."

Tinny smiled wryly. "I'll take that as a compliment. So, what can you tell us today?"

"Right," began Terry; "bear in mind this is over ten years ago, so I can't remember things word for word, but this was basically what happened. I was in the taxi office one day with Yosser, when this fella came in and asked to speak to Neil Hughes. He was wearing a suit and carrying a briefcase, but he was no businessman. The best way I could describe him is he looked like the accused, if you know what I mean."

Tinny grinned. "Terry, I know exactly what you mean."

"Typical Yosser," continued Terry, "he said 'if you're selling something, don't waste my time or yours.' This fella in the suit had walked in full of himself, but right away, he was put on the back foot by Yosser's comment. This fella went on to say he wasn't selling anything, but he was looking to put some business our way. He said he'd heard how reliable we were, and wanted to set up an account with us - but Yosser said we had plenty of cash work, so he wasn't interested in doing any taxi runs which he'd have to wait to be paid for. Then, this fella said he'd pay up front whatever Yosser asked, and then when the money was getting low, he'd pay up front again.

"Anyway, to cut a long story short, everything was set up, and we started doing these runs all over the area. It was going great, because they were usually mid-week nights when it was always a bit quieter, and as they were all pre-paid, it was good business. It all came to a stop when Yosser did one of these runs himself."

Phil took up the story. "I happened to be in the office that night when Yosser walked in, and straight away, he said to the operator not to take any more jobs on that particular account. While I was there, I saw him put a note on the taxi radio, instructing all operators that that account was closed. When I asked him why, he said he was fairly sure we were taking drug dealers from place to place, and they were carrying drugs on them. As soon as he said that, it did cross my mind that every one of them I'd picked up was always carrying a bag of some sort - sometimes a briefcase, sometimes a haversack, or even a sports bag."

Terry nodded his agreement. "When the word went round all the drivers who'd done any of these jobs, it was obvious to all of us Yosser was probably right. I'm not sure why none of us hadn't spotted it ourselves. The next thing we heard, was that the main man had been making threats that he was going to sort Yosser out."

"About a week later," resumed Phil, "I was in the taxi office, when a man walked in, and asked for Neil Hughes. I'm not joking when I say, it felt like the room temperature had dropped about ten degrees when this fella walked in. I couldn't say what it was, but there was something terrifying about him, and I felt pretty uneasy. Anyway, Yosser stood up and said 'I'm Neil Hughes,' then this fella smiled, put out his hand, and said 'I'm Billy Ray Cooder.' That's when my blood really ran cold, when I realised this was "Tex" Cooder. What surprised me was, they obviously didn't know each other, but seemed to greet each other like they were friends."

Tinny frowned. "How do you mean exactly, Phil?"

"Well, Yosser shook hands with him, and asked him if he preferred Billy or 'Tex', and the scary man said 'I much prefer Billy.' Just then the phone rang, Yosser answered it, and said to me 'I've got a little job, if you want it.' 'Too right,' I said, and couldn't get out of that office quick enough."

"So," summed up Tinny, "you didn't hear any of the conversation, but you felt there was no animosity between them?"

"Far from it - as I was going through the door, I heard Yosser say 'I'm just putting the kettle on, if you fancy a brew.'"

"I see," mused Tinny. "How would you describe the man who called himself Billy Ray Cooder?"

Phil shrugged. "It sounds a bit daft, but he looked like a red Indian. He was about five foot ten, slim build, but with broad shoulders. He had a ponytail, and although he was very dark haired, there was a touch of grey at the sides. The thing I really remember, is that there was something about the look in his eyes that was really frightening."

"Yes," agreed Tinny, "that's definitely Billy Ray Cooder. Did either of you catch the name of the man in the suit with the briefcase?"

Terry shook his head. "No, sorry."

"Me neither," said Phil, shrugging.

"Alright then," said Tinny, "well, thanks for taking the time to come in. If you do remember anything else, I'd be grateful if you'd give me a call."

....

Tinny and Gary went into the room next door, where the D.C.I. had been watching the interview.

"Well, what do you think, boss?" asked Tinny.

"We definitely need to speak to Billy Ray," replied D.C.I. Davies; "but, for the moment, we'll treat him as a witness, not a suspect."

Tinny pursed his lips. "I'd love to know who the man in the suit was; however, I can't see any way of finding that out, I'm afraid."

Fred Davies nodded resignedly. "I assume Billy Ray Cooder is still in the land of the living, and we have an address for him?"

Tinny raised his eyebrows. "Now you mention it, I'm not even sure how old 'Tex' is. He's definitely older than you and I, but I certainly hope he's still with us."

"He's fifty-eight, Sarge, and I have an address for him," interjected Gary. "I've got all the information we need on the laptop. Since coming out of prison, he hasn't been in trouble at all, and hasn't even been suspected of any crimes."

Davies rubbed his hands together, and beamed at his two officers.

"I'll leave it to you pair to go and see Billy Ray. It will be interesting for him to meet *two* men who aren't frightened of him." Gary lowered his head slightly, and smiled to himself. "I've been speaking to Pete Jones, Mark and a few of the others in uniform that you worked with," explained Davies, looking at Gary appraisingly.

"I must admit," said Gary, "it will be interesting to meet this man. His background was very much middle-class; his father was a university lecturer on the history of the Native Americans, and his mother held a senior position in a merchant bank. The man himself was well educated; and yet, he took the path that he did."

Tinny snorted. "Well, you're middle-class, and look how you've ended up!"

Gary grinned. "Fair comment, Sarge, fair comment."

………………………………...

As they were sitting in the car, about to set off to interview Cooder, Tinny glanced sideways at Gary.

"I have to say, that laptop you have there is a very fancy looking piece of equipment," he remarked.

"Top of the range, Sarge; the best that money can buy."

Tinny smiled wryly. "A bribe, no doubt?"

"No - my girlfriend bought me this as a birthday present. She's in a really top job, and earns twice as much as I do." Gary's expression was serious.

"Apologies, Gary, I shouldn't have jumped to conclusions," said Tinny, suitably chastened.

At this, Gary looked down, and started to laugh.

"I haven't got a girlfriend, Sarge - it *was* a bribe!"

This set them both giggling like schoolboys, as they had when they were at Matty's sister's house. The D.C.I. happened to walk past the car; he smiled, and shook his head.

"Seeing the boss there has just reminded me of something," said Tinny, after he had composed himself. "After the comment he made about Cooder meeting *two* men who wouldn't be frightened of him, I've just been making some discreet enquiries about you."

Gary smiled enigmatically. "I'm a lot tougher than I look, Sarge."

"So I believe. Both Pete Jones and Mark said that if they had you alongside them, they were quite happy taking anyone on."

"Strangely enough, I've got my father to thank for that."

Tinny raised his eyebrows, and folded his arms. "You don't say? Well, that's the second time you've got me intrigued – you'll have to tell me the full story."

"Right away, Sarge," grinned Gary. "Well, needless to say, I had a private education, as did my father, and public schools are very keen on extra curricular activity. My father and his friends regularly go shooting and, when I was about thirteen years old, he wanted me to go with him. I refused; I told him that I found shooting living things distasteful, and would have no part of it. Anyway, he attempted to embarrass me in front of his friends by saying that I'd probably be frightened of the guns going off, because I was such a mummy's boy." There was a contemptuous tone to Gary's voice. "Suffice it to say, he didn't succeed in embarrassing me; but it did make me determined to put him in his place."

Tinny nodded. "So what did you do?"

"While I was at school, I took up clay pigeon shooting and boxing," replied Gary. "At the risk of sounding conceited, I was very good at both, because I was determined to be; by about age seventeen, I was pretty accomplished. At that point, I challenged my father and his friends to a competition at a clay pigeon shooting range; they all thought it would be quite funny but, by the time we'd finished, they weren't laughing." Gary paused briefly. "I also took the opportunity to tell my father, in front of all his friends, that if he ever called me a mummy's boy again, I'd put him on his back."

"I see," murmured Tinny. "And *did* he ever call you a mummy's boy again?"

"Nope," said Gary firmly. "That's when the bribes started. When he discovered he couldn't bully me, he assumed he could buy me. I'm afraid my father thinks that everything has a price, whether it's a commodity, loyalty, or affection; well, nobody can buy me, and especially not him. He may be academically intelligent, and shrewd in business; but he remains, in my opinion, a very stupid man."

Tinny simply nodded understandingly, not feeling that it was his place to express agreement; but, from everything he had learned about his younger colleague, it certainly seemed to him that Gary's father must be a very stupid man indeed.

"Right," he said briskly, "let's go and see what Billy Ray Cooder has to say for himself, bearing in mind what the D.C.I. said about him."

"The fact that he's a good liar?"

Tinny chuckled cynically. "Oh, he could win trophies for it. He's not just a good liar; he's the best."

....

Tinny and Gary pulled up, got out of the car, and walked towards the house; as they got nearer, Tinny was somewhat surprised to note that the fearsome Billy Ray Cooder was innocently occupied, working in his front garden. He saw them approaching, looked up, and smiled.

"Tinny Smith! It's nice to see you - what brings you round these parts?"

He offered his hand to Tinny as he spoke, so Tinny returned the smile, and shook hands with him.

"I'm involved in a case at the moment," he explained, "and I'm hoping you may have some information which could help us. I must admit, I'm surprised you recognised me after twenty-five years."

"You haven't aged a bit in all that time, Tinny."

Tinny laughed. "You were always a good liar, Billy, but I know you're lying now."

Billy grinned. "You're right. I saw you being interviewed on television a few months ago, when you were involved in that abduction case; and I thought, bloody hell, he sure has aged since I last saw him."

All three of them laughed at this. "Anyway," continued Billy, "come in gents, I'll put the kettle on. I could do with a break from this anyway; my back's killing me, I'm not as fit as I used to be."

Tinny glanced around at the beautiful, neat front garden. "I've got to say Billy, I'm very impressed with your gardening skills; they're a damn sight better than mine."

"It's a real passion to me. Wait until you see the back garden; in the good weather, that's where I spend a great deal of my time."

"Can't wait," said Tinny. "Anyway, I'd like to introduce my colleague before we go in: this is Detective Constable Gary Ward."

Gary nodded, shook hands with Billy, and said "Mr Cooder."

Billy smiled, and turned to Tinny. "People of my age say that there's no respect any more from the youngsters nowadays; I don't believe that to be true." He turned back to Gary. "Billy will do fine."

....

As Billy entered the living room with a pot of tea and three cups on a tray, Tinny said "I've just been looking at some of the photographs you have on the fire surround; I assume this young man is your son, and I take it these are your grandchildren?"

"That's right," replied Billy. "I love spending time with the grandkids. I missed out on raising my son, so I feel I've been given a second chance of doing all the things I should have done with our Ray."

After he had catered for his visitors, Billy sat down, cup in hand, and said "So, what can I tell you gentlemen?"

"Billy, I need you to cast your mind back ten years," began Tinny; "you met a man called

Neil Hughes, also known as 'Yosser.'"

Billy shook his head. "I knew a few fellas called 'Yosser' - what more can you tell me about him?"

"He ran a taxi office called Cumfycars," said Gary; "you visited him not long after you came out of prison."

Billy's face lit up. "Of course, I remember him - he was a good guy, I really liked him."

Tinny nodded. "So, what was your connection to him?"

"He'd been having some trouble with a low-life drug dealer; I offered to help, but he said he was okay."

Tinny frowned. "Are you saying that you knew each other before that occasion when you called at the taxi office?"

"No, that was the first time I'd met him; we had a mutual friend, who I owed a big favour to." Billy paused slightly. "It'll make more sense if I tell you the whole story."

Billy took a deep gulp out of his teacup, and began.

"Not long after I was sent down, my wife died as a result of an overdose; I don't know if you remember, but she was a heroin addict. My boy Ray was put into care, and he was only five years old; he was moved about from one children's home to another, and one foster home to another. Anyway, luckily, when Ray was about seven years old, a man called Colin Richardson fostered him, and then, with my permission, adopted him. Colin raised him, and did a better job than I could ever have done; he made sure Ray worked hard at school, he took him to football regularly, and brought him to visit me as often as he could. He did everything a real father should. By the time I got out, Ray was twenty years old, and in a very good job because of his qualifications; he had his own place, and had so much to look forward to, because of the time and effort put in by Colin, raising him properly. It's quite possible that if I hadn't been sent to prison, Ray could have ended up like me.

"Well, Colin was a friend of Neil Hughes. When I told Colin that I'd never be able to repay him for doing such a great job of bringing up my son, he told me about Neil having a problem with a drug dealer, and that I might be able to help. I was only too glad to go along and see Neil, and offer any help he may need." He paused. "As you well know, Tinny, I'd made a good living from people being scared of me; so, if Neil Hughes had wanted me to, I'd have paid this drug dealer a visit. It's safe to say that, had he known that Neil Hughes was a friend of mine, that would've done the trick."

Tinny nodded. "But Neil Hughes didn't take you up on the offer?"

Billy shook his head. "He said he'd deal with it himself, but thanked me anyway." He took another gulp of his drink. "You know, it's a funny thing," he mused, "when I look back now, prison didn't change me; it was getting to know people like Colin Richardson and Neil Hughes. These were real, genuine people who had values, not like the trash I'd spent most of my life with. That day at the taxi office, talking to Neil Hughes, opened my eyes as to what a fool I'd been. Before I was sent down, I thought I had everything - expensive cars, wads of cash, and lots of so-called 'friends', but I realised that I had nothing compared to people like Colin and Neil. I was there for some time, and had a really good talk with him; he told me all about his family, and his plans for the future. Something else I really liked about him, is that he knew who I was, and what I was, but he wasn't scared of me; he treated me like a real person, and even made me a cup of tea while I was there. I wasn't used to that sort of reaction from people I encountered, and it really impressed me."

"I don't suppose you know who the drug dealer was, by any chance?" asked Tinny.

"I did make a a a few enquiries, just in case," smiled Billy; "but when I found out it was a scumbag called Steve Jones, I knew there wouldn't be a problem. Steve Jones thought he was something, but he was nothing. If he'd been dumb enough to go against Neil Hughes, he would've regretted it."

"Are you still in touch with Mr Richardson?" asked Gary.

"No, unfortunately; the last I heard was that he moved abroad, because he'd taken early retirement. I never did get the chance to repay him for everything he'd done for me and my son."

"Well," said Tinny, "in my opinion, carrying on being a proper father has probably been the best way you could ever have repaid him."

Billy smiled in acknowledgement. "Thanks for that, Tinny; you were a gent when I first met you, and you still are."

"Well, I don't know as my wife would agree," smiled Tinny, as he rose from his seat. "Anyway, thanks for your time, and the information; if you can think of anything else, I'd be grateful if you could get in touch."

"Actually," remarked Billy, "you didn't tell me what this is all about, so I'm not sure whether I could be of any more help."

Tinny considered for a moment; then, he seemed to come to a decision, and resumed his seat. He recounted all that had happened to Neil Hughes, including Debbie's detailed description of what she thought had been done to him; both officers could see that their host was very much affected by what he was hearing.

"They strapped him in to the cab and set fire to it?" He spoke quietly, but the tone of his voice suddenly had the ring of cold steel; he paused slightly, as though he was controlling his emotions. "I'll find out what I can; but if you find these people, and can't make a case against them, let me know."

....

As they got into the car, Tinny turned to his colleague.

"First impression - what did you think of Billy Ray Cooder?"

"Well, Sarge, I would have to say that I liked him and, for most of the conversation, I couldn't see what it was about him that was so frightening; however, when you told him what happened to Neil Hughes and I saw his reaction, I could certainly see it then."

"So, did you feel he was telling the truth?"

Gary considered for a moment. "Yes, I did."

"So did I," agreed Tinny. "The problem is that there are no witnesses to the conversation between Billy Ray and Neil Hughes - so where do we go from here?"

"All we need to do is contact the local authority, speak to the relevant department concerning fostering and adoption, get the contact details for Colin Richardson, and then he can confirm or deny the story Billy Ray has just told us. Even though he's moved abroad, they'd still have to know how to contact him, in case anything were to crop up from when he was a foster carer."

"Fine," nodded Tinny, "I can leave that to you; meanwhile, I'm going to speak to the drugs squad, and see what they can tell me about Steve Jones. I suspect that, potentially, he could be a very interesting line of enquiry."

Gary looked at him curiously. "But Billy Ray said he was nothing; do you think he may have something to do with this?"

Tinny smiled sagely. "Someone who is nothing to 'Tex' Cooder could be a very dangerous man to you and I, and the rest of society. It will be interesting to find out as much as I can about this particular character."

....

Neil was up quite early and, after showering and going downstairs, was not surprised to find Caroline already in the kitchen, drinking tea.

"I thought you'd probably be up early this morning," he commented.

"I'm just so excited," said Caroline; "I'm really looking forward to seeing more of my old customers again. Even if it turns out that only some of them need a hairdresser, at least I'll feel that I'm doing something."

"So, all being well, this will be a huge success, and I can be a kept man for the rest of my life?"

"Only until I can find a younger and more handsome one," said Caroline airily.

"I see; so, once the money starts rolling in, I'll be getting ditched?"

"In a split second, big ears!"

Neil started laughing, and sat down. "Ah, well - any chance of a brew before you turf me out?"

Caroline grinned, poured a second cup, and handed it to him. "On second thoughts," she continued, "maybe I won't turf you out; I'll need someone to look after the house, and do all the washing and cleaning for me." She looked him up and down, as if measuring him up. "Hm. I *might* get you a little French maid's outfit."

"No smut if you don't mind, there's men drinking tea here," remonstrated Neil, as Caroline started chuckling; "and don't you be picturing *me* in a French maids outfit!"

"Too late!" said Caroline from behind her hand, her shoulders shaking.

"Well, that's it, I've got to get myself a job as soon as possible - it looks like being a kept man may not be all it's cracked up to be," said Neil, affecting a forlorn look.

"Don't worry, you're quite safe!" she reassured him. "On the odd occasion over the years, if ever I was ill, or when I was having Michael and Paul, you did your best as far as household chores were concerned; but, the fact is, although I did appreciate your efforts, when it comes to cooking, cleaning, ironing and washing dishes, you make a very good taxi driver."

"So, to sum things up," sighed Neil, "I'm no good round the house, I'm no good at do-it-yourself and, because of the memory loss, I'm not even any good in the garden, because I don't know a plant from a weed at the moment."

"All in all, I think that's a very good summary of the situation, big ears; but I still love you anyway, and wouldn't swap you for the world."

"Fair enough," grinned Neil. "But I'm still going to try and find a job, in case you change your mind."

"At least now, I feel it's taken some of the pressure off, which makes things easier for both of us," said Caroline.

"You're right," he agreed, "it means we're looking to the future, and not dwelling on what's happened."

"Yes but I'd still like to know who did this to you, and why they did it. Plus, if you're right and you did have money to pay into the bank the following morning, that would have covered the mortgage payment and other things, so it's possible we may have had the time to find an alternative to selling the villa."

"I know," said Neil, "but there's nothing you or I can do about it. Maybe the police will track these people down, eventually."

"Maybe," nodded Caroline; "the trouble is, though, even if they do, whoever it was won't get what they deserve."

Neil shrugged. "It doesn't matter - I'm still here, and still smiling."

"You certainly are," said Caroline, squeezing his hand; "and, on that note, I'm off to see my potential new customers. Keep your fingers crossed, and start looking for a French maid's outfit that'll fit you."

Neil was smiling as he watched Caroline walking to her car, because she was almost skipping along. After she had driven off, he went back to the kitchen, sat down, and began considering his next course of action. Last night, he had almost convinced himself that he should forget what happened, and try and move on; however, after talking to Caroline this morning, his determination had returned, and he realised that he could not let it lie. He had to find out who had attacked him, and why.

Neil drove to the petrol station. As before, he positioned his car out of sight of the CCTV cameras, and settled himself to watch the forecourt. He sighed; it was a tedious business, and he knew he could be there for some time.

....

Suddenly, he jolted forward, and hit his head on the car windscreen, which woke him from the nightmare he had been having; fortunately, there was no-one nearby who could have heard him cry out.

Disorientated, he glanced at his watch – clearly, the boredom of waiting had taken its toll. He got out of the car, and started to walk around, trying to clear his head, and to stop shaking; he was sweating profusely. Thankfully, as he was wearing tracksuit bottoms and a running vest, any passers-by who saw him in that state would simply assume that he had been running.

This time, he had seen more than in his previous nightmares. He knew now that the van driver was the man who had struck him in the face with a baseball bat, and that his name was Callum; however, he was not the person who had stamped on him – while that was happening to him, Neil had seen Callum watching nearby, and laughing almost hysterically. If Neil were to see him again, he would have to stay calm, in order to find out who the other attackers were.

Feeling colder, he walked back to his car, and reached inside to get his jacket; as he straightened up, he saw a van pull in to the petrol station. He almost held his breath, as this looked exactly like the van he had seen days before. When the driver stepped out of the van, Neil calmly put on his jacket, and waited; this was the man he had hoped to see.

While his attacker was putting fuel in his vehicle, Neil's mind was racing but, inwardly, he was very calm; he decided that the best thing to do was to follow this man and, hopefully, he would lead Neil to his fellow attackers. He was now satisfied that there were three people involved and, whilst it would be preferable to tackle them one at a time, he was now fit enough to take them on together - should that prove necessary.

The van driver had, by this time, gone into the shop. Neil started the car, and waited for his quarry to emerge; however, the driver was inside for longer than he would have expected. Eventually, Neil switched off his engine, and got out of the car to see what was going on.

Just then, he saw the van driver walk out, followed by two men who evidently worked at the petrol station. Neil was too far away to hear what was being said; however, it was obvious that there was a dispute or argument going on. The van driver turned to face the other two, and appeared to be challenging them to some sort of fight; at this, both men went back inside, and locked the door.

As the driver headed towards his van, there was a smallish, elderly man walking towards him, on the way to pay for his petrol; as he tried to step out of the way of the van driver, the latter pushed him so hard, that the unfortunate man was knocked over on to the ground. Neil gritted his teeth; in any other circumstances, he would have raced over, and dealt with this bullying behaviour immediately, but he had to stop himself getting involved – his priority had to be to find his attackers. Cursing to himself, Neil got back into the car, started the engine up, and waited for the van driver to pull away from the forecourt.

As the driver attempted to exit the petrol station forecourt, however, he had to brake sharply, as a works van pulled straight across in front of him, and blocked his way; four young men jumped out of this second vehicle, and started shouting at the van driver. Neil could see what was happening, and made a very quick decision.

He drove nearer to the scene, still making sure that he could not be picked up on the CCTV cameras; then, he stopped the car, got out, and walked over to where the confrontation was taking place. As he came into view of the van driver, and the four young men who were facing him, Neil took off his jacket, and threw it on the floor behind the van driver.

The biggest of the four men was shouting. "We saw what you did you pikey bastard! Try pushing one of *us* over, and see what happens!"

"You gyppo scum aren't welcome round here!" interjected one of the others. "Why don't you crawl back to one of your filthy sites?"

As Neil had been throwing down his jacket, he noticed that the van driver, who only appeared to be about twenty-five years old, was not remotely frightened of, or intimidated by, the four men; if anything, they appeared to be source of amusement to him. He was clearly more than willing to take them on. Neil also noticed that he had a weapon, which looked like a hammer, in the long pocket of his jeans; he had no doubt that the man would have no qualms about using it.

Neil now took up a position standing next to the traveller, and faced the four young men.

"Four onto one, I don't think that's very fair odds so let's try four onto two and we'll see how it goes from there," declared Neil, in his most convincing traveller accent.

The largest of the four men stepped forward, clearly about to say something, but he did not get the opportunity. Neil quickly jumped towards him, and used the palm of his hand to strike him on the forehead; he knew that the blow would do no permanent damage to the man, but would certainly be hard enough to knock him to the ground. The big man lay on the floor, dazed, as the other three stepped back slightly.

Neil smiled. "Three onto two, I think there's people passing who would have a few pounds on us now. Who'd like to step forward so I can make it two onto two, or maybe you're not quite as brave as you thought you were?"

As the three men helped their friend to his feet and bundled him back into their van, Neil hoped that the headache caused by his blow would not last too long. He felt guilty for what he had just done to his unlucky victim; however, he could not waste the opportunity to befriend his attacker and, hopefully, get close enough to him to get the information he required.

Watching as the works van drove away, Neil ensured that he was standing at the front of the traveller's vehicle, so that he could not be seen on the CCTV cameras; he then bent down, picked up his jacket, and put it on.

"I could have taken those four myself." The traveller's accent was not as strong as that used by Neil.

Neil simply looked him up and down, nodded, and turned to walk away.

"Even so," continued the traveller, "I believe I owe you a drink."

Neil turned, faced the other man, and scrutinised him, almost with disgust. "You owe me nothing."

"In that case, I think I'd like to *buy* you a drink."

Neil continued to examine him. "Well, that's a different matter."

"Do you know the Brown Horse?"

Neil shook his head. "I don't."

"I'm heading there now, but I won't be stopping long - if you want to follow me, I'll see you there." Neil nodded.

As he walked back over to his car, Neil was surprised at his own self-control, now that he was certain that this van driver was one of his attackers; he had seen progressively more and more through his nightmares, and was aware, not only how violent had been the attack upon him, but also the great pleasure his assailants had taken from his suffering.

As he followed the other man in his car, his concern now was how he was going to conduct himself in the pub. The traveller's assertion that he would not be staying there long was, in some respects, just as well; Neil was not looking forward to drinking alcohol, but he realised that, in the circumstances, it was something he was going to have to do. He had been told that he did not like the taste, which was irrelevant; if, however, it made him feel ill, that could prove to be awkward.

Over the last few days, Neil had been making discreet enquiries amongst some of the cab drivers as to where the local traveller sites were situated, and where the travellers tended to drink. He was aware that the Brown Horse was a popular pub with the local travelling community, and knew exactly where it was, as he had been there days before. His reconnaissance had revealed that the only CCTV cameras inside the pub were trained on the tills, not on any of the customer areas; he had also checked the routes to and from the pub itself, and ascertained which roads were, and were not, covered by CCTV. He was still unsure exactly what he proposed to do; however, at least he could be confident that there would be no record of his having been there.

As they arrived, the van driver stepped out of his vehicle, and stood by the entrance to the pub as Neil was locking his car; as Neil approached him, he held out his hand.

"Callum Flynn." Neil shook the hand offered to him.

"Declan," he replied.

"That's not a particularly impressive car you've got there, Declan."

Neil had seen how much of a bully this man was, and knew the level of violence he was capable of; clearly, he was used to saying what he wanted, without fear of anyone. Neil therefore decided to establish who was in charge of the present situation.

"I could say the same about the van you're driving, but I've never judged a man by what he's got, or hasn't got. I judge a man by what he is, not what he thinks he is."

Callum nodded. "You're right, Declan. I'm not used to people standing alongside me when it comes to trouble, I'm used to people standing against me. I apologise if I've offended you."

Neil remained stony-faced. "Callum, you'd soon know if you had offended me."

Callum looked at Neil suspiciously; then he said "I too am a good judge of men, and I think I prefer you as a friend rather than an enemy. I already have plenty of those."

For the first time, Neil smiled. "You and me both."

Callum walked into the bar of the Brown Horse, followed by Neil, and the latter could immediately sense the change of atmosphere; the noise of people talking and laughing on one side of the room stopped, and Neil could see the men standing by the bar move away, as Callum walked towards it. Neil almost felt as if he was in a scene from an old wild West movie, as the gunslinger enters the saloon.

Callum called to the barmaid. "A pint of your best bitter....... Declan, what are you having?"

This was the part Neil had been dreading. "I'll have the same."

Callum passed the first pint to Neil; while the barmaid was pouring the second one, he said "Declan, what do you normally drink?"

"When I'm not paying, whatever's put in front of me. I have to say, I'm not a big drinker - I like to be aware of everything that's going on around me, at all times."

Callum nodded. "I wish I had your sense - unfortunately, I do like a drink, and there certainly have been times when I've regretted it."

"I was the same when I was your age. I have a scar on my left shoulder, which I wouldn't have if I'd been more sober."

"I noticed that scar before when you took your jacket off. Would I be right in thinking that the man who gave you that scar was sorry for his actions?"

"He was, as were his friends and his family. I bear a grudge."

Callum looked hard at this man; as far as he could remember, this was the first time in his life he had been fearful of anyone. He had grown up with the protection of his father and uncle, who were the toughest two men he had ever known - the Flynns were well-known in the travelling community, and were feared by everyone; and yet, the longer Callum was in the presence of Declan, the more he felt that this was not a man to cross.

Callum raised his glass. "Good health, and I hope I never do anything that would cause you to bear a grudge against me."

Neil smiled, resisting the temptation to say "Too late." As he drank the beer, he was surprised to find that he enjoyed the taste after all, which was something of a relief; he simply hoped that Callum did not drink like Jacko - otherwise, Neil would still have most of his pint, while Callum's glass would be empty.

"I have no money on me," pointed out Neil, "so I'll have to buy you a drink another time."

Callum raised his hand. "I'm not a man who invites someone for a drink and expects them to pay. I only have time for the one today, but would be quite happy to have a drink with you again."

Neil acknowledged this with a nod. "I don't expect to be in this area for very long, so when I've finished the business I have here, I'll be moving on. I expect I'll still be in the area tomorrow afternoon, and will be in here having a drink - hopefully, with a great deal more money on me than I have now."

Callum hesitated, as though considering whether he should ask the next question; then he decided to proceed.

"Declan, I could tell when I shook your hand you don't make your money from manual work. Do you mind if I ask how you do make your money?"

"Callum, I don't mind you asking, as long as you don't mind me not telling you. It depends on what you describe as manual work - I certainly don't get my hands dirty, if that's what you mean."

The tone of voice made Callum feel that it would be unwise to aggravate this stranger in any way, so he did not pursue it, and simply nodded. He drained his glass.

"Well, Declan, I'll be here again tomorrow afternoon and would be glad to share a drink with you again."

As Callum turned to leave, Neil said "You said you had some business to attend to - would you be needing any assistance?"

Callum smiled. "No. But I'm grateful for the offer."

As Callum left, once again, Neil detected a change in the atmosphere inside the pub; he therefore decided to take his time with his drink, and see what he could find out about Callum Flynn. As he stood by the bar, it was not long before one of the travellers, who had been sitting on the other side of the room, approached him.

"Would I be right in thinking you are a friend or relative of Callum's?"

"No, I've only just met the man." Neil went on to explain what had happened at the petrol station; he soon observed that his lack of association with Callum Flynn made a difference as to how this man viewed him. When Neil had finished speaking, the traveller immediately held out his hand.

"Paddy, Paddy Rafferty."

Neil shook his hand. "Declan."

"Would you like to join us, Declan? You'd be more than welcome."

"I have to say Paddy, I have no money on me now, so I'd rather wait for a time when I do. Then I'd be only too glad to have a drink with you."

"Well, I'd like to buy you a drink, and I've no doubt there will come a time when you can buy me one. Would it be a pint of the best bitter?"

Neil smiled and nodded; he drank what remained of his pint, then walked over to the table with Paddy, carrying his second free drink. At the table, Paddy announced "This is Declan," and repeated to his friends how Neil had come to be in the company of Callum Flynn.

Neil put his pint on the table, and said he was going to the toilet; he needed to give himself time to think how he was going to approach this situation. He had to find out as much as possible about Callum and his family and, ideally, which site they were on at the moment. So far, things had gone quite well - his traveller accent had clearly convinced the genuine travellers, and he was pleasantly surprised to find that he could handle the alcohol; but he could not afford to relax. He needed to find a way of obtaining as much information as possible, without asking too many questions.

As Neil emerged from the toilet and walked back to the group of travellers, one of the men at the table said "So, Declan, we've not seen you round here before, where've you come from?"

"I've just come from the gents - I'm surprised you didn't see that from where you're sitting. Paddy, I think this man's had enough, but next time I'm in, I'll have a pint of whatever he's drinking, it's obviously good stuff."

Everyone in the group, including the man who had questioned him, started laughing.

"I see we're going to have to be on our guard with you, Declan," chuckled Paddy.

Neil sat down with the company of travellers, and spent some time laughing and joking with them, until he felt that he had been sufficiently accepted; then, keeping his tone jovial, he commented "Correct me if I'm wrong, but I felt Callum Flynn is no friend of yours."

Paddy was the first to speak. "He's no friend of anybody's. The Flynns are hated and despised by everyone in our community."

Neil sat back and listened intently, as everyone in the group gave their reasons for not having anything to do with the Flynn family. He soon realised that, even if only half the stories he heard from these men were true, he would only be able to take on any of the Flynns one at a time; even with his abilities, he would have no chance against all three.

"Callum's father, Patrick, used to call himself the King of the gypsies because he never lost a fight," said Paddy.

One of the other men laughed. "Don't you mean Callum's uncle?"

Neil looked questioningly at Paddy, who provided the explanation. "Patrick's wife had Callum about twenty-five years ago, and everyone assumed Patrick was his father. But as Callum got older, it was obvious to everyone that Patrick certainly wasn't the father."

"So if Patrick isn't his father, who is?" asked Neil.

"Patrick's brother, Sean," replied Paddy. "Patrick is an evil man, and it was well known he beat his wife savagely, almost from the day they were married. Patrick's wife turned to Sean for sympathy, but she got a lot more than that. When it became obvious to everyone that Callum's father was not Patrick, there was a terrible accident," he finished enigmatically.

At this point, one of the other men carried on with the story. "Supposedly, Patrick's wife fell and hit her head on the stove, but died before the ambulance got there. Everyone has always believed Patrick killed her, and he did it in front of her sons."

"Sons? Callum has a brother?"

"Kieran. He's about ten months younger than Callum, and is very much his father's son."

"Declan, are you a religious man?" asked Paddy.

"I am indeed," said Neil.

"If the Devil were to appear in human form, I believe he'd look like Patrick Flynn. It's not just that the man is evil, he looks evil. If you ever have the misfortune to meet him, you'll know what I mean." Paddy's expression was grim. "And Kieran is the Devil's son, there's no question about that in my mind." All the men around the table nodded in agreement.

"Kieran hasn't been seen for a few weeks, and there's a rumour he may have been killed," volunteered another of the travellers. "God forgive me for saying this, but I hope that's true."

Paddy said "if it is true, there's a fair chance it could be a jealous husband. Kieran is a nasty piece of work, but he certainly knows how to charm the ladies."

Neil was intrigued; he had managed to obtain quite a lot of information today, but he decided not to push his luck, and chose this moment to take his leave.

"Well, thanks for the drink, Paddy, I hope to be able to buy you one soon. I have some business to attend to, so I'll be on my way. God willing, I'll be here tomorrow, and would be only too glad to share a laugh and joke with you gentlemen again."

....

As Tinny and Gary were driving back to headquarters, Gary was working feverishly on his laptop.

"This is interesting, Sarge: round about the time Neil Hughes sold his taxi business, Steve Jones and three others were arrested, and charged with the supply of class A drugs."

Tinny nodded slowly. "Let me guess - did Jones get a ten year stretch?"

Gary smiled his assent. "He got out two months ago; the other three were let out years before, but they were just the runners - he was the main man."

"I don't suppose it says who was in charge of the case at the time?"

"Certainly does," confirmed Gary; "it was a Detective Inspector James James."

"Brilliant - Jimmy James is an old mate of mine, and has got a fantastic memory for detail; he'll be able to give us chapter and verse on the Steve Jones arrest. This is looking very interesting."

Gary raised an eyebrow. "James James?"

"I know, I always thought it was a mean trick of his parents to give him the Christian name James, when his surname was also James."

"It could have been worse, Sarge - they could have called him Homer."

Tinny chuckled. "We should have thought of that as a nickname for him years ago."

When they arrived back at headquarters, they went straight to the briefing room, and began making a series of phone calls; shortly afterwards, D.C.I. Davies came in.

"You two are looking very pleased with yourselves," he remarked.

While Gary was still on the phone, Tinny explained what had happened that day.

"What did Jimmy James have to say?" asked Davies.

"He received an anonymous tipoff which led to the arrests. Naturally, Jimmy was well aware of what Steve Jones was, although he'd always kept slipping through the net; however, Jimmy said that the information he was given was very detailed - whoever gave them the tipoff was able to supply names, addresses, times the drugs were being moved, absolutely everything he needed."

"Do you think it could have been Neil Hughes who gave him the information?"

"I don't think so, boss," replied Tinny; "from everything we've learnt about Neil Hughes, I would say that's just not his style. Finding Steve Jones and punching his lights out would, in my opinion, have been the most likely way in which Neil Hughes would've dealt with the problem."

"You're probably right," agreed Davies; "but Steve Jones himself may have thought it was Neil Hughes who ruined his empire."

"Very true, boss. Steve Jones lost everything when he went to prison, so it's fair to assume that he'd be looking for revenge, as soon as he got out."

As Tinny finished speaking, Gary had finished his telephone conversation, and walked over to join them.

"Well, Billy Ray Cooder was telling the truth," he said. "I've just been speaking to Colin Richardson, and he confirmed everything that Billy told us. Mr Richardson was initially concerned that Billy may be in some sort of trouble, but I assured him he wasn't; I hope I wasn't out of order there, Sarge?"

"Definitely not, Gary," replied Tinny. "I'd stake my reputation on Billy Ray not having anything to do with the attack on Neil Hughes."

"Good – because, when I told Mr Richardson that Billy Ray felt he had never got the chance to repay him, his response was quite interesting."

"Oh? Interesting in what way?"

Gary smiled. "I don't know how you do this, Sarge; but Mr Richardson said, practically word for word, the same as you did – that Billy now being a good father was repayment enough."

Tinny shrugged. "I believe that to be true."

Gary looked slightly sheepish. "Well, anyway, I rang Billy Ray, and told him what Mr Richardson said. Needless to say, he was very pleased; he also stressed that, if he could find out anything that would help us, he'd be in touch."

Fred Davies turned to Gary, and gave him a thumbs up. "Good man - there are people out there who'd never speak to us, but would certainly confide in someone like Billy Ray Cooder."

"The Sarge and I were talking the other day, about the possibility of Mr Hughes getting his memory back, and dealing with his attackers before we got to them. I dread to think what would happen if Billy Ray Cooder got to them first."

Davies looked around the briefing room, as if he was checking that no-one else was in earshot; then he leaned forward.

"If we don't catch them, I hope he does," he said quietly; then he straightened up."By the way, Gary, I didn't say that."

Tinny hid a smile; Gary simply shrugged his shoulders. "Didn't say what? Sorry boss, I wasn't listening," said the younger officer innocently.

"No wonder you two get on so well," declared Davies, smiling at Tinny. "Okay, let's get Steve Jones and the other three in as soon as possible; the only trouble is, it might take a bit of time tracking them all down."

"No it won't, boss," assured Gary, opening his laptop; "I've got addresses for all four of them here."

"Is there any information you *haven't* got on that laptop?"

"There is, actually - I can't find out how the Sarge got the nickname Tinny."

Davies grinned at Tinny. "So you haven't told him yet?"

"Not yet, because we had a deal," explained Tinny obscurely; "however, I have to say, Gary is certainly heading in the right direction, with regards to keeping his side of it."

"Let's get the rest of the team together, then, and see who's up for a bit of overtime," said the D.C.I.

"You're going to pull them in now?"

"Why not? The sooner the better as far as I'm concerned; plus, I think Gary's right. If Billy Ray thinks these people could be involved in the attack on Neil Hughes, we definitely need to get to them first."

"I was thinking that Gary and I should go along to see Neil Hughes tomorrow," added Tinny. "As far as we know, he still has no memory of the night of the attack, and nothing before that, either; but I just thought we might have a word, and show him a few mug shots."

Davies nodded. "Do you think he *may* have got his memory back?"

"Maybe, maybe not; however, from experience, I can usually tell when someone recognises a face from a photograph, regardless of what they say. So I'll take along photos of Gareth Davies, Matty and Degsy, Carl McCabe and a few of his associates, Billy Ray Cooder, Steve Jones, and his three runners who did time."

"Well, I agree it's worth a shot, Ron - you never know."

Chapter 11

As Neil drove away from the Brown Horse, he was very pleased with the way things had gone; the information he had managed to obtain certainly answered a number of questions, but he knew that there was still much more he needed to discover.

He was now certain that it was the Flynn family who had attacked him, but the reason eluded him; he wondered if, perhaps, they had been hired by someone else to attack him, because he could not see how their paths would otherwise have crossed. Admittedly, his fellow taxi drivers had told him that he picked up travellers on a regular basis, but there had never been any indication of any animosity towards him – on the contrary, his taxi colleagues informed him that he, Neil, got on really well with travellers. Why, then, would a family like the Flynns have tried to kill him?

There was, however, something Paddy said which had, at least, explained a part of his nightmare. Neil was not a religious man in any way, and did not believe in heaven and hell, or God and the Devil; and yet, the thing that had terrified him the most was the look in the eyes of the man who was stamping on him. Although Neil was still unable to see the face, in the context of his nightmare, he thought it *was* the Devil. This had confused him; however, after Paddy's description of Patrick Flynn, it now made sense.

Although Neil had been very careful when speaking to Callum and the other travellers, he had been unable to discover upon which site the Flynns were presently based; he also knew that there was no point in following Callum as, by his own admission, he was not going straight back to the site. As for Paddy and his friends, Neil was satisfied that they, quite genuinely, had no idea where the Flynns could be.

He now realised that he needed to consider, very carefully, what to do next. The desire for revenge was certainly not as strong as it had been; on the other hand, he still believed that he could not really move forward until he discovered why the Flynns had tried, not only to kill him, but to heap such suffering upon him.

....

When Neil arrived home, the house was empty; he therefore took the opportunity to go to the training room, and set about the heavy bag as though he hated it. He then moved on to the punch-ball, and finally the speedball, which he worked on for some time. Although he was sweating profusely, he found that he was not tiring; he knew that the power of his punches would do a great deal of damage to anyone he came up against.

When he heard Caroline arrive home, he shouted to her "I'm in the training room - I'll just have a quick shower, and I'll be down in a minute."

"I'll be in the kitchen," she called back to him. "Do you want me to make you a cup of tea?"

"Yes, please."

When Neil came downstairs in due course, as soon as he walked into the kitchen, he could see how happy and excited Caroline was.

"I get the distinct impression that your day went well," he commented, as he sat down.

"It was just brilliant," she said eagerly. "As it turned out, I didn't get to see very many of my old customers, because I spent so much time with each one that I did see; even so, not only was it really nice to catch up with them again, but each and every one I have spoken to, so far, would love me to come and do their hair for them." She sipped her tea contentedly. "Of course, I talked a lot about you and the boys; I took the smaller photograph with me to show them, because most of them have never seen Michael and Paul, and haven't seen you since before we were married."

"Did you tell any of them that I look quite different from that photograph, now?"

Caroline looked slightly guilty. "Actually, I didn't," she confessed. "I'd got so excited telling them about this house, buying the villa in Spain, and how happy we'd been, it just didn't seem right telling them what had happened to you; I thought I'd leave that for another time. Does that sound awful of me?"

"Not at all," he assured her, "far from it; it would just upset them unnecessarily. You weren't being awful, you were just being kind. No doubt, at some point in the future, you'll get the opportunity to tell them that I look different; but you still don't need to say I was attacked. You could just say I was in an accident, and had to have plastic surgery."

Caroline looked unsure. "Honestly?"

"Absolutely; particularly after you described what happened when you told Alice about my being attacked."

"Yes, that's true," admitted Caroline. "She was heartbroken; she really sobbed, and I felt awful for upsetting her so much."

"Exactly. I don't believe that a problem shared is a problem halved; a problem shared is a problem doubled. It would be different if it were something that the other person could help with; but if they can do nothing about what's happened, telling them is just cruel. I think you did the right thing - if it were me, I would've done exactly the same."

Caroline looked reassured. "Talking about the photograph has just reminded me of something," she digressed; "you were so delighted with it, you kept it in the taxi, showing it to everyone - all your mates on the cabs, as well as some of your regular customers. Anyway, did Mike and Paul tell you about the two fellas from Manchester, who came to the hospital?"

"Dean the Manc and Jonjo? They did, yes; the problem, of course, is that I've got no idea who they are. Why do you ask?"

"Well, Michael said that the two men seemed to know who he and Paul were, yet he was certain that he hadn't met them before. After Michael told me about them, it occurred to me that you must have shown them the photograph of us all."

"Could be," mused Neil. "Thinking about it, it was lucky I didn't have it in the cab on the night I was attacked, otherwise it would have been destroyed with everything else. I know we've got the big photograph on the wall, and the two photos are identical; but it would still have been a shame, if the smaller one had gone up in flames."

"I know. It was strange, really; about a week before you were attacked, I found it face down on the coffee table, but I never got a chance to ask you why you'd stopped carrying it around with you."

"Well, we may never know," shrugged Neil; "but I'm heartily glad that I took it out of the taxi."

"Definitely," smiled Caroline. "So, how did your day go?"

"Nothing much to report; I'll have to go for a second fitting on the French maid's outfit but, other than that, certainly not as exciting as your day. Anyway, it seems that Mike's coming round later with his mate Rob, the lad who works at the hospital."

"Great," said Caroline; "he's grown into a really nice young man. I'll just do a bit of tidying up, then, before they arrive."

"There's nothing to tidy up," smiled Neil. "When I got home, I thought that, at least, I could wash the dishes; but there were no dishes to be washed. I then looked around to see if there was anything else I could do, but there wasn't. I must say, when it comes to keeping this house immaculate, you're very efficient."

"Ha! Don't be trying to talk yourself out of the French maid's outfit, matey; I know your tricks."

Neil started laughing. "Go careful on the ribs," he pleaded, "they're still a bit sore from last night."

"We did have a laugh last night, didn't we?" she remarked. "Alright, I'll let you off. In that case, do you fancy some more tea, and something to eat?"

"I'm not particularly hungry, to be honest - are you having anything?"

Caroline leaned back in her chair. "Definitely not," she sighed; "I've gone through a mountain of cake and biscuits today, so I couldn't eat a thing."

For the next hour or so, Caroline chatted away merrily, and Neil realised that this was probably the happiest he had seen her, since coming home from hospital. One thing was certain to him now; even if he never regained his memory, he would probably fall in love with Caroline anyway - he certainly could not imagine loving anyone else.

....

When Michael and Rob arrived later, everyone adjourned to the living room.

"Do either of you fancy a beer?" asked Caroline. "I've restocked the supplies; but you'd better grab some now, in case Jacko turns up in the near future."

Meeting with an assent from the two young men, she went out of the room to get the drinks; meanwhile, Rob turned to Neil.

"Have you been watching the Braithwaite soap opera on television?" he asked.

Neil shook his head. "I don't really watch television as such, but you've lost me - what Braithwaite soap opera?"

"As we were on our way here, Rob was telling me about a woman who'd been involved in a serious car accident, and had terrible facial injuries," explained Michael.

"That's right," said Neil, nodding. "I remember your saying, Rob, that Braithwaite made sure her family gave him permission to publicise the work he was about to do; I assume, then, that it was a success, and is now worldwide news?"

"Oh, yes indeed," said Rob, wryly. "He's done a fantastic job, again; but it's the way he's presented it - it's almost sickening."

Neil looked vacant. "Sickening? In what way?"

"You wouldn't believe it," replied Rob. "He's been appearing on chat shows, early morning television, daytime television - in fact, anything and everything he can find, to show off his work. They've been showing photographs of this woman when she was a little girl, her wedding photographs, video footage of when the bandages were removed, and her husband's reaction to her new face. Braithwaite has not missed a single opportunity to gain the fame he so obviously craves."

"Well then, we've got to put the telly on now, to see if there's anything about it," said Michael, reaching for the remote.

"I can guarantee that it'll be on at least one of the channels - and it will certainly be on the news channel," assured Rob.

Caroline came back into the room with a pot of tea, and two beers for Michael and Rob, to find that the three men's eyes were glued to the television; Neil explained to Caroline what they were watching.

"You might not want to look at it, though," he warned her. "They might show the woman's injuries, which won't be very pleasant."

"Her injuries weren't as bad as yours," said Rob; then he saw the expressions on the faces of both Neil and Michael and, silently, cursed his own tactlessness.

Rob's prediction was accurate; the story of the injured woman was on every news channel, as was a preening Braithwaite, being interviewed at a press conference. Caroline watched the footage intently; as she saw the woman's bandages being removed, Caroline realised that she was envious of the woman's husband – because, as the woman regained consciousness, the first thing she saw was her husband smiling, and looking happy.

"You can't see very clearly what she looks like," said Caroline, screwing up her eyes as she looked at the screen; "but it's obvious that her husband is happy with the job Braithwaite's done."

"Well then," said Rob, "I think you'll find the next bit quite interesting, assuming this is the same press conference I saw this afternoon. Braithwaite brings this woman into the room, and parades her in front of all the cameras, as though she's some type of celebrity."

Caroline, Michael and Neil continued to watch the television screen and, sure enough, Rob was correct in his description of what followed; however, none of them were prepared for what they saw when the woman appeared.

"Bloody hell!" exclaimed Michael. "Dad, she looks like your twin sister!"

When he saw the woman's face, and realised that Michael was right, Neil was horrified; however, he did not betray his feelings to the others.

"Well," he said, smiling, "I've been struggling to find work recently; all I need to do is put on a bit of make-up, wear a wig, and I'll pinch her job."

"So much for his new method of facial reconstruction, if he can only create exactly the same face on everybody," said Rob, mockingly. "He's hardly going to make his fortune in Hollywood, if all the actors end up looking the same."

"Mind you," said Caroline, "it would be difficult pinching her job if she was a pole dancer, or something like that."

Neil laughed. "Ah, but I could always wear my French maid's outfit."

Caroline also started laughing, to the confusion of Michael and Rob, so Neil had to explain.

"Anyway," he continued, "Braithwaite was taking a bit of a gamble there, by filming the bandages being removed."

Rob shook his head. "No, he wasn't. He knew how well it was going to turn out, because he used exactly the same method on this woman as he did with you. This sounds harsh, but you were a guinea pig, really."

"Or, at least, a handsome gerbil," said Caroline, glancing at Neil; as soon as their eyes met, they both collapsed into laughter again.

Once again, Michael and Rob looked completely bemused, so Neil provided the explanation.

"Blimey," said Rob; "do you *ever* have any serious conversations in this house?"

"The fluctuating price of banana splits," said Michael and Neil, almost simultaneously; that set everybody laughing, including Rob – although, in truth, he had no idea what he was laughing at.

"Oh no, look at that poor woman's face," said Caroline, suddenly.

Everyone looked at the television screen, just in time to see the photographs which had been taken when the woman was first brought into the hospital.

"Dear God," said Rob; "they should have put a warning up on screen before showing those."

"Actually, I think they did, but I wasn't really taking any notice," said Caroline vaguely, still looking at the screen. "They do that for blind people, you see."

After a few moments, she became aware that the others were looking at her in a bemused fashion. "What?" she said, bewildered.

Michael repeated to her what she had said. "Pretty good for deaf people as well, I'm told," he added, smirking.

At this, Caroline put her head in her hands, and began shaking with mirth.

"Mike, just have a taste of your mum's cup of tea, and see what she's been slipping in it," instructed Neil confidentially, patting Caroline on the shoulder. "I'll just go and search the kitchen, to see if there are any bottles hidden in brown paper bags."

"Blind people," Caroline muttered from behind her hands, and shook even more.

This set the tone for the rest of the evening so that, by the time he and Michael got up to leave, Rob's sides were aching; he could not remember the last time he had laughed so much.

"Thanks," he said to Neil and Caroline; "I've had a brilliant time. I'm definitely coming here again – that is, if you'll have me?"

Neil smiled, and shook his hand. "You're welcome here any time," he assured him. "Anyway, with a bit of luck, we may be having a little party here soon for our wedding anniversary; so, if we do, I'll tell our Mike to give you a shout."

....

"Me and my big mouth - I'm sorry about before, when I said that your dad's injuries were worse than the woman's," said Rob, as he and Michael drove away.

"Don't worry about it," said Michael, although he had a look of concern on his face. "You know, I can't imagine how bad dad's face must have looked, if it was worse than what we've just seen."

"I have to say, I really don't know how your dad has managed to stay so positive after what was done to him; I'm not sure I could."

Michael shrugged. "Dad's always been a bit of a Jekyll and Hyde character; he's great when he's at home with the family and, as you saw tonight, he's very funny. But, it's got to be said - if he were to catch up with the people who did this to him, you'd see a completely different side to his personality."

"I hope he does." Rob's expression was serious.

Michael nodded. "So do I, mate."

....

Neil came back into the living room.

"While I think on," he said, "I was filling in that form today to apply for a doorman's license, but I'll need your help with some of the questions."

"No problem," said Caroline.

"I take it I haven't got a criminal record?"

"You haven't even got a speeding conviction, let alone a criminal record," Caroline assured him.

"That does surprise me; I'd have thought that, working as a taxi driver, being caught speeding would've been an occupational hazard."

"You've always been very careful, particularly in built-up areas where there are lots of parked cars. When you were teaching me to drive, you used to stress the importance of taking my time in those sort of areas; you always said you never know if a child could come running out."

"Well, I suppose that makes sense, really. So, I can put down no criminal record, and no spent convictions. There are a few other things on it concerning previous employment, national insurance number and stuff like that, but I'd imagine the accountant would have all the information. I'm guessing that you'd have no idea, as far as those things are concerned?"

"Wouldn't have a clue - you were always the office manager, and I made the tea."

Neil smiled. "*And* kept the office immaculate as well."

Caroline laughed, "You just don't want to go for that second fitting, do you?"

"Curses, foiled again," he responded. "Ah, I've just remembered something else - the police are calling round tomorrow morning, with some photographs of suspects for me to have a look at."

"That seems a bit pointless, don't you think?"

"I did explain to them that I've still got no memory of the night of the attack; but I gather that the idea is to find out whether my seeing a picture of someone, who *may* have been involved, might jog my memory. The policeman who rang was Scottish; I think it's Jacko's mate, a bloke called Tinny Smith. From what Jacko tells me, he's a sound fella; so," continued Neil, "you're going to have to really get this place tidied up, it's an absolute disgrace."

"I know," said Caroline, sighing; "I thought I'd lined up a French maid to help out, but that's not looking very promising now."

"They're like that, French maids - almost as unreliable as taxi drivers. Anyway, shall I put the kettle on, and make a fresh brew?"

"Yes, please - you'll find the instructions by the tea pot."

....

As Neil was standing on his own in the kitchen, he was mentally cursing Braithwaite. If Callum Flynn were to see the woman who had been in the accident, he could put two and two together, and realise who 'Declan' really was; Neil had to assume that the Flynns would know that he had survived; also, that they would be well aware of the damage they had done to his face.

As if that were not enough, Braithwaite's boasting had supplied all the information needed to identify Neil: announcing at the press conference that this was his *second* successful facial reconstruction but, due to the fact that his first patient had been attacked, saying that it was inappropriate for that patient to appear on television – even though the man's new face was a complete success. Neil was surprised that Braithwaite failed to throw in the fact that his first patient was a taxi driver.

As much as he was cursing Braithwaite, however, he was cursing himself even more. Neil had congratulated himself for what he had achieved earlier today because, at that point, he believed that time was on his side; now, it was evident that he should simply have followed Callum, in the hope that he would, eventually, lead Neil to the other attackers.

As things stood now, although he was still unsure exactly what he would do when he confronted the Flynns, Neil knew that he must act quickly. One thing was certain; he had to find out where Callum, Patrick and Sean were living at the moment – so, he had no choice but to go to the Brown Horse the following day, and meet up with Callum again.

....

Neil brought the tea into the living room.

"What are your plans for tomorrow?" he asked, casually.

"I'm here in the morning, but I'll probably be going out about midday."

"Well, if tomorrow goes anything like today, you'll be even more excited - if that's possible," said Neil, smiling.

"*And* I'll be about half a stone heavier!"

....

Gary arrived at Tinny's house, and was about to get out of his car, when he saw Tinny walking down the path; as Tinny reached the car, he shook his head.

"I'm not sure whether I'm going to be able to get in this!"

"It's bigger than you think, Sarge," said Gary, through his open window; "it's just not as easy getting in or out, as it is with your own car."

"You're not kidding," muttered Tinny as, with some difficulty, he got into the passenger seat.

"Which reminds me," added Gary, "where is your car?"

"My son borrowed it last night, and it broke down; it's now in the garage and will, no doubt, cost me an arm and a leg to have repaired."

"Then it's just as well you're independently wealthy, Sarge, and only doing this job for a laugh."

"That's yourself you're talking about, certainly not me," said Tinny, with a wry smile.

"That's right, I got a bit confused there," grinned Gary. "So, what do you think of the Porsche?"

"I must admit, it's very swanky; I don't think I've ever been in a Porsche before. I hope you don't drive like a lunatic?"

"Far from it, Sarge. I do get some very strange looks when people see the car being driven by someone as young as me, sticking to the speed limits, and slowing down so that little old ladies can cross the road."

"Relieved to hear it, Gary," said Tinny. "Alright, then; we'll head straight to Neil Hughes's house, show him the mugshots, and see if any jog his memory. I spoke to him on the phone yesterday, so he's expecting us."

....

As they pulled up outside the house, they sat for a few moments, admiring what they saw.

"Well, I was impressed, yesterday, with Billy Ray's garden; this one could win competitions."

"The house is pretty impressive as well, Sarge."

As they walked up the path, a smiling Caroline opened the front door.

"I was in the front room, and saw you arrive. I assume you're the policemen?"

"That's correct," replied Tinny, as he and Gary produced their warrant cards. "I'm D.S. Smith, and this is D.C. Ward."

"Come in, I'll put the kettle on. I'm Neil's wife, Caroline, but just call me Caz." She showed the two officers into the living room. "Take a seat; I'll just give Neil a shout to tell him that you're here."

Tinny and Gary were both examining the large family picture on the wall when Neil came into the room; they both immediately turned, and Tinny held out his hand.

"Good morning, Mr Hughes; I'm Detective Sergeant Ron Smith, and this is Detective Constable Gary Ward."

Neil nodded, and shook hands. "Good morning to you. Neil will do fine."

Although outwardly calm, Neil's mind was racing. He had been considering, both the night before and that morning, what he should do if one of these photos he was about to see was of

Callum Flynn; although, what with recent events, it might be the sensible move to have Callum arrested, there was something nagging at the back of his mind, telling him that he should deal with it himself, and not have the police involved.

"Take a seat, gents," he said genially; "I can guarantee that Caz will be in shortly, with a pot of tea. I take it you're 'Tinny' Smith, Jacko's mate?" Tinny just smiled, and nodded.

"And am I also right in thinking that you're the Constable who was first on the scene, on the night of the attack?"

Gary also nodded, and looked uncomfortable; Tinny looked appraisingly at Neil. "*We* are supposed to be the detectives here," he remarked; "how could you possibly have known that?"

Neil shrugged casually. "Since coming out of hospital, I've seen the different reactions from people who knew me before that night, as compared to the people who actually saw the damage done to my face. The best way I can describe the difference is that those people who knew me before are pleasantly surprised; whereas, people like Gary, the firefighter Jane, the paramedic, and Mike Bates, the ambulance driver, have a look bordering on disbelief."

Gary lowered his head slightly. "Unfortunately, when I saw your face, I was sick – which, I regret to say, was very unprofessional of me."

"Being professional, I'd imagine, is an important part of your job," acknowledged Neil; "however, I think having compassion is equally important. Tinny can tell me if I'm right or wrong here; but, to be a good policeman, I would have said that caring about the victim must be a huge part of the reason why you want to catch whoever caused them to *be* a victim."

"You're absolutely right, Neil," agreed Tinny. "If we reach the stage where we no longer care, then we're in the wrong job."

"Right, tea up everybody," said Caroline, coming into the room with a tray. "Help yourselves to milk and sugar; if you'll excuse me, I'll leave you to it, as our sons will be here shortly, and they'll want feeding, as usual." She smiled, and went back to the kitchen.

"Thanks, Caz," said Neil. "Okay then - let's have a look at the pictures, and see if I can spot anyone."

Neil gave all his concentration to the photos, and therefore did not notice that Michael and Paul had arrived, until they walked into the living room; swiftly, he turned the pictures face down onto the coffee table. Tinny and Gary immediately rose to their feet as the two young men came into the room, and Neil made the introductions.

Paul said nothing; he simply stood and glared at the two police officers, which made them both feel very ill at ease. Michael shot a warning look at his brother.

"Are these pictures of whoever may have attacked dad?" Michael asked, addressing the officers.

Before Tinny had a chance to reply, Neil spoke. "They could be, or they could be totally innocent people; they could even be the 1966 World Cup winning team. Either way, you two aren't getting to see them."

Michael glanced at Tinny and Gary; then he turned to his father, smiling. "Well, let's have a look - I'd spot Bobby Charlton straight away, and his brother Jackie for that matter."

"Not a chance. Tinny and Gary are the professionals - leave them to do their job."

Paul's face was unsmiling, and he was about to say something when Neil cut across him.

"That's the end of the conversation. Now, bugger off - I think your mum's in the kitchen."

Michael put his arm around Paul. "Come on, kid, let's go and scrounge some breakfast."

As Paul walked ahead of him out of the room, Michael turned, and looked at Tinny and Gary. "You need to catch these people before we do."

Neil looked sternly at his son, and was about to retort, when Michael held up his hands. "Okay, I'm going - but I think I'd spot Gordon Banks as well."

"The Germans were robbed," declared Tinny, in an attempt to lighten the tone. "That ball was never over the line."

Michael laughed. "Spoken like a true Scotsman," he said, as he went out, closing the door behind him.

"Thanks for that," said Tinny, sitting down again. "I wouldn't like to see your sons getting themselves into trouble."

Neil sighed. "Nor would I; but I do understand their desire to get even. The strange thing is, with having no memory at all, I'm only just getting to know my wife and sons." He paused reflectively. "And I tell you one thing, Tinny - I don't think I'd like those two coming after me."

"I'm with you there - I thought I pushed my luck a bit, saying that the Germans had been robbed."

Neil laughed. "I actually watched that game, on DVD, for the first time in my life the other night; I know that sounds strange, but with no memory, I'm seeing so many things for the first time. Well, Jacko said that you had a good sense of humour, and now I know it - that ball *was* well over the line! Anyway, let's get back to these photographs."

Neil studied each one, but was relieved to find that there was no picture of Callum Flynn amongst them. "Sorry," he said finally, "there's nobody here who looks in any way familiar."

"Ah, well," said Tinny, shrugging, "it *was* a long shot; from what we've been told by the crime scene investigation people, even if you were to get your memory back, it's likely that you were unconscious for most of the time anyway."

Neil nodded. "From what I was told at the hospital, it may be better if I never remember that night, as it could be too traumatic; but I certainly want to remember my life from before the attack, because losing those memories has messed things up completely." He went on to explain all that had happened, including the loss of his taxi plate and badge, and the problems he was now having, trying to find employment.

"Anyway," he concluded, "at least I've been getting in plenty of training; beating hell out of the heavy bag definitely makes me feel better."

Gary's eyes lit up. "You've got a heavy bag?"

"I've got a training room upstairs with a heavy bag, a punch-ball, a speedball, and several other pieces of equipment; you can come and have a look, if you like."

Gary turned to Tinny. "Can I, Sarge?" he asked, almost like a child.

"Absolutely," smiled Tinny. "We're in no rush - as long as Neil has the time?"

"No problem at all," assured Neil.

As the three of them were going upstairs, Neil said "I take it you're interested in boxing then, Gary?"

"I did a little bit when I was at school."

Neil could see the excitement in Gary's eyes as they entered the training room. "That's all the equipment I've got at the moment," he said. "So, what do you think?"

"This is absolutely brilliant," enthused Gary; "this equipment you've got here is top notch, and I must say, I like that sign you have on the wall."

"Well," smiled Neil, "if you want to take your jacket off and put on the gloves, you're more than welcome to have a go."

Gary turned to Tinny; however, before he had a chance to say anything, Tinny grinned. "You're best taking your shirt off as well, if you're really going to get stuck into this stuff," he advised.

Gary could not remove his jacket and shirt quickly enough; he donned the gloves, and started on the speedball. Neil watched him for a few moments; then, he walked to the top of the stairs, and shouted down. "Mike, Paul - come and have a look at this!"

Neil came back into the training room, and continued to watch Gary. "You did a lot more than a *little* bit," he observed.

Gary continued working on the speedball and, without getting out of breath, replied "The school were only able to teach me so much, so I joined a local amateur boxing club."

As Gary said this, Michael and Paul walked into the training room, and watched him with a great deal of admiration.

"That must have been interesting," remarked Michael, grinning; "joining a boxing club with that accent."

Gary stopped, turned, and smiled at Michael. "You're right. When I first joined, everyone wanted to knock the posh kid all over the place."

"And did they?" asked Paul.

"They did to begin with, so I just trained harder."

For the first time since Paul had arrived at the house, Gary saw him smile. "So you didn't back down - you stood your ground?"

"As far as I'm concerned, that's the only option," said Gary. "By the time I left that club, I could beat everyone, including the bigger lads."

"Okay then," said Neil, "let's see what you're like on the heavy bag. I'll hold it for you."

Gary was more than willing; and, as he started hitting the heavy bag, to everyone's surprise, he did so with considerably more power than his appearance would suggest.

"You've got a hell of a punch on you there," declared Neil; "I'm surprised you didn't take the boxing any further."

"The trainer in the boxing club would have liked me to," replied Gary, continuing to pummel the bag; "however, I explained to him that there was only one job I ever wanted to do."

Neil nodded. "Want to have a go on the punchball, now?"

Gary demonstrated great agility as he worked on the punchball; to his onlookers, it was evident that he was no stranger to that piece of equipment.

"Well, I must say, I'm very, very impressed," said Neil, as Gary finally took a break from his workout. "In your job, being professional and caring about victims are pretty good traits in themselves; but I reckon being able to handle yourself, in the way you've shown, must be a big advantage - given some of the scumbags you have to deal with."

Gary's smile was non-committal. "Well, I'd better stop now, or I'll be sweating - and that will really mess up my shirt, when I put it back on."

Paul handed Gary a towel. "*I* would have been well sweating by now - you're a lot fitter than me."

Neil was gratified to note that this young man who, earlier on, had prompted only an aggressive attitude in his son, had obviously risen a great deal in Paul's estimation; he was well aware that Paul was capable of doing twice what Gary had just done, without breaking sweat.

"By the way, is that your Porsche outside?" asked Michael.

"It is, indeed," replied Gary, as he put on his jacket.

Paul looked even more impressed. "That must be an absolute babe magnet - the women must be throwing themselves at you."

"Oh yes, I have to beat them off with sticks - it's a complete nightmare," sighed Gary, exaggeratedly straightening his tie, which caused them all to laugh.

"Well, I think it's time we let these good people alone," said Tinny. "Thanks for your time, Neil; it's been a great pleasure meeting you and your family, and I hope you start getting a bit of good luck for the future."

The two officers shook hands with Neil and his sons; they then went downstairs, and said their goodbyes to Caroline as she saw them out.

....

"When you shook hands with Neil Hughes," said Gary, as the two men walked down the path, "did you notice anything?"

Tinny shook his head. "To be honest, I didn't."

"*I* certainly did," asserted Gary, as they were climbing into the car. "I'd describe his hands as weapons."

"Well, we do know what he's capable of - both from what we've been told, and seeing the footage outside the kebab house."

"Yes, Sarge; but now that I've actually seen his hands, and also shaken hands with him, I understand how he's able to do so much damage. The heel of his hand - the area of the palm below the thumb - is absolutely rock hard; also, the skin on his knuckles is very tough."

"Yes; now you mention it, I did notice that and yet both Michael's and Paul's hands seemed to be rougher than Neil's."

"That's right, Sarge; that's caused by the manual work they do, whereas the skin on Neil's hands is not at all rough."

"I'm confused now, Gary," said Tinny, scratching his head; "are you saying that the skin on Neil's knuckles is tough, but the skin on the palm of his hand isn't?"

"Exactly."

"So how would that come about?"

"By doing press ups on your knuckles, it serves a number of purposes, but there are two main ones: firstly, it hardens the skin, so that you're less likely to cut them; secondly, it strengthens the wrists, so that you're less likely to break your wrist when delivering a blow."

Tinny was intrigued. "You also said that the heel of his hand was rock hard; how would he achieve that?"

Gary smiled. "By constantly hitting a hard surface, usually wood, with the palm of your hand; until, eventually, it stops hurting."

"I see," said Tinny. "I take it, then, that you wouldn't fancy getting into the ring with him?"

"Well, I don't think I'd stand much chance against him in a boxing ring as it is; but I'd definitely *not* want to get into a bare knuckle fight with him."

"Basically, you're saying that you wouldn't like to cross him?"

"Only if I had my shotgun, Sarge," grinned Gary; "and if that jammed, I'd be in real trouble."

"You've got a shotgun?"

"Only because I carried on with the clay pigeon shooting, and I now enter competitions; I still wouldn't consider shooting a bird or a rabbit, or any other innocent creature, for that matter – although, in the last two years, I've had dealings with some people who I could blow away quite happily."

Tinny laughed. "I know exactly what you mean - but that's another comment you need to keep to yourself, otherwise you might get fast tracked straight into prison!"

"I'm exaggerating, Sarge," assured Gary; "I wouldn't really blow them *away,* naturally; I'd just maim them a little bit."

"That's all right then," smiled Tinny. "Incidentally - did you believe Paul when he said you were fitter than him?"

"Not for a second, Sarge," said Gary, firmly shaking his head; "however, it was nice of him to say it, and I did appreciate it."

"You did a good job there, getting them on our side," commented Tinny.

Gary was silent for a moment; then he said "I envy Michael and Paul."

Tinny looked at his colleague in surprise. "*Envy* them? In what way?"

Gary looked pensive. "To a degree, Sarge, it goes back to the story Jacko told us - about Paul knocking out the man who called his father stupid. I must admit that, at the time, I was slightly bewildered, but impressed; and now, seeing those two young men today, desperate to see the photographs of the people who may have attacked their father, it made me realise the difference between my life and theirs." He paused briefly, then continued. "Another thing that struck me today was that, when the boys came into the living room, Neil Hughes immediately flipped over the photos, so that they couldn't see them. It was clear to me that he didn't want his sons to get into any sort of trouble; and yet, by his own admission, as a result of the memory loss, he's really only just getting to know them. That level of love and affection is something of which I have no experience; I envy them for that."

Tinny looked at Gary with a degree of sadness; and yet, he could see that Gary was not remotely self-pitying – on the contrary, he gave the impression of being quite cheerful, as he articulated his thoughts.

"Well," said Tinny, "I'm pretty sure that Neil Hughes didn't recognise any of those faces in the photos - which leads me to believe that, either he still has no memory of the attack, or none of those people were involved. There is something, however, that I'm very annoyed about."

"I know what you're going to say, and I agree," said Gary. "That business over the taxi plate is an absolute disgrace; there's obviously some jobsworth in the council offices, who's taken it upon themselves to stick to the rules way too rigidly."

"Not to worry; I'll speak to Jacko first, but I've got a mate who's got something to do with issuing plates and badges, and I'll see if there's anything he can do."

………………………………………………………………

As they were driving along, Tinny seemed to be deep in thought.

"Just pull over here; I've got a few questions for you."

"Okay, Sarge," said Gary, as he brought the car to a halt. "What do you want to know?"

Tinny paused for a moment. "Tell me - what did you think of Neil Hughes?"

"Well," replied his companion, "he wasn't what I was expecting, Sarge. I know everyone we've spoken to have all said what a nice, polite, and well-mannered man he is; however, after seeing the way he dealt with Carl McCabe, and listening to the story Matty Grant told us, I was expecting someone louder and more aggressive." Tinny nodded, as Gary continued. "What struck me, was how quietly spoken he is; and I concluded that, not only was he a gentleman, but also a gentle man, if you catch my drift - which completely contradicts what we know him to be capable of."

"I know exactly what you mean," agreed Tinny. "I've discovered over the years that the truly tough men don't bully people, don't throw their weight around, and generally avoid trouble, if they possibly can." He smiled. "The best example of that is my mate Jacko. When we played rugby together, as you can imagine, we would come up against some very aggressive types and, naturally, they were big lads; time and time again, the biggest bully in the opposing team would try and goad Jacko into fighting, but he would simply walk away. It was only when he was put in a position where he had no choice that he would deal with them – and, needless to say, not only would the bully get their just desserts, but so would any of their teammates who were foolish enough to get involved."

"Yes," said Gary, "I would say that Neil Hughes was that type of man. It also seemed to me that he had an inner strength, as well as his obvious physical attributes; a self-confidence, without being arrogant. I can't put my finger on it, exactly, but he reminded me of someone - not in looks, but in the way he conducted himself."

"I think I know who." Tinny was impressed at the astuteness of his younger colleague.

"I know that he and Billy Ray Cooder have completely different pasts," continued Gary, "and yet I felt that there were similarities between them. I did a lot of research on Billy Ray, before we went to interview him; apparently, in his prime, he could fight anyone. There were many examples of that, but there was one in particular that caught my eye, which happened when he was still a young man in his twenties. It appears that he took on six men outside a nightclub in Liverpool and, according to the reports at the time, he laid all six of them out, and walked away from it without a scratch – which is more than could be said for his opponents."

"Yes, it's funny - as soon as Neil Hughes entered the room and started speaking to us, I could also see the resemblance to Billy Ray." Tinny paused reflectively. "You know, I like to think I'm a good policeman, and a good detective; I'm not great at either, and have never professed to be. I do believe, however, that to be a good detective, you need to have an instinct for certain things. That instinct - some people may call it a gut feeling - can't be taught; you've either got it, or you haven't."

Gary nodded; for his part, he had discovered, from speaking to a number of people, that his Sergeant had the respect of everyone he had ever worked with, and that Tinny Smith's instinct was so often correct.

"To sum up, then," continued Tinny, "since we've been involved in this case, we've met some, potentially, very dangerous men, both good and bad guys. Jacko, some of the other taxi drivers, Neil Hughes and his sons - they all fall into the good guy category; Matty and Degsy, in certain circumstances, have been known to be quite dangerous; while Carl McCabe, his associates and, of course, Steve Jones and his crew, who we saw last night, are all in the bad guy category. As for Billy Ray Cooder, he was definitely in the latter category twenty-five years ago; now, I'm not so sure – however, he still has the capacity to be a very dangerous man. Would you agree with all of that?"

"Indeed I would," said Gary.

"Alright then," said Tinny; "there's no right or wrong answer to my next question, so take your time with it."

Gary nodded; he was fairly certain as to the nature of the question, and already knew what his answer would be.

"Of all the people I've just mentioned," said Tinny, "who do you feel is, probably, the most dangerous?"

"Michael Hughes," replied Gary, without hesitation.

A smile of satisfaction crept over Tinny's face, and he nodded; then, he seemed to come to a decision.

"Very well - if I remember correctly, we had a deal, and you've now fulfilled your part," he announced. "So, it's my turn – to tell you how I got the nickname Tinny. Now, I must forewarn you, it's not a particularly exciting story; in fact, it's rather dull - but a deal is a deal."

Gary did not mind if it turned out to be the dullest story he had ever heard; the very fact that Tinny was prepared to tell him was better than any compliment anyone could have paid him.

"When I joined the police," began Tinny, "I wasn't married then, and still lived at home with my mum and dad. Now, in those days, all the police stations had their own canteens which were subsidised - but, due to a slight oversight on my part, I failed to mention this to my mum. I think it's fair to say it would be unlikely for you to see me nibbling on a piece of lettuce and a water biscuit. I rather like my food; so, my mum used to do a carry out for me – I assume you know what a carry out is?"

Gary grinned at the picture that came into his mind of Tinny, nibbling on a water biscuit. "Like a packed lunch, Sarge."

"Exactly; but this was a carry out to end all carry outs. There'd be, at least, two pork pies, two sausage rolls, loads of sandwiches, and a good few biscuits as well. The trouble was, she couldn't find a container big enough, so she used a big biscuit tin; at the start of each shift, I would appear with this huge biscuit tin under my arm, and therefore got the nickname Tinny. At first, of course, it annoyed me, thinking that I was being laughed at, and made fun of; but I soon realised that being given a nickname meant that I'd been accepted as part of the team." Tinny grinned mischievously at his younger colleague. "Anyway, I like to think that when they put a major incident team together, it's not at its strongest unless 'Tinny' Smith is there."

With all that he now knew of his Sergeant, Gary was certain of it.

"So, you see, being given the nickname Morse doesn't necessarily mean people are mocking *you*," pointed out Tinny. "If you cast your mind back, when you made the suggestion concerning the CCTV coverage, Fred Davies used the nickname as a compliment. Just remember that, regardless of what rank you eventually achieve, the important thing is the respect that you earn – so that, when an M.I.T. is put together in the future, your colleagues will feel that it's not at its strongest unless 'Morse' is on the team."

"I'll do my best, I can promise that," said Gary "I'm a great believer that if you're going to do anything, you should do it to the best of your abilities."

"I agree totally," said Tinny. "Right, let's head back to the nick, and see how they're getting on with Steve Jones and those other low-lives. I know they were all giving each other an alibi when they were being interviewed last night but, hopefully, one of them will crack."

Gary started the car, and they continued their journey to the headquarters.

"By the way, Sarge," said Gary, as they were travelling along, "on the subject of my being fast tracked to prison – well, I've got something to tell you; as we were knocking off last night, I went to see the Chief Super, and asked to be taken off the fast track program."

Tinny looked at him in surprise. "What possessed you to do that?"

"Ambition, believe it or not," said Gary. "My ambition has always been to be a police detective and, eventually, I'd very much like to be a senior police detective; however, I'd have to feel that I was being promoted on merit and ability, not because I was part of a scheme. If I get no further from this point, then that will mean I don't deserve to."

Tinny pondered this for a moment. "Well, I admire you for making that decision; I only hope that it doesn't backfire in any way. What was the Chief Super's reaction when you told him?"

"Oddly enough, he seemed to be pleased; although I'm not entirely sure whether it was because he thought I wasn't much good anyway, or because he believed that I could get to the top on merit."

"I wouldn't worry," assured Tinny. "Chief Superintendent Turnbull can sometimes be a bit of a pompous man; but, make no mistake, he's a good policeman himself, and knows a good policeman when he sees one. I suspect that, like me, he feels you have the makings of a top detective."

"Thanks for that, Sarge," smiled Gary; "mind you, one thing is for sure - I have no intention of marrying an ugly woman to further *my* career."

"Very wise!" said Tinny, chuckling.

"Talking of which," continued Gary, "I can see what Mark meant about Mrs Hughes. As well as being very attractive, she was a nice woman."

Tinny nodded. "Yes, Jacko had told me how pretty she was, and he was absolutely right. I take it Mark had made a similar comment?"

"It was that night when I was knocking off, and Mark and Jill were just starting their shift; I was talking to them, and they were explaining everything that they'd been told, by Mrs Hughes, about her husband. Mark made much of how pretty she was, how attractive she was, and even began one sentence with 'that beautiful woman said......', and so forth. Jill and I looked at each other, and smiled; he had, clearly, taken a real shine to Caroline Hughes."

"I see - that explains something to me now," remarked Tinny. "That day when we arrested Matty and Degsy, Mark cracked Matty as he was tackling him; I was surprised because, although Mark is a tough lad, I've never known him to be in any way vindictive. However, as we know, Matty was a prime suspect at that point – so, from what you say, that explains Mark's behaviour."

"Do me a favour, Sarge? Don't tell Mark what I've told you, as it would only embarrass him, and I like the fella; besides which, Mark Walker is certainly not a man with whom you would want to fall out."

Tinny grinned. "Well then, it looks like we've got a new agreement; as long as no biscuit tins appear anywhere near my desk, I won't grass you up to Mark. Deal?"

Gary laughed. "That's a *definite* deal, Sarge!"

Chapter 12

Tinny and Gary got back to the headquarters and walked into the briefing room, to find D.C.I. Davies looking very gloomy.

"No luck with Steve Jones and his cronies, boss?" asked Tinny.

Fred Davies wearily shook his head. "It's not looking good, Ron. Either these fellas are telling the truth, or they've planned the whole thing very cleverly - and are sticking, rigidly, to their story."

"When you say 'planned the whole thing', do you mean that they couldn't have attacked him themselves?"

"The four of them were definitely at Steve Jones's house on the night in question," elaborated Davies. "Apparently, every Tuesday night since Jones came out of prison, they all get together for a game of cards and a drink. We've checked CCTV footage, spoken to the taxi companies that they used, and made various other enquiries; the upshot is that they couldn't possibly have been in the area where Neil Hughes was attacked at the time in question, given that it's at least an hour's drive from the industrial estate to Jones's house."

"I see," said Tinny; "but do you think it's possible that Jones was behind the attack in some way, and has made sure he had the perfect alibi?"

"I think there's a very good possibility of that; unfortunately, however, if that's the case, I don't know where we go from here."

"So it's a similar position to Carl McCabe," pondered Tinny; "they both had motive, but unless we can find out who they used, we're stumped."

"That's exactly the situation, Tinny," sighed Davies. "I don't suppose you had any luck with the mugshots you showed to Neil Hughes?"

"I think I can safely say that he didn't recognise any of the people I showed him."

"Great." Fred Davies turned to Gary. "Any bright ideas, Gary? Because we are really struggling now."

Gary's own line of enquiry was looking very promising, but there was one more piece of the jigsaw to put into place. He could see the disappointment in the faces of these two men, for whom he had a great deal of respect, but he decided that he needed to complete his enquiries, before telling them anything at all; therefore, he simply shrugged his shoulders, and shook his head.

....

After Michael and Paul had left, but before Caroline went out, Neil was in the training room, ruminating over his best course of action regarding Callum Flynn.

He had arranged no specific time to meet, but got the impression that Callum would be in the Brown Horse from mid to late afternoon; he therefore decided to get to the pub slightly earlier, in the hope that some of the other travellers would be there, from whom he might be able to obtain extra information about the Flynns. After the conversation he had had with them yesterday, he now felt able to ask them a great deal more, without drawing attention to himself.

Neil smiled as he watched Caroline, almost skipping down the path to her car; she stopped, turned, and gave Neil a huge smile as she waved goodbye. As she drove away, the sight of her happiness strengthened Neil's resolve; he must track down the Flynns, find out why they attacked him, and then decide what, if anything, he was going to do about it.

....

Neil arrived at the Brown Horse by early afternoon, parked in the car park, and then walked round the outside of the pub, looking for Callum's van; however, he saw no sign of it. He walked into the bar, to find it was almost empty; then, as he approached the bar, he heard a voice from the corner of the room. He turned, and saw Paddy, sitting on his own.

"What are you having?" shouted Neil to him, using his traveller accent.

"I'm on the cider today," was the reply from Paddy.

Neil nodded. "I think I'll try a drop of that myself."

Neil duly ordered two pints of cider, hoping that he would be able to handle drinking this today, as successfully as he had managed the bitter yesterday; he took the drinks, and went over to the corner table.

"Good health, Paddy," he said, sitting down.

Paddy smiled. "Cheers, Declan, and good health to yourself."

Even before Neil had time to ask anything, Paddy took a draught of his pint, and leaned over the table confidentially.

"I didn't get chance to tell you yesterday," he said, "but I'd steer well clear of Callum Flynn and his family, if I were you. Not just for the fact that they'd stab you in the back as soon as look at you, but because for the last few weeks, there've been a group of very dangerous men trying to track them down."

Neil took a mouthful of his cider, and was pleasantly surprised to find that he liked the taste of this as well. "Dangerous in what way, Paddy?"

"From what I've been told, there've been two separate groups of armed men visiting sites looking for the Flynns. It's fair to say the Flynns have definitely fallen out with the wrong people, not for the first time - but from what I've heard, this could be their last time."

"When you say armed, what sort of weapons do you mean?"

"Sawn off shotguns - and from all accounts, these people, whoever they are, are more than willing to use them."

"You say 'whoever they are' - does anybody know what this is all about?"

"The word is there are about ten of them, probably from Manchester, because the main man who's been doing all the talking has a Manchester accent."

"You said there were two separate groups?"

"There's been talk of another crew, tooled up with guns, but those fellas are Scousers. You know yourself, Declan, in normal circumstances, if people come onto a site looking for trouble, they'll soon find it. But there's no-one I know of who'd be willing to get themselves shot for the sake of the Flynn family."

Neil thought for a moment. "Does anyone know where the Flynns are now?"

Paddy smiled. "There's two things you can be sure of - they certainly won't be on an official site, and any site they do move on to, it won't be long before they're on their own. Not because of the present problem, it's just that that's always been the case with the Flynns. They move onto a site, and within days, everyone moves off." Paddy's expression became serious. "I can't stress enough to you Declan, these people are evil, and cause nothing but trouble wherever they go."

"So, as far as you know, this isn't the first time the Flynns have crossed the wrong people?"

"If it's not ten years ago, then it's not far short of that, a gang of Manchester men came looking for Kieran, but I don't know if it's the same people now. One thing I can say, it's not just the guns that make them dangerous. You must know big Michael Dougherty?"

This question put Neil in an awkward situation. If he said that he did not know the man, Paddy might doubt that Declan was a true traveller; on the other hand, if Neil said that he did know him, Paddy could ask him something which he would be unable to answer. Finally, he simply nodded, and replied "I know of him."

"Then you'll know what a tough man he is. Something you probably don't know is that big Michael came the nearest to beating Patrick Flynn in a fight, and that was before Patrick's heart attack."

Neil raised his eyebrows, and smiled. "From what you've told me, I'm surprised the man has a heart."

"That was the joke that went round the whole community at the time," affirmed Paddy, "but even though he had a serious heart attack, it's not stopped Patrick Flynn starting trouble with anyone, as he just makes sure he's got his brother and sons backing him up."

"So big Michael almost beat him?"

"The fight went on for over twenty minutes, but eventually, Patrick got the upper hand. When big Michael was on the ground, Patrick tried to do his usual trick and stamp on him, but was stopped by big Mike's family. The rest of the Flynns then got involved and it was a mass brawl.

Did you notice, yesterday, the hammer in Callum's pocket?"

"I did."

"In most people's hands, you'd describe that as a tool, but in Callum's hand, you'd describe it as a weapon. That particular hammer has hit a lot more than nails."

"When I was at the petrol station, I thought he was about to use it then, but when I hit the big man and knocked him down, the other three didn't seem too keen to take us on."

Paddy nodded. "Declan, I know this wasn't your intention, but you probably saved those four young men from a great deal of damage. There's no doubt in my mind that Callum would have fought them, beat them, and then done as much harm to them as he possibly could."

"I didn't know that, I was just standing by a fellow traveller," said Neil, shrugging.

Paddy immediately raised his hands. "Don't misunderstand me, Declan, we all thought you did the right thing. You didn't know anything about Callum Flynn or his family because if you had, you would've driven straight past."

"What made you ask me about the hammer, Paddy?"

"That day when the Flynns fought with the Doughertys, Callum took one man's eye out, and another had his cheekbone shattered."

"So Callum is the toughest of the four?"

"No," replied Paddy, shaking his head, his expression grim. "He's the weakest of the four, that's why he carries a weapon - the other three don't need weapons."

"You said yesterday that Kieran had disappeared - is he still missing?"

Paddy nodded. "He's not been seen for over a month now, and we're wondering if these men with the shotguns have already got to him, and are looking for the rest of the family."

"When you were talking about the men with the guns," said Neil, "how come you asked me if I knew Mike Dougherty?"

"Well, when these Manchester fellas walked onto the site where big Mike and his family were, Michael made it clear he wasn't frightened of them. He even said to the man, who everyone said seemed to be in charge, that if he wasn't holding a gun, Michael would soon show him who the tough man was." Paddy paused, as if for effect. "Bearing in mind it took Patrick Flynn over twenty minutes to beat big Michael, this man handed his gun to one of the other men, and put big Michael down with one blow. The man then stepped back to allow big Mike to get up again, before putting him down a second time. In less than a minute, big Michael Dougherty was out cold on the ground, after the third blow. The Manchester man then said to everyone on the site that he had no fight with them, he was just looking for the Flynns."

Neil thought for a moment. "So, from everything you've told me about this family, then maybe they're going to get what they deserve - I just hope that there are no innocent people caught in the crossfire."

Paddy nodded emphatically. "Declan, that's my concern too - that's why I said you'd be better staying well clear of them."

"I appreciate your concern, Paddy," smiled Neil, "but I'm not bad at standing up for myself."

"Declan, I've no doubt about that," laughed Paddy. "After you left yesterday, we all said that if ever we were in any trouble, we'd very much like you to come round the corner."

"Well, if I were to, you can take my word that I would certainly stand by you and your friends against anyone."

"I don't doubt it, Declan, I don't doubt it. Now, would it be a pint of cider?"

Neil smiled, and tried to look guilty. "I'm on these tablets and I'm not supposed to drink, but one more won't do any harm. The trouble is, I keep having to go to the gents, so I'll be back in a minute."

While he was in the toilets, Neil considered everything he had just heard. If it was all true - and he could think of no reason why Paddy should lie - he now wondered whether it would be wiser to abandon any attempt to find the Flynns, and simply leave it to the Manchester men, or the other crew from Liverpool, to deal with his attackers. Admittedly, he would never find out why he was targeted; but, in the circumstances, and from what he had learned about the Flynns, he would stand no chance against all three of them anyway – and time was against his being able to deal with them individually.

....

As Neil rejoined Paddy in the bar, they could both hear raised voices, coming from the back door of the pub; one of the bar staff came over to their table, looking agitated.

"Paddy, Callum Flynn's outside, drunk, and is looking for trouble because the landlord won't let him in."

Paddy looked up, and shrugged. "Well I certainly wouldn't be able to stop him, ring the police, and get them to sort it out."

Neil swore inwardly; the last thing he wanted, now, was any police involvement. He had been scrupulously careful to ensure that Neil Hughes could not be connected to the Brown Horse pub, or to the travelling community; depending on what Neil decided to do regarding the Flynns, it could certainly involve the police - but if so, they would have some difficulty tracking down 'Declan.' There was only one thing to do.

Neil stood up, and spoke to the barman. "I'll deal with it, don't ring the police."

"Declan, be careful," warned Paddy, "he's a nasty piece of work sober - when he's drunk, he's far worse."

As Neil walked towards the back door of the pub, both Paddy and the barman followed, keeping a safe distance behind him. Neil could see Callum standing in the pub car park, swaying slightly from side to side, and holding the hammer in his hand; the landlord was positioned in the doorway, holding an iron bar. Neil nodded to him.

"I'll speak to Callum and take him home, and I don't want the police to be called - is that clear?"

The landlord was about to say something; then he hesitated, when he saw Paddy quickly shake his head. "Declan will deal with this, one way or another," asserted Paddy, sharply.

The landlord nodded his agreement, and then stood back to allow Neil to go out into the car park; as the other three men looked on from the safety of the pub, Neil walked up to Callum.

"Callum," he said, smiling, "put the hammer away, you're just going to get yourself into trouble."

Callum was, clearly, extremely drunk. "That man is stopping me having a drink with you, Declan," he said, slurring his speech, and using the hammer to point in the direction of the landlord.

Neil continued to smile. "Callum, we can have a drink another time - we both need to get away from here, before the police turn up."

The younger man, swaying where he stood, looked somewhat confused. "But you haven't done anything wrong, Declan."

Neil laughed. "Callum, I have in the past, and if the police recognise me, it could be a very long time before you and I could have a drink together - so put your hammer away, and let's get you home."

Callum, in his drunken state, looked unsure as to what his next move should be; Neil therefore decided to be more direct.

"The hammer," he said, his tone measured, but firm; "I'll not tell you a third time."

This had the desired effect; Callum lowered his gaze, almost like a naughty boy who had just been disciplined by an adult. He put the hammer back into his pocket, and continued to hang his head. Neil then walked over to him, and put his arm around his shoulder.

"Good man, let's get you home."

Callum staggered towards his van, feebly searching his pockets. "I don't know what I've done with my keys," he muttered, "they must have fallen out of my pocket."

As they reached the van, however, Neil noticed that the keys were still in the ignition. "Your keys are here, but you're certainly not driving the van in that state," he informed Callum. "We'll lock it up, leave it here, I'll get you home now, and in the morning I'll bring you back over to collect your van."

Neil then turned in the direction of the landlord, who was still standing in the doorway, holding the iron bar. "Have I got your word that Callum's van will be safe here till the morning?" he called to him.

The landlord nodded. "Absolutely, Declan," he called back.

Neil guided Callum over to his own car, held open the passenger door, and installed him safely inside; at that point, the landlord walked over to Neil.

"Thanks for that, Declan, I think we all owe you a drink," he began, smiling; then his smile vanished as Neil fixed him with a menacing look.

"I'll tell you what you owe me: this didn't happen, I've never been here, and you've never heard of anyone called Declan. Make sure the barman and Paddy understand the situation. Have I made myself clear?"

The landlord, visibly taken aback, nodded his head mutely. He stepped back and watched, as Neil got into the car and drove away; then, slowly, he walked back to the pub to rejoin the others.

………………………………………………………

"He's a bit of a man of mystery, your friend Declan," noted the barman, laughing uncomfortably, after the landlord had repeated what Neil had said to him. "What do you know about him, Paddy?"

"Absolutely nothing, which suits me fine," declared Paddy, which prompted all three to laugh.

"Well," said the landlord, "I just hope Callum doesn't turn nasty on Declan."

"I hope he does."

The other two men looked at Paddy in surprise. "But I thought Declan was your friend?" remarked the barman.

"He is. But if Callum were stupid enough to turn on Declan, I don't think we'd be seeing Callum Flynn again - and that would suit me fine as well."

…………………………………...

"Just direct me from here," said Neil to his passenger, as he drove out of the car park, "and then in the morning I'll pick you up, and bring you back to get your van. We can have a drink tomorrow, but maybe somewhere other than the Brown Horse."

"We've got a bit of business on tomorrow night so I'd better stay out of the pub tomorrow," mumbled Callum; his speech was still slurred, and Neil was having to listen intently, to pick up what he was saying.

"It must be serious business if you need to stay sober for it."

Callum snorted derisively. "More like unfinished business that needs to be sorted out."

"Unfinished in what way?"

Callum appeared to be thinking, as if clearing his head before he said anything else; then he seemed to come to a decision.

"I know I can trust you, Declan, you've proved yourself to be my friend, and I haven't had many of those over the years. What I'm about to tell you is between you and me, but I think you're a man like myself, and so won't be shocked in any way."

"Anything you tell me is definitely between you and me and no-one else's business. After the things I've done in my life, nothing shocks me."

"Just as well." An unpleasant smile spread over Callum's face. "As soon as we get the address, we are paying a visit to someone. We left for him dead, but he didn't die, and so we are going to finish the job."

As he heard these words, Neil almost felt the blood freeze in his veins. He knew he had to stop the car, on any pretext, to give himself time to decide what he was going to do now.

"I'm just pulling over here for a minute, Callum," he said, with a calmness he did not feel, "I think one of my back tyres must be a bit low. I won't be a minute so don't fall asleep, otherwise I'll never get you home."

Callum clapped Neil on the shoulder. "You're a good man, Declan, and a good friend."

Neil got out and walked round to the back of the car; he crouched down, let some air out of the tyre, and then said "It's a bit low but I've got a foot pump here, so this won't take too long." His mind was racing. The chances of the Flynn family leaving someone for dead, and it not being himself, were pretty slim; he must find out as much as he could from Callum, and stop them, by any means. This was no longer about revenge – it was about survival.

He finished re-inflating the tyre, got back into the car, and set off again; as they were driving along, trying to make his voice sound casual, he asked "Do you need any help with the task? I'll gladly stand by you again."

Callum shook his head. "I appreciate the offer, but this is something we have to do ourselves."

Neil nodded. "But you said you don't have the address yet, how are you going to come by that?"

"At some point tomorrow night we should get a call with all the information we need. There are a lot of people who we've done jobs for in the past, who in turn have some good connections, if you know what I mean." Callum said this smugly, apparently in the hope that it would impress Neil.

"Having good connections is never a bad thing," agreed Neil. "How many people are you expecting to be going against?"

"There's only the one man and I don't know how he survived last time, we should've finished the job there and then."

"My only concern, Callum," said Neil evenly, "is that if you're going to his house, he may have a big family, who could make things difficult for you."

"From what we've been told, he has a wife and two sons, but the sons don't live there, so that won't be a problem."

"And what about the wife, from a witness point of view?" Neil almost held his breath.

Callum laughed mirthlessly. "I think they call it collateral damage, there'll be nobody coming out of that house alive, by the time we've finished."

It took Neil every ounce of his self-control not to stop the car, drag this man out, and strangle the life out of him, there and then; however, as he needed to know where to find Patrick and Sean Flynn, somehow, he managed to stay calm - but he was already formulating in his mind what he was going to do. He could see that Callum was now starting to sober up slightly, so decided not ask any more questions.

As Neil was driving along a narrow country lane, Callum pointed. "If you slow down here, Declan, you'll see a gap in the trees where you need to turn in."

Neil did as instructed, and was surprised to find four caravans on a piece of waste ground, hidden from the road by the trees surrounding it; there were three parked quite close to each other at one end of the waste ground, and one standing alone at the other end.

Neil smiled. "Which one is yours, Callum?"

It came as no surprise to Neil when Callum pointed to the solitary caravan and, as they drove nearer to it, Neil could see two men standing outside. He observed both of them reach under the caravan and, at first, he could not see what they were holding. Only when he stepped out of the car could he see that one of the men, whom he recognised from Paddy's description as being Patrick, was holding a pickaxe handle; the other man, whom he guessed must be Sean, was holding a baseball bat.

Neil walked round to the passenger side of the car, opened the door, and helped Callum to his feet; Patrick approached, the pickaxe handle still in his hand.

"And who might you be?"

Callum, who was still swaying somewhat and slurring his speech, answered for Neil. "This is Declan, the man I told you about from the petrol station."

It was immediately apparent to Neil exactly what Paddy had meant, when he had described Patrick Flynn; even without the memory of his previous life, he found it difficult to believe he could ever have encountered a more evil looking man. Patrick's eyes seemed almost black, and he appeared to have a fixed expression of hatred in them. The way in which this man was now regarding him made Neil wonder whether he knew who Declan really was; however, when he observed the cruel gaze that Patrick turned on Callum and Sean, it was clear that the look of hatred in his eyes was permanent.

Patrick glared at Callum with contempt. "Get inside, I'll deal with you later," he snapped; he then turned his cold eyes back to Neil. "No doubt this drunk has been shooting his mouth off."

Neil could see the fear in Callum's face as Patrick said this. "He's not been shooting his mouth off to me," replied Neil, shrugging, "I was lucky to keep him awake to get the directions from him. The van is in the Brown Horse car park, he wasn't fit to drive it - I'll take him in the morning to collect it."

He then threw the keys to Sean, nodded, and started to walk towards his car; as Sean caught the bunch of keys, he called out "Declan, we didn't catch your second name!"

Neil, as he turned round to face him, suspected that the look of hatred in his own eyes was as profound as that in the eyes of Patrick Flynn.

"That's right - you didn't."

Without another word, he got into his car, and drove away. He had decided what he was going to do. Taking the Flynns individually on neutral ground, as he had hoped to do, was now impossible. He needed to speak to Jacko before he got home; he therefore telephoned him, arranging to meet at the taxi rank.

....

As Neil pulled up by the rank, Jacko saw him, walked over, and leaned over to speak to him through the car window.

"What's up?"

"Have a sit in the car, Jacko. I'm going to ask you to do something for me, but I'm not going to tell you why."

Jacko was about to make a joke, but he could see by the expression on Neil's face that this was not the time; so he simply nodded, and got into the car. "Tell us what you need me to do."

"About teatime tomorrow, I need you and a few of the lads round at our house."

"No problem, which lads do you want there?"

"I'm going on instinct here, of course, because I don't know them well; but I want Big Griff, Colin Holmes, and the Mackie brothers. Michael and Paul will also be there."

Jacko raised his eyebrows, but said nothing; relenting, Neil felt that he should, at least, give him some sort of explanation.

"It's possible there could be two or three unwelcome visitors tomorrow night, and I may not be there to deal with them."

"Who are you expecting, the S.A.S?" said Jacko, curiously. "Because, even if it was, they'd still come off second best to the crew that'll be in your house."

"That's basically the idea. I'll give you a call if I don't need them, but if you hear nothing from me, I'd appreciate you being there."

"I'll bring our kid along as well." Neil looked at him questioningly; "I mean our John, my brother," explained Jacko.

"Do I know your brother?"

"You do, but you haven't seen him since coming out of hospital. He's a farmer and used to come round to your house, with me, pretty regularly. Our John is a handy man to have alongside you if there's a bit of trouble. He's not as tough as me when it comes to a stand up fight, but is far more dangerous than me when it comes to dealing with people he doesn't like."

"In that case, he sounds like the sort of man I need. Basically, you're there to protect Caz."

"Then I can guarantee, he'll be there like a shot."

"All being well," continued Neil, "you'll get a call off me tomorrow to say everything's okay. If you don't, and if someone does turn up at our house, kill them."

The blank expression on Neil's face told Jacko that he was completely serious; he therefore nodded, and shook Neil's hand.

"You can bank on it."

....

Neil drove away from the taxi rank, and headed towards home; on the way, he decided to pull over, and run through the sequence of events for tomorrow.

Firstly, he intended to make sure that Caroline would leave the house before he did, and to stress to her not to get home too early; he had an idea how he could achieve that. Then, as soon as she was safely away from the house, he would get the baseball bat from the shed, make his way to the site and, hopefully, catch the Flynns by surprise - they would not be expecting an attack from Declan. On confronting them, he intended to let them know exactly who he was, in order to prevent them going to his house that night; however, he knew that he could not eliminate that risk altogether – so he was satisfied, at least, that the presence of Jacko and the lads at his house should keep Caroline safe.

Paddy and the other travellers had emphasised to him how fearsome was the reputation of the Flynn family. As individuals, it seems that they had never lost a fight and, collectively, they had never lost a battle; but Neil simply smiled to himself. They would now be fighting Neil Hughes - not sneaking up behind like cowards, but having to stand face to face with him. Neil was not frightened, as he knew that the only way they could stop him was to kill him; and, as they had tried that once and failed, they would fail again tomorrow. Even though he was one man against three and, therefore, the odds were against him, that was not the point - the Flynns would only be fighting for their own lives, but Neil would be fighting for Caroline's.

And after that? Should he survive the confrontation, he wanted answers. Why was he attacked? If the Flynns had been hired by someone else to kill him, who was that person? From whom were the Flynns going to obtain his address? The answer to the second question could be the same as the third.

As Neil arrived home, he was relieved to find that the house was empty; he had been dreading having to appear normal and cheerful as soon as he came in, and show no sign of anything being wrong, but Caroline's absence gave him some time to prepare himself. He felt that he had, at least, come to terms in his own mind with what needed to be done – so, when Caroline came home, he was reasonably satisfied that she would have no idea that tomorrow would be any different from any other day; and, hopefully, it would not.

He took the opportunity to retrieve the baseball bat from the shed, put it in the boot of the car, and then strolled back into the kitchen; he put the kettle on, and stood, motionless, staring out of the window.

He thought about the various situations he had faced since he left the hospital, and had been surprised at the extent of his own self-control; there was a calmness about him now, which he could not explain. He knew what he had to do, and was not afraid; in fact, he was almost looking forward to going against the Flynns.

....

"So, it's back to square one again," summed up D.C.I. Davies, to everyone in the briefing room; "I don't know where we go from here."

Just then, Tinny walked into the room, and caught the D.C.I.'s remark. "I don't like to kick a man while he's down, but I've got more bad news, boss," he said apologetically.

Davies smiled wearily. "Can there be any more bad news?"

"I've just had it, on good authority, that Steve Jones isn't in any way connected to the attack on Neil Hughes."

"Oh?" Fred Davies raised his eyebrows. "What 'good authority'?"

"Billy Ray Cooder. He just rang me, to say that Jones wasn't behind the attack; apparently, about three months after he was sent down, Jones found out who actually tipped off the drugs squad."

"Did Billy Ray know who it was?" asked Gary.

"A rival drug dealer who, effectively, took over all the business that Steve Jones ran previously. Anyway, I rang Jimmy James, and gave him the name I had been given by Billy Ray, to see what he knew; Jimmy told me that he'd always suspected the rival drug dealer to be the informant, because he was the one who had most to gain from Steve Jones going to prison."

"So, if Steve Jones is looking for revenge, it will be aimed at the rival drug dealer," said the D.C.I. speculatively; but Tinny shook his head.

"Doubtful, boss; shortly after Jones found out who it was who helped to put him away, the informant disappeared, and has never been seen since. Billy reckons that he's now part of the foundations of that massive office block, built in town a few years ago."

Dave raised his hand. "Isn't it possible, boss, that Steve Jones *is* behind the attack; that it was Billy Ray Cooder, plus two or three associates, who actually carried out the assault on Neil Hughes; and that Cooder is simply trying to point us in the wrong direction?"

Gary shook his head. "Doesn't work, Dave. It was Billy Ray who told us that Steve Jones was the drug dealer who'd been to Neil Hughes's taxi office; the taxi drivers we interviewed didn't know the name of the man and, when we went to speak to Billy Ray, we asked him if he knew who the drug dealer was."

"Gary's right," confirmed Tinny. "When I asked Billy Ray that question, he could have simply said he didn't know – in which case, we would never have known that it was Steve Jones. I believe Billy Ray is telling the truth, and Jimmy James is absolutely certain of it."

Dave looked perplexed. "So why did Cooder take the trouble to give us this information?"

"Because he'd very much like us to catch the people who attacked Neil Hughes," smiled Tinny; "and, as far as he's concerned, he wouldn't like us to be wasting time and resources, investigating the wrong people, when the real culprits are still out there."

"Well, one further point," said the D.C.I.; "I take it we still have no idea of the whereabouts of Carl McCabe?"

Paula raised her hand to speak. "This, I think, is a mixture of rumour and speculation, boss; but the word is that he's fallen out with his uncles, and has certainly not been seen since that day he was followed to his uncle's club."

"I've heard the same," nodded Gary. "I was talking to Mark; and he was told that Carl McCabe won't be seen again."

D.C.I. Davies sighed, rubbing his forehead. "Okay then, that's it for today; fresh start tomorrow - let's keep our fingers crossed that something turns up."

…………………………………...

Just as the kettle was boiling, Neil heard Caroline come in.

"You timed that nicely," he said, putting his head around the door, "I'm just making a brew. Put your feet up, and I'll bring you a nice cup of tea."

As Neil walked into the living room with the tea tray, he fully expected to find Caroline sitting there with a huge smile on her face; he was not disappointed.

"Another successful day, I presume?" he ventured.

As Caroline recounted the marvellous day she had had, and spoke of her anticipation of an even better day tomorrow when she would see even more of her old customers, Neil was pleased with himself that he showed no sign of what was on his mind, and no hint that there was a problem; then, when he considered that she had covered the whole day's events, he said, offhandedly, "So, what are your plans for tomorrow?"

Caroline beamed. "Well, I'm out quite early, and will be busy until mid-morning; then I was going to pop home for a couple of hours; and then, I'm going to visit Alice."

"Here's an idea," said Neil brightly; "instead of coming home, you should go and have a swim, and see if you can remember where I've got the hidden stash."

Caroline chuckled. "I'm not sure if there ever *was* a hidden stash; and, even if there had been, if I knew where it was, there'd be nothing left of it anyway."

Neil laughed. "Good point! Mind you, something else occurs to me - if you've been eating another mountain of cakes and biscuits today, you might need the swimming to keep you in shape."

"Actually," said Caroline, sitting up, "you're right; all joking aside, I probably could do with the exercise. In fact, that's exactly what I'll do," she said decidedly, "so I'm not likely to be home before teatime."

"Tell you what, then," smiled Neil, "don't rush home from Alice's; if possible, I'll try and meet you there."

"That's a great idea! Alice will be really excited to see you, believe me," said Caroline, smiling broadly; "she'll probably talk the hind leg off you!"

"Well, in that case, I'll prepare myself by getting a good night's sleep," grinned Neil, getting up, and kissing her on the cheek; "I'll see you in the morning."

....

Neil lay on the bed, running through everything in his mind again and again, until he felt mentally prepared for what was going to happen on the following day. One thing was certain, at least: physically, he was more than prepared. If he was to lose his life, then he fully intended to take one or two of the Flynns with him – suffice it to say, he would give them the fight of their lives.

....

Neil was up very early the next day. He went out for a run, spent some time in the training room, then got into the shower; he closed his eyes and thought about the impending battle, as he let the water pour down over his face.

Caroline was in the kitchen as he was coming downstairs. "Any chance of a cup of tea?" he shouted to her.

"Might be," she called back, with gaiety in her voice.

She turned and smiled at him as he walked into the kitchen but, almost immediately, her smile faded. "Are you all right?"

"I'm fine," shrugged Neil; "don't I look all right?"

"Yes," she replied, doubtfully; "I don't know what it is, you just look sad."

"No, I'm not sad," he assured her. "I didn't sleep very well last night though, so maybe I'm still a bit tired."

To Caroline, however, his eyes held the same expression as they had on the night when he had been to the site of the hospital, where his father had died; it was a dull, bleak gaze, completely devoid of emotion. Since that night, bit by bit, she had thought that the old Neil was coming back to her, despite the fact that he still had no memory; but now, she looked at him, and was worried.

"I've got to go shortly, but I don't like leaving you like this," she said, concern in her voice.

"Honestly, I'm fine," he insisted. "All being well, I'll see you later at Alice's – but just in case I can't make it, don't tell her I might be coming, so she's not disappointed if I don't turn up."

Caroline frowned. "Are you *sure* you're okay?"

"Definitely," smiled Neil, "just a bit tired. I might go back to bed for a couple of hours, and I'll see you later."

Neil followed her to the front door and, as she turned to speak, he embraced her tightly; ordinarily, this would have delighted her, but now, she felt even more concerned.

"Don't worry," said Neil, as he held her; "I'll see you later."

Watching Caroline walking slowly towards her car, Neil was annoyed with himself for not disguising what he was feeling, as he had managed to do the night before. She turned to wave goodbye, and Neil fervently hoped that this would not be the last time he ever saw her; for her benefit, however, he smiled, and gave a thumbs up sign to her, before she got into the car.

....

Once Caroline had been gone for a reasonable time, and he was satisfied that there was no likelihood of her coming back because she had forgotten something, Neil got into his car and set off.

He reached the end of the lane and turned on to the main road. As he was driving along, he was focusing so intently on the coming confrontation with the Flynns, he was oblivious to the fact that the Porsche, reflected in his rear view mirror, had been following him since he left home.

....

Neil parked his car in a small layby, near to the site entrance. He got out, took the baseball bat out of the boot, and proceeded to walk along the outside of the trees enclosing the site, until he reached the area nearest to the Flynns' caravan; he concealed himself behind one of the trees, while he took a look at the scene.

Unexpectedly, Callum's van was already parked by the caravan; so, Patrick or Sean must have collected it the night before, or first thing that morning - but it made no difference to what was about to happen. Neil remembered what the other travellers had told him, as to the presence of the Flynns on a site frightening others away from it; he was not surprised, therefore, to note that there was only one of the three caravans, which had been there last night, now remaining at the other end of the waste ground. He had tried to think of a way of hiding the baseball bat, until he was near enough to the Flynns to use it; however, as he was so close now, it hardly mattered.

The man who was following Neil had stopped out of sight, when he saw Neil pull into the layby; as Neil was walking along the line of trees, his observer got out of the car, took a shotgun out of the boot, carefully loaded it, and put the remainder of the cartridges in his pocket. He then took up a position where, if he was needed, he could take immediate action.

....

As Neil cut through the trees, he could see the three Flynns sitting outside the caravan around a small table. He strode purposefully towards them.

The three men did not notice Neil until he was right on top of them; as soon as they saw him, they all stood up quickly.

"Declan!" greeted Callum, smiling. "I didn't need a lift after all, but I didn't know how to contact you." Then his expression changed. "What are you doing with the baseball bat?"

"It's not Declan, it's Neil," was the response, the pretence of the traveller accent abandoned. "I'm the taxi driver you were going to visit tonight. I thought I'd save you the trip."

The effect of his words was immediate. Callum grabbed the hammer from his pocket, Neil swiftly knocked it out of his hand with the baseball bat and, simultaneously, stepped to one side and kicked Sean in the chest, knocking him over the table; in those few seconds, a warning bell rang in Neil's head - everything he had been told about Patrick was that he stood and fought and yet, in his peripheral vision, Neil saw him running towards the caravan.

He raced after him to the door, and the double barrelled shotgun appeared, even before the man holding it; Neil's instinct told him that the other two men were, at the same time, closing in behind him. He swung hard with the bat and, as it made contact with the gun, both barrels were discharged; in an instant, three against one became two against one, as Sean dropped in his tracks. Neil was chilled to the bone to see on Patrick's face, not an expression of shock, but of disgust, as he looked down on his dead brother.

A second later, out of the corner of his eye, Neil saw Callum raising the pickaxe handle, so he swung the baseball bat with all his strength. Both men made contact with each other at exactly the same time - one dropped down, almost certainly dead; the other was still standing. Two against one had now become one against one.

Patrick was now holding the gun by its barrel and swung it at Neil, but Neil was too quick for him - he caught the gun in mid-air, and wrenched it out of Patrick's hands. He then threw the gun away, and smiled at Patrick Flynn; the glare that Patrick returned was filled with hatred.

"I knew you'd come for me one day, but you won't take me to hell without a fight. Only the Devil could take a blow like that and survive."

Neil continued to smile. "I'm not the Devil, I'm Neil Hughes - the man you stamped on, kicked, beat with weapons, strapped into the taxi, and left to burn to death. So I want to know why - and I may even let you live."

"You're not Neil Hughes, because he'd know why we wanted him dead - but whoever you are, I'll see you in hell!" spat out Patrick, viciously.

He charged at Neil almost like a bull, but Neil quickly sidestepped and tripped him, sending him sprawling, face first, onto the gravel; but Flynn was immediately back on his feet, blood pouring from the wounds on his face.

"So, I've been told you call yourself a hard man, and yet you killed your wife in front of your two sons." Neil's voice was filled with contempt.

"That whore deserved to die, and that drunk was never my son!" shouted Patrick, spitting out blood. "That's his father there, who I should've shot years ago! If you were Neil Hughes, then you'd know what happened to Kieran, my only true son!"

During the whole of this confrontation, Neil was astounded by the fact that he had remained so controlled, and did what he had to do without anger; Patrick, on the other hand, was filled with hate - Neil suspected that, if he encouraged that rage, he may discover the truth from this evil man.

Neil laughed at him. "The King of the gypsies?" he taunted. "Are you sure that's not the Queen?"

"You're a brave man with a weapon in your hand!"

Neil dropped the baseball bat. "Alright, now's your chance - let's see how good you are."

Patrick raised his fists and stepped nearer to Neil, but he did not see the blow coming as Neil punched through his guard, and broke his nose; enraged, Patrick kept coming forward but, every time he did so, was picked off by perfect blows from Neil - as Patrick became more angry, it became childishly easy to knock him back.

"You are never going to win this fight," declared Neil. "Tell me why you wanted me dead or who hired you, and I'll walk away."

Suddenly, he saw a look of absolute terror in Patrick's eyes; somehow, he sensed that he had seen that look once before in his life, even though he had no memories of that life. As he watched, Patrick grasped his own left arm, dropped to his knees, and then fell face forward onto the ground. Patrick Flynn was dead.

Neil, slowly, walked over to the prostrate figure on the ground; then he crouched down, and removed the mobile phone from the dead man's pocket.

....

Neil stood, motionless, and then exhaled deeply. His first feeling was an overwhelming sense of relief that Caroline was safe; but then he looked around at the three bodies. What the hell was he going to do with those?

Just then, a Range Rover appeared at high speed, and stopped within yards of him. Four men leapt out of the vehicle, all carrying weapons; Neil was surprised to see that it was Paddy, and the other three travellers with whom he had been drinking in the Brown Horse.

Neil smiled, picked up the baseball bat, and walked towards the four armed men; however, they all immediately dropped their weapons. "Declan, we haven't come to fight against you, we came to fight alongside you," assured Paddy.

"How did you know I was here?" asked Neil, slipping easily back into a traveller accent.

"Mary rang me to tell me what was happening, so we got here as quick as we could."

As Paddy said this, a woman emerged from the caravan at the other end of the site and walked towards them; Neil was taken aback when the woman came straight up to him, and gave him a hug. "God bless you, Declan," she murmured.

Paddy provided the explanation. "Mary's on her own, but shortly after the others had left the site, and Mary was about to follow them, she found her tyres had been slashed. She didn't know who to turn to - then last night the Flynns paid her a visit."

Neil nodded his understanding, and held the unfortunate woman tightly. "Well, they'll never bother you again, or anybody else for that matter."

Paddy was looking at him curiously. "I have to ask, Declan, what in God's name did they do to you or your family, to make you go against all three of them on your own?"

Neil glanced, dispassionately, at each of the three bodies. "They didn't do anything, I just didn't like the look of them."

One of the other men laughed nervously. "Declan, if ever you don't like the look of me, if you could give me a bit of notice, then I can guarantee you'll never see me again."

"Once I've got rid of these bodies, you'll never see me again either."

"You leave that to us, Declan," offered Paddy, "we've got the very place for these three."

"And I need to know where that place is," said Neil.

Paddy nodded. "They'll be at the bottom of the Manchester ship canal, and will be well weighted down - so unless the canal gets drained, which I don't think will happen in our lifetime, they'll never be found."

"Then I'll be on my way."

"The Flynn's property and possessions are yours now, Declan," said one of the other travellers. "What should we do with them?"

Neil smiled. "You came here to help me - I know how frightened you all were of the Flynn family, and you're now going to get rid of these bodies for me. As far as I'm concerned, this property is now yours, do what you like with it."

"Well, this is going to be an interesting game of cards tonight," laughed Paddy. "By the way, Declan, we think we know the truth now about Kieran, and the armed men from Liverpool and Manchester."

Neil frowned. "So what's the story?"

"Kieran is dead. He was killed by a bare knuckle fighter from Liverpool," explained Paddy.

"Yes, that fighter was another man we'd have liked to have had a drink with," interjected one of the other travellers. "Kieran was just like his father, if not worse, he should've been drowned at birth."

"They all should," said Mary quietly. "I hope they rot in hell."

"Anyway," continued Paddy, "although this man killed Kieran in a fair fight, the Flynns tracked him down and killed him, but he was well connected to some very dangerous people in both Liverpool and Manchester. These are the people with the sawn off shotguns who've been trying to get their revenge on the Flynn family."

Neil shrugged. "Well I've done the job for them, let's hope this is the end of it."

"I was on the site that day, when I saw how that Manchester man dealt with big Mike Dougherty," volunteered Mary. "I didn't think I'd ever see someone fight like that again, until I watched you against Patrick Flynn."

Neil shook his head. "Patrick wasn't tough, he was just evil. Anyway, be lucky - and if any of us ever pass each other in the street, keep walking."

Everyone laughed at this, as Neil headed back to his car; he got in, started the engine, and was about to drive away, when Paddy shouted "Declan!" and came running over, the baseball bat in his hand. Neil opened the window.

"I believe this is yours, you never know when you may need it again," said Paddy, handing the bat to him. "Oh, and I've just remembered the name of the bare knuckle fighter from Liverpool - he was called ScouseNeil. Look after yourself."

As Paddy was walking away from the car, he could not know the significance of what he had said, or that it had caused his listener, temporarily, to pass out; after a few moments, feeling dizzy and disorientated, Neil opened his eyes.

The therapist at the hospital had said that a name could trigger the return of his memory, and she was absolutely right. As soon as he heard the word 'ScouseNeil', a tidal wave of memories came flooding through Neil's mind – it began with how desperately he loved Caroline and how, when he discovered that she was having an affair, his whole world fell apart; seeing her kissing another man, being held tightly in his arms, had led inexorably to a sequence of events which had ended in tragedy.

Neil sat in his car and, in his mind, replayed again and again those events which had culminated in his being left for dead. He was no innocent victim of an unprovoked attack; he got everything he deserved, and would have done exactly what the Flynns did to him, had he been in their position.

Stunned by what he now knew, he drove away, but not in the direction of home - he had to think, and decide what he was going to do next.

....

Neil's observer, who had been about to unload his shotgun when it was apparent that Neil had prevailed over the Flynns, had seen the arrival of Paddy and his fellow travellers. When he noticed that they were carrying weapons, he had left his own weapon armed, and watched what was happening; thankfully, there had been no need to use it.

Now, as the travellers were loading the bodies into the back of Callum's van, they had no idea that they were being watched. When they had finished and were about to drive away, the man with the shotgun returned to his car, carefully unloaded the weapon, started his engine, and waited for them to emerge.

Neither the traveller who was driving the Range Rover, nor Paddy, who was at the wheel of Callum's van, noticed the Porsche that was following them at some distance behind. As both vehicles turned down a rough track leading down to the ship canal, the observer, who knew the area well, took the next turning along from that taken by the travellers; from there, he would have a good view of what - he had guessed – they were going to do.

As the three bodies were being dragged out of the van, the youngest of the three appeared to move slightly, while he was on the ground; one of the travellers went back to his vehicle, took out Patrick's shotgun, held it to the young man's head, and pulled the trigger. The bodies were then taken out, individually, in a small rowing boat, to the centre of the canal; each corpse had what appeared to be a large block of concrete attached to it. One by one, the weighted bodies were tipped overboard, and sank quickly under the murky water.

As the travellers drove away, the observer just nodded his head slightly, and got back into his car.

....

Neil had not driven very far before he found a small piece of waste ground, near to a high bridge which went over the Manchester ship canal. He parked the car, but did not get out; he sat and thought of the last four years which had, ultimately, led to today's events. He had believed that regaining his memory would be the best possible thing that could happen; he now realised that it was the worst.

Unbeknown to his wife, his sons, his closest friends, and everyone who knew him, for the last four years he had lived a double life – one which Neil Hughes, the loving husband, the family man, could never have imagined being involved in. He had always been uneasy about keeping the truth from Caroline, as he had never previously done anything to deceive her; but he had told himself that it would not last forever, and was simply a means to an end – to a new life in Spain, where he and Caroline could enjoy the rest of their lives together in comfort, without his having to work night and day. It would have served no purpose, and worried her unnecessarily, had she known what he was doing to achieve this dream.

He could remember, as though it was yesterday, how it all began – with the night he first met "Dean the Manc." Dean was ten years younger than himself, yet Neil considered him to be one of the most remarkable men he had ever met in his life, and certainly the toughest. As a result of that meeting, Neil had been introduced to a way of life which was dangerous, exhilarating and, most of all, lucrative; he believed that the risks he was taking were worth the prize at the end – but then it all went wrong.

Jerking his thoughts back to the present, he remembered that he must contact Jacko, to tell him that there was no longer any need for him to call at Neil's house that night; he did not want Caroline worried for no reason. Getting no reply from Jacko's phone, he rang Danny; luckily, Danny confirmed that he would be meeting up with Jacko in the next hour, and would pass on the message. There was something further - now that he had recovered his memory, Neil knew the identity of the armed men who had been trying to find the Flynns; he therefore made two more calls, thus ensuring that the traveller sites would not be getting any more visits from men carrying shotguns.

He switched off his phone as, by this time, the battery was getting low; he left it in the glove box, got out of the car, and began walking along the side of the canal. He had a lot to think about.

....

Gary entered the briefing room, smiling.

"You're looking rather smug," remarked Tinny; "did you get your bit of business sorted out?"

"Certainly did, Sarge; I think I've cracked the case."

Tinny gave a satisfied nod. "I knew you'd been up to something, almost since this case started; however, as I've got to know you, I reckoned that you'd tell me when the time was right."

"Well, Sarge, the time is right now."

Gary went on to explain to Tinny how he had been conducting his own investigation, in his own time; when he had finished, Tinny raised his eyebrows.

"Well," he said, "the D.C.I. has got to hear this."

They duly went to Fred Davies's office, where Gary repeated everything that he had discovered to the senior officer. Davies listened intently, and finally shook his head.

"I think we need to speak to Neil Hughes."

Chapter 13

Neil walked along the side of the canal almost in a trance, as he thought back four years to that night in Chester………..

……………………………………………………………………………..

It was in the early hours of the morning. Neil had just dropped off his last fare, and had decided that it would be his final job of the night; he therefore set off home.

As he was driving, further along the road, he noticed what appeared to be a fight in progress. Previous experience had taught Neil to keep driving, if he saw people brawling in the street; often, on previous occasions, he had pulled in and tried to stop a fight, only to find that everyone would turn on him, and he would end up doing far more damage to them than they would ever have done to each other. This situation looked different, however; four men appeared to be attacking one man on the ground, and one of the attackers appeared to have a weapon, possibly a baseball bat.

Neil knew that he did not have the heart just to ignore this, and drive past; that was someone's son on the floor, possibly someone's brother, or even a young child's father. He gritted his teeth, and prepared himself; as he got nearer he speeded up, put the headlights on full beam, mounted the curb, and drove straight at the assailants. He slammed on his brakes just before he reached them, and jumped out of the cab.

Two of the attackers ran away, while a third looked startled, and seemed unsure what to do; however, the fourth man, who was holding the baseball bat, was obviously willing to stand and fight. Neil ran at this man, who was considerably taller than himself, then jumped through the air and butted him in the face, breaking the man's nose in the process, and sending him sprawling on the ground; as soon as Neil had landed on his feet, he turned and punched the other man so hard that he also fell where he stood.

The man who had been punched waited until Neil stepped away from him, then scrambled to his feet, and ran off in the same direction as the other two; the taller man remained on the ground holding his face, blood pouring from his broken nose, as Neil looked down at him.

"You've got two choices, kid - get up and walk away, which would be sensible, or get up and have another go. If you want to have another go, I'll put you down again, and the next time you move, it'll be when you're being lifted onto a stretcher. It's your choice."

Neil was smiling to himself because, as he had spoken, he had used a strong Liverpool accent, which was contrary to the way he normally sounded. It was strange; but whenever he was in a confrontational situation, his 'scouse' accent was much stronger than normal. He suspected that he did it because it made him sound more menacing - especially as he did not look particularly fearsome.

The man on the ground tried to reach for the baseball bat, but Neil simply stood on it.

"I think I'll keep this, ace - you'd be far better following your mates."

The man with the broken nose slowly got up off the ground, then carefully backed away from Neil, before turning and running; when he had got a reasonable distance away, he turned and shouted. "I'll get you for this, you Scouse bastard, only next time I'll have a gun!"

Neil raised his eyes upwards and shook his head; he then turned to assist the victim of the attack, but was surprised to find him standing up, showing few signs of injury. The young man smiled, and stepped forward, holding out his hand.

"Cheers for that - any chance of a taxi home?"

Judging by his accent, Neil assumed that he must be from Manchester; he was very smartly dressed, and looked more like a young businessman than a nightclub reveller. Neil shook the hand that was offered to him.

"Certainly," he replied; "although, there's a hospital not far from here with an A. and E. Department - I'll get you round there first so they can check you over, and then I'll take you home."

"Honestly, there's no need," assured the other man. "I'll just have a few bruises tomorrow, but I know there's nothing broken."

"Are you sure? I was knocking off anyway, so I'm not in any rush. They definitely got a few kicks in, and the big lad hit you at least twice with the bat."

"I'd protected my head so I was okay. I was just waiting for them to step back and admire their handiwork, then I'd have got up and knocked hell out of the four of them."

Neil laughed. "Fair enough! Where's home?"

"Manchester, not far from the airport."

Neil nodded. "I'll get on the M56 and head for the airport, then you can direct me from there. I'm Neil, by the way."

"And I'm Dean. Have you got to drive back to Liverpool, after you've dropped me off?"

"No, I live in Cheshire. I'm originally from Liverpool, but moved over here years ago."

"Right," said Dean, nodding. "So, how long will it take us to get to the airport?"

"Roughly, about half an hour."

"Great," said Dean. "I've just got to make a phone call and then we'll shoot off, if that's okay with you."

As Neil picked up the baseball bat and put it in the boot of the cab, he could hear Dean's phone conversation. "Jonjo, I've had a bit of mither in Chester, I got jumped by four fellas, so have the doc there to check us over, I'll be there in about forty minutes...... I'll tell you all about it when I get back....the fella bringing me back is a Scouse taxi driver called Neil, while I was on the ground he took two of them out and the other two ran away.......that's right, get the good stuff ready." He then rang off, and walked back to where Neil was waiting.

"Right then, Neil, whenever you're ready."

As they were driving along, Neil found it easy to chat to his passenger, talking about his family and his job, and his hopes for the future.

"When we get back to the warehouse," said Dean, "you'll have to come in and have a quick drink with us before you head back."

"The warehouse? Is that some sort of club?"

"No - I live in an actual warehouse, or at least, a converted warehouse," explained Dean. "It doesn't look much from the outside, but wait till you see the inside - I think you'll be impressed."

"I'll gladly come in and have a drink with you, but it'll have to be tea, coffee or a soft drink."

"Is that because you're driving?"

"No, I don't drink alcohol at all. I don't like the taste of it, and it doesn't agree with me; it makes me feel ill."

Dean laughed. "Well, you must be the first teetotal Scouser I've ever met!"

"I don't smoke and I don't gamble either; in fact, thinking about it, I'm a right boring bastard, really," grinned Neil.

Dean laughed again. "You can certainly fight though, can't you? That was an absolute beaut you took the big fella out with, and I think the other lad has probably never been hit so hard in all his life."

Neil shrugged. "This sounds a bit strange, but I actually avoid trouble if possible," he confessed; "but you're right - if there's no alternative but to fight, I can and I will."

"Don't mind me asking, Neil, but how old are you?"

"I'm thirty-six," replied Neil; he smiled as he saw the look of confusion on Dean's face. "I know I look older than that, but I am honestly only thirty-six."

"Well, you're ten years older than me, but you do look a bit older than that," remarked Dean; "although I don't think it bothers you, does it?"

Neil shook his head. "Doesn't bother me a bit - never has, never will."

Just then, Dean's phone rang. "It's fast Eddie," he told Neil; "I'll have to answer it, or he'll just keep ringing." He took the call, listening and nodding his head, until finally he said "I'm sound, Eddie, I'll be there shortly - get the kettle on, Scouse Neil doesn't drink alcohol................... I know, that's what *I* said!" Dean was laughing as he finished the conversation.

For the remainder of the journey, Neil's dry humour kept his passenger entertained to such an extent that Dean began to wonder whether he was aching from the beating he had received, or from laughing at the things Neil had been saying. Finally, they arrived at their destination; as Neil drove on to the industrial estate, Dean directed him down a gap between two warehouses, where Neil could see a large metal gate in front of him. The gate was electronic, and opened automatically as they approached.

"I'm already impressed," smiled Neil, as he drove through the opening. "How did you do that?"

"We've got surveillance cameras all around the warehouse, so the lads will have seen you driving down," explained Dean. "If there's no-one in, we just enter the code in the box on the wall."

Glancing in his rear view mirror, Neil saw the gate automatically close behind him; initially, the area was poorly lit, but as he drove further along, a series of floodlights switched on, enabling him to see exactly where he was going. Shaking his head, he turned to Dean.

"I don't think I'd like your electric bill."

"We can afford it." Dean's tone was matter-of-fact; as they pulled up at the door of the warehouse, Neil looked admiringly at the expensive cars parked outside, and concluded that Dean was not exaggerating.

They got out of the cab just as the door to the warehouse opened, and two men emerged; observing them as they walked towards himself and Dean, Neil decided that they were not the kind of individuals with whom he would like to fall out.

"This is Jonjo, and this is Eddie," said Dean, indicating the two men in turn.

At five feet ten, Neil had never thought of himself as being small; but as he noted that both Dean and Jonjo were over six feet in height, he was glad that Eddie was no taller than himself.

Both men shook his hand, and Eddie smiled.

"Welcome to the warehouse, Neil! Come in, and I'll put the kettle on."

Neil took to this man immediately; Eddie had a sparkle in his eye, and looked like he was permanently up to mischief.

"Deano was just saying that you took the baseball bat off those cowards and put it in the boot of your cab?"

"You never know when it might come in handy," replied Neil.

"Now I would have taken you as being more of a rounders man, myself," remarked Eddie, grinning.

Neil shook his head. "To be honest, Eddie, hockey's my game - the short pleated skirt sets off my thighs nicely."

"You'll do for me!" laughed Eddie, slapping Neil on the back. "You've got to come here on a regular basis, because you and I could have some laughs."

As they all went into the warehouse, Jonjo turned to Dean. "I think we've got two of a kind there - Eddie won't want Scouse Neil to go home."

Dean smiled his assent. "He had me in stitches on the way back. I can tell you now, Jonjo, he's a sound fella."

Jonjo nodded. "And a brave fella. Most people would've driven past when they saw it was four onto one."

"Make no mistake, he's just like us."

As he entered the warehouse, Neil was somewhat taken aback to see an interior which, to him, looked more like a hotel lounge. Sitting in one of the leather armchairs was a middle-aged Asian man, who immediately stood up and came towards them.

"Right, Dean," he said briskly, "jacket and shirt off - let's have a look at you."

Dean nodded. "I think you'll find there's nothing broken, doc, but I thought it best to get you to check us over, just in case."

Neil was intrigued by the fact that Dean was able to call on the services of a doctor at this time of night, and because it was apparent that the two men knew each other well. In addition, when Dean had removed his jacket and shirt as instructed, Neil was very much surprised, and impressed, with the physique of the younger man; he had always prided himself on keeping fit and staying in good shape, but Dean was, clearly, in a different league. Neil had assumed that Dean had been joking earlier, when he had said he was waiting for the opportunity to get up and 'knock hell' out of his four attackers; surveying him now, Neil realised that it had been no empty threat.

"How many blows?" asked the doctor.

"I was kicked nine times, stamped on twice, and hit with the bat three times."

The precision with which Dean described his assault, being able to differentiate between the types of blows, intrigued Neil still further; his admiration for this resilient young man was growing.

"Neil, I believe you did a certain amount of damage to the two fellas who didn't run away?" enquired Jonjo.

Neil nodded. "As for the one with the bat, his nose is never going to look the same again; and the other one won't be able to see out of his left eye for some time."

"Is right!" declared Eddie, with a big beaming smile.

Concluding his examination, the doctor gave a satisfied nod. "You're right, Deano, nothing broken - just take it easy for a few days."

"Will do, thanks doc," replied Dean, as he got dressed.

When the doctor was about to go, Neil noticed Jonjo handing him something which the doctor put in his pocket; he then smiled, shook hands with Jonjo, and took his leave. Neil assumed that Jonjo had just paid him, but concluded that it would be indiscreet to ask; despite the fact that he felt comfortable in the company of these men, his instinct told him that it would be unwise to get on their wrong side. He decided that it was time to leave, and stood up.

"Right, I'll make a move - I'm up early in the morning."

Dean nodded to Jonjo who, in turn, stuffed some money into Neil's shirt pocket.

"There's no need," protested Neil; "this was my good deed for the day."

"I know there's no need," said Dean; "that's not for bringing me home, or saving my life, it's for you to take Caroline and the boys out for a nice meal. Please accept it."

Neil smiled and said. "Okay!"

"Do you work days as well as nights, or have you got to be up early for something else?" asked Dean.

"I do a mixture of days and nights," explained Neil; "but I've got an early run to the airport, so I'd better get in a couple of hours sleep."

"What time's your airport run?" interjected Eddie.

"I'll be dropping them off at about eight o'clock; but I need to set off in good time, because the traffic can be quite heavy at that time in the morning, even on a Saturday."

Eddie's eyes lit up. "Brilliant! You could dive round here after you've dropped them off, and I can give you a full tour of the warehouse."

"We have the weightlifting competition in the morning, so you'll get to meet the rest of the lads," encouraged Dean.

"That would be great," nodded Neil. "I used to do a bit of weightlifting at school, so it'll be interesting to see what sort of weights you fellas can lift."

Eddie rubbed his hands together. "Bring your gym kit, and you could have a go as well."

Neil gave Eddie a crooked smile, and nodded slightly. "That's definitely a plan. I'll see you gents in the morning."

"Is right!"

Dean shook Neil's hand. "Give us your mobile phone number, so I can contact you if there's a change of plan."

As they all exchanged numbers with Neil, Dean remarked "I've already got a Neil on my contact list, so you'll be Scouse Neil."

"I'll store yours as 'Dean the manc.'"

As he was driving along the motorway heading home, Neil looked forward to the prospect of visiting the warehouse again; he felt that in Dean, Jonjo and Eddie, he had found some kindred spirits.

After Neil had driven away, Dean walked back into the warehouse.

"So, what went on at the meeting?" asked Jonjo.

"We've got the whole contract," replied Dean; "not just the doors, but the security on the premises as well."

Eddie nodded. "How many clubs is this Chester fella talking about opening up?"

"As things stand, three of them - each in a different part of Cheshire."

"Good bit of business there, if we're doing the lot," mused Jonjo.

"I think he'd made his mind up that he was going to use us, even before I got there," said Dean. "Apparently, one of the proposed clubs is not far from a particularly rough estate. I was asking Scouse Neil about it, and he was able to give me some good information."

"Talking about Neil," said Eddie, leaning back and folding his arms as he looked at Dean, "how did you manage to end up on the ground, when there was only four of them?"

"Oldest trick in the book, and I fell for it." Dean shook his head ruefully. "As I was heading for the taxi rank I spotted, as I thought, three lads attacking another on the ground. As soon as I ran over, the three quickly backed off but, stupidly, I turned my back on the big lad on the floor." Jonjo and Eddie looked at him in disbelief. "I know, I just wasn't thinking. Anyway," continued Dean, "needless to say, he was hiding the baseball bat underneath him, and caught me with it just behind the knees. As I went down, the four of them were all having a go, but they were getting in each other's way; I'd protected myself properly, and was about to get up and sort them out, when Neil came hurtling down the pavement in his cab."

Eddie laughed. "I'd have loved to have seen that!"

"It was brilliant. He put his headlights on full beam, dropped it down a couple of gears so that the engine was really loud, and then slammed the brakes on, just before he got to them. As he jumped out of the taxi, there wasn't a moment's hesitation as he judged the fella with the bat to be the main threat, took him out straight away, and then turned and cracked the other one."

Jonjo was nodding appreciatively. "Do you think Neil was lucky that the other two ran away?"

Dean smiled as he shook his head. "I think the two who ran away were the lucky ones," he said decidedly.

"Is right!" enthused Eddie.

"Well," resumed Dean, "this estate that Neil was telling us about is called the Rockford, so we'll do the usual before the new club opens: all ten of us will go down there, find out who the troublemakers are, have a quiet word with them, and then probably do the doors ourselves for a couple of weeks, until we reckon it's safe to have regular doormen working there."

Jonjo looked at him speculatively. "Do you think the four that jumped you were in any way connected to this deal?"

"I'm sure of it. There's a local gangster who controls most of the doormen in that area, and those fellas were definitely bouncers. Well," shrugged Dean, "if this fool tries to go against us, we all know what the outcome will be."

....

As soon as Neil had deposited his passengers at Manchester airport, he headed straight for the warehouse, and was really looking forward to the weightlifting competition. Neil had been somewhat modest about his own ability, as he had not wished to appear to be boasting to his hosts at the warehouse; in point of fact, he had done a great deal of weightlifting at school, as it was one of his favourite sports.

As Neil drove towards the electric gates they opened automatically, indicating that he had been picked up on the security cameras. He had admired the cars that he had seen parked outside the warehouse on the previous evening; now, he was amazed at the number of top of the range vehicles he could see, as he came to a halt outside the entrance to the building. Just as he was stepping out of the taxi, out walked a smiling Eddie, followed by Dean.

"There's some fancy looking motors out here - my cab looks quite shabby by comparison."

"Those London cabs aren't cheap to buy though, I bet," suggested Dean.

"Brand new, they're a lot of money," agreed Neil; "but to be fair, they're built for the job, and as long as you look after them, they'll go on forever."

"Right," said Eddie, "first job, tour of the warehouse - then when you've met all the lads, it's the weightlifting competition."

Neil had not appreciated the sheer size of the warehouse, when he had been there the night before; now, as he was being shown around by Eddie, he understood what Dean had meant when he had told Neil that he would be impressed. In addition to the room which was to house the weightlifting competition, there was another which Eddie described as the training room; this had a number of pieces of equipment you would expect to see in a boxing club. The training room, in turn, led to a much larger area, which Eddie described as the fight room; as well as a conventional boxing ring, it contained a large circular area, with a wooden floor. Neil made no comment during this tour, as he was overwhelmed; not only was he astounded by the quality of the equipment, but by the fact that everywhere was immaculate. Eddie concluded this part of the tour at the far end of the warehouse, by showing Neil the swimming pool.

"So, that's the downstairs," said Eddie; "come and have a look at the upstairs accommodation."

On the upper floor, the first room Eddie showed Neil was obviously an office and, once again, Neil remarked to himself how efficiently everything was organised; then Eddie opened the next door along.

"This is Jonjo's bedroom," he announced.

Neil hesitated slightly. "Are you sure Jonjo won't mind me looking in his bedroom?"

"Far from it," smiled Eddie; "wait till you see his trophy cabinet."

Glancing around the room, Neil smiled to himself at the thought of how Caroline would love these young men, for being so neat and tidy; but when he examined the contents of the trophy cabinet, he could scarcely believe his eyes.

"Are these all Jonjo's?"

"Impressive, isn't it?" grinned Eddie.

There were trophies for football, rugby, karate, boxing, basketball and swimming, together with various athletic trophies, ranging from long jump and triple jump to 400 metres; and these were only the ones that Neil could see. There were so many that Neil could only see the tops of some of the trophies at the back of the cabinet, and therefore could not make out what they were for.

Eddie then showed Neil his own bedroom, followed by that belonging to Dean, and another used by someone called Tommy; Neil, again, felt slightly uncomfortable about this, particularly as he was yet to meet this man. There were several other bedrooms, but these did not appear to be in use.

As the pair returned to the top of the stairs, and began to descend, Eddie turned to Neil. "So, what do you think of the warehouse?"

Neil shook his head in admiration. "It's absolutely stunning. Looking at it from the outside, you'd never know it was such a fantastic place inside."

Eddie looked suitably gratified. "When we first took it over it was derelict, but with a lot of hard work, and a hell of a lot of help from friends and family, we finally got it the way we wanted it."

"So you, Dean, Jonjo and Tommy actually live here? Do you own it outright?"

"It's owned by Warehouse Boys Security, which is our company. People refer to us as the 'warehouse boys', sometimes 'warehouse lads', or even 'the warehouse crew.'"

"I'm guessing, judging from the cars parked outside, that Warehouse Boys Security is doing well," observed Neil.

"Over a reasonably short period, it has really built up," confirmed Eddie. "That's because we've got a very good reputation, and it's going from strength to strength. Talking of which," he added, "let's get down to the weight room, and you can meet the rest of the lads."

"Great," smiled Neil. "How many warehouse boys are there?"

"There's ten of us altogether. Dean, Jonjo and me you already know - the other seven are downstairs, waiting to meet you."

When Eddie said this, Neil felt slightly nervous, and hoped that the reception from the other seven would be as welcoming as it had been from Jonjo and Eddie the night before.

As the two of them entered the weight room, Neil came face to face with nine of the biggest, toughest looking men he had ever seen in his life. Not one of them was below six feet tall, and all looked in perfect physical condition. Neil looked down at the floor.

"Am I standing in a hole here?"

"It's because they're all wearing platform training shoes."

Neil glanced at the feet of the men standing in front of him, which caused Eddie to start laughing. "I can't believe you looked!" he spluttered.

Neil started chuckling. "I know, I couldn't help it!"

Dean, who was also laughing at this little scene, said "Gentlemen: this is Scouse Neil, the man I was telling you about."

Each one of these large, formidable looking men stepped forward in turn, introduced himself, and warmly shook Neil's hand; he just hoped that he would be able to remember all of their names. The first was called Andy, the next was Joe, then Tommy (he, Neil noticed, simply nodded to him, where everyone else had smiled), followed by Carl, Phil, Rod and, finally, Earl. They ranged in height from at least six feet, but Earl towered over all of them; Neil guessed that he must be about six and a half feet tall.

"Okay," said Dean, "this is the way the competition works: you get on the scales to see what weight you are, and then you try and lift as much over your own body weight as you possibly can." Neil nodded, and was secretly relieved; had it been a simple test to see who could lift the heaviest weight, he knew he would have no chance against these men.

After everyone, apart from Eddie, had stepped on to the scales, Dean beckoned to Neil. "So, you're the lightest, Neil - you're first up."

Neil turned to Eddie. "How come you're not taking part? Are you injured or something?"

Andy, the first man to shake Neil's hand, offered the explanation. "He's not injured, he's barred."

Neil looked perplexed, so Dean elaborated. "We started doing this a while ago, not long after the warehouse was complete. Someone suggested we all put in a hundred quid each, and the winner takes all. Eddie won the first week, then the second, then the third, and so on."

"It wasn't 'someone' who suggested it," said Jonjo, pointedly; "it was Eddie."

Neil gave a wry smile, and looked round at Eddie who, somewhat unsuccessfully, was trying to look innocent.

"Which was when we realised that Eddie isn't just strong, he's freakishly strong - so we barred him," continued Dean.

Neil glanced at a smiling Eddie, who simply shrugged his shoulders. "Jessies!" he retorted.

"Anyway," concluded Dean, "without Eddie, the competition's really fierce, and there's very little to choose between the nine of us."

"Okay," said Neil; "I'll be Eddie's champion, and just hope I don't come last!"

However, although Neil went on to lift a reasonable amount above his own bodyweight, and was fairly pleased with his efforts, he did, in fact, come a resounding last; even so, he was surprised at the reaction of his companions, who all seemed to feel that he had done remarkably well.

At the end of the competition, which Jonjo won, everyone went into the large lounge area at the front of the warehouse. Neil sat down in a particularly comfortable leather armchair, and took in his surroundings; as he was doing this, Dean came over to speak to him.

"So, what do you think about everything you've seen here?"

"Well," replied Neil, "you said last night you thought I'd be impressed, but that doesn't begin to describe my reaction - this place is absolutely fantastic. That training room you've got is superb; it's got me thinking that I could convert one of the upstairs rooms in my house into something similar. I imagine you'd know the best place to go, in order to buy the equipment I need?"

"You could be in luck there," smiled Dean. "We're just about to replace some of our equipment, so you'd be quite welcome to the stuff we're getting rid of."

"That would be great," said Neil; "you'll have to show me what you're replacing, and we'll see if we can come to some sort of deal."

"The deal is simple - you can have it. I certainly don't want any money for it."

Neil held up his hand, and shook his head. "Show me what you're replacing, and then we'll sort something out. I wouldn't be comfortable not paying you for it."

Dean nodded. "Okay - come and have a look at what we're getting shut of."

As they entered the training room, Dean showed Neil the various pieces of equipment that were being replaced; it included one of the heavy bags, a punch-ball, a speedball, and various other items, including the weights that they had just used in the competition.

"There's got to be over a thousand pounds worth of equipment here," pointed out Neil; "I'd have to give you something for it."

Dean just smiled. "Let's go back into the lounge, then, and speak to Jonjo - he's the money man."

They rejoined all the others in the lounge, and Dean explained to Jonjo his proposal regarding the equipment.

"Scouse Neil here insists on paying for it, though, and won't take no for an answer."

"There's no need," assured Jonjo. "The new stuff we're buying goes down as a business expense, and comes off the tax we pay. I think I can safely speak for all of the lads here, and say that you're more than welcome to it."

"I appreciate what you're saying, but that equipment you've got there is the best on the market," insisted Neil. "I've been looking through catalogues recently, and what you're proposing to give me would cost about one and a half thousand pounds."

"Ah, but that's if you were buying it brand new," said Eddie; "this kit's second-hand."

Neil was not convinced and was determined to pay for the equipment.

"Fair enough – five hundred pounds to a charity of your choice," suggested Jonjo.

Neil smiled. "Fine - I'm happy with that, as long as all you lads are?"

All the warehouse boys nodded. "Okay then, Neil," said Dean, "it's your money - you choose the charity."

"Help for Heroes," replied Neil, without hesitation.

"Is right!" said Eddie emphatically, thumping the arm of his seat.

As Neil looked at the faces of all the men surrounding him, it was obvious that his choice was met with universal approval.

"By the way, Jonjo, I was just admiring your collection of trophies," said Neil; "just out of curiosity, is there any sport you *haven't* got a trophy for?"

Jonjo paused slightly before speaking, as though considering his answer. "Ice hockey - I can't skate!" he declared. Everyone laughed at this.

"Well, on that note," said Neil, as the laughter subsided, "I'll make a move and get back to work. Thanks for letting me take part in the weightlifting competition."

All the warehouse boys stood up, and each in turn shook hands with him; Dean and Tommy then followed him out to his cab.

"I'll give you a ring when the new equipment's arrived," said Dean, "then we can sort something out with the stuff you're having."

"Are you any good at do-it-yourself, Neil?" asked Tommy.

Neil shook his head. "Absolutely useless!"

"No problem," said Tommy; "I can bring all the stuff over to your house and fit it for you - my uncle's got a good sized van, so I can do the lot in one trip."

Neil smiled. "Cheers Tommy, you're a gent." He then turned to Dean. "Give us a bell when you get the new stuff, and I'll be over to sort things out."

As Neil drove away, he felt pleased at Tommy's offer of help. When he had been introduced to the warehouse boys, it had seemed to Neil that Tommy was not quite as welcoming as the others; however, he now realised that he was wrong - it was merely that Tommy seemed to be the most serious of them.

"What did you all think of Scouse Neil?" asked Dean, when he and Tommy had rejoined the others back in the lounge.

At this, everyone in the room started nodding their heads, with comments such as "sound bloke", "good lad", "top man".

"In that case," continued Dean, "I was thinking of inviting him to come and train with us; but I wanted to run it past you lads first."

Eddie was the first to speak. "Great idea, I'm all for it."

Jonjo also nodded in agreement. "I was really impressed with the weight he lifted, when you consider the amount of hours we spend training, compared to the amount of hours he spends driving the taxi. He wasn't that far behind us."

"I know," said Dean. "He was telling me that he works, on average, about seventy hours a week."

"Seventy hours?" exclaimed Earl. "Is he heavily in debt or something?"

"No, far from it," assured Dean; "he's a real grafter, and does it because he's got some big plans for the future."

"So he's willing to work hard in order to achieve his goals," commented Phil. "Good on him."

"So I think it's fair to say we're all for Scouse Neil training with the warehouse boys?" Eddie paused slightly, but everyone in the room knew what was coming next. "Is right!"

…………………………………......................................

A few days later, Neil got the call from Dean to say that the new equipment had arrived, so he arranged to call up at the warehouse that afternoon. As he arrived, he was greeted by Dean and Tommy, and jumped out of his cab.

"I'm just a big kid really," he explained. "I got so excited when you rang before."

"We're just as excited at the new stuff we've got," smiled Dean. "Come and have a look at it and, while you're here, you can sort out with Tommy when it's convenient for you to set up your own personal training room."

"It's really whenever it's convenient for you," said Neil, turning to Tommy.

Tommy shrugged. "Whenever you like. If you include the time it takes to get the equipment from the van, carry it upstairs and put it all in place, I can get it done in about three hours."

Neil looked slightly guilty. "Don't suppose there's any chance of this Sunday? Caroline and the lads are going over to her cousin's in North Wales for the day, so the house will be empty. If possible, I'd like it to be a surprise, particularly for the lads."

"Fine by me," nodded Tommy, "but I wouldn't be able to get over till the afternoon."

"Perfect – that'll give me the morning to shift the stuff that's in the room now into the loft."

"What exactly have you got in the room now?"

"That's very much a matter of opinion," said Neil obscurely. "In my opinion, it's stuff that may be of some use in the future; in Caroline's opinion, it's junk."

"So your missus won't be bothered that you've converted one of the bedrooms into a training room?"

"Far from it, she'll be well pleased. Firstly, she'll be able to get the vacuum cleaner into the room; secondly, all the so called junk will be out of sight in the loft; and thirdly, there's plenty of chrome on this equipment for her to polish, which is something she really enjoys. My wife is a serial cleaner and polisher."

After Neil had seen the new equipment, they all went back to the lounge, to find Jonjo and Eddie there.

"Tommy was saying you're not much good at D.I.Y.," was Eddie's opening shot.

"Not much good is an understatement - I'm a dangerous man with an electric drill in my hand." Neil paused slightly. "Even worse if I plug it in and switch it on."

Eddie chuckled. "Well, Tommy's your man for all that sort of stuff. So far, we've yet to have a problem in the warehouse that Tommy can't fix."

"That's good to know," said Neil. "Anyway, Dean's just asked me if I'd like to come and train here as well, and I said I'd love to."

Neil was reasonably certain what Eddie's reaction would be, and he was not mistaken. "Is right!" came the response.

Neil grinned; turning to Tommy, he said "I'll get back to work now, and I'll see you on Sunday?"

"Certainly will," replied Tommy.

"And here's a cheque for five hundred quid, made out to Help for Heroes," continued Neil, handing the cheque to Dean.

Dean smiled, took the cheque, and shook Neil's hand. "Any time you'd like to come over and do a bit of training with us, just give us a bell."

Neil worked the cab solidly leading up to the Sunday morning, in order to make up for the time he knew he would lose sorting out the training room. He arrived home only about an hour before Caroline and the boys got up and, as soon as they left, he began moving everything into the loft.

Tommy's timing was perfect, as he arrived just as Neil had finished clearing the room; they worked as a team, carrying all the equipment upstairs, and then Tommy set about putting it all in place. "I just need to go up into the loft, to see where the joists are," he said, and disappeared up the loft ladder.

"Unbiased opinion," said Neil, when Tommy re-emerged from the loft, "is Caroline right? Is it all junk, or do you think any of that stuff is worth keeping hold of?"

"Well, I'm a bit like you, inasmuch as I don't like throwing anything away - but I think it's fair to say that most of the stuff you've got up there is junk."

For the rest of the afternoon, helping in whatever way he could, Neil observed and admired Tommy's professionalism, as he erected and secured all the various pieces of equipment. In addition, while they were talking, Neil further revised his assessment of Tommy's character; he realised that Tommy was not only serious by nature, there was also a sadness about him, which made him seem much older than his years. It turned out, to Neil's surprise, that there was only eighteen months' difference in age between the oldest and youngest of the warehouse boys, and only Eddie was younger than Tommy.

When Tommy had put the last piece of equipment in place, he turned to Neil. "What do you think - looks good, doesn't it?"

Neil breathed out a sigh of satisfaction, as he surveyed the result. "It's absolutely tremendous - the way you've positioned everything is spot on. Our Mike and Paul will love this; all three of us will be able to train in here, and not get in each other's way."

"How old are your sons?"

"Michael's fifteen, Paul's thirteen."

Tommy nodded. "Good age for them to get in to some serious training. It doesn't do any harm for them to be able to stand up for themselves."

Neil smiled. "To be honest, they're both already pretty good at that. I'm hoping they'll work off some of their aggression in here, particularly Paul."

"And you're sure your wife will be happy with your new training room?"

"Definitely," Neil assured him; "the lads will now be spending a lot more time at home than they do normally, which will please Caroline no end." He shook hands with the other man. "Cheers for this, Tommy - you've done a brilliant job. What do you think of the sign I had made to go up on the wall?"

Tommy just smiled and said "Perfect!"

As Tommy drove away, Neil gave him a thumbs up sign, and then went back up to his new training room; he went round with the vacuum cleaner, and was also able to clear some cobwebs from the corner that Caroline had always been unable to reach, due to the amount of (as Tommy had confirmed) 'junk' in the way. He surveyed the room with immense satisfaction, rubbed his hands together, and went downstairs.

Neil hoped that Caroline and the boys would be home soon, and found himself pacing up and down in the living room, looking out of the window so he could see them arrive; eventually, the car pulled into the drive, and Neil raced to the front door as his wife and sons came in.

"Right, everyone upstairs, I've got a bit of a surprise," he announced.

Caroline looked slightly startled. "What sort of a surprise?"

"It wouldn't be a surprise if I told you what sort it was, would it?" grinned Neil. "When we get to the spare room, you must all close your eyes, and not open them until you've stepped inside."

"With all the junk you've got in there, I'm not sure all four of us would fit in," said Caroline drily.

Neil gave what he hoped was a mysterious smile. "Just close your eyes, she of little faith, and wait and see."

They all accordingly trooped upstairs, and closed their eyes as they stood outside the spare room; Neil opened the door, and guided each one carefully into the room, stressing that they had to keep their eyes closed.

"Okay," he said, once they were all inside, "you can open your eyes now."

The gasp of surprise from all three was just what Neil had hoped for; although, admittedly, Caroline's first words were not quite what Neil was expecting.

"Brilliant! I'll be able to clean those windows properly now," she declared; then, glancing over at the speedball, she added "I see you've managed to get that cobweb - that was really annoying me."

Neil gave a lopsided smile as he turned to the boys. "So, your mum is obviously happy – what about you two?"

Paul, visibly excited, said "This is fantastic, dad! Would I be able to bring some of the lads round?"

"Absolutely – I'd far sooner you and your mates were punching this stuff, rather than anything else."

Michael, always the calmer of the two, simply smiled as he looked round at the equipment. "Dad, this is spot on - it must have set you back a few quid."

"I did a good deal with a fella from Manchester."

"Who put it all up?" asked Caroline.

Neil tried to look hurt. "I did, of course!"

Caroline, looking suitably impressed, said "Did you really?" The two boys exchanged smiles, while Neil tried to keep a straight face; in the end, he gave up. "That's what I love about you, you are so gullible," he said, smirking.

Caroline just looked at him in disgust. "Please tell me you took all that junk to the tip."

Again, Neil's face took on a serious expression. "No, I've stored it all in our bedroom for the time being; it should be okay, as long as you don't mind sleeping in the wardrobe?"

"Right, that's it, you're in trouble now!"

As Caroline said this, Neil had a look of mock horror on his face; he ran round the far side of the heavy bag and, as Caroline chased after him, he ran out of the room and down the stairs, shouting "Help! There's a mad woman chasing me!"

Caroline ran down the stairs after him, as Michael shoved his hands in his pockets, and turned to his brother.

"Tell me again," he said, "who are supposed to be the kids in this house?"

……………………………………...................................

A little over a week after Neil had the training room installed, he took the opportunity to visit the warehouse again, and was really looking forward to his first training session with the warehouse boys. On arrival he was met by Dean, and they went inside.

"Now," said Dean, "don't take offence at this, because I know you can fight - but we are going to teach you how to *really* fight."

Neil was very much intrigued by this statement; however, he said nothing, and simply followed Dean into the training room.

As they walked in, Jonjo was working on the speedball, while Eddie was dancing round the punch-ball, delivering both punches and kicks. Neil could see why Eddie was often referred to as 'fast'; he was amazed at the speed of his movements, and the power of his blows.

"The first thing we're going to work on, Neil, is your defence," said Dean. "I'll show you my style of fighting and the way I defend, then in turn you'll work with Jonjo, Eddie, Tommy, and all the other lads; that way, collectively, you'll learn a great deal, and discover which style suits you best."

Neil was still unsure what to say; he therefore simply nodded and smiled his acknowledgement, as Dean continued. "So, the first job is as follows: you and I are off to the fight room, where we'll get into the boxing ring, and you're going to try and hit me."

Neil finally found his voice. "I'm not a hundred per cent sure I'd like to hit you, in case you decide to hit me back."

Dean laughed. "Two things: firstly, I can guarantee I wouldn't hit you back; secondly, that's because I can also guarantee you won't be able to hit me."

"Okay, let's give it a go," said Neil. He followed Dean into the fight room. "Where are the gloves?" he asked, when they were standing by the boxing ring.

"Don't need them, because no-one is actually going to get hit - trust me."

Although Neil gave no sign of it as he climbed into the ring, he felt quite uncomfortable with the situation; he therefore decided he would try to avoid making contact while sparring, despite Dean's confident assertion that he would not succeed in hitting him. After less than a minute, however, Dean held up his hand.

"I've got to stop you there," he said. "This can only work if you are genuinely trying to punch me. Believe me, try your best – you'll miss me every time."

Neil glanced at Eddie, who was standing nearby. "He's not joking, Neil. Try your best to land one on him, and I'll give you a thousand quid if you catch him with one."

Finally, Neil accepted in his mind that the only way of learning from these men was to do what he was told, so he set about trying to hit Dean; they continued for five minutes, after which Neil was pouring with sweat, not having succeeded in laying a finger on the other man.

"Let's take a short break," suggested Dean.

"How the hell do you do that?" said Neil, panting, and shaking his head. "Some of those punches only missed you by inches, and yet sometimes you hardly moved!"

"There's a number of things involved, but I can teach you how to do it; so next, you are going to try and do the same as you've just been doing, but when I get the opportunity, I'm going to hit you."

"Cheers, I'm really looking forward to that," smiled Neil.

"Needless to say, I'll be putting the boxing gloves on and, of course, I'll just be making contact, not hitting you with any force," elaborated Dean. "Don't feel I'm trying to humiliate you in any way, but as I make contact, I'll just simply say 'pop'; this will show you the effectiveness of my method of defence, because I'm always so close to my opponent."

For the ensuing five minutes, Neil tried his best to catch Dean with at least one punch, but to no avail; meanwhile, he lost count of the number of times he heard Dean say 'pop'. Finally, Dean held up his hands. "Okay, time for another break."

As Neil was wiping the sweat from his face, he noticed that Dean had not broken sweat at all. "That was incredible - you must've 'hit' me over thirty times."

Dean nodded. "In a real fight, some of those blows would've just hurt a bit - but some of them would have knocked you out."

"And you can really teach *me* how to fight like that?"

"Absolutely, I can guarantee it; and there'll come a time in the future, when you and I get into the ring, where I'll need to make sure you're wearing gloves - because you will be able to hit me."

Jonjo had been at the side, watching. "When you're ready, Neil, I'll show you how I defend myself, which is a different style to Dean's," he offered.

"Let me guess," said Neil, leaning on the ropes; "I won't need gloves on while I'm trying to hit you, either."

"Exactly," said Jonjo. "You'll have to do the same as you did with Dean, and try your very best to punch me. I'll put the gloves on straightaway, and see how often I can hit you."

Eddie and Dean watched as Neil sparred with Jonjo; frustratingly for Neil, he had no greater success in landing any punches. The main difference between the two styles was that Jonjo either blocked Neil's punches, or simply diverted them; however, Jonjo's style had the same effect, inasmuch as he was able to 'hit' Neil many times. At the end of this session, Neil felt as if he had run a marathon, as he was so tired from swinging punches to no effect; he sat on the stool in the corner of ring with his head hanging down, and his arms resting on the ropes.

"Are you okay?" asked Eddie, looking slightly concerned.

Neil slowly lifted his head; as he did so, the others could see a big beaming smile spread across his face.

"That was absolutely brilliant," he declared. "I've got to come here again, and learn how you fellas do this."

"Glad to hear it!" said Eddie, smiling. "Anyway, before you have a shower, I just want to show you something - one of the things I'll be teaching you."

Neil followed Eddie, Jonjo and Dean back into the training room. "Jonjo, just stand by the heavy bag, the one we use for the kicks," instructed Eddie.

Jonjo duly positioned himself alongside a bag which was higher than all the others, and which was marked with a piece of black tape.

"Okay Neil," said Eddie. "Jonjo's about six foot three; so the area just above his head, where you can see the black tape, is roughly the head height of someone around the six foot six mark." Neil nodded. "Alright then – watch this!"

Eddie stepped forward, and appeared to bounce off the floor, as he jumped and kicked the area with the black tape with a tremendous amount of power; Neil could scarcely believe his eyes. "What sort of kick do you call that?"

"That's a roundhouse kick," explained Eddie; "I'll be able to teach you that, and several other very effective kicks, which are particularly useful if you're going against taller opposition."

"Remarkable," said Neil, shaking his head. "I can't wait."

"Well, I daresay you want to go and have your shower Neil - we'll see you back in the lounge," said Dean.

....

"Eddie was explaining to me the other day about Warehouse Boys Security, and how you employ security guards, as well as night club doormen," said Neil, when he had joined the others in the lounge.

"Yes," said Dean; "although, strictly speaking, only the security people are employed by us. The bouncers are self-employed, and we just take a percentage when we get work for them."

Neil nodded. "So effectively, W.B.S. acts as an agent for the doormen?"

"Exactly," said Jonjo; "but we get a great deal of work, so we have a lot of bouncers on our books."

"And, judging from the cars parked outside and the equipment inside, you're doing very well," commented Neil.

"We certainly are," confirmed Dean. "We have our own accountant, our own solicitor, we pay corporation tax, and everything is legal and above board."

Neil was smiling and nodding his head. "But would I be right in thinking that you have a little sideline which is *not* exactly legal and above board?"

Dean, Jonjo and Eddie all smiled non-committally. "Is there much money in bare knuckle fighting?" pressed Neil.

Dean turned to Eddie and Jonjo. "I told you nothing gets past this fella."

"Well," replied Jonjo, "to answer your question, Neil, there's a lot more money in it than you'd think."

"Then you'll have to tell me all about it, next time I'm here," said Neil; "for the moment, I need to get back to work, and earn some money myself."

"We can do better than tell you," offered Dean. "I've got a fight in Bootle next week, against some fella from Kirkby – you'd be more than welcome to come along."

"So, all the stuff you've just been showing me, I could see in action? Wild horses couldn't keep me away from it."

Eddie slapped Neil on the back. "Is right!"

Chapter 14

Neil had arranged with Dean to meet in a pub which they both knew, situated just outside Bootle, an hour before the fight was due to take place; he duly travelled over in his cab, sat in the car park, and waited. He was unsure whether Dean would be on his own, or accompanied by some of the others; so he was pleased to note that when a large minibus, emblazoned with 'W.B.S.' in gold letters on the side, pulled into the car park, all ten of the warehouse boys emerged from it. He locked up the taxi, and walked over towards the minibus, to be greeted by Dean.

"Okay," said Dean briskly, "we'll shoot in here for half an hour, which will give me time to explain how these things work."

Neil grinned. "I'm glad about that; I almost made a list of the things I wanted to ask you."

"No problem," assured Dean, returning the grin. "The best way to answer your questions is for me to explain the whole process, and then if there's anything I've left out, you can just ask me accordingly."

Neil nodded in acknowledgement, and followed the other men into the pub. The bar area inside was quite large; this allowed the group to sit together, in an area which was well away from the other customers and bar staff, in order to speak freely without being overheard.

"Right," began Dean. "These fights are organised by a third party; tonight's has been organised by big Joe from Bootle. The venue will depend on how many people are expected to attend; but it can vary from something as small as a village hall, right up to an empty warehouse and, occasionally, they could even be outdoors in a farmer's field. Tonight, it's a warehouse.

"Now, these fights have rules; they are not just simply a brawl. You can hit your opponent with your hands, fists, elbow and forearm; you can also knee them, kick them, or even butt them, provided you can get close enough. However, holding is not allowed, and there are two referees who will immediately pull the fighters apart if that happens; also, if either fighter is deliberately holding his opponent, he'll receive warnings, the second of which is final – so, if he were to do it a third time, the fight, and therefore the prize money, would be awarded to his opponent.

"When you knock your opponent down, you must immediately stand back. You cannot, under any circumstances, attack someone who's on the ground; if you do, then the fight's immediately given to your opponent. The man on the ground has thirty seconds to get back up, and resume the fight. There are no rounds or breaks of any sort, so the fight is over when someone goes down, and doesn't get back up; and that applies regardless of whether he's unable to get up, or he chooses not to. If a fighter stays down for more than thirty seconds, then he loses."

All this time, Neil was listening attentively, and mentally ticking off each one of his questions, as Dean continued his explanation.

"The extent to which the fighters are evenly matched or, in some cases, their actual style of fighting, will determine how long the fight will last. The organisers will always try to get an evenly matched pair because, obviously, no-one wants to pay out good money to see a fight that only lasts thirty seconds, or where the men fight dirty; as I said before, this is not a brawl. People who come to watch are not interested in watching two men rolling around the floor, trying to bite each other's ear off - you can see that any Saturday night, in every town centre throughout the country. A lot of the people who get involved in this are big, strong, fighting men although, admittedly, they're not athletes; I'll often spend the early part of a fight just keeping out of the way of any blows aimed at me, and wait until I see my opponent tiring - then I'll step in, and put them down.

"Which brings me to the prize money, the amount of which depends on the number of people who've come to watch the fight. The organiser - in tonight's case, big Joe - takes a cut of the gate money to cover his costs, which includes the security, the referees, and the cost of the venue itself; after that, all the remaining prize money goes to the winner, and the loser gets nothing - that way, you're guaranteed a real fight. I spoke to big Joe today, and he thinks the prize money will be about a thousand pounds; but the real big money is made on the betting. There'll be a bookmaker there tonight, possibly two, who'll be taking bets on the outcome; so, when Jonjo gives me the nod that he's got the best odds on me, and he's laid the bet, I'll put this Kirkby lad down."

"So, I take it you're reasonably confident that you'll win?" commented Neil, smiling.

"I know you don't gamble, Neil," interjected Jonjo, "but have you got any money on you now?"

"I think I've got just over two hundred pounds."

"Well," said Eddie, "when the fight starts, give that two hundred pounds to Jonjo - and I can guarantee he'll give you back more than that, once the fight's over."

"Gambling," said Dean, with a smile, "is when you're betting on the possible outcome of a race, a football match, a boxing match, or whatever; putting two hundred pounds on me to win is no gamble." He said this with no suggestion of arrogance on his part, but as if it was a simple statement of fact.

"To put things into perspective," added Jonjo, "as soon as I know I've got the best possible odds, I'll be putting 20 K on Dean."

Neil swallowed, and raised his eyebrows. "Twenty thousand pounds?"

"I'll start the fight as favourite, I always do," shrugged Dean. "I'll try and make it look like this fella's in with a chance against me; hopefully, if we can get the odds down to where I may only be 2/1 on, then that's the best we can hope for."

"You'll have to excuse my ignorance in these matters," said Neil apologetically; "but, if you are 2/1 on, and Jonjo bets twenty thousand pounds, what do you actually come away with?"

"30 K," replied Dean. "That's the 20 K we bet, and 10 K winnings."

"You still look a bit confused," observed Eddie, as he saw Neil shaking his head.

Neil laughed. "No, I'm not confused; I've just been trying to calculate in my head how many hours taxiing I'd have to do, to come away with ten thousand pounds."

"Well strictly speaking, I'm going to come away with eleven thousand, because I'll have the prize money as well," pointed out Dean, as the other warehouse boys grinned.

"That's it, you've taken me into next year now!" complained Neil; at which, his companions burst into laughter.

"Okay," concluded Dean, "let's head down to big Joe's place, so I can knock this Kirkby lad into the middle of next week."

As they arrived at the venue, a large warehouse on an industrial estate in Bootle, Neil followed the minibus to the rear of the building; here, there was a small compound, in which were already parked a number of vehicles.

"Your cab will be safe here," Dean assured Neil, once they had also parked in the compound. "Big Joe has one of his men on the gate, for the entire time the fight's in progress."

They entered the warehouse through a back door, and Neil was immediately taken aback with the size of the interior, and the number of people inside; but he was even more surprised to see such a cross-section of society in attendance - not only male and female, but ranging from young thugs with shaved heads, to elderly gents in expensive suits. As Neil was taking in his surroundings, he observed a giant of a man walking over to his group, and was relieved to see that he was wearing a welcoming smile; he appeared to be in his early sixties, with a face that looked like as if it had been chiselled out of granite, and in height, he stood well over six and a half feet tall.

"Evening Joe," greeted Dean; "this is our friend Scouse Neil, the taxi driver I was telling you about."

Big Joe looked down at Neil, and held out his hand. "Any friend of the warehouse boys is a good friend of mine - pleasure to meet you, Neil."

"How did you get the nickname big Joe?" asked Neil, wryly, as he shook hands.

Big Joe laughed. "Dean said you and fast Eddie get on well - I can see why!"

"Separated at birth, I reckon," agreed Dean, also laughing. "Right then, Joe, down to business - how many bookies are here tonight, and what are the odds at the moment?"

"Well, I've got two here now, because the crowd is even bigger than I expected. At the moment they're both showing the same odds, and obviously you're well the favourite."

"And what do we know about this fella I'm fighting?"

"He's a street fighter - no boxing or martial arts background, and has spent more of his adult life behind bars than on the outside. He's a bully, and has got a bit of a temper." Big Joe paused slightly, with a knowing smile. "So, he'll be right up your street."

When Neil heard this description of Dean's opponent, in his mind, it did not sound like good news at all; and yet Dean himself appeared to be very pleased with this information.

As he and the warehouse boys walked over to where the crowd was standing, Neil could see an area in the centre which was, he assumed, where the fight was going to take place. There were many rubber mats laid out neatly on the floor, surrounded by a number of long wooden benches, with an approximate gap of six feet between the edge of the matted area and the benches. Neil looked enquiringly at Dean.

"I assume the mats are there so you don't injure yourself, if you're knocked down?"

Dean nodded. "A young fella died because he hit his head on the ground and cracked his skull, so big Joe always has mats down now."

For the first time, it began to dawn on Neil how potentially dangerous bare knuckle fighting could be; he realised that, should a promoter make a mistake and pitch together two fighters who were not evenly matched, the outcome could be tragic. Earlier, when Dean and Jonjo mentioned about the possible earnings to be had, it had occurred to Neil that it might be something he would consider doing himself; however, as he now looked across the matting and saw Dean's opponent, he changed his mind. The man was about six feet four, his head was shaved, he was covered in tattoos, and had massive biceps; the only way Neil would consider fighting him was if he was threatening the life of Caroline, Michael or Paul. Neil could not understand how Dean appeared so calm, and completely unafraid, at the prospect of facing this monster.

As the crowd was filling up, Neil suddenly saw a face that he thought he recognised; he immediately walked over to big Joe.

"I may be wrong here," said Neil, "but I've just seen someone who I think is police. I sometimes go to functions with a mate of mine who's a serving police officer in Merseyside, and I've just seen someone who I'm sure was at one of these functions. I find that police tend to socialise with each other, so there's a fair chance I'm right, and he is police."

Big Joe nodded. "Point him out to me, Neil."

Neil pointed to the far side of the matted area. "That fella there with the glasses, wearing the Crombie overcoat."

"Yeah," said Joe, peering at the man Neil indicated, "you're right, he is police, but he's not on duty now - he's a regular at the fights, and is quite a big gambler. Sometimes he has his missus with him, and occasionally he brings his fancy woman. There's been the odd time in the past when I've had to cancel a fight because of the information he's passed to me. So he's okay, he's one of us." Neil nodded, and was about to walk away, when big Joe continued. "Neil, thanks for the warning - it's appreciated, and remembered."

"No problem," smiled Neil, as he turned to rejoin the warehouse boys.

As he walked back to the arena, where Dean was making ready to engage his opponent, Neil noticed that the rest of the warehouse boys appeared to have spread themselves about amongst the crowd, with the exception of Jonjo, who was standing roughly halfway between the two bookies. Neil chose a suitable vantage point from which to view the fight; the two referees called the opponents together into the centre, said something to them which Neil could not hear, and then the referees stepped back.

The fight started more slowly than Neil had imagined, as both men seemed to be sizing each other up, with speculative swings of fists and feet which were making no contact. Neil observed that Dean was wearing a gumshield, whereas his opponent was not – although, in any event, the latter had few teeth left to protect, which made him look even more fearsome. Suddenly, Dean appeared to lose his footing slightly, and was caught with a punch which knocked him over. Neil was concerned for his safety as, for a split second, it looked as if the Kirkby man was about to attack him while he was on the floor; however, Dean simply stayed on one knee for about twenty seconds, then stood up, and the fight resumed.

The Kirkby fighter was swinging wildly at Dean, and Neil feared that, if one of those blows made contact and knocked him down, Dean might not be able to get back up again. At this point, Dean appeared to be keeping well out of the way of the punches and kicks that were being aimed at him, which was contrary to the way he had shown Neil in their first training session. Neil was just wondering whether that style of dodging blows was too risky in a real fight, when he noticed that Jonjo had walked to the edge of the matted area, and saw him nod to Dean.

Immediately, Dean launched a sustained attack on his opponent. The Kirkby man was desperately trying to defend himself; as he guarded his head, Dean was punching and kicking to the body and, as Dean's opponent dropped his guard, the onslaught under which he came could only be described as merciless. Neil was amazed that this man stayed on his feet as long as he did, but it was only a matter of time before he went down and, as he did, Dean calmly stepped back; even more astounding to Neil was to see that, after twenty seconds, the man got to his feet and tried to resume the fight.

The second attack from Dean was even more ferocious than the first and, to Neil's eyes, what he was witnessing had ceased to be merely a fight; it had become a demolition. He marvelled at the way in which Dean was able to stay so close to his opponent and deliver powerful blows, while avoiding any defensive shots by inches. When, inevitably, the Kirkby man was knocked down again, Neil was reasonably certain that, this time, he would not get back up; and, sure enough, he was correct. Whether Dean's opponent was unable to get up, or had decided against it, was not evident; either way, he stayed down for over thirty seconds, and the fight was over.

Dean walked over to Neil, to be joined by Jonjo. "2/1 on was the best I could get," said Jonjo.

Dean nodded. "That'll do; 10 K is the best I could have hoped for. I don't know how that fella came into this fight undefeated - Eddie's girlfriend could've beat him."

Jonjo laughed. "Eddie's girlfriend could beat *us* if she put her mind to it."

Neil was intrigued. "I'll ask this while Eddie's not in earshot - but is she a bit of a bruiser, then?"

"Far from it, she's an absolute stunner," replied Jonjo, "but you wouldn't want to fall out with her. Why do you think Eddie's as fast as he is?"

As the three were laughing, they were joined by the remaining warehouse boys.

"Everything okay?" asked Dean; all the men nodded. Dean turned to Neil. "When big Joe said that there were more people here than he expected, he may not have had enough security of his own, if there'd been any trouble," he explained, for Neil's benefit.

"What sort of trouble?"

"Occasionally, some of the fighters bring a large group of supporters with them, who aren't happy when their man loses; so the lads here were just keeping an eye on the crowd for any potential troublemakers."

"So, I take it there weren't any troublemakers here tonight?"

"There was one stood by me who got a bit mouthy," mentioned Phil, "so I had a quiet word with him, and he seemed to calm down."

Neil looked at Phil. "A quiet word?"

"He knocked him out," elaborated Andy, laughing.

Phil shrugged. "Like I say - it *did* calm him down."

"Well, I must say, Dean," said Neil, shaking his head, "this has been a real eye-opener; you've shown me a world that I didn't know existed. But now, I'm afraid I need to get back to the real world, and earn some money - so I'll make a move."

"Don't forget your winnings," Jonjo reminded him; "here's your two hundred pounds stake, and a hundred pounds profit."

"Of course," grinned Neil; "with all the excitement, I'd forgotten about that. Cheers, Jonjo - that hundred quid is probably more than I'd have earned tonight anyway. Wednesday nights can sometimes be pretty slow."

"And that's the first time in your life you've ever gambled?" asked Dean.

"Gambled?" replied Neil, affecting surprise. "I didn't gamble!"

"Is right!" barked Eddie, cheerfully.

"In that case, seeing as how you aren't out of pocket, why don't you have the rest of the night off, and come down the Dingle with us?" suggested Dean.

Neil smiled. "You're not fighting someone down there as well, are you?"

"No, that's enough fighting for one night," Dean assured him; "we're going to see an old friend of ours who's got a little pub in the Dingle, and you'd be more than welcome to come along."

Neil considered for a moment. "Okay then, why not? I was born not far from the Dingle, and I haven't been there for years; it'll be interesting to see if the old neighbourhood's still standing."

Just then, big Joe came over to join them. "Good fight, Deano," he remarked, "he wasn't as tough as I'd been led to believe. I know you could've done a lot more damage to him, and I appreciate the fact that you didn't."

Dean made a dismissive gesture. "You know me, Joe, I'm not malicious - I just do what's needed to win. Anyway, we're off to Macca's pub in the Dingle, if you fancy coming along?"

Big Joe paused slightly. "You know, I haven't been over there for years. Is there room for a little 'un in your battle bus?"

"There is, but it'd be a bit of a squeeze."

"I can take you in my cab, Joe, there's plenty of room in there," offered Neil.

"Cheers, Neil, that would be great."

Outside in the compound, Neil got into the taxi, started the engine, and waited for big Joe, who had indicated that he needed to make a phone call before they left; however, it was not long before big Joe climbed into the back of the cab.

"I believe you don't know this pub, so I'll direct you," suggested Joe. "I bet you we get there before the warehouse boys, even with their fancy satnav system."

"I wouldn't bank on it Joe - I'm quite a careful driver. I like to take my time, and get there in one piece."

"We'll see," insisted Joe; "I used to drive a cab in Liverpool, donkeys years ago, so I know all the short cuts."

This proved to be no idle boast; Neil had always thought that he was thoroughly familiar with the city, but soon realised that he knew it nowhere near as well as big Joe.

"Told you we'd get here first," declared Joe, as they got out of the cab.

Neil looked around him, and shook his head. "I can't believe how little there's left of this area; as we came through, I noticed that my old street's gone, and so many other streets I used to play in have also been demolished."

"I know what you mean," agreed Joe. "I haven't been round here for years myself, so I was surprised to see how much waste ground there is, where there used to be houses. Years ago, it used to be a close knit community, the Dingle - but it looks like a ghost town now."

As they walked in to the pub, the man behind the bar stopped what he was doing, smiled, and said "Big Joe? You must have taken a wrong turn - this isn't Bootle!"

"How are you doing, Macca?" said Joe, with a big beaming smile. "It's great to see you."

"Likewise, Joe - what brings you down this end of the city?"

"The warehouse boys are on their way over, so I thought I'd join them for a drink." He turned, and indicated his companion. "This young man here is Neil - he's a friend of the warehouse boys, and a good friend of mine."

Joe turned to Neil. "Dean tells me you don't drink alcohol, so what would you like?"

"Glass of orange with a load of ice would be great, cheers Joe."

"Single malt for you, Joe?" Big Joe nodded and took out his wallet, but Macca held up his hand. "Put your money away, this is on me."

Macca then turned to the rest of the people in the bar. "Listen up, everybody," he instructed. "There's a crew of Manchester lads arriving shortly, who are good friends of mine. I'll warn you now - if anyone does or says anything stupid, then two things will happen: firstly, you'll never get a drink in here again as long as I own this place; secondly, if you cross these fellas, I guarantee you'll be taken out of this pub on a stretcher."

Neil glanced around the room, and could see that there were some tough looking men in the place; nevertheless, he hoped that they had the good sense to heed Macca's warning. He and Joe had just sat down with their drinks when the door opened, and in walked the warehouse boys.

"Brilliant!" exclaimed Macca. "Thanks for coming down to see us - what are you all having? It's on the house!"

The warehouse boys duly collected their drinks from the bar, and joined Neil and big Joe.

"What did you think about tonight then, Neil?" was Dean's opening enquiry, after he had taken a mouthful of his drink.

"Unbelievable," replied Neil, sincerely. "What surprised me most was the mixture of people that came to watch the fight. Is that typical?"

"To be fair, it's down to big Joe," explained Dean. "Some of the people you saw there tonight you wouldn't see at other bare knuckle fights. If the fights are not well organised, there's the risk of a police raid, or even a big battle at the end of the fight."

"Over the years," added Joe, "I've built up a lot of good contacts, so when I put on a fight, people from all walks of life know that they can attend safely, with no risk of being arrested, or getting involved in any sort of brawl."

As Joe was speaking, Neil noticed a man walk into the bar, whose appearance was even more fearsome than that of Dean's opponent earlier.

"Look out, it's little Albie!" announced Eddie, as he stood up with a welcoming smile.

Neil examined the new arrival; he estimated that the man was in his late thirties, possibly early forties, but as to the term 'little' – Neil smiled to himself; 'little' Albie was as tall as Jonjo, and as broad as Dean. He was a popular man with the warehouse boys, if their reaction was anything to go by; and he, in turn, seemed genuinely pleased to see them.

"Evening gents," greeted Albie, as he came over to join them. "I just got a call to say there were ten big Manc lads in Macca's pub so I knew it had to be the warehouse boys. It's great to see you lads, how are you all doing?" He took a seat by big Joe. "Dad's going to be pig sick when he finds out he's missed you, Joe - you haven't been down our end for years."

Big Joe looked slightly shamefaced. "It was a spur of the moment thing, Albie - how is your dad?"

"He's great, he's in Turkey at the moment. He seems to spend more time there than he does at home."

"Albie, this is Scouse Neil," interjected Dean; "he's a friend of ours."

"And a good friend of mine," added Joe.

"'Scouse' Neil?" enquired Albie. "What's a Scouser doing drinking with a bunch of Manchester riffraff?"

All the warehouse boys smiled at his words, but Neil suspected that if anyone else in that pub had described the warehouse boys as 'riffraff', the outcome would have been quite different.

"Strictly speaking, I'm not really drinking, this is only orange juice," confessed Neil; "and although I was born in Liverpool, I actually live in Cheshire now."

Albie scrutinised him, almost suspiciously. "Why are you drinking orange juice?"

"I don't drink alcohol," shrugged Neil in reply.

Albie was now frowning. "So, you don't drink, you live in Cheshire, and you talk a lot posher than me or big Joe - are you sure you're a Scouser?"

"Albie!" Neil could see immediately that when Dean said this, little Albie gave him his full attention; he had not realised that Dean had been listening intently to their exchange. "This is the taxi driver I was telling you about, from that night in Chester."

Albie examined Neil with renewed interest. "Four of them?"

"Two of them ran away," corrected Neil, diffidently.

"But you didn't know they were going to do that when you decided to go against them. Dean said they were all bigger than you, and one of them had a baseball bat. You were willing to go against four fellas, one of them armed, to protect someone you didn't even know?"

Neil's response was simply to smile, and shrug his shoulders.

Albie then seemed to sit up in his chair, and look around the pub as though he was searching for someone. "Who's trying to say that this fella's not a Scouser? They'll answer to me first." Everyone laughed as Albie said this, he then looked at Dean, almost for approval; and it was evident that he believed he had received it, when Dean simply nodded his head.

"I've got to ask this," ventured Neil; "you must be about six foot three - so if you're little Albie, how big is big Albie?"

"About five foot seven!" grinned Albie. "Big Albie's my dad. We're both called Albert, so when I was growing up, he was big Albie, and I was little Albie. I think I was about twelve years old when I caught up to his height, but our names have stuck with family and friends."

"Right," laughed Neil. "By the way - you said before to Joe that your dad spends a lot of time in Turkey; has he got a place over there?"

"Yeah - he's got a villa, swimming pool, the full works."

"The reason I'm asking is that I'm thinking about maybe, one day, buying a place in Spain - but I've got no idea how you go about buying somewhere abroad."

"Alright, next time dad's home, I'll find out what I can. If you give me your mobile number, I'll pass on any info that might be useful."

"Cheers, Albie," Neil thanked him. "This is still a bit of a dream really, and it may never happen; but the more information I can get, the better chance there is of me being able to do it."

"Well, if I can help, I'll be well pleased. I'm a great believer that if you want something hard enough, then anything's possible."

Neil nodded his head, leaned over and shook hands with Albie, and then stood up.

"Right lads, I'm going to slide off," he announced. "I'll see you all soon." As he was shaking hands with the rest of the party, he remembered about big Joe; however, Albie offered to give him a lift home, so Neil said his goodbyes, and left the pub.

"How's the training going at home?" asked Dean, as he followed Neil back to the cab.

"Well, I've started doing press ups on my knuckles in the shed, seeing as that has a wooden floor; as the knuckles toughen up, I'll start doing the press ups in the garage, which has a concrete floor. I've also set up the two blocks of wood in the garage, and have been practising hitting them with the heel of my hand. I've got to say now, it's very painful."

Dean nodded in acknowledgement. "It is, to begin with; but, progressively, the palm of your hand will get tougher and tougher, to the point where you'll be able to hit the wood as hard as you like, and feel nothing."

"I also went running the other night, and found it takes me, on average, thirty minutes to run that circuit I told you about - roughly five miles."

"So, the next step is to run the same circuit carrying a ten kilogram weight in a haversack, making sure that the inside of the haversack is well padded, so that the weight isn't bouncing on your back. Once you can get your time down to thirty minutes, increase the weight to fifteen kilograms. You'd be surprised how that extra five kilograms will slow you down; but you just keep working until, eventually, you get back down to thirty minutes – then do the same again, upping the weight to twenty kilograms."

Neil nodded, secretly wondering whether he would ever reach that point.

"Once you reach that stage," continued Dean, "don't increase the weight – instead, try to better your time. Even if you're only knocking seconds off the time, by running while carrying a twenty kilogram weight, you are really building up your stamina. Also, try to get up to the warehouse as often as you can; an hour's training with us is worth three or four hours spent in that fitness place you've been going to."

"I've been doing some stretching exercises as well - the ones Eddie showed me, to improve the range of kicks."

"Excellent," said Dean. "I told you that we can show you how to really fight; well, you saw me fight tonight - if I'd have wanted to, I could've put that fella away in a minute."

Neil looked annoyed with himself. "I realise that now. As well as fooling the bookies and all the other punters, you fooled me. I genuinely thought you were in trouble at the start of the fight."

"I know," remarked Dean. "I saw you take your jacket off, when I went down."

"It was a bit warm in there," said Neil lamely, looking slightly uncomfortable.

"Was your wrist warm as well?" enquired Dean, raising one eyebrow. "Because I saw you take your watch off, and put it in your jacket pocket."

Neil grinned sheepishly. "I thought for a minute he was going to attack you, when you were on the floor. I was the nearest of all the lads, so I thought, if he does, I'll take him out."

"Interesting," commented Dean. "Before the fight, you told me you thought that he looked really fearsome, and wouldn't fancy crossing him yourself; and yet, when you thought I was in danger, you were willing to take him on?"

Neil looked almost embarrassed. "I know. Doesn't make sense that really, does it?"

"It makes perfect sense to me," Dean assured him. "We can teach you to be stronger, fitter, faster, more powerful, and to be ten times the fighter that you are now - but we could never teach heart or bravery. Fortunately, you've got tons of that."

The two men shook hands, then Neil climbed into his taxi, and drove away; Dean watched him go, and then rejoined his companions in the bar.

"Everything okay?" asked Albie. "Scouse Neil wasn't offended by what I said before, was he?"

"Not at all," replied Dean, dismissively; "it was just two Scousers having a bit of banter."

Albie looked relieved. "The lads were saying that he's training with you. I've never known you allow anyone to train with you before."

"That's because he's the first man we've ever met who's just like us," explained Jonjo.

"He's a warrior," agreed Eddie. "We'll teach him to be a better one."

Albie noted that all the warehouse boys were nodding their agreement.

"I think that probably answers your question," said Dean.

…………………………………...

Neil called in at the warehouse as often as he could, and stuck rigidly to his training regime at home. He had always thought of himself as being fit and in good shape for a man of his age, but surprised himself by how much fitter and stronger he was becoming. All the warehouse boys were only too pleased to give up their time whenever Neil was there, to help with his training.

In addition to the work he was doing on his defence, he was also now working on his attack. He was amazed at how much he was learning from these young men who, in turn, seemed to be really impressed with how quickly Neil was progressing, and how powerful he was becoming. Amongst other things, they taught him how to attack when his back was turned to an opponent; this was a particularly effective ploy when fighting against someone who had a good defence.

During this spell of training, Neil attended a fight involving Jonjo, which gave him the opportunity to see, at first hand, how effective was Jonjo's defence; as with Dean, Jonjo demonstrated that he could end a fight whenever he chose. However, by far the most exciting to watch was fast Eddie; although he did not demonstrate the same level of power as some of the other warehouse boys, Eddie could deliver so many blows so quickly during a fight that opponents stood no chance against him.

Dean's next fight was against a young man from Blackburn who, from all accounts, was likely to prove far more testing than the Kirkby opponent. The Blackburn man had a martial arts background and, the warehouse boys had discovered, was far more of an athlete than the usual bare knuckle fighter. The meeting was due to take place in a large warehouse, on the other side of Manchester.

Shortly before the time he knew the boys would be setting off from their own warehouse headquarters, Neil arrived, and went straight into the lounge.

"You may as well leave your cab here, and come over with us in the battle bus," suggested Jonjo.

"Okay," agreed Neil. "By the way, I've been meaning to ask this for ages - why do you call it the battle bus?"

"Well, actually, we've got two of these minibuses," explained Jonjo indirectly. "Whenever there's a night in the city where we're expecting more trouble than normal, five of us are in one bus, and five in the other. If any of the nightclubs or pubs that have our doormen outside get any major problems, we get there as quick as we can to sort it out. By having the two buses, either group of the warehouse boys is likely to be near enough to deal with it."

As Neil was boarding the minibus, he realised that Dean was absent, as were Tommy, Phil and Joey; Jonjo saw the confused look on Neil's face. "In case you're wondering, Dean's meeting us there," he volunteered. "He's been over in Yorkshire today, sorting out a possible security contract with a number of hospitals."

"Ah, right," said Neil. "Did he take Tommy and the lads with him in case the nurses gave him a hard time?"

"It'd take more than four of us to deal with the nurses," sniggered Eddie. "No - Phil, Joe and Tommy are doing a private function over your way. It's at a big posh house in Cheshire in a marquee, and the owner doesn't want any uninvited guests."

They arrived at the fight venue, which was in an area called Crumsall; as they were parking, Jonjo was frowning as he looked around outside, seemingly searching for something.

"That's strange," he observed; "I'd have thought Deano would've got here before us. He should have come over the M62, and as far as I know, there've been no problems as far as traffic's concerned. I'd better give him a ring."

Neil stood by the entrance while Jonjo attempted to call Dean, but it was clear by the way he was shaking his head that he was getting no reply. "Voicemail," he said, an element of frustration in his tone. "It's very unusual for Dean to have his phone switched off."

They decided to go into the warehouse, where Neil was confronted by a large, menacing looking man, who thrust his open palm at him.

"Fifty pounds!" he demanded.

"Sparky! He's with us," remonstrated Jonjo.

The man called Sparky took a step back, and held up his hand in what was almost a defensive gesture. "Sorry, Jonjo, I didn't realise," he said contritely.

"Fifty pounds?" Neil remarked to Jonjo, as they walked away. "That's a bit steep, isn't it?"

Jonjo smiled. "It would be if we had to pay it - but we never get charged at any of the fights, when one of our lads is involved."

"That's not bad," noted Neil. "How've you managed to get that arrangement?"

"Because if anything kicks off, we'll help the security fellas sort it out. That's a big help to the organiser, so not charging us for entrance is his way of repaying us."

"At fifty pounds per head, Dean will be picking up a good wedge in prize money," mused Neil; "let alone what you win off the bookies."

"That reminds me - I assume you've brought your standard two hundred pounds with you?"

"Certainly have!" said Neil cheerfully, as he handed the cash to Jonjo.

"With a bit of luck, I might be able to double that for you tonight," offered Jonjo. "This Blackburn lad is no pushover, so we may be able to get even money on Dean."

Now that he had a better understanding of odds, Neil was impressed that this new opponent was possibly good enough to keep Dean at even money, instead of odds on favourite as normal. He was just reflecting about his likely winnings, when it occurred to him that there was still no sign of Dean; as he and Jonjo joined the rest of the warehouse boys, Jonjo looked at them all, shrugged his shoulders, and shook his head.

Eddie looked troubled. "I've just been checking the internet on the phone, and there's no mention of any accidents or hold-ups on the 62."

While the warehouse boys were speculating as to what could have happened to Dean, Neil was watching his friend's opponent doing various stretching exercises; it was clear that this young man was far more of an athlete than any of the previous adversaries that the warehouse boys had fought.

The organiser of the fight walked over to Jonjo, in an agitated state. "Where's Dean?" he demanded. "This crowd's getting restless. Have you tried ringing his mobile?"

Jonjo regarded him with an expression of disgust. "I would never have thought of that," he replied sarcastically; "I'll give that a try."

The man's expression changed from concern to fear. "Sorry Jonjo - that was a stupid thing to say, sorry mate."

Meanwhile, Neil began to notice that the Blackburn fighter, and his large group of supporters were, ostentatiously, making fun of the warehouse boys.

"No sign of the tough guy yet?" shouted Dean's opponent, derisively. "Warehouse boys? Warehouse fairies, more like! I told you that Dean fella wouldn't fight me, he's too much of a coward!"

Almost without realising, Neil had found himself walking towards this loud mouth and, as he got closer, felt the blood pumping in his head.

"I'll fight yer, kid!" Neil flung at the other man, in his strongest Liverpool accent.

The Blackburn fighter turned; he surveyed Neil with open contempt.

"I haven't come here to fight an old Scouse dwarf!" he sneered. "Walk away, old man, you're not in my league."

Neil gritted his teeth. "There's only one way of findin' out what league I'm in - or are yer too scared?" he hissed. "Seems there's only one coward round 'ere."

The Blackburn man's features hardened. "Okay, fool - I'm going to punish you for that remark."

As Neil walked back over to the warehouse boys, he began to shake uncontrollably.

"I don't know what I'm shaking for," he told them, "because it's not fear."

"It's the adrenaline, you need to calm down." Jonjo looked concerned.

"Stay cool," advised Earl; "stay cool."

Just then, one of the Blackburn supporters shouted across to them. "Look, the Scouser's quaking in his boots!"

This barb inflamed Neil's temper still further; Eddie gripped Neil by the shoulders, and made him face him.

"Alright, if you're going through with this, then listen," he instructed. "Whatever you do, don't fight angry - he'll just pick you off. Stay focused on what needs to be done, concentrate, and remember everything we've taught you. Words will never harm you – but he will, if you let him get to you."

"Eddie's right," said Jonjo. "Now, get the gumshield in. Stay out of the firing line to begin with, give yourself time to settle down, and then start fighting him. Don't go piling in thinking you're going to knock him straight out, because you won't. Take your time, concentrate, focus, and ignore what his fool supporters are shouting. Bravery isn't enough here - you need to put into practice everything you've learned."

Meanwhile, the bookie had shouted to everyone that all bets were off, and the odds were now changing; the Blackburn fighter was now odds on favourite, and Scouse Neil was 6/1 against.

Neil walked to the centre of the fighting area; he was aware that the referee had said something to him, but he had no idea what it was, as all he could do was glare at his opponent.

"You're going to be sorry you ever opened your mouth, Liverpool scum," spat out the other man, to the baying approval of his supporters.

No sooner had the fight started when - so fast, that he did not see it coming - Neil took a powerful blow to his mouth; it felt as if his mouth was on fire, and as he felt the blood flowing from it, running down his chin, and then his neck, he was grateful for Jonjo's insistence that he use a gumshield. Still angry, however, he foolishly kept going forward and, as a result, received an incredibly painful kick to his side, which felt as if it may have cracked his ribs; going forward again, a second kick landed in almost exactly the same spot, winding him – but it knocked him to his senses. He took a moment to get his breath, fought to suppress his anger, and started to concentrate on what needed to be done.

Neil continued to focus, thinking calmly, and managed to avoid the blows that were being aimed at him, all the while formulating how to mount an attack of his own. When he began his offensive, however, Neil discovered that the other man's defence was excellent, and soon found that he had left himself open to a counter-attack, when his young opponent caught him with a blow to the side of the head. Neil was almost swung around with the impact, so the Blackburn man stepped forward with the intention of finishing Neil off – but in doing so, the former dropped his guard, and Neil saw his chance. He kicked backwards into the midriff of his opponent, almost doubling him over, and immediately followed through with an elbow, straight into the other man's face; then, turning to face him, Neil could see that the young man was dazed – and swiftly delivered a roundhouse kick to his opponent's head, a move of which even Eddie would have been proud.

As his opponent hit the floor, Neil was up on his toes, ready and waiting for the man to get up, knowing that he would put him back down; now that he had his emotions under control, he knew he could beat him, and was almost willing his adversary to get to his feet. Then, suddenly, he felt a hand on his shoulder, which caused him to jump; he turned round, and found he was looking into the smiling face of Jonjo.

"He's not getting up, mate." Neil gazed at Jonjo in disbelief for a moment; then he turned, and looked back at his opponent, still on the floor. He was out cold.

"That's right, it's all over," confirmed Jonjo. "Come on, let's get back to the lads."

Neil followed Jonjo back to where the rest of the warehouse boys were standing, almost in a daze at what had happened; they welcomed him like a conquering hero.

"We need to get you back to the warehouse, to get the doc to check you over," advised Jonjo. "Let's have a look at your mouth, and see if it's still bleeding."

Neil submitted to his examination gratefully, as his jaw was aching. "Have we heard anything from Dean yet?" he asked.

Jonjo merely shook his head, and carried on attending to Neil's wounds, wiping the blood from his face and neck; after he had finished, Neil was putting on his shirt, when he noticed that big Joe was heading towards them.

"Alright, Joe," Neil hailed the big man. "I don't know how I missed you in the crowd."

As big Joe reached Neil, he simply looked down at him, almost like a father who was very proud of his favourite son; then he leaned forward, and stuffed a wad of money into Neil's top shirt pocket.

"You've just won me a very large amount of money," he informed him, "so please accept this as a thank you."

Neil looked at him in amazement. "You didn't bet on me, did you?"

"I brought a large sum with me, expecting Dean to be favourite," he admitted; "although, I have to say, the lad you've just fought is a good fighter. He was undefeated, keeps himself in shape, and is very professional, even though he's a bit mouthy."

Neil smiled. "So what possessed you to bet on me?"

Again, big Joe seemed to regard Neil with a genuine affection. "Because you've been trained by the warehouse boys, you've got the heart of a lion, and you're a Scouser; you couldn't lose."

"Is right!" declared Eddie, as he clapped Neil on the shoulder, with equal affection.

Jonjo had stepped aside, to answer his phone; everyone fell silent, and were relieved to discover that the call was from Dean. Jonjo's responses suggested that there was no cause for concern, and that Dean would meet them back at the warehouse.

"What was the problem?" asked Neil, after Jonjo finished the call.

"Something to do with the electrics on Dean's car," said Jonjo. "It seems that, as he was coming along the motorway everything died on him, and because he was charging his phone at the time, that died as well. Anyway, it's all sorted now, and he's on his way to the warehouse."

Just then, the organiser of the fight came over with the prize money; he looked extremely pleased to be handing the money to Neil.

"I'm so glad you dropped that mouthy bastard," he asserted. "It was a good turnout tonight, so there's a reasonable wedge there for you. Well done, mate!"

……………………………...

The doctor was at the warehouse when they arrived, and gave Neil a thorough check over. Luckily, his ribs were intact, although most of his side was very badly bruised; his mouth was also quite swollen, but the doctor assured him that it would look better in two or three days. As everyone sat down in the lounge, Tommy, Phil and Joey arrived, followed shortly afterwards by Dean.

Meanwhile, Jonjo offered to work out the night's takings. "You've got a good wedge there," he told Neil; "plus, I've got your twelve hundred pounds winnings, and your two hundred pounds stake. Altogether, including what big Joe gave you, there's just under five grand here."

"You bet on me as well?" Neil was astounded. "I thought you'd have put the two hundred quid on the other fella, so that if I lost, at least I would've come away with a couple of bob, even though I'd have got battered."

Tommy, who was standing behind Jonjo, put his hand on Jonjo's shoulder. "Only a fool bets against the warehouse boys - and Jonjo's no fool."

Before Eddie could open his mouth, Dean rapped out "Is right!" At this, everyone started laughing, including Neil; this caused him to groan and hold his ribs which, in turn, increased the laughter. Neil simply groaned even more loudly as he held his aching side.

"Isn't there a saying about laughter being the best medicine?" remarked Eddie. "Well, right now, not in Scouse Neil's case it isn't!"

This comment led to even more laughter; however, as much as Neil was genuinely in pain, the laughter was the best medicine he could have wanted; he also felt a great deal of pride, at being looked upon as one of the warehouse boys. Dean, it seemed, must have been reading his thoughts; when Neil looked across the table, he saw Dean smiling and, almost imperceptibly, nodding his head.

"Anyway, what's your missus going to say when she sees your mouth?" wondered Eddie. "You've got lips like Mick Jagger at the moment."

"I'll try and dodge her for the next couple of days."

"How are you going to manage that?" was Joey's question.

"Sometimes we go days without seeing each other, it's the job," shrugged Neil. "There are times when I get in so late of a night that Caroline's already in bed, asleep; then, I'm up so early the following morning, I've gone out before she gets up. Very often, I don't even go to bed - I just have a doze downstairs and then go back out to work."

"Yes - but what if she does clock you, while your mouth's like that?" enquired Phil.

Neil grinned. "I can, more or less, tell you how the conversation will go. Caroline will say something like 'Neil, what's happened now?' And I'll say something along the lines of 'A bit of a problem with some drunks.' Caroline will then say 'Neil, you've got to do something else.' Then I'll say 'But what else *can* I do?' And that will be the end of the discussion."

"Caroline's good at remembering your name, then," chuckled Eddie.

"To be fair, she has had a few years practice," said Neil, in mock reflection.

At that point the banter started, and the rest of the evening was spent laughing and joking Neil and Eddie, in particular, had the rest of the warehouse boys nearly crying with laughter; the two were almost like a double act.

Chapter 15

Neil arrived at the warehouse quite early, and was surprised to find that only Rod and Eddie were there, in the lounge.

"Well, did you manage to avoid your good lady wife?" asked Rod.

Neil nodded emphatically, as he sat down. "I did indeed. By the time I got home last night, Caroline was well away, so I grabbed a couple of hours' sleep downstairs on the couch, then left before I knew she'd be getting up."

"Well done!" said Eddie "Does Caroline know you come here training?"

"Definitely not. If I told her I was training with a group of men who sometimes work as security guards, bodyguards or nightclub bouncers, and who make extra money from bare knuckle fighting, she'd be frantic; every time I went out of the house she would be fretting. Caroline's bad enough as it is, worrying about me when I'm working nights on the taxi – I don't want to add to that."

"Fair enough," said Rod. "Does anyone know you come here?"

Neil shook his head. "You see, occasionally, Caroline and I go out with some of the other taxi drivers and their wives. If any of the lads knew what I was involved in, they might let it slip by accident, or tell their wives, who in turn could tell Caroline." He shifted uneasily in his seat. "To tell the truth, I feel a bit deceitful keeping this from everyone, but it would just worry Caroline unnecessarily."

"Whatever's easiest for you," shrugged Eddie. "But don't your mates on the taxis wonder where you've been, when you go missing for a couple of hours?"

"Well, that's the great thing about driving a taxi - I'm a complete free agent. I'm not answerable to anyone, I'm not accountable in any way, and I work when I like. During the average day, I might only see my mate, Danny, half a dozen times - either passing on the road, or having a quick chat on one of the ranks; but if someone were to ask him if I'd been working all day, he'd assume that I had, even though he'd only seen me from time to time. Effectively, I could be missing for two or three hours, and the other taxi drivers would assume I was working a different rank from the ones they were working."

"I get it," acknowledged Rod; "in theory, then, a taxi driver could lead a complete double life, and no-one would notice?"

"Exactly - and to a certain extent, that's what I'm now doing."

Rod nodded his head thoughtfully. "So, now you've had time to think about last night's events, and your performance in the fight – how would you sum it up?"

Neil had found Rod to be a very intelligent man, and always enjoyed holding a conversation with him; he considered his response for a moment.

"Well," he said eventually, "obviously, where I really let myself down was not controlling my anger. I won't make that mistake again - the next time I'm in any sort of confrontational situation, I'll stay calm."

Eddie, as always, was smiling. "You're right, that could've cost you the fight - but luckily, that second kick to the ribs forced you to concentrate on what needed to be done."

"You finished the fight well," remarked Rod; "we were all impressed with the speed and power of that combination you put together - it was very effective."

"His defence was very good; so, when he caught me with the left hook, I made it look a lot worse than it actually was, to get him to drop his guard. Thankfully, that worked, and I was able to take him out."

Eddie punched the arm of his seat with delight. "I *knew* it!" he declared. "Jonjo thought he'd really hurt you with that shot, but I said he hadn't - I *knew* you were setting him up!"

Rod smiled, slightly sheepishly. "Well, you fooled me as well - because I thought you were really in trouble at that point."

"It's all down to Eddie," said Neil generously. "He and I have been working on that finish for some time, using the backwards kick and the elbow at full force – so, as I turned and saw the lad was dazed, I knew I could take him out with the roundhouse. Again, Eddie has been working very hard with me, improving my kicking technique."

"And it paid off," added Eddie; "but we'll give the training a rest for a while - your ribs are going to be sore for some time."

Neil smiled, and appeared to be deep in thought as he scrutinised his companions, as if wondering how to broach a subject with them.

"Something else on your mind?" asked Rod, astutely.

"Well, as a matter of fact, yes there is," replied Neil. "Since I've got to know you lads, I can see there's obviously a bond between all of you, a closeness which I've never seen before amongst a group of mates. If you don't mind my asking - what *is* the connection?"

Rod and Eddie exchanged a look, and smiled.

"Afghanistan," replied Rod, simply.

Of course, Neil reflected, these men were ex-military. Everything he had seen and heard now made sense - how neat and tidy the warehouse was; how smart and well turned out the warehouse boys were in themselves, always clean-shaven, never scruffy; the camaraderie between them; and their reaction to Neil's choice of charity for the five hundred pound donation.

"Stupid of me, I should've realised," said Neil. "Did you all serve together?"

"We did," confirmed Rod; "but it wasn't just the fact that we served together that created the bond between us. It was a particular incident in Afghanistan."

Eddie's eyes lit up. "Have you ever seen a film called 'Zulu'?"

"Dozens of times," said Neil, enthusiastically; "it's my most favourite film by a long, long way."

"Mine too," said Eddie. "Well, then, you're going to love this story."

Rod took his cue. "We'll just stick to the basics, otherwise we could be here for days," he said. Neil listened expectantly.

"It all started when we were behind enemy lines, and were cut-off from the rest of the troops," began Rod. "There were seventeen of us, trapped in a small compound, surrounded by Taliban fighters. Our radio had been shot to bits, so we had no communication; but fortunately, we had plenty of ammunition, and didn't expect to be there too long before help arrived."

Eddie took up the story. "The compound we were in was quite small, with three reasonably high walls, and one low one; that wall only came to just above our waists so, obviously, that was the side of the compound where we were coming under the heaviest attack. Anyway, we were pinned down without any means of escape, and there was nothing we could do about it; we were well outnumbered and, although we were taking out a lot of them, we were losing some as well." He paused, and it seemed as if a cloud had passed over his normally cheerful countenance. "Macca and Jimmy were the first to be killed," he said flatly; "they were good lads, tough lads, frightened of nothing, typical Scousers."

"Jimmy was hit as he was standing by the low wall," continued Rod; "it caused him to fall forward and out of the compound, so Macca was over the wall like a shot, and tried to lift him back in."

"And then, Macca was shot in the back, as he was trying to lift Jimmy up," said Eddie, bleakly. "Macca once told me that him and Jimmy had been best mates since they were little kids; it's not much consolation, but at least they died side by side."

"That's why we went down to the Dingle, the night Dean had been fighting in Bootle," explained Rod. "The fella who owns that pub is Macca's older brother, and we always like to look in on him whenever we're over that way."

"Over the next twenty-four hours, we lost five more, including the captain," resumed Eddie. "He was a top man - talked dead posh, but was one of the lads. He never expected anyone to do something that he wasn't willing to do himself."

Rod was nodding his agreement. "A grenade came over, and the captain just dropped on it; he took the full blast, but his actions saved four or five of us."

Both men fell silent at this point. Neil observed the haunted look on Rod's face as he finished speaking; and, for the first time since they had met, he did not detect the mischievous spark in Eddie's eyes, which he had assumed was permanently present. He began to regret that his curiosity had caused them to revisit their sadness, but felt obliged to say something.

"I take it, then, that the surviving ten men are now the warehouse boys?" Rod and Eddie simply nodded. "How did you manage to escape?"

As he asked this question, he was glad to see the lively expression coming back into Eddie's eyes. "This is the part that you're going to like," Rod assured him, whose mood also visibly brightened.

"I'd already said to the lads that we should call the compound Rorke's Drift," said Eddie, "so I suggested we start singing Men of Harlech; trouble was, none of us knew the words, and I don't think there's a song called Men of Manchester - so we thought it was probably best to just keep shooting."

"However, we were starting to get low on ammo at this point," added Rod. "The frustrating thing was that there was a 240 there, but it was jammed."

"Sorry for my ignorance," interrupted Neil, "but what's a 240?"

"The M 240," replied Rod; "it replaced the M 60. Although it's a bit heavier than the M 60, it's a much better piece of equipment."

This left Neil feeling none the wiser. "Sorry, Rod, but I've got no idea what an M 60 is either."

"It's a machine gun," explained Rod; "a heavy machine gun, which is normally operated on a stand, and generally used by the US Marines. When we found the 240 in the compound, we assumed that there must have been some sort of battle there before, and the weapon had just been left because it was jammed. There was plenty of ammo with it, but that was no good, because we couldn't get it to fire."

"At this point, the Taliban had stopped attacking the three high walls of the compound, because they were getting nowhere - so all their attacks were coming at us from the same direction," continued Eddie. "While this was going on, Tommy had stripped the 240 down, cleaned it, and put it back together - but it was still jammed."

"The next bit still makes me shudder," remembered Rod. "Dean had been checking everyone's ammo while there was a break in the fighting, then he said 'When they come at us again and start firing, don't fire back.' I just looked at him and thought he'd gone mad. Dean, of course, was as calm as you like, and explained why. He said 'We need them to think that either we're all dead, or we've run out of ammo. That will draw them out into the open ground, and bring them much closer to the compound. We're so low on ammo now, we have to make every shot count.' I could see his logic; but the thought of allowing the enemy to get so close was terrifying." As Rod was speaking, Neil was intrigued to note that Eddie appeared to be chuckling to himself. "And the worst part was that Dean told us that no-one should start firing until Eddie decided to shoot."

Neil glanced at Eddie, and raised his eyebrows questioningly. "I'm the world's worst shot," confessed Eddie, grinning. "Deano knew full well that, if I decided that *I* could hit one of the enemy, all the other lads would definitely be able to hit one as well."

Rod smiled at Eddie. "It wasn't just the fact that he's a rubbish shot," he told Neil. "Eddie is the bravest of all of us, and Dean knew that Eddie would leave it till the last second before firing. We've all talked about it since that day, and every one of us, including Dean, was praying Eddie would take that shot."

Eddie winked at Neil. "Jessies!" he grunted.

Neil shook his head with admiration at the bravery of the younger man. "So you were waiting until you could see the whites of their eyes?" he ventured.

Eddie snorted. "I was waiting till I could see how many nose hairs they had!"

Rod hanged his head, groaning slightly. "You know Neil, I don't think he's joking."

Neil, meanwhile, was laughing at Eddie's audacity. "So, when you took your first shot, were you successful?"

"Certainly was!" replied Eddie, his eyes now back to their normal expression. "And I've always hoped that the first one I got was the one who shot Macca."

"As soon as Eddie fired," continued Rod, "we all started shooting, and we were really picking them off; but there were so many of them. Suddenly, Tommy shouted 'Deano, I've unjammed the 240 - it'll fire, but I can't find the stand for it!' But then Dean just said 'Give it here!' Then he simply lifted it, stood up, and just let rip at the Taliban fighters."

"You've never seen anything like it in your life," Eddie said to Neil. "The 240 is a fair old weight just to lift - but to see Dean actually lift it, fire it, and yet keep it under control, was unbelievable; and bearing in mind, he actually stood up, in full view of the Taliban, and just kept firing. We all stopped shooting because we couldn't see - the shells from the 240 were hitting the ground, kicking up one hell of a dust storm."

"When Eddie says 'hitting the ground', this was after the shells had gone straight through Taliban fighters," pointed out Rod. "Dean just stood there, the sweat pouring off him, and his eyes were red raw from the dust cloud - but he just kept firing, until he ran out of ammunition."

"Even when he'd run out of ammo, Dean just stood there, glaring out as though he was showing the Taliban he wasn't frightened of them." Eddie's admiration for his friend was obvious. "As we looked over the wall, we could see the rest of the Taliban fighters running back up to the high ground - literally, running for their lives."

"It was only then that we realised how outnumbered we were," reflected Rod. "There were bodies everywhere; some had even fallen on top of each other, as they'd been shot. Without doubt, none of us would be here to tell the tale, if it hadn't been for Dean's actions."

Eddie smiled, and shook his head. "And then," he told Neil, "Deano carefully put down the 240, sat down next to it and said, calm as you like, 'Once it goes dark, we'll take it in turn to go over the wall, and collect the weapons and ammo from the Taliban.' It was as though he regularly stood up and shot a hundred Taliban, like it was no big deal."

"It was very strange," mused Rod; "it's true, he wasn't excited, angry, or wound up in any way - he was so matter-of-fact, and spoke without emotion."

"So I said 'I'll go and get the weapons, I'm the fittest, fastest and the smallest,'" grinned Eddie; "the thing was, if the Taliban had a sniper up in the hills, he'd have thought it was his birthday if some of the big lads had gone over the wall."

Rod nodded his agreement. "I've got to admit, at any other time, Eddie saying that he was the fittest would've caused an argument - but there was no argument on that day."

"And then Dean said to me 'you best take a blade, just in case.' But I just smiled, because I already had a knife on my belt."

"Did you need it?" asked Neil.

"No, they were all well dead." Eddie grimaced. "The 240 had almost cut some of them in half. By the time I finished getting all the weapons and ammo it was nearly light, and I had so much blood on me, I looked like a butcher."

Rod took up the story. "We sorted out all the weapons and ammo, so that each one of us was so well equipped, we were ready for anything. The weapons the Taliban had been using were a bit old-fashioned by our standards, but they were still good enough to do the job."

"They all had wooden stocks," added Eddie; then he chuckled. "Which turned out quite well, really."

"The stock is the part that goes into your shoulder," interjected Rod, when he saw Neil's quizzical expression.

"So, we waited and waited, but there was no sign of them," continued Eddie. "Finally, it must've been about midday when Andy got fed up – he started slapping the wooden stock of his gun, and chanting 'Come an' 'ave a go if yer think yer 'ard enough!'" Neil could see the spark in Eddie's eyes as he remembered. "The next thing, Deano stood up, looked out across all the dead Taliban, and joined in the chanting, which was all we needed - me and Jonjo were on either side of him, and we were up like a shot as well."

"Imagine counting to four at normal speed," said Rod for Neil's benefit, "but rather than counting, slapping the stock of the gun; it made a real 'crack' of a sound, which echoed across the valley. Well, needless to say, within a second all ten of us were up, side by side, shoulder to shoulder, chanting 'Come an' 'ave a go if yer think yer 'ard enough!' crack, crack, crack, crack "Come an' 'ave a go if yer think yer 'ard enough!'"

"But they never did." Eddie smiled grimly. "Then, it was while we were chanting that we heard the Chinook - but we just carried on."

Neil, embarrassed by his ignorance, was reluctant to ask what a Chinook was; luckily, however, there was no need.

"When the helicopter was overhead," continued Rod, "I'm not sure if the Americans saw us in the compound from the air, but they certainly would've seen all the dead Taliban. It was quite funny, because they landed on the other side of all the bodies, then looked over at us - but we just kept chanting."

"The Yanks were obviously unsure what to do, because we're still chanting 'Come an' 'ave a go if yer think yer 'ard enough!' Then we all started laughing," remembered Eddie, grinning. "As they walked over to us, one of them said to Jonjo something like 'You Brit guys don't know when to give up!' Jonjo just looked at him straight in the eye, and said 'We don't know how to give up.' I can't remember what I said at that point," he concluded, scratching his head.

Neil laughed. "And was giving up an option?"

"Not really - some of the Taliban aren't exactly 'au fait' with the Geneva Convention," remarked Rod, wryly.

Eddie was mystified. "'Au fait?' What's 'au fait' when it's at home?" Neil provided the explanation. "Apologies, Roderick," smirked Eddie; "carry on with the story."

"Roderick?" enquired Neil. "I thought Rod was short for Rodney."

"Don't ask, mate, don't ask," replied Rod, shaking his head ruefully.

"So – after all that, the ten of you got away unscathed?"

"Not exactly," Rod informed him, as he pulled his T-shirt across to show Neil a scar on his shoulder.

"Is that a bullet wound?"

"Straight through. Fortunately, though, the bullet missed any important bits," said a smiling Rod.

Neil winced. "That must have hurt."

"It did chafe a bit."

"And after that grenade going off, my hearing's never been the same since," sighed Eddie.

Neil looked concerned. "In what way?"

Eddie looked at his watch. "Half past nine!" As the other two collapsed into laughter, Eddie rubbed his hands together. "Got ya!"

"Anyway," recommended Rod, grinning at Eddie, "we all got in the Chinook; and then, as we were taking off, Eddie shouted 'God bless America!' - which went down well with our hosts." Neil, shaking his head, turned to look at a laughing Eddie, who then simply shrugged.

"Well, it seemed like the right thing to say at the time, particularly as they took us to an American base, seeing it was the nearest to where we were," Eddie pointed out. "Tell you what though, Neil, you should've seen it - comparing their base with ours was like comparing a five-star hotel to a bed and breakfast. Anyway, after the de-briefing, we all went to have something to eat, because we were absolutely starving."

Rod looked pensive. "It was quite strange," he reflected. "As we all sat eating, nobody spoke; it was as though it had just hit us, exactly what we'd been through. Although that wasn't the first fire fight we'd been involved in, it was one that none of us should ever have survived."

"That's when Dean announced he was getting out," continued Eddie. "He said that the next time he put his life on the line, it would be for his benefit, and not someone else's. We all agreed with him - and that's where the basic idea of Warehouse Boys Security was first thought of."

"That's right," murmured Rod; he pondered for a moment. "It was almost as though we'd cheated death, and were therefore determined to enjoy every day in the future - always to stand side-by-side, shoulder to shoulder, for the rest of our lives."

The two men fell silent for a minute, and Neil reflected on what he had heard; he could now understand the unbreakable bond that must have formed between these brave men, and felt privileged to have heard their story.

"So," he said, "how did you get the business off the ground?"

"Well," began Eddie, "in the early days, we did security work, working the doors on pubs and clubs, and we got involved in the bare knuckle fighting - basically, anything to raise the money to set up the company."

Rod was nodding his agreement. "Everything we were earning was just going into the one pot; there was no 'Dean's money', or 'Jonjo's money' - it was all Warehouse Boys' money."

"To a certain extent, then, it was a co-operative?"

"No, no....... we weren't selling fruit and veg, or anything like that," replied Eddie.

Neil lowered his head, hiding a smile. "When I said a co-operative, I meant......."; however, as he looked up, Eddie had the mischievous look in his eyes. "Got ya *again*!" he declared, giggling.

Just then, as all three men were laughing, Dean and Jonjo walked in, looking very smart.

"How did it go?" asked Eddie, as the new arrivals sat down.

Dean gave a thumbs up sign. "We've got the security contract for the whole shopping centre."

"Brilliant!" commented Rod. "We've just been telling Scouse Neil about Rorke's Drift."

"Oh?" smiled Jonjo. "The first one, or the second one?"

"Afghanistan," replied Eddie. "That was the first one," he elaborated, turning to Neil.

Neil raised his eyebrows. "So where was the second one? I'd love to hear the story of that as well."

Dean appeared to give a sign to Jonjo, who then began the tale.

"It was in a pub car park, just outside Manchester," he explained. "When we first started working doors, there was a local gangster who controlled most of the doormen in the area. As we got more and more work and built up our reputation, this gangster asked us to meet him in one of his pubs, with what he called a business proposal."

"We had a good idea what his business proposal was," Dean continued, "so we all went up to this pub; me and Jonjo went in to speak to him, the rest of the lads stayed outside in their cars. As we expected, once the two of us were inside, this fella said if we knew what was good for us we should work for him." Dean smiled. "I politely pointed out to him that we did know what was good for us, and we'd be working for ourselves. I also – again, politely - made it clear to him that if he decided to go against us, he'd regret it. Anyway, while this was going on, Eddie rang me to warn us that there was a large group of doormen waiting for us outside."

"When you say a 'large' group - how many?"

"It was difficult to say exactly, because the car park wasn't well lit," Eddie informed Neil; "but I'd say, between thirty and forty."

"Suffice to say," said Rod, "as Dean and Jonjo walked out of the pub, we were all out of the cars, and were ready to take them on."

"It was simple enough - they were the enemy," shrugged Eddie. "When we put them down, if they had the sense to stay down, they were safe. If they got back up, we'd put them down again. The only way they could escape was to crawl away from the fight, and then get up and run. In a matter of minutes there were only ten men left standing."

Dean smiled at Neil. "The message went out clearly that night; the warehouse boys won't be bullied. If anyone is fool enough to go against us, they'll lose."

"The funny thing is, quite a few of those bouncers we put on the ground work for us now," added Jonjo.

"So they're your mates now?" ventured Neil.

Dean shook his head, his expression grim. "No, they'll never be our mates, because they went against us. We get work for them, and take a percentage - and that's the only dealings we have with them."

Throughout the rest of that day in the warehouse, various people came and went. As for Neil, he was pleased to have the time, and the opportunity, to chat to each of the warehouse boys individually; in doing so he discovered that, although their characters were quite different, as a collective, they held the same values – of standing together, and always looking out for each other. Finally, as the end of the day drew nearer, only Neil and Dean remained in the lounge.

"I suppose you and the lads must have picked up a medal or two, from Afghanistan and Iraq?" suggested Neil.

"We've got a box full of them upstairs," acknowledged Dean; "but medals don't put food on the table, and they don't pay the bills."

"So will they ever see the light of day?"

Dean smiled. "I've got quite a stack, so I'll probably give them to my son, when he's grown up."

Neil was taken aback. "I didn't know you had a son. I apologise if you've mentioned him before, and I wasn't listening."

Dean made a dismissive gesture. "It's okay, I haven't spoken about him before now."

Somewhat relieved, Neil was now curious. "I see; so, how old is your son, and what's his name?"

As soon as he said this, Neil detected a profound sadness in Dean's eyes, and regretted asking the question. "Sorry if I've touched a raw nerve," he apologised; "if you don't want to talk about it, that's fine."

"No, it's alright," Dean reassured him. "Well, he's two years and seven months old; in my mind, his name is Dean, the same as me - but that's not what his mother calls him, and I've never seen him."

"Will you ever get to see him?"

Neil's question seemed to lift Dean's spirits a little because, almost imperceptibly, he seemed to raise his shoulders. "Hopefully, one day - when he's old enough to make his own decisions."

Neil nodded. "Understood. Again, I'm sorry to have brought it up - it must be tough to talk about."

Dean seemed to come to a decision, as he squared his shoulders, almost as if preparing to stand up to an enemy.

"I don't mind telling you the story," he began. "Dean's mother, my ex, is called Rebecca; she comes from a wealthy background, and both her parents are barristers. Well, the father is a real bully - not in the physical sense, you understand, he wouldn't last five minutes in a real fight – but a bully, nevertheless. He does it by using his wealth and position, to get his own way. Anyway, when he and I encountered each other for the first time, he soon realised that he couldn't bully me; so, when he discovered that Becky was pregnant, he made sure that I'd have nothing to do with bringing up his grandson.

"It went to court but, of course, I was on a loser straight away; with that family's connections, it was obviously a done deal, even before I put my case forward. I was described in court as a 'street fighting thug', as well as various other things, before the judge decided I'd have no access to my son at all." Dean's expression hardened. "At the time, I had no money as such, so couldn't afford legal representation; well, in the future, that situation will change. Currently, all the money earned from fights still goes into the W.B.S. pot whereas, in just under two years, we all effectively become free agents; after that, for those of us who carry on with the bare knuckle fighting, any money made will belong to the individual."

Neil frowned. "But surely the lads would have understood the situation over your son, and would have let you use whatever money you earned to fight the case?"

Dean shook his head. "We all made a deal at the start of this, and agreed that, no matter what happened, we would stick to the deal. This situation is my problem and so I'll sort it out myself," he said with emphasis. "Apart from that, none of the lads know about my son."

Neil's perplexed look now changed to one of surprise. "Have you not told anyone of this? But these are your mates - I'm sure they'd understand that this is an exceptional situation you've found yourself in."

Dean smiled. "To a degree, it's difficult to describe both the closeness of the warehouse boys, and their individuality. On the one hand, I'd give my life to save any of them, and I know they'd do the same for me - certainly, when it comes to a fight, we'll always stand shoulder to shoulder; but on the other hand, I'd never worry them with a personal problem of mine – and I know that every one of the others has the same attitude."

"Well, I must admit, I'm of a similar mind," confessed Neil; "I've never believed that a problem shared is a problem halved. For what it's worth, I've no doubt that, when you're ready, you'll take on and beat the people who are keeping you from your little lad; one thing is certain – he'll be proud to have you as a father, because any child would be."

Dean smiled appreciatively. "Cheers mate, I knew you'd be the best person to tell. I knew you wouldn't feel sorry for me, or pity me in any way."

"I don't think sympathy or, worse still, pity, is much use in this situation. You're obviously already making plans on how you're going to go against them. If you fail on the first attempt, you get up and go again; and no matter how many times you get knocked down, you just keep getting up till you win. When you're in the right, and if you fight hard enough, you will prevail."

As Neil was saying this, his face wore a grim, determined expression. Dean looked at him appraisingly.

"You would've made a great commanding officer," he observed.

Neil's expression suddenly changed, to be replaced with one of embarrassment. "Sorry - I started giving a bit of a speech there, didn't I?"

"Don't apologise," Dean told him; "that was the reaction I'd have expected, since I've got to know you. You're absolutely right, by the way - I won't give up, no matter how long it takes me." He paused for a moment. "Now, I've got a question for you - and I believe the answer has some connection to what you were talking about just then."

Neil regarded him warily. "Ask your question then, mate."

Dean looked him straight in the eye. "Why don't you drink?"

Neil smiled wryly, glanced down, then immediately looked up again at Dean, and reflected what a remarkable man he was. People who had known Neil for many years had never questioned the reasons he gave for not drinking – including Caroline and the boys; yet Dean, a relative stranger, but with wisdom beyond his years, somehow knew that he was hiding the truth.

"Nothing gets past you, does it?" remarked Neil. "Well, hope you're sitting comfortably - because this may take some time."

He paused a moment, as if wondering where to start.

"When I was younger, as I mentioned, I lived in Liverpool with my family - mum and dad, my younger sister Sally, and my brother Ian, who's five years older than me. Well, when he was nineteen, he looked to have a bright future – he was in a very good job, drove a really flash car, and had a lovely girlfriend, who he was going to get engaged to. Then something happened, which changed everything.

"One evening, Ian was driving home from work; it was light, the weather conditions were good, and he wasn't speeding. Then, all of a sudden, a little girl ran out between two parked cars, right in front of him, and he hit her; he didn't even have time to put his brakes on, and the poor little tot was killed instantly. As it turned out, there were plenty of witnesses around who saw what happened; they all said that there was nothing Ian could have done about it, including the little girl's mother." Neil paused for a moment. "But then, when the police arrived, Ian was breathalysed, and found to be almost four times over the legal limit." He shook his head. "All of us in the family knew he liked a drink; but we had no idea, until it came out later, about the extent of his drink problem."

Dean nodded. "They reckon there's a fine line between liking a drink, and needing a drink; once someone crosses that line, they're in big trouble."

"Exactly – and Ian had crossed well over it. They found half bottles of vodka in his office, in the glove box of his car, at home in his bedroom - he even carried a hip-flask full of vodka. So, of course, he was charged, pleaded guilty, and went to prison – although, because of the witness statements, his sentence wasn't as long as you would have expected. But that wasn't the end of it.

"At the time, my dad worked away a lot; he'd go where the work was, rather than stay local and be unemployed. Well, within a week of Ian going to prison, I was at home with mum and Sally in the front room, when all of a sudden we heard shouting coming from outside; the next thing, a brick came through the window, and missed Sally by inches. Sally was terrified, screaming from the top of her voice, and mum grabbed her, holding onto her to try and calm her down – but I could see the fear in mum's eyes as well. I ran straight outside to see who'd done it.

"The house we lived in at the time was on an old street in Liverpool; there was no front garden, so when you opened the front door, you just stepped out onto the pavement. Anyway, when I got outside, there were three lads there, shouting that our Ian was a murdering bastard, and that he should have been hanged for killing an innocent little girl. I'd never seen these lads before; they certainly weren't locals, so I'd no idea where they came from - but I couldn't tolerate it." Neil paused, and smiled grimly. "You have to bear in mind that I wasn't a fighter then, I'd always avoided trouble; I wasn't a coward, but I just didn't get involved in fighting. My passion at the time was football - so that's all I did, and left the fighting to other people. But I wasn't going to let these lads get away with what they did. It wasn't so much what they were saying about our Ian - it was more the fact that they had terrorised my mother and sister.

"So, I went for them; and although I was getting battered, I wouldn't stop. Every time I went down, they kicked hell out of me - but as soon as they stopped, I got back up again and attacked them. This went on for some time, and I was bleeding from my mouth, my nose, my ear, and one of my eyes was almost closed, but I couldn't stop - and I knew then that I wouldn't stop, not until I beat them." Neil paused reflectively. "The strange thing is that I was crying, while I was fighting them. Not because I was hurt or frightened in any way - I couldn't tell you why; but the only way they could've stopped me was to kill me. Funny, I was remembering that, when Eddie told me what Jonjo said to the American at Rorke's Drift - because I'm the same. I don't know how to give up either."

Dean looked at Neil with a knowing smile. "Let me tell you, when I was shooting the Taliban with the 240, I had tears running down my face. As far as I was concerned, these people were attacking my family - because the warehouse boys *are* my family. You know my history; these lads are the only family I've ever known. I know exactly how you felt when you were fighting, because you were standing up for *your* family."

"Well," sighed Neil, "unfortunately, that was just the start of it. A few weeks later, me, mum and Sally were at home, when something was thrown at the front door. Mum tried to stop me, naturally - but I was out there like a shot, ready to take anyone on.

"This time, the lads were bigger and older than me, and one of them had a rounders bat, so I went for him first. I just flew straight at him, grabbed him round the throat, pinned him up against a wall, and just kept butting him till he dropped the bat. While I was doing this, his mates were punching and kicking me from behind, but it was almost as though I couldn't feel it. Once I had the bat in my hand, it was a different story; I started laying into all of them, and even when they tried running away, I caught up with them, and hammered them with the bat.

"At one point, I was laying into one of them, when someone grabbed me from behind; so I quickly butted backwards, turned, and was about to attack whoever it was, when he stepped back quickly, and put up his hands. 'Neil!' he said, 'I'm on your side, but you've got to stop, or you'll kill them!' Turns out, it was one of our neighbours; but what seemed strange to me at the time, considering I was still only fourteen, and he was a big tough lad in his twenties, was seeing the look of fear on his face."

Dean nodded, but made no comment.

"Anyway," continued Neil, his tone subdued, "things only got worse after that. Sally would come home from school in tears, because the kids were being horrible to her for what Ian had done; and I was getting into more fights in my school, because the word had got round about the trouble in our street, so the tough guys in the school wanted to take me on. Needless to say, these lads weren't as hard as they thought they were – but, of course, I was getting into trouble with the school for fighting all the time. It got to the stage where dad was having to refuse good work, if it meant him being away from home; so, finally, him and mum decided that we should move away – and that's how we ended up living in Cheshire, miles from family and friends, but at least mum and Sally felt safe.

"The whole thing affected us in different ways. Sally was okay, because she just made new friends; as for me, basically, I carried on where I left off, because the school I went to was quite tough, and the lads there wanted to see how hard the Scouser was. They soon found out." Neil said this without any hint of satisfaction. "But the saddest thing was seeing the deterioration in mum and dad. Where we lived in Liverpool, we were surrounded by both mum's and dad's families, so I was forever at one of my cousins', or they were at my house. Apart from that, mum and dad regularly went to a local social club, where they met up with their family and friends; but once they started living in Cheshire, they were just on their own. Initially, I think they both blamed themselves for what happened regarding Ian; then in time, unfortunately, I think they started to blame each other as well. Although it was never spoken of, it continued to hang over them, and I could see them moving further apart. Dad now has heart problems, and mum is in the early stages of dementia – and I don't think it's too much of a stretch to conclude that the business over Ian contributed to their ill health.

"So, as you can see," concluded Neil, "that's why I don't drink. I'm convinced that the alcohol didn't only ruin Ian's life, it ruined my parents' lives as well. Ian was away for five years, and was let out shortly before I got married; he just crawled back into the bottle, and has been there ever since."

"And do Caroline and the boys know about Ian's history?" enquired Dean.

"No. As far as I'm concerned, it's not my place to tell them what happened; it's up to our Ian himself, and he's always chosen not to."

"Did you ever think of moving back to Liverpool?"

"Oh yes, I had every intention of moving back; but then I met Caroline. All her friends and family lived in Cheshire or North Wales, so I stayed in Cheshire."

Unusually, Dean's expression became almost mischievous.

"I've got to tell you this," he confessed, "but me and the lads talk about you when you're not here. We are all, to a man, so envious of how much you love your wife. A few of the lads thought they loved their partners, until they listened to you talking about Caroline, and realised that your feelings for her are on a whole different level."

"Yes, I admit it - I'm passionately in love with my wife, and have been from the moment I saw her. Everything I've done in the past, and all the plans I'm making now for the future, are to make her happy. It sounds like a cliché, I know; but if Caroline's happy, then so am I." A look of sadness flickered across Neil's face. "The worst time was when she was told she could never have any more children, because she'd always desperately wanted a daughter. I know I said that offering you sympathy or pity about your son was no use to you, because you'll eventually find a way to see him; however, in Caroline's case, there was nothing I could do to make it right, and all I could do was hold her, while she sobbed and sobbed. Since then, I've done everything in my power to shield her from any upset, and I always will." It seemed to Dean, for a moment, that Neil had a haunted expression in his eyes. "I don't know whether it's a good or bad thing to love someone as much as I love Caroline; but I've no control over it. I've always known that I'll love her till the day I die, and I'm not ashamed to say so – in fact, I'm proud of it."

Just as Neil had finished speaking, Eddie and Jonjo walked into the lounge.

"So, Neil," said Jonjo, dropping onto one of the couches, "you came away with a good wedge last night. Are you going to go mad and buy yourself a better phone?"

Neil laughed. "There's nothing wrong with this phone I've got now, thanks. I'm going to squander the money on premium bonds."

"I've heard of premium bonds, but I don't really know what they are," mentioned Eddie.

"It's basically a government saving scheme which started in the 1950s," explained Neil. "One bond is worth a pound, and you have to buy a minimum of a hundred pounds' worth. Each bond has its own number, there's a monthly draw, and if one of your numbers comes out, you win a cash prize."

"So it's a bit like the lottery?"

"Well, only in so far as you can win cash prizes, because lottery tickets are otherwise worthless. If I've got five thousand pounds worth of premium bonds, regardless of whether I win the draw, I've still got five thousand pounds in savings. I could put the money into a savings account and get interest, but realistically, that wouldn't be much; whereas with the premium bonds, although I'm not getting interest on them, there is the possibility of winning a large amount of money. Any winnings I do get, I just plough back into more bonds, increasing the savings."

"So if you have any extra money, you save it, or spend it on the house?"

"That's right, because the house is also an investment," confirmed Neil. "I work too hard for the money to waste it. All being well, the time will come when I won't have to work at all; and then, Caroline and I can really enjoy our life together."

Eddie looked slightly quizzical. "Don't you and Caroline ever fall out?"

"Never," declared Neil; "we get on really well, and have a laugh. We don't necessarily always agree on everything, admittedly - but we don't fall out when we do disagree."

"Well, I envy you that," admitted Eddie shaking his head. "When Julie and I disagree, it's a nightmare, and sometimes we don't speak to each other for days afterwards. That's why I moved back into the warehouse - because we couldn't live under the same roof without getting on each other's nerves."

"Hm," said Neil. "Just out of curiosity - do you and Jonjo always agree with each other?"

"Most of the time, but occasionally we do disagree."

"And do you fall out with each other, when you disagree?"

"No we don't," admitted Eddie, grinning. "Point taken! You are a wise man, Scouse Neil. I'll make you a deal - I'll carry on teaching you to be a better fighter, and you can carry on teaching me how to be a grown up!"

"Sounds like a plan," said Neil, returning the grin. "Well, gentlemen," he continued, rising from his seat, "on that note, I'll make a move. Expect me tomorrow when, hopefully, my lips won't be quite as big as they are today."

....

"Jonjo, I didn't really get chance to ask you last night," said Dean, after Neil had left, "but what decided you to let Neil fight?"

"I'm not a hundred per cent sure I could've stopped him if I'd tried. When that Blackburn lad called you a coward, I thought Scouse Neil was going to throttle the life out of him."

"Jonjo's right," agreed Eddie. "We need to work on Neil's temperament, to make him the complete fighter that we all believe he can be. I've got to say, I was concerned with the damage done to Neil in the first few seconds - but it was obvious to me that no matter what that Blackburn fella did, he was never going to stop Neil coming at him."

Dean nodded thoughtfully. "So, was I right? Is he as brave as us?"

"At the very least," asserted Jonjo. "Possibly braver."

Eddie laughed. "If he'd been at Rorke's Drift with us that day, he wouldn't have wasted bullets. He'd have just jumped over the wall, and taken them on with his fists."

"I think you're right," commented Dean, nodding. "Did Tommy tell you about the sign Neil has up on the wall in his training room? Make no mistake - he's just like us."

Driving home from the warehouse, Neil was reflecting that he had often wished it was possible to go back in time, and meet the men from the original Rorke's Drift; but now, after hearing the story told by Eddie and Rod, he believed that he had met their twenty-first century equivalent – and, in addition, he had the privilege of training with these men, and the honour of being considered their friend. One day, when the time was right, he would have great pride in introducing these men to his family.

Chapter 16

Over the next few days, Neil was able to avoid Caroline until his face looked sufficiently normal not to arouse her suspicions; however, he also took the precaution of getting undressed in the dark when going to bed, as his side was still badly bruised. Although he had only missed two full days' work, he put in the extra hours in order to make up for the loss of earnings.

A week passed before he was able to resume training with the warehouse boys. He began with some light workouts, but was soon ready to get back to sparring; after that, he progressed to learning some new moves and methods of attack from all of the warehouse boys, but especially from Dean, Jonjo and Eddie. They also concentrated on helping Neil to control his temperament, to ensure that he could remain calm at all times.

At the end of one of these training sessions, Neil, Dean and Eddie were sitting in the lounge drinking coffee.

"Well, after today, you won't see me for two weeks," announced Neil; "and when you do see me again, hopefully, I'll be a good bit browner."

"You're not going swimming at that gravy factory again, are you?" asked Eddie.

"Certainly - Dean said it's good exercise, and a vital part of the training," replied Neil, glancing at Dean with a mischievous look in his eye.

"I lied," declared Dean, adopting his best poker face. "I've got a mate who works in the gravy factory, and I bet him a hundred quid that I could get a daft Scouser to swim through it - but he didn't believe me."

Neil adopted a crestfallen expression. "Do you mean that going to the farm and juggling horse droppings won't improve my eye/hand coordination either?"

"I won two hundred quid off the farmer for that one," said Dean to Eddie in a confidential tone, and winked.

"Deano," said Eddie, shaking his head, "you're getting onto our wavelength now - you do realise that's a challenge we can't refuse?"

After that, each of the three men tried their best to make the other two laugh while keeping a straight face, but the result was a foregone conclusion - Eddie won hands down.

"Alright, I give up," laughed Neil, rising from his seat, and holding up his hands. "I know when I'm out of my league. I'm off to Spain - I'll see you in a couple of weeks."

Eddie followed Neil out to the cab, leaving Dean still chuckling.

"That's the best laugh I've had with Deano for years," remarked Eddie.

"He did have a real look of mischief in him - it was great to see."

"Anyway, make sure you keep your training up while you're abroad," instructed Eddie. "I know you're on holiday - but early morning runs on the beach are good training, and then later, swimming in the Atlantic will be excellent exercise."

"I'm impressed that you know it's the Atlantic, rather than the Mediterranean."

"Ah, well, Deano told me, to be honest," confessed Eddie, grinning. "I thought all southern Spain was on the Mediterranean."

"I think most people do; but between Gibraltar and the Portuguese border, it's actually the Atlantic. We love it down there - and if I ever were able to buy a place abroad, that's the area I'd be looking at."

"Well, mate, enjoy yourself," said Eddie, shaking Neil's hand. "Stay fit - and keep thinking positive, because that way, one day you'll have a place of your own over there. See you in a couple of weeks."

....

While Neil was on holiday, Dean arrived at the warehouse to find that everyone was there, and called them together into the lounge.

"I bumped into that Blackburn fighter last night," he told them, "and he said he wants a rematch with Scouse Neil."

"Oh?" said Jonjo. "What did you say to him?"

Dean shrugged. "I just told him I'd pass the message on; but I did point out that Neil may not want to do it - not because of fear, naturally, but simply because Neil would've considered the previous fight a one-off."

"And what did he have to say to that?" asked Eddie.

"He got a bit gobby then," replied Dean, "saying he'd been conned into thinking that Neil couldn't fight, and so took it easy; according to him, Neil caught him with a lucky shot. He claims that, if he fights Neil again, he'll really punish him."

"Well," said Jonjo, rubbing his chin, "as much as I'd like to see Neil drop him again, I've got to say that, to a degree, he's right in saying that he was conned."

"That's why I wanted to discuss it with all of you. I didn't see the fight, as you know, and although I know how brave Neil is, I don't want to put him in a position where he's got no chance."

Tommy spoke up. "I didn't see the fight either, but I don't think it's up to us whether Neil fights him or not - that's got to be Neil's own decision. I reckon you should tell him."

"I think he's got a point, Deano," agreed Eddie. "Imagine if he finds out that the Blackburn fella wanted to fight him, and that we knew about it, but decided not to tell him - how do you think he'd feel? I, for one, wouldn't be able to look him in the eye."

Rod joined the discussion. "In my opinion, Neil could beat him again," he asserted; "but my concern is the amount of damage this fella could do to him in the fight. Remember, Neil's self-employed - if he's not driving his taxi, he's not earning any money, and he's got a family to support and bills to pay."

"Yes," nodded Dean; "from what I've gathered, this fella from Blackburn can be a nasty piece of work. Recently, he fought the big lad from Kirkby who I beat the other week –but he didn't just beat him, he slaughtered him. From what I've been told, that Kirkby fella will be in hospital for some time; I don't know whether there was bad blood between them before the fight, but the Blackburn lad really did a number on him."

"Well, even so, I think Tommy's right," volunteered Carl. "It's got to be Scouse Neil's choice."

"Okay, a simple show of hands," suggested Dean. "All those who feel I should tell Neil, raise their hand."

In an instant, ten hands were raised. "Is right!" was Eddie's conclusion.

"Is absolutely right!" agreed Dean, smiling and clenching his fist. "As soon as Neil's back off holiday, we'll train him to knock that mouthy bastard all over the show."

Phil laughed. "I take it you weren't overly keen on this young gentleman from Blackburn?"

"That's the understatement of the year," grunted Dean, gritting his teeth. "Before Neil went on holiday, I was working with him on staying calm and keeping control. Well, I needed all those skills myself when I was talking to that toerag from Blackburn, to stop me from ripping his head off. When I pass the information on to Neil, I'll try my best to give the impression that I don't care whether he fights this lad or not; but I can tell you now, I hope he decides to – and batters the hell out of him."

....

Neil returned from holiday and, as soon as he was able, paid a visit to the warehouse, looking forward to getting back to training with his mates; however, as soon as he joined them in the lounge, he could sense a different atmosphere amongst the men.

"I take it something's happened while I've been away?" he suggested.

Dean shrugged, and frowned slightly. "Nothing of any importance," he replied casually. "It's just that the Blackburn fighter you beat the other week wants a rematch. Now, it's entirely up to you – you're not under any obligation to accept his challenge, it's your choice. Have a think about it, and then decide."

Neil's reply was quiet, but emphatic. "I'll fight him any time he likes, anywhere he likes. In fact, if you've got a number for him, I'll go over to Blackburn now, and fight him in his own backyard."

Eddie brought his fist down so hard, he nearly broke the table. "Is right! Let's get training!"

....

Neil was like a man possessed while he was training, focussing on the upcoming fight. After an excellent training session, he walked back into the lounge.

"How was the holiday, then?" asked Jonjo.

"Absolutely brilliant," enthused Neil. "I'm more determined than ever to buy a place, and live over there."

"Have you told Caroline yet of your plans, or are you still keeping it quiet?" queried Dean.

"I haven't said anything yet; if I were to tell Caroline too soon, and then it fell through, she'd be so disappointed. I'd rather wait until I'm in a position to make it happen - then I'll ask her if she's up for the idea."

"Do you reckon she would be, then?" was Eddie's question.

"I'm pretty sure of it, and even more so after this trip. We were at one of our favourite places, a cliff-top restaurant looking out over the ocean; and she said 'Wouldn't it be nice to live here?' I was dying to tell her my plans, but I just laughed, and said something like 'I'll have to work harder, then!'"

Andy joined in the conversation "What about the lads? Do they like going over there as well?"

"They certainly do. Although we go abroad as a family, once we get there, Caroline and I hardly ever see them – we've been going to the same place since they were little, so they've got a group of mates in the area. The only time they show their faces is when they need money!" This remark caused some amusement amongst his companions.

"And so, back to reality for now," proposed Dean. "When do you want to fight the lad from Blackburn?"

"When you and the lads consider I'm ready," replied Neil. "And don't worry about my temper - I can guarantee that, no matter what he says, I'll stay calm."

"I've got to warn you though, Neil, this guy is no pushover," advised Jonjo. "It's unlikely you'll be able to pull the same stroke as last time - he'll really be on his guard."

"I know that," nodded Neil; "and he'll need to be on his guard – because, this time, I'll be coming at him with everything, and I'll beat him." His tone was matter-of-fact. "He'll regret wanting to fight Neil Hughes."

....

"Was it just me, or did anyone else's blood run cold when Neil said that fella will regret wanting to fight Neil Hughes?" Eddie glanced quizzically around at the other men, after Neil had driven away.

"I know what you mean," confirmed Jonjo. "As much as Scouse Neil's a nice bloke and a gentleman, when he said that, I suddenly realised there's something very menacing about him."

Carl nodded his agreement. "Over the years, we've fought against some tough men in Iraq and Afghanistan; but I can tell you now, I would not like Scouse Neil as an enemy."

"Nor would I," said Andy. "I suspect that, because we've trained with him, got close to him, and found out what a great fella he is, to a certain extent we've lost sight of the fact that he's a weapon of a man. Deano, you're the closest to him - what do you think?"

"I've no doubt the lad from Blackburn *will* regret wanting to fight Neil; whether Neil can beat him or not is a different matter - but I'm pretty sure Neil will do a lot of damage to him."

....

Big Joe was staging the fight in the Bootle warehouse, in accordance with Dean's arrangements, and informed Dean that the Blackburn fighter was bringing a huge amount of support with him. Dean found himself speculating that the Blackburn man might not be as confident of an easy victory as he had claimed, and needed his cronies to back him up.

"It wouldn't be right to use W. B. S. money to bet on Scouse Neil," Dean informed the other warehouse boys. "If anyone wants to put a bet on him, then bring the cash in tomorrow night, and sort it out with Jonjo. I've found out that the odds are heavily against Neil; the general feeling amongst the people in the business is that Neil was lucky in the last fight, and doesn't stand a chance this time."

The following evening, the warehouse boys duly met up again. "Right gentleman, pass me your money, if you're having a bet on Neil," instructed Jonjo.

Phil, Joe, Carl, Andy, Earl and Rod produced one thousand pounds each, while Tommy, Eddie, and Jonjo himself, laid down two thousand pounds apiece.

Jonjo looked down at the cash, nodding his head in satisfaction. "Twelve grand - I'm impressed! Deano, are you chancing a couple of quid?"

"I might do," smiled Dean. "I'll just make it up to a nice round figure, I think - check that for eight grand, Jonjo." He tossed a wad of notes into the mix.

Jonjo also smiled, but raised his eyebrows. "I've got to admire your confidence in Scouse Neil," he remarked; "but this Blackburn lad's a hell of a fighter, from what I've been told."

"I daresay he is," shrugged Dean; "but is he a hell of a *man*?"

…………………………………..........................

Neil drove straight to Bootle in his cab, and arrived at big Joe's warehouse before Dean and the others. As he entered the warehouse from the back door, he was met by big Joe himself.

"Well, your prize money is going to be good tonight," Joe informed him.

"When you say *my* prize money," said Neil, "I take it that means you're confident I'm going to win?"

"I am, as it happens," Joe assured him, grinning. "But what I'm saying is, if the Blackburn lad were to win, the prize money he would get would be minus the cost of the premises, security, and the referees. This warehouse belongs to me, Macca and little Albie are the referees, and the warehouse boys are doing the security - so, when you win, you'll get every penny of the gate money."

"Well then, let's hope it's a good turn out," said a smiling Neil, "because I will win. It won't matter how long it takes, or what damage is done to me - but I can guarantee, I'll beat him."

"Dean was telling me that this lad *wanted* to fight you." Joe paused slightly. "What a fool."

……………………………………………………………

As the warehouse was filling up, Neil was standing, alone, at the edge of the fight area, when he heard a jeering voice from over the other side.

"Aren't the warehouse pansies bothering to come and see the Scouse dwarf get wasted?" Neil ignored this, and began doing his stretching exercises.

"You're going to get punished tonight, scum, you'll be going out of this warehouse on a stretcher!" was the next barb from his opponent. Neil had no intention of rising to the bait; he merely concentrated on what he was doing, but also focussed on planning his strategy for the forthcoming battle.

As the warehouse boys arrived, little Albie was just about to call the two fighters together; Dean hurried up to speak to Neil. "Sorry, hold-up on the motorway," he explained. "Now, remember: stay calm, concentrate, pick your shots, stay out of trouble, don't get into a war – focus on what needs to be done."

While dispensing this advice, Dean was concerned to note that there was a look in Neil's eyes he had never seen before; it was a complete lack of expression – a dullness, almost a blankness. As Neil walked to the centre of the fighting area, Dean turned to Jonjo and Eddie. "I don't like that look in his eyes," he confided; "I've never seen that in Neil before. It wasn't fear, or anger. I'm not sure what it was."

"Eddie and I have seen that look before," Jonjo told him, "but not in Neil's eyes. We've seen it in yours."

Dean looked at his friends questioningly.

"At Rorke's Drift," elaborated Eddie. "When you took the 240 off Tommy, and were about to stand up, you had exactly the same look in your eyes. I'd describe it as pure hatred. This Blackburn fella's got no chance."

Dean puffed out his cheeks. "What were the odds with the bookies?" he asked Jonjo.

"Scouse Neil is 5/1 against. There's a huge crew from Blackburn who've bet heavily on their man. Needless to say, I put the bet on straight away - we're not going to get better odds than that. Obviously, I apologised to big Joe for the delay but he said it was no big deal, his two minders did the door and there've been no problems."

....

The young Blackburn fighter looked down at his opponent, as the referee, little Albie, was reminding both fighters of the rules.

"When one of you go down, you've got thirty seconds. Macca will shout when there's five seconds left - if you're not up in that time, then the fight's over."

Neil simply nodded his understanding; his opponent, however, was more vociferous. "There's only one man going down in this fight," he sneered, "and you won't be getting back up again, Liverpool scum."

To the younger man's surprise, his threats and abuse did not have the desired effect. He had assumed, learning from their previous encounter, that goading Neil was the key to making him wide open to attack; yet now, he did not appear to be angry in any way. If anything, he seemed calm, and with a look in his eyes which the young Blackburn fighter found slightly disturbing; but he dismissed any concerns. With his martial arts background, he was satisfied that he could beat this man quite easily – after all, he was smaller, possibly double his own age, and almost certainly not as fit and strong, or with the same stamina, as himself. He formed his own strategy: he would allow Neil to attack him, simply keeping out of the way and picking him off with the odd shot - and then, as his opponent tired, he would really punish him. The signal was given, and the fight began.

The Blackburn man was pleased with himself, having correctly guessed that his opponent would attack him; what surprised him was the ferocity of Neil's opening assault, given that he had seemed so calm earlier. The young martial arts exponent was having no difficulty avoiding or blocking the blows that were being rained down but, so far, he found that he was unable to deliver any himself; nevertheless, he continued to bide his time, keeping out of the way, hoping his attacker would start tiring - when, suddenly, out of nowhere, he took a blow to the head. He had to backpedal swiftly, to avoid a second blow; but he had to quickly rethink his strategy, as his opponent's attack was relentless. It was at this point that he was glad to have brought so much support with him; having his supporters chanting his name, almost like a football crowd, certainly spurred him on - because he realised that this fight was not going to be as easy as he had expected.

He decided to mount an attack of his own, confident that this was where his greater strength lay; at the same time, he would be able to assess the effectiveness of his opponent's defence. He was therefore concerned to find that, as he was attacking Neil, he was being picked off himself with some damaging shots – whereas, the blows he was delivering seemed to be having little or no effect on the tough Liverpool man. He began to wonder whether Neil was very skilled, or just very lucky; many of the blows the younger man was delivering were only missing contact by inches - he was also having no success with any head shots, and the body shots seemed to be having no effect whatsoever on this hard man, who simply kept coming at him relentlessly.

The Blackburn fighter eventually stopped trying to attack, as he was receiving too many blows himself; he decided simply to defend, and hope that his opponent would eventually slow down. At this point, he realised that his supporters had stopped chanting, and there was an uncomfortable silence in the warehouse; this thought had barely registered with him, when he received another savage blow to his face – and heard a lone voice in the crowd say "Is right!"

Reeling from the blow, the young man was beginning to regret insulting his opponent, insulting the warehouse boys and, most of all, wanting to fight this man. If he could only deliver one effective blow, he thought in desperation, it might give him an opening. Suddenly, his wish came true - a speculative kick to Neil's midriff almost doubled him over; but as the young man quickly stepped forward to follow up with a more damaging blow, he failed to see Neil's elbow, which caught him on the side of the head. Before he knew what was happening, he felt a powerful kick to his ribs, then another to his solar plexus; then, as he was staggering from this onslaught, he received another straight kick to his face - and as he was falling, he just hoped that the cracking noise he heard was his gumshield, not his nose or jaw, because he was now in so much pain, he could no longer tell.

As the young man hit the ground, he cursed himself for his own stupidity, thinking he could possibly do anything which would hurt this monstrous fighting machine. He immediately rolled onto his chest, so as not to choke on his own blood; then he dragged himself up on all fours, facing the ground, and could see the large pool of blood forming below him. He spat out his cracked, previously white, gumshield - and was shocked to see that it was now pure red.

The Blackburn man looked up at his opponent, and observed that blank gaze in his eyes, which had been there before the fight began. He wondered whether this was the look of a murderer, just before they killed; and he realised that he was now afraid, in considerable pain, and that there was nothing he could do to stop this man from killing him, if the fight continued. He heard the referee shout 'Five seconds!'; he looked again at Neil, then at his supporters, gently shook his head, and finally looked back down at the floor. It was with a great sense of relief that he heard the words "Fight over!"

"Are you alright, mate?"

The Blackburn fighter raised his head, somewhat dazed, and for a moment he thought he was seeing things; he was looking at a smiling man, with a concerned look in his eyes, holding out his hand to help him up – and that man was Neil Hughes.

"You fought well," continued Neil; "showed a lot of bravery, and tried your best, so there's no disgrace in losing." The young man continued to look nonplussed, so Neil repeated his initial question. "Are you alright?"

The young man felt as though a trick had been played on him. How had the cold-eyed, invincible juggernaut been replaced by this gentle man, with a look of kindness on his face? Still incredulous, he took the proffered hand, and was helped to his feet.

"I am, now you've stopped attacking me." His tone was almost sulky, and Neil saw only a disappointed young man. He patted him on the back.

"Well done," said Neil, simply; then he turned, and walked away to rejoin the warehouse boys.

....

"Well, I thought that went well," shrugged Neil, when all of them were gathered.

"We've all been involved in some good fights in our time, and watched each other fighting – but you just delivered the greatest display of aggression I've ever seen in my life!" enthused Eddie, chuckling. "You're not just a warrior, Scouse Neil - you are a gladiator!"

Neil laughed at Eddie's boyish delight. "Now, I wouldn't go *that* far."

"I'm not exaggerating - everyone who's here this evening will be talking about that fight for years to come, believe me."

"Well, gladiator or not, we need to get you back to the warehouse, so the doc can give you a good check over," advised Jonjo.

"I think I'm okay - I don't think he caught me with much."

Phil smiled at him. "You're not joking, are you?"

"Honest, I feel all right - he caught me with a couple of body shots, but nothing worth talking about."

Several of the warehouse boys were exchanging amused glances, and shaking their heads.

"One of the kicks he caught you with would've knocked me down," pointed out Earl, grinning.

Andy was laughing. "He could have wanged you with a lump of four be two, and it still wouldn't have stopped you!"

"Jonjo's right, though," added Tommy, "you still need to get checked out."

"My face is all right though, isn't it? I don't remember him hitting me in the face."

Dean nodded. "Your face is fine – don't worry, you won't need to dodge Caroline, but you've got to hope that she doesn't hug you in the next few days." He added, confidentially, "*Are* you alright?"

"I'm fine. That was me, that's how I fight." Neil looked almost guilty. "I am what I am."

"Then you need to be proud of what you are," Dean told him. "I and all the other lads would certainly have been proud to put on that display - it was awesome. I knew you were tough, but I didn't realise you were *that* tough."

Just then, big Joe appeared. "Neil, that was incredible," he said, slapping him on the back, which made Neil wince. "I know from what Dean has told me that this fight is probably a one-off but, if ever you were to decide to take this up, I can guarantee two things – you'll never get 5/1 against again, but you'll always fight to a packed house. I've been trying to get across to you since the fight finished, but kept being stopped by people asking when you're fighting again. A good few of them said they would've paid double to see that exhibition."

"Where did that last kick come from?" asked Eddie. "It certainly isn't one that I taught you."

"What did you think of it?" Neil looked gratified. "I've been working on that one at home for a few weeks now, but was waiting until I perfected it before I showed you. The opportunity presented itself tonight, so I thought I'd give it a try."

"And that doubling over, when he kicked you in the stomach, was a ruse, I take it?" said Rod.

Neil nodded. "He would never have fallen for that trick earlier on in this fight, not after the last time; so I just had to wait for the opportunity. I've been working a lot on my stomach muscles; my two sons have great pleasure in regularly bouncing a medicine ball on my stomach. When he kicked me, it had no effect at all - but I knew the time was right to make him think that it had."

Jonjo looked at him in admiration. "You fooled me last time, and you fooled me again this time. I really thought he'd hurt you with that kick."

"By that point, I decided it was time to finish the fight. I knew I was going to beat him - without sounding conceited, I always knew that - it was really a question of minimising the damage to myself. I think if I'd put him down earlier in the fight, he may have got back up again - whereas by the time he did go down, I was reasonably confident that he'd stay there."

"I think he was wise to stay down," said Tommy, seriously. "He couldn't possibly have won – he'd only have suffered more."

Shortly afterwards, they were joined by Little Albie and Macca. "Well fought, Neil," complimented Macca. "You can tell you've been trained by this crew. When that fool called you Liverpool scum, if it had been me or Albie, we would've torn his throat out."

Neil smiled. "So, I believe you two gentlemen will not take payment for this evening's soiree?"

"See, I told you he was posh!" said little Albie to Macca, laughing. "That's right – you owe us nothing," he continued, turning back to Neil. "We're privileged that we were here to watch you and be part of it - and if you never fight again, we'll always be able to boast that we saw Scouse Neil fight."

"Is right!" declared big Joe.

"Oy, that's my line!" said Eddie in mock outrage, and everyone laughed.

"Anyway, Neil," said Dean, "are you all right to drive back to Manchester? Or would you rather go in the battle bus, and I'll drive the cab back?"

"You're alright, I'll be okay driving," Neil assured him. "I think you'll find that when the doc checks me over, there's nothing broken. I'll just be a bit sore for a few days."

"Well, as promised," announced big Joe, "I've got a tidy sum of money for you here."

"Cheers Joe - if you'd care to pass it to Jonjo, then he can start putting all the Queen's heads the same way, while we're heading back to Manchester."

"I just can't help it, it's got to be done," agreed Jonjo, to the amusement of all of them.

Just as Neil and the warehouse boys walked out of the building, a voice was heard saying "Here he is now!"

Everyone who had witnessed the fight, including the Blackburn crew, was waiting outside the warehouse – and, to Neil's great embarrassment, as soon as the crowd caught sight of him, they started cheering and clapping.

....

By the time they had returned to the warehouse, Neil was quite sore, and fairly certain that he would not be driving the taxi for a couple of days. After the doctor had given him a thorough checking over, he sat and relaxed in one of the comfortable armchairs in the warehouse lounge.

"Right Neil, this is slightly embarrassing," said Jonjo, looking awkward; "I'd like to give everybody their winnings, but everyone won more on the fight than you did."

"Fine by me," said Neil, with a dismissive wave of his hand; "in fact, I'm very flattered that any of you took the chance and bet on me at all. The reason I only put five hundred pounds on myself is because, if I'd bet any more than that, I wouldn't have been concentrating on the fight – I'd have been more concerned about the money I might lose. That's why I'm not a gambler by nature. It wouldn't have bothered me losing five hundred quid, because I know I could soon make that up by doing extra hours on the taxi for a few weeks."

"Fair comment," said Jonjo. "Anyway, I got 5/1, so you've got two thousand-five hundred, plus your five hundred stake - so there's another three grand, to go with your prize money."

"Great," said Neil. "Better than a poke in the eye with a pointed stick."

"I find most things are," said Eddie, smirking.

"And as for the rest of you gentlemen," continued Jonjo, "Andy, Joe, Earl, Carl, Phil and Rod, five grand each; Tommy and Eddie, ten each for you; and ten for me."

"This is brilliant," said Neil; "since I've known you lads, I feel it's all been one-way - you've all given up so much of your time to train me, plus you wouldn't take any money for doing the security tonight. At least now, I feel as if I've paid you back in a small way."

"Well, if that's the case," smiled Jonjo, "I'd say you've paid Dean back in a big way. Deano, forty thousand pounds to you. Don't spend it all in the one shop." Neil glanced at Dean, smiled, and shook his head.

....

"Simple question - did you enjoy the fight?"

The other warehouse boys had left to go out socialising with their wives and girlfriends, and only Dean and Neil remained behind in the lounge. Neil pondered over his reply.

"To be perfectly honest, I'm not sure," he said thoughtfully. "I was glad when the young fella went down - but not for my sake, for his. If he'd got back up, I'd have attacked him again. It's difficult to describe; but it's almost as though the 'fighting' Neil Hughes is a different person to me. Does that make sense?"

"More than you know," replied Dean, who had been nodding while Neil was speaking. "So, I assume the money earned tonight will be squandered on premium bonds again?"

"Definitely," agreed Neil. "The taxi work has been poor recently, which would normally bother me - but I've just received the equivalent of about three months' takings for fifteen minutes' work. Admittedly, I received all the gate money tonight, which isn't how it normally works; even so, I can see that there's still a great deal of money to be made, if I were to carry on doing this."

"And are you going to carry on?"

"Yes I am," said Neil decidedly. "I'll take part in the fights myself for the next two years; then, what I'll probably do is get involved in running and organising the fights for about another two years – and I think that will be it."

"Sounds like a plan," commented Dean. "When did you decide all this?"

"A great deal of it when I was on holiday - but I only really made the final decision in my head about ten minutes ago," admitted Neil. "It occurred to me that you don't become a free agent yourself for a couple of years - but there's nothing to stop you betting on me, until you're able to bet on yourself, to get the kind of return you made tonight. You'll need a great deal of money to go to court over your son, because you'll have to have the very best on your side." Dean seemed surprised at Neil's implied offer to assist him. "Helping you also helps me," Neil continued, by way of explanation; "I want to move to Spain, and be able to spend all my time with Caroline, as soon as possible. I could achieve it by driving the taxi night and day, but that could take years. I'll make the money quicker by fighting; and while I'm reasonably ferocious when fighting for myself, if I was fighting for you and me, I'd be unstoppable."

"I see what you mean," said Dean. "But will you ever tell Caroline or the boys about this part of your life?"

"Only when I'm no longer involved in it; which, if everything goes to plan, would be round about my twentieth wedding anniversary. I'm a pretty good organiser and planner, and I've already calculated that the extra money I need, to realise my dream, can be raised over the next four years." Dean nodded his understanding. "And in your case, for the first two of those years, you can build up a good amount of money on your winnings from my fights, which will then give you a good platform to work from - because you can guarantee, your ex-girlfriend's family know the judicial system, and are likely to drag the case out for as long as they possibly can, hoping that you run out of funds."

"Well, I've got Scouse Neil on my side now - I can't lose, can I?"

"Dean the manc and Scouse Neil - a formidable duo."

They both smiled, nodded to each other, and said simultaneously "Is right!"

…………………………………..

From that point onwards, Neil drove the taxi as often as he could; otherwise, he simply trained and fought. Each fight seemed to be more difficult than the one before, but that did not stop him. As time went on, and as his reputation grew, the only men willing to fight him were much larger than himself, although he knew that to be inevitable - one of the reasons he had given himself a deadline as a fighter was because he knew that, eventually, the only fights he would get would be ones where he was risking his life.

During this period, Michael and Paul had gone on a holiday with their school, so Neil and Caroline took the opportunity to spend a week in Spain on their own. Neil rented a villa, with a swimming pool, situated very close to the beach.

"This is nice," he remarked, as they pulled up outside.

Caroline stepped out of the car. "This is more than nice – it's spectacular," she declared. "Just imagine owning something like this."

"Let's have a good mooch round," suggested Neil. "From the outside, it looks a fair size."

After they had finished looking around the villa, they sat out by the swimming pool with a cold drink.

"You're right, this is spectacular," sighed Neil, contentedly. "I think we've got to have one of these."

Caroline snorted derisively. "If only!"

"I'm serious! I can say now that, at some point in the future, we'll be able to own a villa like this."

Caroline looked at him. "You're not joking, are you?"

"I've had the idea for a while, and been making enquiries on how to go about it. I know now, definitely, that it can be done – and, although I can't be sure exactly how long it will take me, if all goes well, we could own a villa like this within the next couple of years; and soon afterwards, if we wanted to, we could move over here altogether. What do you think?"

"Neil, it would be absolutely brilliant!" said Caroline, leaning forward in her chair. "It's always been a secret dream of mine - but I never thought it could be done."

"Well, I can say now, categorically, that not only can it be done, it will be - I just needed to be certain that it was what you wanted as well."

Caroline's eyes started to fill up with tears. "Don't start, or you might get me going," groaned Neil.

As they both stood up, Caroline hugged him so tightly that Neil was grateful not to have had a recent fight – otherwise, he suspected that he would now be in a great deal of pain.

"So you think it's a crap idea?" he gasped, as Caroline was squeezing the breath out of him.

Caroline was laughing and crying at the same time. "You've come up with some rubbish ideas over the years," she spluttered happily, "but this one takes the biscuit!"

…………………………………..

Neil was eager to get to the warehouse after his holiday, to tell Dean and the boys about

Caroline's reaction to his proposal; all of them were genuinely pleased when he told them the news.

"I know how much of a cunning man you are," commented Dean; "was there a reason why you stayed at that particular villa?"

"I've said this before - nothing gets past you, does it?" said Neil. "Well, you're quite right - the villa we stayed at was built by a particular builder who was recommended to me, and I wanted to see the quality of his workmanship. It was absolutely spot on - the woodwork, the tiling, the roof, the walls, everything was perfect. Tommy, you'd have loved it."

"How did you hear about this fella?" asked Tommy.

"Well, a tip I got from little Albie which he'd got from his dad, and from another fella I know who owns properties abroad, was to get a good local solicitor. It was through the solicitor that I found out about the builder."

Eddie was grinning from ear to ear. "So you've got a solicitor over there now as well?"

"Certainly have. I've also opened a bank account over there, to start transferring money on a regular basis - so when I eventually move, I'll have a bank account with a good few quid in it."

"That's great," said Jonjo. "So, at what point are you going to stop fighting, and start promoting the fights?"

"About another nine months of fighting, I reckon. Then I'll speak to big Joe, and get as much advice as I can from him; I'll do about two years of promoting, and after that, I'll be finished with it altogether."

Eddie looked somewhat crestfallen. "When you're finished with it, will we not see you again?"

"Far from it," Neil reassured him. "Before I move abroad, you'll get to meet Caroline and the lads; then when I do move over to Spain, you can come and see me as often as you like. I very much hope that you'll all visit, frequently; Caroline will love you boys, and will be really pleased if she has guests all the time."

"Surely she wouldn't want guests *all* the time?" laughed Andy.

"Oh yes she would - she loves entertaining. Whenever we get visitors now, I see her eyes light up. When we were talking about owning a villa in Spain, I said we may get the odd visitor, and she was delighted. I can tell you, if we owned a villa like the one we stayed in, it would be immaculate; and Caroline would be itching to show it off to as many people as possible."

"Listening to your plan is brilliant," said Dean. "We're as excited as you are - and I can guarantee, we'll definitely all be coming to see you on a regular basis. It'll be nice for us to climb onto a plane without having to carry a gun!"

"Is not wrong!"

Everyone started laughing at Eddie's contribution, and then, as always, the joking started. As Neil looked round at the group of men, he hoped that they would always be part of his life.

………………………………..

Neil had arranged that, shortly after his final fight, he would travel to Spain, to put in place the next stage of the villa buying process; on his return, he would speak to big Joe about being a fight promoter. As soon as the word circulated that this was probably the last chance anyone would get to see Scouse Neil fight, the crowd was huge.

The fight followed its usual course, with Neil relentlessly attacking; he was very much impressed with this particular opponent's resilience, and the fight lasted for some time but, inevitably, Neil prevailed, and even managed to finish the fight relatively unscathed - in stark contrast to his opponent, who looked as if he had been hit by a truck. Once the fight was over, as always, Neil reverted to his human side, as opposed to the evil-eyed warrior. He looked at the condition in which he had left the other man, and was glad that this was to be his last fight; sometimes, even he was disturbed at his own propensity for violence. Remarkably, his opponent was smiling – because, as he said, he could now boast that in his battle with Scouse Neil, he had fought him for longer than any other man.

As Neil was standing with the warehouse boys, big Joe came over. "I've got a nice little bonus for you here," he told Neil. "I didn't want to tell you before the fight but, basically, I doubled the entrance fee tonight - needless to say, though, nobody complained. So there's a very good wedge for you here, which no doubt you'll fritter away on more premium bonds, and I'll see you when you get back from Spain."

Neil returned to the warehouse in his cab and, on arrival, was checked over by the doctor; but he knew that he had suffered very little injury. After Jonjo had paid him, Neil had a quick word with the doctor before he left, and then rejoined the warehouse boys.

"That was one tough fella you just fought," said Dean.

"I know – I could swear he was made of stone. All the work I've done, toughening up my knuckles, and hardening the palms of my hands, was certainly needed against him. I've got to say, I'm relieved that it was my last fight; I'm thirty-eight now, and getting too old for this."

"Are you going to keep training?" enquired Eddie.

"Absolutely. I don't intend on fighting anymore; but there again, while I'm involved in promoting, if a really good fight were to crop up – one which would draw a big crowd – I might consider taking it on. So, to be on the safe side, I'll keep myself in good shape."

"And what will you be up to in Spain next week?" asked a smiling Dean.

"I'm meeting up with the solicitor and the builder I told you about and, hopefully, we'll be able to do a deal on buying a villa off-plan – that is, the builder will show me the piece of land, and I can tell him exactly the type of villa I want built on it. After that, it's down to sorting out a price; assuming we can come to an agreement, I'll pay him twenty-five per cent upfront, and the balance once the villa is built, subject to me being satisfied with it."

"I assume you've got a price fixed in your mind?"

"I've been looking in the area where we want to live, and pricing up villas which are similar to what I want; buying off-plan is a huge saving, so when it's built, it will be worth far more than what I eventually pay for it."

"Assuming you can do a deal, how long will it take to build?" asked Joey.

"Somewhere between twelve and eighteen months, I reckon. I don't plan to rush him - I'd sooner he took his time, and did a good job."

"How will you pay the balance, once it's built?" asked Jonjo. "Surely you wouldn't be able to save that in the time you've got?"

"I've got together the deposit in the past two years from a combination of grafting in the taxi, and taking part in the fights – but I knew I couldn't raise the balance in the same way. So, I'll do it by remortgaging the house. It's worth a lot more than what I owe on the existing mortgage, and it still will be, even after remortgaging."

"I get it," said Tommy; "when you move over there, you'll sell your house over here, clear the mortgage, and still have a lump sum to take with you?"

"Well, that *was* my original plan - but I now have something in place which means I won't have to sell the house at all," said Neil, brightly. "A few weeks ago, I picked up a fella in the taxi, an agent for some of the big companies in Cheshire; he finds properties for overseas executives and their families, while they're temporarily based in this country. Anyway, he told me that, for as long as I wanted, he could guarantee finding such tenants for my property – and the rent I could charge would more than cover the mortgage, and all the other costs of keeping the house."

"Of course," said Tommy, nodding; "after seeing your house, and where it's situated, I've no doubt that companies would pay top dollar to put their executives there. The age of the house, and all the original features, would be particularly attractive to people from abroad – especially Americans."

"Exactly. So, provided everything goes to plan, we'd still own the house and the rent would pay the mortgage as well as everything else, and we'd own the villa outright. I've also got a few ideas on how to create income over in Spain, without actually working, as such."

"Caroline must get pretty excited, when you tell her all this stuff," smiled Dean.

"She probably would, if she ever listened to me when I'm talking to her," laughed Neil. "It must look bizarre to other people - when I've been talking at great length about Spain, and

Caroline says something about how worrying it is. I'll look at her, totally confused, and then realise she's been thinking about something completely different."

"Doesn't that annoy you?"

"Far from it," said Neil, smiling indulgently. "I'll finish speaking, then Caroline will come out with an absolute corker, which bears no relation to what I was talking about - it really creases me up. Once I start laughing, Caroline realises what she's done, and that sets her off as well."

"You just don't fall out, do you?" remarked Phil.

"We're a long time dead," pointed out Neil, shrugging; "so we need to make the most of what we've got now."

"Is right!" agreed Eddie. "Next time Julie gets mad with me, I'm going to smile, and give her a big kiss."

Dean laughed. "You need to be careful, Eddie - she might think you're making fun of her, and then you'd really be in trouble!"

"You're right," sighed Eddie; "I'll make sure I'm wearing a crash helmet, just to be on the safe side."

"Eddie, you're barking mad," chuckled Neil. "Okay, I'm off - all being well, next time you see me, I'll have paid twenty-five per cent deposit on my dream villa."

Chapter 17

Neil had been home from Spain for several days before he had the opportunity of visiting the warehouse; and so, as he arrived and walked into the lounge, there was an air of expectancy as he looked at all the smiling faces.

"Well, gentlemen, I've got good news and bad news," he announced.

"Good news first!" instructed Eddie. "Always got to be good news first, that's the rule."

Jonjo interrupted. "What rule? Who says that's the rule?"

"That's always been the rule. It's well documented, and has been for many years - good news always comes first."

"Well I've never heard of it before, I think you're just making it up."

"Hang on a minute, I may have got this wrong - come to think of it, the rule is that bad news always has to come second." Eddie looked triumphant.

"That sounds more like it to me. So, Neil - what's the good news?"

Neil frowned and scratched his head. "Are we doing the good news first? That's pretty unusual."

By this time, all the warehouse boys were sniggering, including Dean. "Don't you start, we'll be here all day - tell us the good news quick, before these two get going again."

"Well, you'll be pleased to know that I've got nowhere near as many premium bonds as I used to, and very little money left in my Spanish bank account."

Eddie shook his head decidedly. "That doesn't sound like good news to me, more like bad news. Jonjo - get the rulebook out, I need to check on something here."

Neil laughed, and turned to Dean. "It would have been quicker just to say that I had two things to tell you, wouldn't it?"

"On reflection, that may have been the wiser course of action," agreed Dean, wryly.

"So you did the deal then?" Earl got to the point, wearing a beaming smile. "Well done, mate."

Tommy, typically, wanted the detail. "Were you able to stipulate everything you wanted, at the price you were willing to pay?"

"Yes - it all went like clockwork. The solicitor was absolutely invaluable; her English is better than mine, so I was able to explain to her in detail what I wanted, which she, in turn, translated for the benefit of the builder."

"That's good," said Tommy; "because it did occur to me that if there was any confusion over a translation, you could end up with something that you didn't really want, or not get something that you did want."

"I know, I had the same thought - but it all went perfectly, thanks to my solicitor's language skills. The builder himself is a few years older than me, and both his sons work for him; one of his lads had a laptop with him, so as the solicitor explained what I wanted, he did a 3-D image of what she'd said." Neil was now warmed to his subject. "If you pass me a laptop, I can show you exactly what my villa will look like. We can even do a virtual tour of the interior."

"Here, I'll do it," offered Andy; "pass me the laptop, and we'll get the images up on the big screen."

Andy duly set up the screen, and they all spent some time viewing Neil's virtual villa, murmuring approval at the images.

"You're right, that is absolutely stunning," said Tommy, once the show was over.

"It's great being able to see it on a large screen - and the design ideas, both inside and out, are pretty much Caroline's." Neil was clearly proud to sing her praises. "The builder and his son were very much impressed and told us, through the solicitor, that they were going to enjoy building it; they even asked if they could photograph the finished article, to show any future clients they may have. I reckon Caroline was well pleased, to get professional approval of her vision for the villa."

"The problem is now, I'm dreading the bad news," sighed Eddie. "I'm sure we should have had that first."

Dean chuckled at Eddie's affected look of gloom. "So, what's the bad news?" he asked Neil.

"This news *is* serious, I'm afraid," replied Neil. "I picked up a gang of lads last night in the taxi; they were very drunk, and talking about an impending attack on the nightclub near to the Rockford. Over the next few nights, I'll be able to get all the information - so I'll have chapter and verse on when it'll happen, how many are involved, and how they're going to do it."

All humour had now evaporated from the faces of the warehouse boys, and they were listening intently.

"Okay," said Dean briskly. "Can I give you a list of things I'd like you to find out? If you can do that, and pass it back to me as soon possible, we can decide on the most effective course of action - the more information we've got, the better."

"No problem," said Neil. "The beauty of driving a taxi, is that the people in the back often forget that you can hear what they're saying; plus, the likes of the fools I picked up last night think it makes them look tough if they talk about stuff like this, even though they're not personally involved."

"Do your best," advised Dean; "ideally, we'll try and get to these people before they even arrive at the club."

"Don't worry," Neil assured him. "I can guarantee now, I'll get everything you need to know - either by asking the right questions, or getting hold of one of them, and knocking it out of him. I've got no problem with doing that – as far as I'm concerned, the kind of people who are involved in stuff like this are scum, and should be treated accordingly."

....

Days later, Neil arrived at the warehouse late one evening, to find only Dean and Jonjo in the lounge.

"Right, I've got everything you need to know," he told them. "There'll be about forty in the gang, and they're meeting in a pub on the Rockford, called the Spread Eagle. This particular pub is on the edge of the estate, within easy walking distance of the nightclub, which is how they plan to get there."

"Brilliant. Jonjo - get the map of the area up on the laptop, so Neil can show us exactly what route these fellas will take. What night is this attack planned for, Neil?"

"Next Wednesday, which is 'student night' at the club. From what I've been able to find out, as well as trying to do as much damage to the premises that they can, they also intend on attacking as many innocent people as possible - so that the students, or anyone else for that matter, will be too frightened to go there in the future." Neil looked at Dean astutely. "I assume you've already guessed who's behind this?"

"We were expecting something like this to happen," confirmed Dean; "it was always a question of when, rather than if. The beauty of it now, though - with you being able to give us all this information – is that we'll have the element of surprise."

"Take a look at this map, Neil," said Jonjo, as he turned the laptop screen towards him, "and show us exactly where the pub is, in relation to the club."

Dean was peering at the screen, as Neil traced the route. "Is that a football pitch there?"

"It is - and they'll definitely walk across it, as it's not surrounded by fencing; it's just a local council pitch, hardly used, but on the most direct route from the pub to the club. Also, the route they'll be taking is very poorly lit; so, as long as they're reasonably quiet, they won't attract too much attention - not that there's many round there that would bother ringing the police, anyway."

Dean, having shared a nod of agreement with Jonjo, said "Then that's where we'll take them."

"What will you do - get a big load of your doormen, and outnumber them as they're crossing the football pitch?"

"The ten of us will deal with them." Dean smiled in anticipation.

"It will be Rorke's Drift three," added Jonjo, brightly.

Neil was bemused. "I can understand you having to fight when you were well outnumbered for Rorke's Drift one and two - but surely, in this situation, there's no need to be outnumbered?"

"The numbers are irrelevant," pointed out Dean. "I need to know, in a situation like this, that the men I'm fighting alongside would give up their life for me, as I would for them. If I was on the ground and surrounded by ten attackers, with only Jonjo here left standing, I can be certain that he would lay into them without any consideration for his own safety. It's true, we've got some pretty tough bouncers on our books - but I don't know if I could count on them, as I can on the warehouse boys."

"Dean's right. The warehouse boys will never stop fighting while they can draw breath. We'll always stand by each other, regardless of the odds."

Neil realised that this loyalty and fearlessness was what he liked most about these men. Eddie had described Neil himself as a 'gladiator' – but to Neil, the warehouse boys were the real thing.

The lounge door opened, and in trooped the rest of the warehouse crew. "Gather round lads," ordered Dean; "we've got all the information we need now. There'll be about forty of them, and I've pinpointed exactly where we can take them down."

"I'll probably be able to give you an exact number on the night," volunteered Neil. "I'll just wait in the cab on the Spread Eagle car park, and do a head count as they're coming out. It'll take them about five minutes to walk from the pub to the football pitch - but in the cab, I can be there in two."

"You don't have to do that," said Dean; "it doesn't matter how many there are, we're still going to take them."

"Still," mused Tommy, "it wouldn't do any harm if there was eleven of us."

Eddie nodded emphatically. "Is right!"

"Hold on there," cautioned Dean; "my concern is that some of them that we're going against may know Neil, and could go after him in the future, when he's on his own."

"Are you saying that it's my decision, whether or not I fight alongside you?" was Neil's question to Dean.

Dean nodded, but clearly had reservations on Neil's behalf.

"Then there's eleven of us," decided Neil. "And if any of those fools want to take me on after the event - I can guarantee, no matter how many there are, they would regret wanting to fight Neil Hughes."

"That's it, then," smiled Dean. "We've got Scouse Neil on our side - we can't lose!"

Eddie was grinning like a schoolboy. "I was just going to say something then, but I can't for the life of me think what it was."

"Not 'Is right!' by any chance?"

Eddie affected to look mortally offended at Jonjo's remark. "'Is right'? That's a stupid expression - you wouldn't catch me saying *that*."

As everyone burst into laughter, Neil felt a real surge of pride that he was going to fight alongside these, modern-day, warriors. Remembering Dean's words, he realised that he also would fight to his last breath to defend any one of these men, secure in the knowledge that they would do the same for him. To Neil, this was very much Rorke's Drift three – and he was honoured to be part of it.

....

Neil parked his cab by the warehouse boys' minibus, then walked over to the centre of the football pitch to join them.

"We should start seeing them coming through that gap by the garages in the next two minutes," he informed Dean. "As it's so dark, they won't see us until they're quite close."

Dean nodded. "As soon as they're close enough, we'll launch the attack."

"And the strategy: if they stay down they're safe, but if they get back up we attack them again – and their only means of escape is to crawl away?"

"That's the way it works. I'll allow them to crawl back to the goalposts, then they can get up and run way."

"You're just a big softy really, aren't you?"

Dean turned to look at Neil, and raised his eyebrows. "Well, I can't help it, can I? I'm a soft touch – it's the way I am."

As the large group of thugs got nearer to the warehouse boys, and discovered that there were eleven men standing in their way, the leader of the group stepped up to them.

"Get out of our way or you'll get hurt," he began, intending to say more, but he was deprived of the opportunity; Neil quickly ran forward, jumped through the air, and butted him squarely in the nose. As Neil landed, he followed up by punching another man in the face while, simultaneously, kicking a third in the head. All this took only seconds; and, for an instant, the warehouse boys had time to smile in admiration at Neil's actions, before they launched their own assault.

The Rockford estate crew, who had considered themselves to be hard men, realised all too quickly that they were completely out of their league. The warehouse boys' fighting strategy was terrifying and relentless; although Neil himself was concentrating on taking down as many of the opposition as he was able, he could still see how formidable were the warehouse boys, when it came to this sort of fight.

The battle was soon over. Eleven men remained standing, looking down on their opponents; of these, those not lying motionless on the ground were, slowly, crawling away to a point of safety. Neil then noticed that Dean nodded to Tommy, who quickly walked over to the minibus, took something from under the back seat, and threw the article through the air to Dean, once he was close enough to him; it was a sawn off shotgun. Dean caught it with one hand; then, stepping forward to the big man that Neil had butted earlier, he stood on the man's throat, and forced both barrels of the shotgun into his mouth.

"This will be your only warning," said Dean quietly. "If you or your mates ever cause any trouble at my club, I'll come looking for you. I know who you are, where you live, and where your family live; go against me again, and I'll kill you and all your family. Be very clear about this; you're out of your league. I'm going to let you get up now, so that you can run away from me as fast as you can. If I think you're not running fast enough, I'll shoot you in the back."

Dean stepped back accordingly, and allowed the man to get to his feet, turn, and run away; watching him, Neil was fairly certain that he could not have run any faster. At one time in his life, Neil would have frowned upon someone threatening another person with a sawn off shotgun – but his involvement with the warehouse boys had given him a whole new perspective. Knowing what the Rockford estate gang had planned to do to innocent people, Neil believed that Dean had dealt with the gang leader correctly.

Once all their enemies had crawled, and then ran, from the scene of conflict, the warehouse boys walked back over to their minibus; before he headed back to his cab, Neil walked alongside Dean. "Did you recognise the one I butted?"

"You like rearranging his nose, don't you?" was Dean's observation.

Neil laughed. "As soon as I realised it was him, I just couldn't resist it."

Eddie, walking nearby, overheard their exchange. "Was that the fella with the baseball bat, from that night in Chester?"

Neil chuckled. "Certainly was – although, when I last saw him, his nose did look quite different."

Dean, who has also laughing, said "Well, I'm sure he was grateful for you helping him to reshape it."

"Is right! Neil – you're all heart!"

……………………………….......................................

Three days after the events at the Rockford estate, Dean received a phone call from Neil, to say that his father had died, and that it would therefore be some time before they would see him at the warehouse, while he dealt with his father's affairs. Later that day, Dean explained what had happened to the others, when they were all together in the lounge.

"It's unfortunate really," said Eddie, more soberly than was usual for him. "I feel that we should all attend the funeral - but in the circumstances, that would make it difficult for Neil."

"I know, we're not exactly inconspicuous," agreed Dean; "so his friends and family are bound to ask who we are, and that would put him in an awkward position. He's halfway through his plan to get to Spain, and us turning up at the funeral could mess that up for him. He'll understand us not being there."

"Do you know whether Neil's spoken to big Joe yet, about getting involved in promoting fights?" enquired Jonjo.

"Not yet. I spoke to big Joe before; Neil had told him about his dad, so they're going to meet up at some point in the future. Like us, Joe decided it was wiser not to attend the funeral."

"Let's just hope Scouse Neil doesn't think that none of us care," cautioned Andy.

Tommy put his hand on Andy's shoulder. "Don't worry, Neil will know why we're not there. He'll understand, and he'll appreciate us not attending."

Tommy was correct. Neil was grateful for the wisdom of the warehouse boys, and that of big Joe, in staying away from the funeral; he did, however, very much appreciate the two enormous wreaths that arrived – the one with a card endorsed 'W.B.S.', the other with a card from big Joe. Fortunately, no-one asked Neil directly if he knew the people who had sent these beautiful wreaths, and therefore he was saved from having to lie.

A few days after the funeral, Neil telephoned big Joe, and arranged a meeting in a small pub in Bootle. As he arrived, he walked in to the main bar area, and saw two large, angry looking men standing at the bar itself; they moved towards him, staring at him suspiciously, and appeared to be considering confronting him, when a voice shouted from a small side room. "It's okay, this is Scouse Neil!"

Neil was bemused; he recognised the voice as being that of big Joe, but wondered how the big man could have known that it was he, Neil, who had entered the pub. The two 'gorillas' simply nodded to Neil, stepped back to the bar, and continued drinking their cups of coffee; meanwhile, Neil entered the small side room, where he found Joe. The big man stood up, smiled, and shook his hand.

"Hope everything went all right," he consoled. "I knew it would be a problem for you if I'd attended the funeral, if you catch my drift."

"I understand completely. I know this sounds strange, but I appreciate your tact in staying away – and I want to thank you, very much, for the wreath that you sent."

"The least I could do," said Joe, making a dismissive gesture. "I'm flattered that you've come to me for advice on organising the fights. Over the last two years you've developed a great deal of credibility as a fighter - I've no doubt you won't have a problem gaining the same credibility as a promoter."

"Well, I've got a few ideas; and I thought I'd run them past you, to see what you thought, if you don't mind."

"By all means," said Joe, and listened intently as Neil set out his proposals.

"To begin with, as people are entering the venue, I'm going to have someone scanning for weapons, using a hand held metal detector. I heard, recently, about an incident at a fight in Manchester, where a gun was produced; I want people attending my fights to be satisfied that something like that can't happen.

"Secondly, no mobile phones will be allowed inside – each person will hand in their phone at the door, be given a ticket, then they can collect the correct device as they're leaving; I think it's a sensible precaution. A couple of months ago at a fight in Wigan, some fool videoed the whole thing on his mobile; he was arrested for pinching a car a few days later, and when the police checked his phone, all that footage was still there – and the police recognised the two fighters, and a fair few people in the crowd, so they all ended up getting arrested as well.

"Finally, I'll have a doctor in attendance at all of the fights I promote; for the benefit of the fighters themselves, naturally - but that's not the only reason. I've always seen the calibre of people that your fights attract, and I want the same – but it took you years to build up the trust that people have in you, and I haven't got that amount of time. I'm looking at ways of immediately establishing that it's safe to attend one of my fights - to give out the message that I'm professional; that way, I hope to encourage the right sort of people to attend, right from the start."

"I must say, you've certainly given this a lot of thought," said Joe; "and you're right - the more professional you are, the better. The only problem I can see is finding a doctor who'd be willing to attend an illegal fight."

"I've already got that lined up; it's the doctor used by the warehouse boys. I've explained the situation to him, and he's willing to do it."

"Well, I take my hat off to you," remarked Joe, smiling; "this is what this business needs, young fellas like yourself, with new ideas. Needless to say, all my premises are at your disposal - and naturally, you'll get a better deal than anyone else."

There was one thing that had puzzled Neil, and he decided to take the opportunity to bring it up.

"While we're here, I've got another question for you," he told the big man. "Remember that first time I fought the lad from Blackburn? At the end of the fight, you gave me a load of money from your winnings – and as I was leaving, you said to take Caroline, Michael and Paul out for a nice meal."

"I remember it very clearly - you poleaxed him with a roundhouse kick that fast Eddie would've been proud of."

"Yeah, but that's not it," said Neil. "I was wondering - how did you know the names of my wife and family? Because I didn't tell you, and nor did the warehouse boys."

Big Joe looked at Neil for a few moments, gently nodded his head, and smiled.

"Over the years," he said, "I've made a lot of good friends; but unfortunately, I've made the odd enemy as well. You clocked the two lads at the bar on the way in?"

"You couldn't very well miss them."

"You must have noticed that, whenever you see me, there's always two like that nearby, watching my back." Neil nodded. "Well, that first night I met you, and you offered to give me a lift over to the Dingle, I made a phone call. I needed to be sure that you were who you said you were."

Neil now looked confused. "When we left the warehouse, who *could* you have rung to check up on me?"

"As soon as I saw your taxi - and more importantly, the plate number - I was able to ring a mutual friend of ours. He confirmed who you were, told me a bit about you, and spoke very highly of you as well. That's how I found out the names of your wife and family." Big Joe then paused slightly, and shook his head. "Deano said nothing gets past you - you should've been a detective."

"And the mutual friend?"

"Jacko!" said Joe, grinning. "He used to be involved in this business, a few years ago."

"You mean he used to fight?"

"One of the best fighters I've ever seen. The last fight he was involved in was the biggest I've ever put on."

Neil appeared to be mentally calculating. "Was it about five years ago?"

"That's right," confirmed Joe. "Jacko came away with a lot of money from that fight. As well as the prize money, he cleaned up by betting everything he had on himself."

Neil's brow cleared, and he leaned back in his chair.

"Of course," he said; "that explains something to me that's always been a bit of a mystery. You see, five years ago, Jacko told everyone he'd had a big win on the horses with an accumulator; he bought an old cab and plate off one of the drivers, got rid of the vehicle, then went and bought a brand-new cab, all of which would've cost him about fifty thousand pounds. Now, I've known Jacko for some years, and I've never seen him go in to a bookies' once, so I always wondered where he really got the money from – and now I know." Neil nodded to himself, smiling. "Well, then - who was his last fight against? Anybody I know?"

"Little Albie," Joe told him. "It was one of the best fights I've seen, in all the years I've been involved in this. They both went into the fight undefeated, so the crowd was enormous. The fight went on for some time, because each time one was knocked down, they were straight back up again, to carry on. The fight finished when Jacko, literally, knocked little Albie out with a terrific punch. Neither of them fought again, after that."

"And does Jacko know I'm involved in it, now?"

"Oh, no," Joe assured him; "I was pretty vague when I asked him for the information, so he doesn't know there's any connection between you and I. And I'd sooner you didn't let on that you know he was involved himself - he always wanted to keep the fighting separate from his normal life."

"You say you've been involved for years – then, I assume you were a fighter yourself, originally?"

"I was - and even though I say so myself, I was a good one. When I stopped fighting, I was undefeated."

"How did you get involved in the first place?"

Neil sensed a profound sadness in Joe. "Anger!" he declared. "I was a very angry man, and found it was the best way of dealing with it." Big Joe sighed. "My wife died in childbirth, so I brought up my little boy on my own; then when he was five, he died of meningitis."

"I'm so sorry, Joe - I shouldn't have asked."

"It's okay, you weren't to know," said Joe. "Anyway, it took me a very long time before I stopped being angry. We called our son Neil, and if he'd lived, he would be the same age as you are now. That's why I've always paid close attention to what you've been up to, and glad to see how things have worked out." He looked slightly sheepish. "As you've recently lost your dad, I'd be honoured if you thought of me as a replacement - and I can be an honorary grandad to Michael and Paul."

"Absolutely," grinned Neil. "Within the next couple of years, I'll be finished in this business altogether. When I am, you'll get to meet Caroline, Michael and Paul - and when we move to Spain, you'll be able to come over and see us as often as you like. The only problem," he added wryly, jerking his head in the direction of the bar, "is that you'll be paying out for three airfares, every time you come."

Big Joe shook his head, smiling. "I won't need any minders when I come to see you." Neil assumed that he meant he had no enemies in Spain – so he was surprised, and touched, when Joe added "I wouldn't need them. I'll have Scouse Neil watching my back – and I can't think of anyone better."

"Ah, come on," said Neil, "over the years, you must have seen some great fighters. If you had to pick one, who do you think is the best ever?"

Big Joe pondered for some time. "I'd have to say Dean," he concluded eventually; "he's got everything - speed, power, strength, stamina, and above all, heart. I know you and fast Eddie are close with your similar sense of humour, but I also know you and Dean are closer, because you're two of a kind. You're both brave, fearless, natural leaders, and at your most fearsome when you're fighting for someone else."

Neil smiled. "Well, I'd need to go some, to live up to a bloke like Dean," he asserted. "Anyway, I'll make a move now – thanks for taking the time to listen to my ideas." He stood up and shook Joe's hand. "I'll see you soon."

As he walked out of the pub, Neil felt about a foot taller than when he had first gone in.

Neil continued to work hard, kept up his training at the warehouse and at home, and was also doing well on promoting the fights. Meanwhile, the builder's son was, regularly, emailing photographs of the villa as it was being built; each time these arrived, Neil and Caroline almost fought with each other to see them first, like excited children with a new toy.

As they were sitting in the conservatory, and Neil was examining one of the photographs on the laptop, he asked her "What gave you the idea of the archway at the side? It really sets off the whole building."

"I'd done some rough drawings of how I pictured the villa in my mind; then I added the archway on one of the drawings, and it looked so good, I left it in."

"Have you still got the drawings? I'd love to see them."

Caroline was only gone for a minute when she reappeared, the drawings under her arm, which she then handed to Neil. "I started doing these, right after you said we would, one day, have a villa of our own."

Neil spent some time leafing through Caroline's work. "These are fantastic," he murmured, as he looked closely at the detail. "Tell you what - with this talent, you were definitely wasted in hairdressing."

"Well, I wanted to make a good job of designing it, because it was for us," she explained. "I'm not sure if I'd have the same passion, if I were designing something for someone else."

"I always knew, even after eighteen years of being married," said Neil pompously, "that one day, you would be of some use."

Caroline giggled, hugged him, and kissed him passionately.

"I love you!" she declared.

Neil, with a stupid smile on his face, was so glad that she did.

Finally, a letter arrived from the solicitor, to confirm that the villa was complete; when Neil opened it, and they had read the contents, he and Caroline were practically dancing around the house, impatient for Michael and Paul to get home, so that they could tell them the good news.

They flew out to Spain just before their nineteenth wedding anniversary, met up with the solicitor to finalise the purchase, and then hurried over to take a look at their dream villa. As soon as they saw it, they realised that the builder's photographs came nowhere near to doing it justice; it was more than they could have hoped for. Caroline was so overwhelmed that she just burst into tears.

"Well, this is your creation," said Neil, making a sweeping gesture; "you must be very proud of it."

Caroline hugged him. "I've got a horrible feeling I'm going to wake up any minute."

Neil smiled, and gently kissed her on the forehead. "This isn't a dream - this is really ours," he assured her; "and, all being well, in about twelve months' time, we'll actually be living here for good." Ever the practical man, he went on "What we need to do now is sort out some furniture. You can decide what we need and choose it - you've got a much better idea than me."

Caroline started drying her eyes. "And I know the very store I want to go to - it's in Seville. Do you remember the time we went back to the airport early, and spent some time in Seville?"

"Was that the time when me and the lads joined in a game of football in the park, and you went round the shops?"

"That's right – well, I found this furniture store, and I was in there for ages. Funny, now I think about it; but when I was in the store, I was imagining having my own villa, picturing how I would furnish it. And now the dreams come true." She shook her head, still scarcely believing it.

"In that case, we'll go there first thing in the morning," promised Neil. "Will we be able to get everything we need from the same store?"

"Oh yes, it's massive, and there's so much choice for every room in the house - but I already know exactly what I want." Caroline looked smug. "I have drawings."

"Love it! Right then - which restaurant do you fancy going to, this evening?"

"Hm." Caroline thought for a moment. "The little one in town, by the side of the river."

"The first one we ever went to, when we started coming here," mused Neil.

"I think sitting outside that restaurant by the river, on that first trip, was what made me fall in love with this part of Spain. I still can't take it in that we're going to live here, in our own villa."

"If all goes to plan, we'll have a big party for our twentieth wedding anniversary, and that will be our leaving party as well. By that time, Michael and Paul will be nineteen and seventeen, so it'll be up to them if they want to come with us or not."

"That's my only worry," said Caroline, and her expression reflected her words. "If the lads decided to stay in Britain, and if we'd sold the house, where would they live?"

"Ah, but we're not selling the house, remember? I told you about that agent fella I picked up."

"Oh that's right, I remember now - but even so," she pointed out, "if we're renting it out, the lads wouldn't be able to live there."

"Don't fret - remember that, whatever happens, it's our choice. So, if the lads decided to stay and had nowhere to live, I could simply make sure that there was enough money in the bank to cover the costs of the house, for as long as they wanted to live in it."

"Would we be able to afford to do that?"

"Of course. The beauty of the situation is that we could move over here around the time of our twentieth anniversary, but that doesn't mean we have to. We could wait, and come over whenever we like; I'll know when we're in the position when we can afford to do it - but you can be the one to decide exactly when we make the move."

Caroline nodded. " We'll see what happens in the next twelve months."

When they got back home, Neil carried on as usual; and, financially, everything was going according to plan – he was reasonably confident that they would be in a position to choose to move abroad by the time of his and Caroline's anniversary. As time went on, however, Neil could not shake the suspicion that Caroline was having second thoughts about the move; she did not seem to be as excited at the prospect as he was. He began to realise that it was probably the only thing that he ever talked about, and wondered whether he was almost too obsessed.

In fact, unbeknown to Neil, the reason for Caroline's preoccupation was not cold feet about the move, but her increasing concern about Paul's behaviour, and the bad company he was keeping. Neil was therefore unaware that, while he was talking excitedly about Spain, Caroline was worrying about their younger son.

After one particular training session at the warehouse, Neil was sitting in the lounge with Dean, Jonjo and Eddie.

"So, how are the fights going?" enquired Dean. "You've hardly mentioned them since the villa was built."

"Sorry - I'm just so excited about it, and can't wait to get there," replied Neil. "As far as the fights are concerned, they're going okay; I'm either using Joe's place in Bootle, or a place just outside Warrington. So far, it's bringing in the extra cash - which means everything will be in place for moving to Spain in about six months."

"So, all being well, we'll get to meet Caroline and the lads at your twentieth anniversary party, then you'll be sliding off to Spain?" said Eddie.

Neil hesitated for an instant, and suppressed a sigh. "I hope so - we'll have to wait and see."

Dean, Jonjo and Eddie glanced at each other, but said nothing. "Anyway, I'll make a move," said Neil, getting up from his seat; "I'm not sure when I'll be back over, but I'll let you know."

Eddie followed Neil out of the building, and watched him drive away, as usual. He stood there for a moment, pursing his lips; then he turned, and went back inside.

"There's something wrong," he declared, as he rejoined the others in the lounge. "I don't know what it is - but there's definitely something wrong."

"We know," Jonjo told him. "Dean and I were just talking about it while you were outside. Although Neil's really excited when he talks about the villa, you get the sense that there's something not quite right, as far as the move to Spain's concerned."

"Well, we all know the rules," Dean advised them; "we don't pry into each other's affairs. If Neil's got a problem, and he wants to discuss it, then that's different - but as things stand, it's none of our business."

"When did we make that rule?" demanded Eddie. "I can't remember making any of these rules at all."

"Er - that one was your idea," pointed out Jonjo. "It was around the time you and Julie were having loads of problems, and you said you were fed up with everyone asking if you two were all right."

"Well, we need to change the rules, because Julie and I are getting on great - but I'm concerned about Neil. The main reason Julie and I get on better now is because of the advice Neil has given me. If he's got a problem, I owe it to him to try and help."

Dean shrugged. "I know what you mean, Eddie; Neil's been a good friend to all of us in different ways. But it's not our place to poke our nose in to something which is none of our business." His tone was firm. "Let's just keep an eye on things, and hope that, whatever the problem is, it sorts itself out."

Neil was having some work done on the taxi, which was going to take most of the day; he therefore dropped the cab at the garage early in the morning, and jogged home. As he got there, Caroline was just getting up.

"Cup of tea?" he shouted up the stairs. "I'm just putting the kettle on!"

"Yes please, I'll be down shortly."

"Will you stop calling me 'shortly'?" he shouted back. "I'm getting a complex!"

"Sorry, Shortly," said Caroline, as she came into the kitchen soon afterwards; "I didn't quite catch what you said while I was upstairs."

"I can't remember," he said, as he gave Caroline her tea. "Anyway, as I was jogging back from the garage, I had an idea. Why don't we all go over to the villa, and have a small party? We could invite the solicitor and her husband, and the builder and his family. Mike could bring Cathy, and Paul could bring his new girlfriend - she seems very nice."

Caroline's eyes lit up. "Jenny does seem really nice, doesn't she? I think she'll be a good influence on our Paul. I just hope he's got the sense to stay with her, and spend less time with those fools he's knocking round with at the moment."

"So you fancy the idea, then?"

"Yes, it's a great idea - the sooner the better, as far as I'm concerned."

Neil was elated by Caroline's reaction, and set about making the arrangements.

....

It was soon after returning from the trip to Spain that Neil visited the warehouse, and had a good training session with Dean and Eddie; however, it seemed to his friends that he was even more despondent than the last time they had seen him.

Neil told them that he was heading straight back out to work, when Eddie detained him. "I've made you a coffee, if you've got time?"

"Okay then, cheers," agreed Neil. "Actually, I don't know what I'm rushing off for - the taxi work is really crap at the moment. If I wasn't doing so well out of the fights, I'd be really struggling, cash wise."

Once the three of them were in the lounge, drinking coffee, Dean asked "How did your get-together in Spain go?"

Neil tried to look enthusiastic. "It was great," he lied; "the solicitor's lovely, and her husband is a sound bloke. The builder and his family certainly enjoyed themselves as well, so I thought it went well." He paused. "The only thing that spoiled it slightly was one of the solicitor's friends. I'd told her she could bring a friend if she wanted to, so she brought this English couple she knows, who live over there; thinking about it, I suppose she thought we'd get on with them, seeing as they were from our own country. Anyway, the wife was okay - but the husband was a complete tosser; never stopped rubbing it in about how wealthy and successful he was. I can't be doing with his type."

"I often find that sort aren't as wealthy or successful as they would like you to believe," said Dean, sagely. "What does this fella do for a living?"

"Supposedly, he buys property, and then rents it out to holidaymakers; but when I started talking figures with him, it just wasn't adding up. One thing I would say for sure, is that I wouldn't trust him as far as I could fling him - and I suspect anyone who got involved with him financially would have to watch their step." Neil shook his head. "He even had the brass neck to say that if ever I decided to sell the villa, he would like first option. I can't imagine wanting to sell the villa anyway - but I certainly wouldn't sell it to him. Other than the fact that I thought he was a toerag, I don't think he could afford it. I just thought he was full of crap."

"What did Caroline and the lads think of him?" asked Eddie.

"The lads, and especially Michael, didn't take to him at all. What surprised me, though, was that Caroline seemed to quite like him." Neil was clearly nettled by this, his listeners gathered. "She never used to fall for all that flannel years ago. Maybe it was just me being a bit jealous - I've never been able to pour the charm on like that. I was never any good when it came to chatting up women."

Eddie laughed. "Do you think being an ugly bastard had anything to do with it?"

Neil also laughed. "Good point," he conceded, "I think that might have had a lot to do with it. Now you mention it, I've never understood to this day what Caroline ever saw in me."

"She probably thought you had money," suggested Dean, winking at Eddie. "It must have been a terrible disappointment to her when she discovered you hadn't - but she probably felt sorry for you by that time."

"Well, I feel a lot better now," declared Neil, still chuckling; "you can't beat a good vote of confidence to lift your spirits."

"We aim to please," said Eddie, loftily. "Any time you need your spirits lifting, we are the very men to do the job."

"I'll bear that in mind!" said Neil, smirking. "Anyway, I'll head back to the rank – and with any luck, I might get a bit more abuse from the other taxi lads, which should lift my spirits even more."

Neil drove away from the warehouse, giving a thumbs up sign to Eddie and Dean as he did so.

"Well, at least we got him laughing," remarked Dean.

"Which was great to see - but I still reckon there's something wrong," concluded Eddie.

"I agree - but I've no idea what, and I can't see the point of us speculating, because we'd just be stabbing in the dark. Let's keep our fingers crossed that, whatever it is, Neil can deal with it."

After one of Neil's fights at big Joe's warehouse in Bootle, the two men were chatting after everyone had left.

"I believe some of your fights over in Warrington have involved travellers?" said Joe.

Neil nodded enthusiastically. "They're a bit of a wild crew," he admitted, "but the turnout is fantastic when one of the travellers is fighting – and, to be fair, they are damned good fighters."

"I know, but you need to be careful. Some of them can be too wild, particularly when things don't go their way."

"I haven't had any problems so far, but I know what you mean. What gives me a bit of an edge, is that I can talk like a traveller."

Big Joe was taken aback by this claim. "I've got to hear this," he encouraged. "Say something in a traveller accent."

"I'm not quite sure what you'd like me to say, Joe, but when I talk like this, the travellers think it's really funny and I never seem to have any problems with them." Neil said all of this in his most authentic traveller's brogue.

Joe laughed in delight, when Neil finished speaking. "I only understood part of that," he confessed, "but I bet that goes down really well with the travellers. I can see why you get on so well with them. Even so, how come you're arranging fights for them as well?"

"The fact is, that for the last few months, the taxi work's been getting really grim," explained Neil, reverting to his normal speech; "and if I was only relying on that, I'm not sure if I'd ever get to Spain. The particularly big fights involving the travellers have really kept things on course for me."

Big Joe was nodding. "I know you've got about three months to go before your twentieth anniversary - will you be able to move to Spain then?"

"I think I'll be in a financial position to move, yes - whether I do or not is a different matter."

Joe was surprised by his reply. "But what might stop you doing it?"

Neil puffed out his cheeks, and did not answer straight away. "The truth is, I'm not quite sure what's happening," he said eventually; "I get the feeling that Caroline may be having second thoughts about the whole thing - but I could be wrong."

"Well," said Joe carefully, "to be fair, it's a big step, actually leaving the country, and all your family and friends. I know it's going to be easy for people to come over and see you, and for you to come back over here - but it's still quite an upheaval."

"I don't think it's the move to Spain that's the problem," said Neil, shaking his head. "You see, since Caroline and I were married, I've always worked hard, putting a lot of hours in on the taxi; because of that, sometimes, she and I are a bit like ships that pass in the night. My dream has always been that, one day, I'll be able to give up work, and she and I can spend all our time together. Naturally, I always thought that was her dream as well - but I'm wondering now if I was wrong."

Joe's face was now full of concern. "Has Caroline said, or done something, to make you feel that?"

"No; but I can tell that the enthusiasm she had when I first mentioned the villa, right up to when it was built, is not as strong as it was. I've been racking my brains trying to come up with an explanation for her change of heart - and it did occur to me that, maybe, one of the reasons we get on so well, is because we don't see that much of each other." Neil was looking troubled. "I'm starting to wonder if the idea of me being there all time is not what she wants, but she feels that, in the circumstances, she can't tell me the truth. I'm always banging on about how great it will be, how all the years of hard work have helped me achieve my dream. Imagine how awful she'd feel, if she had to say that she didn't share it."

Joe had been listening carefully, and wondering what he could say that would be of any comfort.

"As you say, you could be wrong," was all he could think of. "I wish I could suggest something to you that would help, but I don't know Caroline." He was conscious that this sounded rather lame.

"I'm frightened to ask Caroline directly, in case I'm right, and I force her into admitting it. So, although it's the coward's way out, I'd rather do and say nothing, and hope that I'm wrong. Anyway, we'll just have to wait and see what happens. Hopefully, I'm just being paranoid, and everything will work out okay." He looked at Joe. "Sorry to have bent your ear about this, but you're a good listener. Anyway," he continued, "I'd better get going. It was a good turnout here tonight – thanks, as usual, for letting me use the warehouse."

As Neil left the Bootle warehouse, Joe watched him go with a terrible feeling of guilt, cursing himself that he had been able to offer no consolation to this fine young man, who he had come to look upon as a son. Joe could only fervently hope that Neil was wrong, and that there was some other explanation for Caroline's apparent change of heart.

Chapter 18

After a particularly gruelling training session, Neil, Dean, Eddie, Tommy and Jonjo were all sitting in the lounge drinking coffee.

"Fair play to you, Neil," said Dean; "although you haven't fought for nearly two years now, you've certainly kept yourself in shape."

"I've had a few skirmishes when I've been taxiing - but unfortunately, I don't make any money out of those," said a smiling Neil.

"Are you still doing a lot of hours?" asked Jonjo.

"I've got to. Apart from saving up for Spain, I do pay out a lot each month - between the mortgage, various insurances, utility bills and loads of other things, I need to have plenty of money in the bank account at any given time."

Dean nodded. "Were you able to build up your premium bond savings again?"

"Oh yes, I've done that; I've also been able to transfer a reasonable amount of money over to Spain - not to mention my secret stash," added Neil cryptically.

Eddie's eyebrows shot up. "You've got a secret stash?"

"Certainly have, underneath the shed in the garden. The shed's got a wooden floor, with an old piece of carpet covering one section of it that lifts out."

"When you say 'secret stash', how much have you got there, and who knows about it?" enquired Tommy.

"Well, the amount fluctuates depending on whether I need to pay out a large sum of money for something, such as our Michael's party recently; but, on average, there's usually about three grand in there. And as for who knows about it – the fact is, you're the first people I've told."

Eddie was amazed. "Haven't you even told Caroline?"

"I daren't," replied Neil. "If she knew it was there, at some point she wouldn't be able to resist dipping into it, and then she'd feel really guilty. Mind you, I think she suspects; she must do - given the fact that, when I've needed a reasonable amount of money quickly, I've always been able to produce it."

"What about the premium bonds and the Spanish account?" asked Jonjo.

"Well, I did tell her about those – but I can tell you now, if anyone asked her if we had any savings, she'd say she didn't know," replied Neil, wryly. "I mentioned about the bonds years ago, but I don't think it ever quite registered; and it was obvious, when we were over there doing the deal on the villa, that she hadn't been listening when I told her about the account in Spain either."

Tommy was smiling and scratching his head. "And it just doesn't bother you at all, does it?"

Neil shrugged. "Over the years, I've tried – and failed - to get her more involved in the financial side of things. I suspect she just assumes that, no matter what the problem is, I'll be able to sort it out."

Eddie gave a furtive glance at the other warehouse boys. "By the way, Neil - are you still planning on having a party for your twentieth wedding anniversary? You seemed a bit unsure, when we spoke about it the other week."

"There'll definitely be a party for our twentieth, and I can't wait for Caroline and the lads to meet you lot," confirmed Neil, smiling; "but I'm not sure whether we'll be moving to Spain around the same time. We might put that off until a later date."

Dean looked pleased. "And don't forget, we'll be having a party here, between now and when you have yours."

"I know, but I'll have to check it doesn't clash with the wedding Caroline and I are going to. Her cousin's getting married at a posh hotel in Cheshire, and Caroline's really looking forward to it. For the last three or four years, I've hardly taken her anywhere, because I've been so obsessed with this business over Spain."

"It must be peculiar when you're surrounded by people getting drunker as the night goes on, and you're sober," observed Jonjo.

"It can be pretty funny," agreed Neil. "Caroline herself can start the night quietly, but by the end of it, she's a different person - everyone's her friend, and she manages to be pleasant to people that I know she doesn't like. It's just as well I don't drink, because I'd be the other extreme – deeply *un*pleasant to people I disliked."

"A drunken man speaks a sober man's thoughts," was Dean's pearl of wisdom.

"All the more reason why I'm not sure if I want to come to your party - because I might find out what you really think about this Scouse bastard who's taken up so much of your time, and who ripped you off as far as that equipment was concerned!"

"Which reminds me," said Tommy; "I know you got plenty of use out of your training room - did the lads use it as well?"

"They got more use than I did," asserted Neil. "The way it worked was great; a lot of the things you fellas were teaching me, I taught to Michael and Paul – and then they, in turn, were teaching their mates."

Tommy was clearly gratified. "When I was installing the equipment, you said then that Michael and Paul were pretty good at looking after themselves – so, with the training, they should be even better."

"They are my sons," said Neil with pride, "but if I didn't know them, I definitely wouldn't like to go against either of them. Mike's nineteen, and Paul seventeen, but they're both bigger than me, and still growing. Neither of them are bullies - but if they're in a position where they've got to fight, any fool that crosses them is in big trouble."

"I take it you've seen them in action?" said Dean.

"Indeed I have," grinned Neil. "The thugs on the Rockford estate must hate me and my family. A few weeks ago, Michael and Paul were playing in a cup final against a team from the Rockford; Mike's team won, and after the game, some of the Rockford players and their mates were foolish enough to have a go at my sons. Well, I wasn't too far away - but by the time I got there, there were only two fellas left standing." Neil's eyes twinkled. "I don't need to say which two."

"Is right!"

"If they'd been alongside us on the night of Rorke's Drift Three, believe me, they would not have been out of place," declared Neil. "To a certain extent, Paul is like I used to be, whereas Michael is like I am now; you see, Paul is absolutely fearless, and would go against anyone, regardless of who they were, or how many – whereas Michael is calm and controlled, but considerably more dangerous."

"Yes," said Tommy soberly, "I'm afraid it's important, nowadays, that decent people are able to stand up for themselves - because we seem to be surrounded by scum and low-lifes."

"I couldn't agree with you more, Tommy - I've seen the difference over the years I've been driving the taxi. That's one of the reasons I want to live in Spain; the area where we'll be living is like stepping back in time - people are polite, well- mannered, and the youngsters have respect for the older ones."

"In the short time we've been involved in doing the doors on the clubs, we've seen a difference ourselves," noted Dean. "You don't have to worry about the hard case - it's the head case you've got to look out for." Everyone murmured their agreement.

"Anyway, Neil," interjected Jonjo, "how many more fights have you got lined up before you're finished altogether?"

"Just the two: the first at big Joe's in Bootle, the second in Warrington, and both should attract reasonable size crowds. If they do, then I'll have the funds in place to move to Spain - if I choose to."

As he finished speaking, Neil paused, as if he was about to add something; but then he appeared to change his mind. There was an almost uncomfortable silence for a few moments, before it was broken by Eddie.

"Will you be inviting big Joe to your anniversary party?"

"Definitely," replied Neil, who seemed to brighten up at the prospect. "Joe is really looking forward to meeting Caroline and the lads. Anyway," he continued briskly, draining his coffee cup, and rising from his seat, "I'll make a move - not sure when I'll be back over, but I'll give you a bell."

This time, as Neil drove away from the warehouse with the usual thumbs up sign, it was Tommy who stood and watched the departing taxi, until it was out of sight. Walking back into the lounge, he saw the others look at him expectantly.

"I see what you mean," he told them, and gently shook his head as he was sitting down.

This comment was all Eddie needed. "So you agree - there's definitely something wrong?"

Tommy looked concerned. "There's no question. That spark we've always seen in him, the enthusiasm – it seems to have disappeared."

"Well at least he's going ahead with his anniversary party, which is good news," observed Dean; "but he hesitates now about the move to Spain – I wonder why?"

"Anyway, let's hope he can make our party - all the girls are dying to meet him," commented Jonjo.

"It doesn't seem like five years, since all the work was done on this place," said a smiling Tommy, as he looked at their surroundings.

"We've come a long way in the past five years, and I think we should all be proud of ourselves, with what we've achieved." Dean paused for a moment. "Let's hope Neil can make the party. If he wasn't here for that, it wouldn't feel right."

....

Neil's penultimate fight, at the warehouse in Bootle, could not have gone any better. There was a massive turnout which meant that, even after paying everyone, he came away with a substantial amount of money. He knew that, should his final fight in Warrington be only half as well attended, he would have the funds in place to go to Spain; however, by now, he had more or less convinced himself that it would never happen – because how could he continue to pursue a dream that he suspected Caroline did not share?

The warehouse party was to take place a week before the wedding, so Neil confirmed with Dean that he could attend, but only for an hour; Saturday was the busiest night of the week on the taxi, and he did not want to miss out on the income. He felt somewhat guilty, given that he had no real desire to go to the party; but he knew that the warehouse boys particularly wanted him there, and therefore felt that he must make the effort. It was almost four years since the night he had met Dean and, despite having formed a close bond with the boys, he had avoided any social gatherings; he had always felt uncomfortable leading a kind of double life, and attending a party without Caroline simply did not seem right.

When the evening came, Neil arrived relatively early, hoping that there would not be too many people; however, he was surprised to find that the party was already in full swing. Aside from the warehouse boys, he noticed that big Joe was there, along with little Albie, Macca, and a small, stocky, white haired man; judging by his tan, Neil assumed that this was big Albie. As he approached the group, big Joe immediately stepped forward with his hand outstretched.

"Good to see you, Neil," he greeted; "this is my old mate, big Albie."

"It's great to meet you, Neil," said the stocky man, as he shook hands with him. "Our Albie is a big fan of yours. When you were still fighting, Albie was putting some big bets on you on my behalf – it meant I was able to stay in Turkey permanently, and I'm very grateful!" He smiled. "I believe you've also done well promoting the fights?"

"I've done okay," confirmed Neil, without enthusiasm. "I've got one more fight, and then I'm finished with it altogether. Getting to know people like the warehouse boys, and big Joe, has been great - but to tell the truth, this isn't my world, and I know I'll be glad to get back to living a normal life."

"Excuse me gents," interrupted Dean, who had just joined them, "but I've got to drag Neil away from you." He cleared his throat. "The ladies want to meet him."

The other men laughed, and Big Joe slapped Neil on the back. "You go ahead, son," he grinned; "we wouldn't dream of keeping you from your fan club!"

As he was being shepherded away by Dean, Neil was inwardly cringeing; this was the very situation he had hoped to avoid. Although he was no longer as shy around women as he had been when he was younger, he was still far more comfortable in men's company. The wives and girlfriends of the warehouse boys were sitting together, and looked over expectantly as he and Dean approached; Dean duly made the introductions and, no sooner had Neil seated himself, than he was bombarded with questions, which he did his best to respond to appropriately, earnestly hoping that he did not look a complete fool.

"We've all been dying to meet you," declared Julie, Eddie's girlfriend. "For the last four years all I've heard from Eddie is, 'Neil said this', 'Neil recommended this', 'Neil suggested this' - but don't get me wrong," she qualified, hurriedly, "I'm not complaining, far from it. I think, with your help, Eddie's finally growing up." Neil smiled, but made no comment; in his heart, he hoped Eddie would never really grow up.

As Julie had been speaking to him, it suddenly struck him that, in appearance, she was not dissimilar to Caroline, and it gave him an idea; he felt the need for a short break from being the centre of attention.

"You know, you and my wife could be taken for sisters," he told her; "I've got a nice photograph in the taxi of Caroline, me, and the lads - I'll just nip out and get it."

"Great – we'd love to see it," said Julie, as he got up.

Although this was partly a ruse to get away for a few minutes, he was also very proud of this recently taken photograph, and liked to take any opportunity to show it to anyone and everyone who wanted to see it. Having retrieved it from the cab, as he came back into the warehouse, Neil observed someone standing by little Albie; the face of the man seemed familiar, but he could not place it. He shook his head, and rejoined the girls.

"That's Michael and that's Paul," he said to Julie, pointing to the images in the picture; "and, as you can see, I wasn't joking when I said you and Caroline could be taken for sisters."

Julie held the framed photograph in her hand, and looked at Neil with an almost dreamlike expression. "You think I look like your wife? I'm so flattered!" She seemed amazed. "Eddie!" she called to her other half, who was nearby. "Come and have a look at Neil's wife and sons."

Eddie dutifully came over in response to her summons, and examined the photo.

"My God, you actually could take you and Caroline for sisters," he murmured; then he shook his head. "Not that I believe this is a picture of Caroline at all. I think Neil found a photo of a really good looking family and had himself airbrushed into the husband's place. No woman that beautiful could marry a man this ugly." He winked at Neil.

Neil laughed, but Julie was appalled. "That's a terrible thing to say!" she admonished. "I thought you two were supposed to be mates!" This caused Eddie to start sniggering.

"Let me have a look," instructed Jonjo, and Julie passed him the photo. "Hm," he said, after examining it carefully; "lucky the lads got their mum's looks and not yours."

"Is right!" declared Neil, laughing.

"That's a good expression that - I might start using it myself!" decided Eddie.

"Are they always this horrible to you, Neil?" This came from Kirsty, who was Tommy's girlfriend.

Neil tried his best to look forlorn. "It's constant," he sighed; "sometimes, I leave this place in tears."

"Eddie told me that you asked Caroline to marry you only three weeks after meeting her," said Julie.

"That's right. It took me three weeks to pluck up the courage."

It was Lisa, Phil's wife, who picked up on his meaning. "If it took three weeks to pluck up the courage, when did you actually know you wanted to marry her?"

By this time, all the women were gathered round, and listening intently. Neil felt extremely uncomfortable, and looked to the warehouse boys for a bit of support; however, all he got was the remark from Dean: "If you don't tell them, I will."

Neil shrugged, and spread out his hands. "From the moment I saw her, I knew then that I loved her, and could never imagine loving anyone else."

There was a moment's silence, as his female audience around the table seemed to be stunned by this declaration. Julie was the first to speak.

"Well then, you must tell us the whole story," she ordered, smiling. "Eddie told me you met in a nightclub in Liverpool - and only three weeks later, you proposed? We've *got* to have the rest of the details."

With resignation, Neil took a deep breath, and recounted the story – beginning with how they met, and ending with his proposal to Caroline in the small church in Wales. It went without saying that he had the ladies' undivided attention; but he was surprised to note that even the warehouse boys themselves seemed fascinated by his account. As he finished, there seem to be a moment's silence, before it was broken by Kirsty.

"All the lads were looking at the picture, and telling you how lucky you are – well, I know who *I* think the lucky one is."

"Is right!" said Julie, nodding emphatically.

"Neil, Julie's trying to pinch your saying there!" exclaimed Eddie, which caused everyone to burst into laughter.

"I thought it was Jonjo's?" countered Neil.

"No - I sold it to Dean a few years ago," retorted Jonjo.

As everyone was laughing, Neil noticed that the man he thought he had recognised earlier was heading in their direction, with what appeared to be an angry expression on his face; when he reached the group, he looked at the family photograph almost in disgust.

"Scouse Neil? Gay Neil, more like!" He jabbed a finger at the photo. "She's probably got a proper man on the side, and that's where the lads get their looks from."

This sudden interruption took everyone by surprise; but Neil's response was swift.

"You never know, kid," he said, smiling; "if you drop your wallet tonight, you may be better kicking it to the wall and sliding down to pick it up – because if you bend over, I might be behind you!"

As he said this, everyone's anger from the man's insulting remark was put on hold, and they all started laughing at the uninvited guest.

"What's your problem, knob'ead?" demanded Julie. "Open your mouth again, and I'll punch your lights out!"

Neil could see the fire in Julie's eyes, and had no doubt that she was quite capable of backing up her threat; fortunately, however, the man said nothing further, and simply walked away, throwing a look of pure hatred at Neil as he left.

"What the hell was that all about?" Julie was incensed.

"God knows," said Neil, shrugging. "Well, it's time for me to make a move, I'm afraid - but no doubt I'll see you all again, soon."

"You're not going because of what that tosser just said, are you?"

"No," Neil assured her, smiling. "I need to get back to work, that's all. It was just starting to get busy when I knocked off before. Anyway, ladies, it's been lovely meeting you all."

Dean and Jonjo accompanied Neil to his cab.

"Thanks for coming," said Dean, as he shook Neil's hand. "I've no idea who that fool was, but I was very impressed with your self-control."

"Four years ago, you'd have knocked hell out of him," pointed out Jonjo.

"I'm not sure whether I *could* have knocked hell out of him four years ago – he's a big lad."

"Oh, you could have," smiled Dean. "It just would've taken you some time. Now, you could put him away in seconds, but chose not to. We really have taught you well."

"Battering him would only prove that I was tougher," shrugged Neil. "As I'm already aware of that, it would have been a pointless exercise. Words are never going to do any harm to me."

Jonjo grinned. "That's it - the student has become the master."

As Neil was about to get into the cab, Eddie emerged from the warehouse; he came up to them and nodded to Dean and Jonjo. "Tommy got to him first!"

"There's a surprise," remarked Dean, with a wry smile.

"Where?" asked Jonjo.

"The training room," replied Eddie, grinning from ear to ear. "We've got some cleaning up to do in the morning."

Neil was looking perplexed as he heard this exchange. "Have I missed something here?"

Eddie glanced at Dean, and when the latter nodded, Eddie explained.

"Tommy's just knocked hell out of that fella who insulted you. He shoved him into the training room, and gave him a right good leathering. Then he dragged him along the floor into the lounge, dropped him at little Albie's feet, and said 'If you insult one of us, then you insult all of us.'" Eddie smirked. "You've probably got a good idea what I said then."

"I see," said Neil thoughtfully. "You know, when I saw that fella earlier on, I thought I knew him from somewhere, but still can't remember where. Anyway, I assume he's a mate of little Albie's - what did he say, when Tommy dropped his mate at his feet?"

"Albie could see the look in Tommy's eyes and so, very wisely, said nothing."

Neil shook his head. "I'm sorry to have been the cause of this. I've obviously done something in the past to annoy that bloke, but I've no idea what."

"There's nothing to apologise for," said Dean firmly; "that fool was the problem and, quite rightly, he got what he deserved."

Eddie and Jonjo said their goodbyes to Neil, and went back to the warehouse, but Dean remained; he turned, and looked at Neil speculatively.

"I may be wrong here," he ventured, "but I got the impression you weren't keen on big Albie."

"Well spotted!" declared Neil. "Didn't like him one bit - and I was surprised when big Joe introduced him as an old mate of his, because I don't believe they are, or ever have been, mates."

Dean was smiling, and gently shaking his head as Neil was speaking.

"We often say this about each other - but absolutely nothing gets past you, does it?" remarked Dean. "It took me quite a few meetings, when the two of them were together, before I realised that they weren't mates. Big Joe is a great believer in that saying: keep your friends close, but keep your enemies closer."

"Anyway, hope the rest of the evening goes well, and that no-one upsets Julie." Neil paused and chuckled. "She's really fiery, isn't she?"

"She's great," agreed Dean, "and she wasn't kidding, either. If that fella had said another word, she would've definitely cracked him one. Which reminds me," he continued, "for someone who's not supposed to be very comfortable around women, I thought you did pretty well there tonight."

"Maybe I'm not as ugly as I thought."

"Oh you are certainly ugly, make no mistake," Dean assured him, with an evil twinkle in his eyes; "but you have got a villa in Spain. Don't go and buy yourself a Porsche, for God's sake, or the rest of us will have no chance!"

Neil was laughing as he got into the cab; he drove away, giving his usual thumbs up sign out of the open window, and shouted "Enjoy yourself - see you next week!"

....

The following weekend, Neil and Caroline attended her cousin's wedding. The hotel was very upmarket, and Caroline was clearly having a good time, but Neil knew that she would be suffering in the morning; as for himself, he always felt like a fish out of water at these kind of events, and could only hope that it did not show. He would spend his time people watching, which he found fascinating. He noticed one particular man at the next table, who reminded him very much of his Spanish solicitor's English friend, the one that he and his sons had so disliked; the man he was now watching was a smooth operator with the attractive women, yet dismissive and ignorant when speaking to one of the barmaids who, Neil assumed, the man did not consider as attractive. It was times like these that Neil was glad he did not drink.

The next morning, Neil was up early; he had already been for a run and was back in the training room, when he heard Caroline getting up. As he walked into the bedroom, he could see his beautiful wife looking very sorry for herself.

"Cup of tea and some headache tablets?" he suggested.

Caroline uttered a groaning sound, which Neil took to be an affirmative; he went downstairs accordingly, and reappeared in due course with her hangover cure.

"Well," he said, carefully handing her a cup and some tablets, "you *certainly* enjoyed yourself last night!"

Caroline, with only one eye open, peered at him suspiciously. "I didn't do anything silly, did I? The way you just said that......."

Neil seemed to draw breath slightly. "I wouldn't say *silly*, exactly," he said slowly; "but I was glad I had the credit card on me."

Caroline sat bolt upright. "Oh no, what happened?"

"Now, it wasn't your fault," he consoled her. "I don't think you fell, I think somebody tripped you - it was just unfortunate that the table you knocked over had an awful lot of drinks on it. Plus, I think some of the people at that table weren't being completely honest; they all supposedly had large whiskeys, large vodkas, expensive cocktails, all that sort of business. I only had three hundred quid on me, which wasn't enough, so I had to use the credit card."

"Whose table was it?"

"I think it was your cousin's new husband's family. What *was* funny," continued Neil brightly, "is that while you were still on the floor, you were sick all over the groom's mother's feet."

"Oh my God," whimpered Caroline, as she put her head in her hands; "that's it, I'm never going to drink again."

Neil sat on the edge of the bed, put his arm around her shoulders, kissed the top of her head, and carefully stroked her hair.

"There are so many things I love about you," he whispered; "but you being so gullible is one of my favourites."

"You rotten swine!" she exclaimed, giving him a shove, which caused him to fall on the floor, giggling. "I really believed you, then – ow, my head hurts!" she moaned.

"Okay, I confess, you didn't do anything silly," chuckled Neil, sitting on the bedroom floor. "You had a great time - you got very drunk, you were loving and hugging everyone, and you were the life and soul of the party – as usual!"

....

A few days later, Neil was sitting in the lounge of the warehouse with Dean and Eddie.

"Wedding go alright?" asked Dean.

"Caroline certainly enjoyed herself - she suffered for most of the next day."

"There were a few fat heads after our party last weekend, so that's allowed!" Eddie pointed out, smiling.

"I take it there was no more unpleasantness?" enquired Neil.

"None," confirmed Dean. "Shortly after you left, big Albie, little Albie, and his mate from Birkenhead all left. Big Joe and Macca stayed though, and were here until the early hours – they had a great time."

"What was funny," said Eddie, grinning, "was when big Joe told Julie to take her shoes off, and then stand on his feet, as he danced her round the dance floor. She thought it was absolutely brilliant, and reckoned it was the best night out she'd had for years. She still hasn't stopped talking about you, by the way," he told Neil, "and can't wait to meet Caroline at your twentieth."

"It'll soon be on us," nodded Neil. "I've got my last fight next week, then that's it - I can go back to living just the one life."

"Will you still be coming here to train?" asked Dean.

"Definitely; and after my last fight, I'll be able to tell Caroline and the lads all about the warehouse boys. In future, when I go out of the house, I can tell Caroline that I'm going to work, and then going to the warehouse to do some training. I'll be a lot easier in my mind than I have been for the last four years; although I've never had to lie, I've not told her the whole truth, so I've always felt a bit deceitful. It'll be a relief for that to end."

Eddie looked slightly uncomfortable. "Are you saying that you won't be moving to Spain, after all?"

"I'm not sure, to be honest," confessed Neil. "The main thing was to be in the financial position to be able to do it, which I am; but there was never a deadline on the actual move, so I'll just have to see how things work out."

………………………………….....................................

A few days later, after only a short training session, Dean noticed that Neil looked worried as he was sitting in the lounge.

"Everything okay?"

"Not exactly - our Paul had a crash last night, and the car might be a write-off. I'm waiting on a call from my mate."

"Is Paul all right?"

"He's fine, the airbag did its job - but driving head-on into a big tree didn't do the front of the car much good."

"How did he manage to drive into a tree?"

"Well, it was late, and he was driving down a country road that he wasn't familiar with, when something shot out in front of him; he swerved, but I gather he over-steered, so instead of just going into a hedge, he hit the tree. I set off as soon as he rang me, so I got there quite quickly, and contacted my mate who does twenty-four hour breakdowns." Neil paused. "While we were waiting, I took the opportunity to have a good talk with Paul; he's not a bad lad, but he's been mixing with one or two fools lately, and I told him he needed to ditch them. Anyway, it turns out he's already given them the elbow, so I told him he should tell his mum that. Shortly afterwards, the police turned up and breathalysed him; needless to say, he hadn't been drinking - I know our Paul well enough to know that if he'd had a drink, he would never have driven the car."

"I bet Caroline was upset, when you told her Paul had driven into a tree."

Neil looked somewhat sheepish. "To be honest," he confessed, "I didn't tell her, and I told Paul to keep quiet about it as well. He wasn't injured and, as you say, she would have been upset. I don't like upsetting her unnecessarily."

"Fair comment," murmured Dean, although it looked to Neil as if he wanted to say more.

"Okay, I can see there's something on your mind – what is it?" prompted Neil.

"Look," said Dean, "if I'm out of order here, just tell me, and I'll shut up. Now, I understand, and even envy, how much you love Caroline; but I'm not sure that constantly wrapping her in cotton wool is a good thing. If something were to happen to you – God forbid - how would she cope?"

"Well, I've tried over the years to get her more involved in financial things, without any success," explained Neil; "but you're right - I do try and keep her away from anything that may bother or upset her."

"You know, Neil, you're just coming to the end of a phase of your life that, years ago, you could never have imagined being involved in. After your final fight next week, as you've said, you can go back to living a normal life; so why not take the opportunity, from that point onwards, of getting Caroline more involved in everything - the good *and* the bad?"

"You may well be right," said Neil uncertainly; "but to tell the truth, I reckon it's not just down to how much I love her - it's also the fear of losing her. I've said that I could never understand what Caroline saw in me; and although I say it as a joke, there is a part of me that believes that. This sounds childish, I suppose – but by trying to keep her happy all the time it makes me feel that, deep down, I can't possibly lose her."

"Well," said Dean, "all I can say is, when I walked back into the warehouse after you'd left the party, I wish I'd had a tape recorder so that you could have listened to all the things the girls said about you. I still think you're an ugly bastard, myself," he continued bluntly, "but you've definitely got something that women are attracted to – and it's not the Spanish villa."

"Yeah, right," said Neil sarcastically, grinning. "Anyway, we'll see what the future holds; I seemed to be certain of so many things not that long ago, and now I'm not sure of anything."

Just as he finished speaking, his mobile phone rang. "Alright Jamie – what's the damage?" He listened, nodding his head at intervals. "Cheers, Jamie," he said finally; "go ahead with it, and I'll drop the cash round later." He rang off, and turned to Dean.

"It's going to cost about two thousand-five hundred quid to fix Paul's car."

"Just for hitting a tree?" said Dean. "Is it worth spending that sort of money on it?"

"Well, just about. Had it been over three grand, I probably would've scrapped it - which would have been a shame, as it's a good little car. Paul's always skint," he said ruefully, "so I'll pay the garage, and he'll have to pay me back over a period of time."

"Secret stash, I presume?"

"Possibly. Paying this will certainly clean out the bank account, but there's a couple of weeks before the mortgage and some other bills are due; I should be able to pay some back in from takings in the cab, and make the rest up from the secret stash. I can't use the money I'll make from the fight next week – that's already earmarked to be transferred to Spain."

"Incidentally," said Dean, "Big Joe was telling us your last fight in Warrington involves gypos?"

"One of the fighters is a traveller," corrected Neil; "his opponent is a Welsh lad."

"I've got no time for the pikey scum - none of us have," asserted Dean vehemently.

This was something about the warehouse boys which Neil had always found rather odd. Since he had been involved with them, he had never known them to display any racism or bigotry – unless the subject of travellers came up. If it did, every one of the warehouse boys, to a man, would refer to them as 'gypo bastards', 'pikey scum', or something equally offensive; however, Neil decided it was none of his business, and made no comment over such jibes.

"Well, anyway," he said, rising from his seat, "I'll probably see you between now and the fight next week; if not, I'll no doubt see you shortly afterwards."

"Certainly - and I hope everything goes okay."

As Neil was driving away, he continued to wonder why Dean and the others had such a hatred for travellers.

… … … … … … … … … … … … …..

It was the day before Neil's final fight, and he was sitting in the cab, waiting on the taxi rank for the next job.

As he was tapping his fingers on the steering wheel, he suddenly remembered that he had meant to leave some cash at home, because Caroline was going to a jazz concert that evening, and there was no money in the house. He tried ringing home several times, and could not understand why he kept getting a 'dead' tone; then it dawned on him that they were having the number changed that day and, unfortunately, he could not remember the new number. He therefore tried Caroline's mobile phone; but all he could get was her voicemail, and his battery was now running low. He sighed, and gave up trying to call her; all he could do was either hope that a job would take him near his house, or if not, simply finish work earlier than he had planned, and get home before Caroline was due to go out.

As Neil's day progressed, the taxi was beginning to make a strange sound when he changed gear. He therefore made a detour to his friend Jamie's garage.

"All right, Yosser lad!" greeted Jamie, as he walked up to the cab. "What's the problem?"

"Just jump in the back, Jamie, and I'll drive it round the block. It's making a weird sound when I'm changing gear, and I've no idea what it could be."

Neil had only driven a short distance, when Jamie called to him "It's okay, Yosser - I know what the problem is, just drive it back to the garage."

"It's no big deal," assured Jamie, when they had returned to the garage. "I just need to order the part; that should be delivered in the next half hour, then it'll take me about an hour to do the job. It's just as well you brought it straight to me, because if you'd driven it much further, you'd have done serious damage to the gearbox."

"Okay - so even if they're a bit slow delivering the part, we're looking at two hours tops?"

"Definitely. I'll get it up on the ramps now, and as soon as I've got the part, it won't take me long."

"Well, I've got one or two things I can sort out in town. I'll be back in about an hour and a half."

"If it comes sooner and I get the job done quickly, I'll give you a bell," offered Jamie.

"No point, Jamie lad - the battery's run out on my mobile."

"Yosser," said Jamie, shaking his head, "you've got to get yourself a new one. I reckon that phone's older than me."

"I might get a new battery for it; I don't think the existing one is holding a charge at all anymore."

Jamie snorted. "You'll be lucky getting a battery for that! If you take that thing into a proper phone shop, they'll laugh at you."

"We'll see," smiled Neil. "Anyway, I'll leave things with you – see you later."

Neil had ample time to call in at the bank, and deal with one or two other matters, before strolling back to Jamie's garage; however, as he arrived, he could tell that his friend was looking somewhat irritated.

"What's the problem? You don't look best pleased," observed Neil.

"They sent the wrong part," replied Jamie, pointing at the offending item in disgust. "This one's no good, it's for the new style box. I told them the age of your cab, so they should have known it would have the old gearbox. Needless to say, as soon as the right part arrives, I'll get stuck into the job."

As Jamie was speaking, he noticed that Neil was looking at his watch, and appeared to be slightly agitated.

"You're looking a bit stressed out. Have you got a particular pickup you wanted to do, or something?"

"No, it's nothing like that – it's only that Caroline's out tonight, and I'm pretty sure there's no money in the house."

"Well, they should be here any minute now. How much time have we got, before you've got to be home?"

"I think Caroline's leaving the house in about an hour and a half, but she needs money to pay for her ticket. She's going to a jazz concert, and I think whoever arranged it bought the ticket for her, so she owes them the money."

"How come you're not going?"

"Not my thing. Jazz is probably the only music I really don't like, so when Caroline asked if I wanted to go with her, I just laughed."

"Tell you what, then - if push comes to shove, you can always borrow my van to go home, while I'm fixing the cab."

"Thanks, mate – although I'd sooner go home in the cab, if I can, then I can simply drop the cash with Caroline, and come straight back to work."

Jamie could see how concerned Neil was, which surprised him; Neil was normally the epitome of calm. "Alright – in that case, I'll give them a ring, and see if they've any idea when the delivery driver will get here with the part." He followed up on his suggestion, but after he had rang off, he looked at Neil and shrugged. "They said they were surprised he hadn't already been here," he told him. "They tried him on his mobile, but couldn't get any answer. If he turns up in the next five or ten minutes, we haven't got a problem."

However, when fifteen minutes had passed with Neil impatiently walking up and down, and still no sign of the delivery van, Jamie took a set of keys from his pocket and handed them to Neil.

"You go home in my van," he instructed. "As soon as the part arrives, I'll get the cab sorted out. If I've finished the job before you get back, I'll just leave your keys in the glove box - just park the van up, and shove my keys through the letterbox."

"But If I've got your van, how are you going to get home?"

Jamie made a dismissive gesture. "I don't need the van to get home. If I've finished the job before you get back, I'll just use that little Corsa over there," he explained, pointing, "because I've done the work on it, but it's not being collected till tomorrow. We're both covered by the insurance, so we're okay."

"Are you sure I'm not putting you out? It's not your fault they sent the wrong part."

"It's no problem at all," assured Jamie, "but you're best setting off soon, if you want to catch Caroline - as you know, my van is not the nippiest of vehicles."

Neil grinned his acknowledgement. "I must admit, it is a touch on the slow side. You could only get done for speeding by rolling it down a steep hill." He shook hands gratefully with his friend. "Cheers, Jamie - if I don't see you later, I'll see you tomorrow."

....

Neil set off from the garage, annoyed with himself. He should have made a note of the new home phone number before he left the house that morning; and his refusal to replace a useless mobile phone, by insisting it was useable, was sheer pig-headedness. Thanks to his stupidity, he was now attempting to race home in a vehicle that was capable of no such thing; he just hoped that, if he could not get back in time, whoever bought Caroline's ticket was a good friend, and would understand if she had to leave home without any money. Typically, every traffic light seemed to be on red and, as the traffic was so heavy, it seemed as though he was just leaving one queue to join another; Neil was constantly checking his watch, almost certain he would not reach home in time.

Finally, however, he was in sight of their lane, and was approaching the turning when, suddenly, Caroline's car emerged at the junction with the main road; Neil was cursing to himself, and was about to honk his horn to catch her attention, when he saw her turn left out of the lane, and drive in the opposite direction. He was puzzled- he was sure that she had told him the concert was in Manchester, so he would have expected her to turn right and be coming towards him; there were now several vehicles between Neil and Caroline, so all he could do was keep her in sight, and hope he could catch up to her.

As each vehicle between them turned off, it made it easier to keep track of Caroline; however, as the van was so slow, Neil was unable to reduce the gap between them. He was becoming increasingly confused as to where she could be heading, as she was certainly going in the wrong direction for Manchester; moreover, it was now dark, making it even more difficult to keep her car in view. He just kept going, and hoped she would soon come to a stop.

The next thing he saw was the flashing light of her right-turn indicator, and he began to feel uneasy. He knew this area well, and the only right turn coming up was a country lane with a pub on the corner, an establishment known to be very popular with married couples who were not necessarily married to each other. There was also a small country park, no more than a hundred yards down the lane, and Neil knew that the car park there was far busier at night than it was during the day. He was well aware that he was something of a prude over such things - 'courting couples', as far as he was concerned, was too flattering a term to describe people having sex in the car in such a public place.

Consequently, as Caroline turned into this lane, Neil's stomach really started to churn; to his knowledge, there was only the entrance to the pub car park and the entrance to the country park accessible from there. As he made the turn himself, he could see no lights ahead of him, then abruptly came to a halt as he caught sight of Caroline getting out of her car in the pub car park. As he was about to get out of the van, however, he froze; walking towards Caroline was someone he recognised – the unpleasant man from the next table he had observed, when he and Caroline had been at the wedding party. Neil stared in disbelief at what happened next – he saw his wife in another man's arms, kissing passionately, and the man had his hand on her bottom.

Neil closed his eyes tightly, lowered his head, and had an overwhelming desire to be sick, desperately trying to think of an innocent explanation for what he had just witnessed; but he was at a loss. He sat with his eyes closed, unmoving, for what seemed to be an eternity, although it could not have been more than a few minutes; he then heard an engine start up and, opening his eyes, he saw the man drive out of the car park with Caroline in the passenger seat. They drove straight down the country lane.

Neil immediately started the van and followed, in the desperate hope that maybe there was something else down here, some kind of innocent explanation for what was happening; however, as the car ahead of him turned into the country park, Neil knew he was clutching at straws. He had not been able to watch them kissing, and had no wish to see what was going to happen now. He swung the van round, and drove back to the main road.

As he was driving back to the garage, a kind of numbness crept over him; surely this was just a nightmare, and he would soon wake up. He arrived at the deserted industrial estate where Jamie's garage was situated, and saw his cab parked outside; moving slowly and mechanically, he carefully locked the van, put the keys through the letterbox of the garage, and got into his taxi. For a few moments, he just stared into space; then he put his head in his hands, and broke down, his body racked by violent sobbing.

He cried for a long time, and could not remember a time in his life when he had ever cried more. In spite of what he had seen, he did not blame Caroline; he knew it was completely his own fault. For the last three or four years, all he had ever talked about was moving to Spain; he had paid no attention to her fears and worries about Paul, hardly taken her anywhere, and had taken her love for granted. In despair, Neil knew that he could never compete with the man in the car park, if he lost Caroline to him; he knew the type: tall, handsome, charming, obviously successful in whatever he did, judging by his appearance at the wedding - expensive suit, expensive watch, not to mention the top of the range car he was driving. Neil had always hoped that loving Caroline as much as he could would be enough; it seemed to him now that he had been fooling himself. Those who knew him told him how fortunate he was to have such a lovely house, and a villa abroad; but he knew that, without Caroline, he had nothing.

He stared at the family photograph, of which he had been so proud, going over in his mind the mistakes he had made. Now that his tears had subsided, he found that anger was beginning to creep into his consciousness - not with Caroline, but with the man who had been holding her so tightly. He was beginning to wish that he had got out of the van, and sorted out the smooth-talking creep; the trouble was, he knew full well that Caroline's sympathies would lie with the one who came off worst in the altercation, and that person would not be him – fear of losing her was all that had held him back. But perhaps it was all too late in any event.

Reluctantly, he started the cab, and headed home, hoping that Caroline would be there when he arrived. It was now the early hours of the morning, and he tried to banish the thought that he may arrive home to find her still absent. His anger at the man intensified, as the possibility of this nagged at him; thus, an aggressive and abusive drunk who deliberately stepped out in front of the cab, forcing Neil to stop, found that he had made a great error of judgement. This fool had considered himself to be something of a tough guy; when he regained consciousness some time later, he vowed that he would show taxi drivers more respect in future.

When Neil arrived home, he was relieved to see Caroline's car in the driveway. There were no lights illuminating the lower floor, so Neil quietly crept upstairs; he found Caroline in bed, in a deep sleep.

He went slowly back downstairs, and into the living room. He sat on the couch and, for a few moments, stared down at the framed family photograph that had been his pride and joy; then he carefully placed it, face down, on the coffee table.

Chapter 19

Neil lay down on the couch and tried to go to sleep; but the feeling he had now was more painful than any physical damage he had sustained in any of his fights, making sleep impossible. All his life, whenever there had been a setback, he had always tried to think positive, and do all he could to make things better; but this time, he simply did not know what to do.

At some point, he would need to ask Caroline about what he saw - but how was he to go about it? Would she believe that he had stumbled upon it by accident, that he had only been following her because he thought she had no money? He was so terrified of losing her completely, that he even wondered whether he would be safer saying nothing at all.

He found himself speculating as to how long her affair had been going on. He had assumed that she had met the man for the first time at her cousin's wedding; but he now considered the possibility that they had known each other prior to that. He had thought nothing of it at the time; but when they were at the wedding reception, each time that Caroline went outside for a cigarette, the other man had followed her. Of course! Neil sat up, and put his head into his hands at this realisation; the more he turned it over in his mind, the more upset he became. If the affair had started months ago, it would explain everything – the difference he had seen in Caroline, and her apparent hesitation at the prospect of moving to Spain, which Neil had hoped was caused by her concerns over Paul.

He had been sitting for hours, still with no idea of what to do, when he heard some movement upstairs; he had been so absorbed in his thoughts, he had not noticed that it was now daylight, and Caroline would therefore soon be coming down. He stretched himself out on the couch and decided to pretend to be asleep, because he was by no means ready to get into a conversation with her. As he lay there, he heard her coming downstairs; he did not know whether she had even glanced into the living room but, to his surprise, she went straight out of the house, started her car, and drove away.

He waited, unmoving, for a little longer, in case she had simply gone to one of the local shops; although, in truth, he had no notion of what – if anything - he would say to her if she came back. However, as the time went by, it was clear that she would not be returning, and Neil could not suppress the sickening thought that she had, perhaps, gone to meet her lover.

He heaved a heavy sigh, got up from the couch, and walked slowly out to the cab. He sat there for a few moments, wondering what to do; certainly, he was in no frame of mind to work. He started the engine, and headed to the warehouse.

....

As soon as he arrived, Neil walked straight into the training room, got changed, put on the gloves, and started violently attacking the heavy bag.

Dean and Eddie could hear the thudding sounds coming from the training room, and were surprised that Neil had not acknowledged them when he arrived at the warehouse; they therefore went to greet him, but their welcoming smiles soon changed when they saw the ferocity of Neil's attack on the heavy bag, and the look in his eyes – a look that could only be described as rage. As they watched, Neil seemed oblivious of their presence, and kept punching and kicking the heavy bag with all his power; even though the sweat was pouring from every inch of his body, his attack was relentless, almost vicious, as every blow seemed to be delivered with pure hatred.

Eventually, Dean used his eyes to signal to Eddie to step back out of the training room, and they closed the door behind them; for a few moments, neither of them spoke, both disturbed by what they had witnessed.

"That first night, when Neil fought the bloke from Blackburn," opened Dean; "you all said he really lost his temper – is that what he looked like?" He jerked his thumb in the direction of the training room door.

"Deano, there's no comparison," replied Eddie, visibly shocked. "That night, Scouse Neil was just angry. God knows who that monster is in the training room, now."

"I don't understand it," said Dean, shaking his head. "You saw how calm he was, the other night at the party. We were all mad, and wanted to tear that fella apart, but Neil was totally chilled out. What the hell could have happened to cause this?"

"Well, I can tell you one thing," declared a smiling Eddie, "*I'm* not bloody asking him"

"Me neither," agreed Dean, with a grim answering smile. "Let's slide back into the lounge, and see if he comes and talks to us when he's finished."

Shortly after they had sat down in the lounge, Jonjo joined them.

"I just had a quick look in the training room - what the hell did the heavy bag say to Neil to upset him that much?"

"We don't know what's wrong," responded Dean. "I'm just glad he's only organising the fight tonight, and not fighting himself."

"If he were, I think he'd kill them," said Eddie bluntly, shuddering. "For those two years he was fighting, I thought I'd never see a better display of aggression. But watching him in the training room now, he's terrifying."

They could hear the door to the training room being slammed shut, and Neil's approaching footsteps. "Hold on, he's coming in here," warned Dean, lowering his voice. "I'll just ask him if everything's okay, and leave it at that."

However, when Neil came into the lounge, Dean had no opportunity to speak, "I won't stop," said Neil, "I've got something important to sort out. I'll probably see you later, after the fight."

Jonjo, Dean and Eddie all nodded mutely, realising that they needed to leave well alone; they said nothing further to each other, until they heard Neil start the cab and drive away.

"Let's hope the fight he's talking about is the one he's organising tonight, and not some battle he's got on this afternoon," ventured Eddie.

Dean frowned. "That thought hadn't crossed my mind. Surely he'd tell us, if that was the problem?"

"Well if it is, God help whoever he's battling with," commented Jonjo. "I'm just glad it's not me."

....

As Neil was driving home, he realised that the training session was probably the best thing he could have done; not only did it get rid of a lot of the aggression and anger he was feeling, but it also seemed to make him think more clearly. He resolved that, when he got home, he would open a tentative conversation with Caroline, asking if everything was okay, or if there was anything troubling her. He had no intention of confronting her; if he had to share her, so be it – rather that, than lose her altogether. He could not conceive of a situation where he was no longer a part of Caroline's life. As he got nearer to home, however, he felt his stomach churning, terrified of getting things wrong, and was so annoyed with himself for being so selfish – when all the while, Caroline must have felt completely neglected.

Caroline's car was parked outside the house, which was a relief to him. As he opened the front door, however, it sounded as if the back door closed simultaneously; puzzled, Neil called out, but got no answer. He therefore assumed Caroline was upstairs, and ascended the staircase quickly, but still found no sign of her. He looked out of the bedroom window, and his heart sank; there was Caroline, disappearing out of the driveway in her car. Evidently, she had exited the house through the back door as soon as she heard him come in – and the only possible explanation was that she did not want to see or speak to him.

Neil sank onto the edge of the bed, covering his face with his hands, and was overwhelmed with despair. Had Caroline, somehow, known that he had seen her last night? And yet, surely, that was impossible - where he was parked had been so dark and, even if she had seen the van, she could not have associated it with him. In that case, was she feeling guilty over what had happened, and ashamed to face him? He desperately hoped he was right, as he would forgive her anything, and jump at the chance of changing whatever needed to be changed in order to keep her. But he soon dismissed that small ray of hope; he had to be realistic. Caroline had simply had enough of him, and that was why she was avoiding him now. How could he have got things so wrong? How could he have been so blinkered, and lost sight of what really mattered?

....

Some time later, when Caroline had still not returned, Neil reluctantly set off for the fight in Warrington. As he arrived at the venue, a man walked over to him, with his hand extended.

"I know you're Scouse Neil," greeted the man. "Your normal security crew can't make it tonight, so they've asked me and my boys to fill in for them." Neil merely nodded, not really listening, and carried on walking into the building.

The first thing that struck him was how few people there were in attendance. Normally, when there was a traveller taking part, there was a good turnout; however, when Neil asked one of his traveller acquaintances about this, he was told that both the young man who was due to fight, and his family, were very unpopular with the rest of the travelling community. This information was of no interest to Neil, but the low turnout tempted him to cancel the proceedings there and then; he was just considering this when he heard some shouting coming from the main door, and went over to investigate. All the security men on duty were barring the way of four travellers, who were trying to force their way in. Neil turned to the man who had spoken to him earlier.

"What's going on?" he demanded.

"This crew won't let us search them for weapons, and refuse to leave their mobile phones at the door."

"I'll deal with this." The security men duly moved aside, without argument, and Neil went outside. He stood directly in front of the four travellers.

"I'm sorry gents, but those are the rules," he told them. "You won't be let in unless we're satisfied that you're not carrying weapons. If we do let you in, you leave your mobile phones at the door."

The eldest of the four men, who seemed to be in charge, stepped forward.

"Do you know who you're talking to?" he spat out, aggressively. "We are the Flynns, nobody searches us, and nobody tells us what to do. If we want to keep our mobile phones on us, we will."

As the man fixed him with a glare, Neil thought that he had never, in his life, seen such an expression of pure evil in another's eyes; but he stood his ground. It was almost certain that these men were carrying weapons, so they were not getting in without a search.

"I don't care who you are. We do it my way, or you don't get in."

The other man's eyes flickered slightly, as Neil had spoken these words in a traveller accent.

"I'm Patrick Flynn, King of the gypsies," he announced arrogantly. "Just because you can talk like us, doesn't mean you're the same as us."

"I've no desire to be the same as you," was Neil's retort, still in the traveller brogue. "You're the type that gets all the good travellers a bad name. This is your last chance. You either do it my way, or you go home."

Patrick continued to fix Neil with an icy stare for a few moments; he then signalled to the other three to step away from the door, said something to them which Neil could not hear, after which all four men proceeded to walk over to their van. Neil observed that they appeared to be removing various things from their pockets, and depositing them in the van; that being done, they came back.

"You can search us now."

Neil addressed the security men. "Search them thoroughly," he instructed, in his normal speaking voice. "As long as there are no weapons or mobile phones, let them in." He then turned on his heel abruptly, and went back inside the warehouse.

He had been trying to stay calm while this was going on, but it had been difficult. The travellers' behaviour was not the cause, however; it was the memory of the previous night's events, together with Caroline's behaviour today. The sooner this fight was over, he told himself, the better - he could turn his back on this life, and concentrate on trying to repair the damage he had caused in his normal life, the one that mattered.

Fortunately, the fight was over very quickly. Kieran Flynn - who Neil assumed was Patrick's son - defeated the Welsh fighter with ease, although Neil had to intervene at the end of the fight to prevent Kieran from stamping on his opponent as he lay on the ground.

"You stamp on him and you get no money!" barked Neil, as he quickly pushed Kieran away. "The rules were explained to you at the start of the fight. Walk away – now!"

As he was saying this, Neil suddenly realised that he was very much on his own; there was no sign of the security men, and even the two referees seemed to have disappeared. He surveyed the Flynns with disgust.

"I'll be back with your prize money shortly. It's such a poor turnout, you won't be getting much."

Neil went to the front door of the warehouse. Where the hell were the security men and the referees? Cursing, he realised how stupid he had been. He immediately telephoned his usual security crew, who informed him that they had received information that the fight had been cancelled; consequently, they had not arranged an alternative crew.

In spite of realising that he had been conned, Neil decided that, after all, it was of no real consequence. The profit from this fight had been intended for transfer to Spain; however, in his present frame of mind, that all seemed rather pointless. Luckily, he had enough money on him to pay Kieran; he could pay the warehouse owner at a later date.

By the time Neil walked back to the area where the fight had taken place, everyone had departed, with the exception of the Flynn family. Neil took five hundred pounds out of his pocket, and handed it to Kieran.

"That's your prize money," he said flatly. "Now, walk away."

Kieran quickly counted the cash. "Where's the rest of it, you thieving Scouse bastard?"

"You're lucky to get that."

Kieran stepped forward, seemed to lift his chin slightly, and then spat in Neil's face. The reaction he hoped for, however, was not forthcoming; Neil simply took a handkerchief out of his pocket and wiped his face, but made no other move.

"Just as I thought," jeered Kieran, "typical Scouser - a thief, and a gutless bastard!"

There was still no reaction from Neil, as the Flynns were laughing – but not through fear, or even calmness; it was overwhelming anger which kept him rooted to the spot, anger so intense that he could not even fight. Picturing in his mind what he had seen the night before, it was the man from the car park who had just spat in his face and laughed at him, not the young traveller. In his agitated state, the Flynns' laughter seemed to suggest that they could see his thoughts, and were taunting him because he had closed his eyes and done nothing, while the other man had stolen his wife. Finally, the sound of a door slamming woke him from these thoughts; he realised that the Flynns were gone, and he was alone in the Warrington warehouse.

Neil remained there for some time; he tried to contact Caroline by ringing home, as well as her mobile, but despite repeated attempts, he could get no answer. He therefore secured the warehouse and sat in his taxi for a while, contemplating what to do; finally, he started the engine, and set off in the direction of Manchester, to call in on the warehouse boys.

As he was driving along, he was becoming increasingly angry with himself – partly for allowing himself to be conned by the bogus security crew; but mostly, for not putting Kieran Flynn on his back.

....

Unbeknown to Neil, his usual security team had informed Dean about the swindle.

"I just don't understand this," said Dean, after he had explained it to Jonjo and Eddie. "Neil is always so well organised, and would never fall for a trick like that."

"Well, let's face it, he wasn't himself earlier on, when he was training," pointed out Jonjo. "He was pretty angry. Maybe there's some connection."

"Deano, I suppose the script is as usual - that we can't ask him?" asked Eddie.

"No, we can't," confirmed Dean; "but I'm not quoting warehouse boys rules and regulations here - I've got a feeling there's something seriously wrong. I very much hope he feels he can tell us, and that we might be able to help. But, if he chooses not to, then we've got to respect his privacy."

Eddie sighed, but nodded his agreement.

"Dean's right," added Jonjo. "What if one of us asked him what the problem was, and he told us to piss off, and mind our own business?"

"After watching him this morning? I'd piss off, and mind my own business," answered Eddie, grinning.

"I think we're all in agreement, there," decided Dean, with a wry smile.

Just then, Dean's mobile phone started ringing. "Alright, Neil," he greeted; the others watched as he simply nodded his head in response to the call, until finally he said "Okay, see you soon, Neil – we'll get the kettle on."

"Brilliant!" said Eddie, clearly pleased. "But I'll make the coffee. I don't know how you do it, Deano, but your coffee's terrible."

As Eddie almost bounced into the kitchen, Jonjo grinned at Dean.

"He's never cottoned on to you deliberately making awful coffee so that he ends up making it all the time, has he?"

Dean chuckled conspiratorially. "He nearly caught me out the other week, though. I made one for me and Neil, but Eddie walked in and tasted one of them - so I had to tell him Neil made it."

Just as Eddie emerged from the kitchen carrying the coffee, Neil was pulling up outside in the taxi. As they heard his footsteps approaching, the warehouse trio looked in the direction of the lounge door, wondering which Neil Hughes was going to come through it; but when he walked into the room, it was not an angry man they saw – instead, they observed a sad, almost defeated, man.

"Well, tonight wasn't exactly a great success," he said quietly, as he sank onto one of the couches. "I'm glad that was my last fight. By the time I've paid for the hire of the warehouse, it will have cost me over a thousand pounds to be laughed at, and have someone spit in my face." He went on to explain exactly what had happened. "I feel as though I've let you down."

All three of his listeners looked nonplussed. "Let us down?" queried Jonjo, mystified. "Let us down in what way?"

"That crew will now probably go round boasting that one of the warehouse boys backed down to them," said Neil, bitterly.

"You didn't back down - you just chose not to fight him there and then." Dean's tone was firm. "Tell us when you do want to fight him, and we'll arrange it."

"As soon as possible." Neil's response was quiet, but determined.

"That's the spirit!" barked Eddie, rubbing his hands together. "What's this pikey scumbag's name?"

"Kieran Flynn."

As soon as the words left Neil's mouth, his three companions stared at him as if they had been turned to stone.

"Kieran Flynn?" was Dean's question.

"That's right. The father was Patrick Flynn. As for the other two, I took one to be Patrick's brother, name of Sean; and the other I assumed to be Sean's son, who I think was called Callum."

Dean appeared to be calculating something in his head, before asking Neil for a description and approximate age of Kieran, which Neil supplied.

"Okay, Neil, leave it with us," instructed Dean. "I'll give you a bell when I've got something sorted out. Just as a matter of interest - what stopped you taking the four of them out, there and then?"

"Anger. I was just too angry to fight. I wouldn't have been able to concentrate on what I was doing, so I let them walk away."

Jonjo was frowning. "I don't understand, Neil. I remember that fella spitting at you years ago before one of your fights, and you just laughed at him, and said saliva was never going to do you any harm."

"That's right," agreed Eddie. "People tried all sorts to wind you up, and realised they were wasting their time. What was different about these gypo bastards?"

"In my mind, it wasn't Kieran Flynn who spat and laughed at me."

This cryptic explanation simply made Jonjo and Eddie look at each other with confused expressions, and shrug; Dean, however, who had been looking down as Neil was speaking, raised his head furtively, long enough to catch the look in Neil's eyes. He desperately hoped he was mistaken as to what, he suspected, was behind Neil's words.

Shortly afterwards, Neil announced that he was going home, so Dean accompanied his friend out to the taxi, hoping that he might explain more concerning the terrible sadness Dean had detected in him; however, Neil said nothing further - he shook Dean's hand, got behind the wheel of the cab, and drove away. Dean watched him depart, deep in thought; then he returned to the lounge.

"Did you ring Tommy?" was his immediate query.

"He's on his way now," replied Jonjo. "I warned him that it could be coincidence - but the age and the description certainly fits."

"I've been on to big Joe," added Eddie. "He knows someone who can arrange the fight between Neil and this Flynn fella. Of course, this pikey's going to think he's fighting someone else, because there's no chance of him turning up if he knows it's Scouse Neil. I explained to big Joe exactly what the situation is – and told him only to deal with people who can keep their mouths shut."

Dean said "If it's who we think it is, Tommy will want to kill him. But that's not going to happen while Neil's there. We'll give Neil the opportunity of giving this fella a good hiding – then, we'll get him away."

....

When Neil got home, he was disappointed to find that Caroline had gone to bed early, and appeared to be fast asleep. Neil spent some time downstairs, playing everything over and over again in his mind; eventually, he went upstairs. Michael's old room had been unused since he had moved out, so Neil decided to sleep in there. He lay awake on Michael's bed for some time, despite the fact that he was desperately tired, not having slept for almost forty-eight hours; however, he finally drifted off to sleep.

He awoke abruptly the next morning, having slept far longer than he would normally, to find that the house was empty. He was annoyed with himself for oversleeping; he had wanted to catch Caroline before she went out, to find out what was happening.

He went downstairs, made some tea, and waited in the kitchen, hoping that she would not be gone for long; then, as time went on, and she did not reappear, he decided to ring her mobile phone – but when it connected, he could hear it ringing somewhere in the house. Why had she left it behind? He was now getting seriously worried as to her whereabouts; then, suddenly, he had a terrible thought. He ran upstairs, into their bedroom, and flung open the wardrobe – but to his relief, all her clothes were still hanging there. He sat down on the edge of the bed, now feeling guilty over his suspicion. But what else could he do? He desperately needed to speak to her, but he felt she was slipping away from him, and he was powerless to stop it.

Eventually, he went back downstairs, and decided that he might as well go to work; it was no good moping around the house - the longer he stayed there alone, the worse he would feel. He picked up his keys, and left the house.

....

A couple of hours later, Neil found that driving the taxi had been therapeutic, and helped him to get things straight in his head. Heading back home, he found himself resolving to come up with some sort of plan to keep Caroline in his life. There had to be a way of persuading her to love him again. He must do what he had always done: think positive, and stop feeling sorry for himself. He and Caroline just needed to have a good talk – he was prepared to do whatever he could to save their marriage, and only hoped that it was not too late.

As he arrived home, he was so pleased to see Caroline's car parked outside. He got out of the cab, and took a deep breath as he entered the house, determined to be as cheerful as he possibly could. Walking down the hall, he could hear Caroline in the kitchen, and he called out to her.

"It's only me! Are you making a brew?" But she did not answer; and as Neil entered the kitchen, she would not turn to face him.

"I'm not very well," she muttered, "so I'm going to bed." She then simply walked out of the kitchen, passing Neil without even glancing at him, and went upstairs.

Neil was so stunned, it was almost as if she had struck him in the face. All his resolve evaporated in an instant. What hope could there be, if she could not even bring herself to look at him, let alone speak? He had to face it – she had made her feelings perfectly clear, and there was nothing he could do about it. He sat down at the kitchen table, and even now felt embarrassed as the tears flowed again.

Eventually, almost mechanically, he rose to his feet, and made himself a pot of tea; then, after a while, he went upstairs, took a change of clothes from their bedroom – being careful not to disturb Caroline - and went to Michael's room. He did not sleep for long, however; he got up early, and went to work.

………………………………………………………………

While he was working, Neil received a call from Dean; the fight with Kieran Flynn had been arranged for the following evening.

Neil was almost tempted to call the whole thing off - he had no particular wish to hurt the young traveller, just to humiliate him would be enough. But he could think of no other way of achieving that without fighting him; so, rather than prolong the agony, Neil decided that he would probably just knock him straight out. He was perfectly capable of doing this, naturally; Kieran Flynn was not in his league.

Neil continued to work until very late that night, knowing that Caroline would certainly be in bed before he got back. It was therefore the early hours of the morning by the time he arrived home; he slept for a short time on the couch, got up, had a shower, then went straight back out in the cab. He decided that he would just keep working until it was time to head over to Manchester; then, once this business with Kieran Flynn was out of the way, Neil intended to explain to the warehouse boys what had happened, and hoped they would understand that, in all probability, they would not be seeing him again.

When he arrived at the warehouse, Neil immediately felt a difference in atmosphere; there was a kind of tension amongst the warehouse boys. He could not decide whether he was the cause, or it was something else; either way, something did not feel right – the usual laughing, joking and banter was absent.

"Alright – now you're here, Neil, let's get moving," said Dean, without ceremony.

Everyone got into the battle bus, and set off; during the journey, barely a word was spoken. When they arrived at their destination, which looked like a small barn, miles from anywhere, Neil was surprised to note that theirs was the only vehicle. He was then further intrigued to realise, as they got out of the bus and walked into the barn, that a young man had been travelling with them; Neil had never seen him before. And why were Tommy, Phil, Carl and Joey all wearing long overcoats, despite the warm weather? Well, whatever was going on, he thought, he just wanted to get this over with.

"This isn't going to take long," he said to Dean, and explained what he had decided to do.

Dean nodded. "When they arrive, just keep out of the way until we've locked the door behind them," he instructed. "It'll be a nice little surprise for this scumbag to find out who he's really fighting."

Phil, who was on the door, shouted over to Neil. "There's an old, rusty white transit van pulling up - I take it that's them?"

"There should be four of them," called Neil in reply. "Two of them are mid-forties, two are mid-twenties."

"Right lads, let's do this properly," said Dean briskly. "Search them thoroughly, and make sure they haven't got any mobile phones on them, once they're inside the barn. If they haven't, we'll assume they've left their phones in the van."

Neil moved out of sight as the Flynns entered the barn; however, he could not help but notice that the unknown young man who had accompanied the warehouse boys was pointing at the

Flynns while talking to Tommy, and vigorously nodding his head. The young stranger was obviously a similar age to Kieran, and Neil was curious as to his connection with all of this.

As soon as everyone, including the Flynn family, were inside the barn, and the door had been locked behind them, Dean walked over to the travellers, and surveyed them with open contempt.

"There's been a slight change of arrangements." He spoke quietly, but there was steel in his voice. "The man you thought you were fighting can't make it. We've got a gutless Scouser in his place."

With almost dramatic effect, Neil stepped out of the darkness from the side of the barn, and walked up to Kieran. He fixed him with an icy stare.

"I think we'll find out now who the gutless one is. I'll give you one chance to apologise, but if you don't, you'll regret it for a long time."

"I'll fight you any time you like," blurted Kieran, and was about to lunge forward; but in an instant, both his father and uncle grabbed him, and pulled him back.

"You know my boy's got no chance against you!" spat out Patrick Flynn. "This isn't an even match!"

"I'll settle for an apology, or I could fight all four of you, if you like - if you think you might stand a chance."

Neil could see that the expression of hatred in Patrick's eyes was mixed with one of fear; he appeared to be well aware of Neil's reputation, and was obviously unwilling to fight him. The warehouse boys could also see Patrick's discomfiture; so, by some kind of unspoken agreement, Phil took his cue, sauntering over to the travellers.

"Won't daddy let his little boy fight?" he smirked. "Bless him!"

The warehouse boys started sniggering at Kieran, who was desperately struggling to get free from his father and uncle.

"Aaahh, what's up?" taunted Andy. "Is little Kieran frightened of getting a bloody nose?"

Kieran was almost crying with rage by now, and it took both his father and uncle to hold him, because all the warehouse boys were pointing and laughing at him. As for Neil, oddly, he found he was glad that it had turned out this way; he had not really wanted to hurt the young man, only humiliate him – and the warehouse boys were doing just that, without his help. Neil even started to feel sorry for the lad, realising that it was really the man from the car park whom he wanted to punish, not this young, headstrong traveller. He came to a decision.

"That's it," he declared. "There'll be no fight."

Neil then turned, intending to walk away; but just at that moment, Kieran finally broke free from his relatives and, from behind, landed a punch on the side of Neil's head. Instinctively, Neil immediately spun round, and aimed a punch directly at Kieran's jaw; but the traveller had, in that split second, tilted back his head, intending to spit at Neil – and the powerful blow hit him squarely in the throat.

Kieran instantly dropped to his knees, blood pouring from his mouth, and terrible choking and gurgling sounds coming from his throat. Patrick rushed to his son, and caught him in his arms as he fell; a shocked Neil, frozen to the spot, could only look down at Patrick holding his dying son, hardly believing what had just happened. In seconds, the young man had breathed his last.

With a howl of rage, Patrick launched himself at Neil, followed by Sean and Callum, when all three Flynns were suddenly confronted by Tommy, aiming a sawn-off shotgun; he was quickly joined by Phil, Carl and Joey, similarly armed.

"One more step," said Tommy, "and you three will be joining him."

Neil, in a daze as he looked down at Kieran's body, was still able to detect from the tone of Tommy's voice that he wanted the Flynns to take that step. He dragged his eyes away from Kieran, and looked at the scene around him; there was no doubt, from the looks in the eyes of the warehouse boys, that they would willingly kill these travellers. Neil felt as if he was in the middle of a bad dream; how had it escalated to this? He sensed someone putting an arm around his shoulders and, as though from a long way away, he heard Dean's voice.

"Come on, let's go – there's nothing you could have done."

As Dean guided him outside into the daylight, Neil could see that all the tyres on the Flynns' van were flat; and, scattered on the ground by the driver's side door - the window of which had been smashed – lay the remains of the Flynns' mobile phones. Confused, Neil simply climbed into the minibus, and sat there, half expecting to hear the sound of shots; but no such sound ever came.

The other warehouse boys emerged from the barn, and joined Neil in the minibus. Tommy, being the last to come out of the barn, bolted the door on the outside, padlocked it, and walked over to the minibus, where Dean was waiting for him.

"It'll be some time before they get out of there," said Tommy; "and one thing we know for sure - they won't be going to the police."

....

When they got back to the warehouse, everyone simply filed into the lounge without speaking. Neil felt that he needed to say something, but he had no idea how to begin; he still could not believe what had just happened, and was shocked by the calmness of the men around him. He was well aware that they had all taken lives in a war situation; but there seemed to be no pity, from any of them, for the young man who had just died.

Neil sat down slowly, and remained motionless, staring into space, when he became aware that what looked like a large glass of whiskey was being placed, carefully, on the table in front of him.

"I know you don't normally drink," said Tommy, "but get that down you, you'll feel a bit better. Our Billy has finally got justice, and I'm very grateful." He then walked over to the far side of the lounge, poured a large whiskey for himself, and sat down on his own.

A mystified Neil looked at Dean, hoping for some sort of explanation. "Billy?"

"He was Tommy's younger brother," clarified Dean. "Kieran Flynn and his mates kicked Billy to death, about ten years ago."

Neil, speechless, sat back in his chair, astounded by this revelation.

"We were still serving in Afghanistan when this happened," said Jonjo. "Billy was about fifteen at the time. Well, one Saturday afternoon, him and his mates were by a shopping centre, when these pikeys turned up looking for trouble. The main troublemaker was a lad called Kieran, about the same age as Billy."

Eddie took up the story. "Billy was so much like Tommy - he was a good lad, but as tough as they come, and he had no intention of backing down when challenged by the likes of that scumbag." He shook his head sorrowfully. "Anyway, it was a fair fight, and Billy beat him fair and square. Then, later that same night, Billy was on his way home across a field when he got jumped. When his body was found in the morning, the police forensic people were able to calculate that he'd been set on by four people - they kicked him, stamped on him, and left him to bleed to death." Eddie had to stop speaking, as he was getting so angry.

"But how can you be sure that the Kieran I've just – killed," said Neil, swallowing, "is the same one that killed Tommy's brother?"

Dean supplied the explanation. "The young fella who was with us tonight was a mate of Billy's, and he was with him that day. As soon as the Flynns walked into the barn, he picked out Kieran straight away."

Just then, Dean's mobile phone rang. "It's big Joe," he told them, stood up, and walked away from the table to take the call.

As the phone conversation lasted for some time, Neil reflected on what he had been told. He now understood Tommy's sadness, and the antipathy of the warehouse boys towards travellers. Yet in his mind, he saw the image of Kieran choking on his own blood, being cradled by his father; and, in spite of what he now knew, he was overwhelmed with feelings of pity.

When Dean returned, he looked furious; he called to Tommy to join them.

"I'm sorry Tommy, I should've let you kill them all," declared Dean vehemently. "When Neil gave me the proper names of these people the other day, I asked big Joe to find out what he could because, like Neil, he's got a certain amount of time for this scum." Neil had never seen him so angry. "Joe tells me that it wasn't Kieran and his mates who attacked Billy, it was all four of the

Flynns. And Billy wasn't the only one – Kieran had killed a few people. He'd also raped several girls, who were not much more than kids. Then, two months ago, he threw a petrol bomb into another gypo's caravan – it killed everyone in there, including two children." He looked at Neil, and it was as if he had read his earlier thoughts. "Don't feel pity for him, Neil - I just wish *I'd* killed him."

The stricken expression on Neil's face prompted Jonjo to speak.

"Neil, let's put things into perspective here," he said reasonably. "You didn't set out to kill him. You were actually defending yourself as he attacked you, and if the dirty bastard hadn't lifted his head to spit at you, you would have just given him a broken jaw. In any case, I can assure you, he wasn't going to come out of that barn alive. Be absolutely certain about this - he got what he deserved. It's his victims that are entitled to pity and sympathy, certainly not him or his family."

Tommy had been nodding while Jonjo made this speech, then he put his hand on Neil's shoulder. "The lads are right. Those bastards killed my little brother, but because of you, I now know exactly who they are, and what they look like. I won't rest until I've tracked them down and killed them."

"You mean, when *we* have tracked them down," Dean corrected him. "Ten years ago, we weren't sure who we were looking for. We are now, and we'll find them."

Neil stood up, abruptly, his head swimming. "I've got to go. I don't know when, or if, I'll see you again."

And with that, he walked out of the lounge; the warehouse boys watched in silence as the door closed behind him.

....

Neil was half way home when he pulled onto a small car park; he needed to think. His world had been turned completely upside down. What was he to do? And who could he now turn to?

After what he had heard, although he understood why the warehouse boys had tried to make him see that he should have no regrets about the death of someone like Kieran Flynn, it made no difference. A young man – not much older than his own sons - was dead, and he, Neil Hughes, had been the instrument of destruction. The fact that Kieran may have got what he deserved brought Neil no consolation; all he felt was remorse, and bitter regret.

In his despair, he struck his forehead against the steering wheel. Why the hell had he not just got out of the van, and dealt with the man who had been holding Caroline? Instead, because he was so frightened of losing her, he had sat there with his eyes tightly closed, and allowed his anger to fester; so when Kieran spat in his face, his desire for revenge had led him to that barn. It was irrelevant that he had not intended to kill; as far as Neil was concerned, the result of his fear of losing Caroline was that a young man was dead, and by his hands. Recriminations could never change that.

Wearily, he restarted the engine, and continued on his journey home, in the vain hope that Caroline would be waiting up for him; however, when he let himself into the house, as expected, he found that she had already gone to bed. He therefore went into Michael's room and lay on the bed, staring up at the ceiling.

....

Neil awoke early the following morning, having barely slept, and the reality of his situation struck him like a physical blow; nevertheless, he got up, went for a run, had a shower when he got home, and then went to work. The normality of these tasks seemed ridiculous to him, bearing in mind that his marriage had collapsed, and he had just killed a man; but he did not know what else to do.

All that day, as he ferried passengers around in his taxi as usual, he found that he was analysing his own life, a whole new experience for him. Since he had first started to stand up for himself as a boy, he had neither wanted, nor needed, anyone's help; in fact, it was he that his family and friends came to, when they were in trouble. He was the hard man, frightened of nothing and no-one, both the immovable object and the unstoppable force; but now, for the first time, he realised how lonely it was to discover that he had no-one to turn to. Who could he tell of the terrible guilt he was feeling, about his part in the ending of a young man's life – a guilt made stronger by the fact that Kieran's death took second place in his thoughts to the loss of Caroline?

So he just kept working; it was all he knew. The day moved into evening, and eventually to night; and, in the early hours of the following morning, he picked up Matty and Degsy from the town rank, and dropped them off as usual on the Rockford estate.

In normal circumstances, he would have taken more care getting out of the cab on the Rockford at that hour, but his mind was full of how stupid he had been to lose Caroline; consequently, as he squatted down to check his front tyre, he was oblivious to the fact that Callum Flynn, armed with a baseball bat, was coming up behind him………..

…………………………………...

Neil shuddered, as he dragged his mind back to the present.

He glanced at his surroundings; he had walked for some time along the canal, at one point crossing over a bridge, and then headed back to where he had started. It was almost a metaphor for the journey his mind had taken, as he had played back his memories of the past four years.

As he stood on the high bridge looking down, he realised, now, how lucky he had been to survive that night. The violence of the attack, now a vivid memory, should have killed him; and it was pure chance that the flames had eaten through the seatbelt, enabling him to get out before he was burned alive.

But was it only luck? As he remembered every blow that the Flynns rained down on him, he remembered something else - what had been going through his mind. He had willed himself to stay alive, refusing to give in, no matter how savagely he was beaten; and then, as he had launched himself out of the cab, in agonising pain, he vowed to himself that he would get his revenge. He could recall, clearly, lying on the ground, and thinking: they should have made sure I was dead. Leaving me alive was the wrong choice.

Well, now he had got his revenge – and what had it achieved? Four men had died, and he had lost everything that mattered to him. Reminding himself of the image of Caroline, being held tightly by the other man, he now had a further sickening thought: what if her behaviour towards him after he came home from the hospital was not because of his changed appearance – with what he now knew, could the true explanation be that she had already ceased to care for him, before he was attacked? Admittedly, she had begun to show some affection towards him recently, but that could have been from a misguided sense of duty on her part - or worse still, pity. Neil knew that he was a survivor by nature; but he could never live with that.

Looking down from the bridge, Neil could see why it had become a popular spot with attempted – and, to his knowledge, in every case, successful – suicides. For his part, he had never been able to understand how anyone could be so desperate that they should want to take their own life; yet at this moment, as he stared down at the concrete far below, and for the first time in his life, he experienced that depth of despair.

As he stood peering down from the high bridge, unbeknown to Neil, he was being watched.

………………………………………………….

As Dean arrived at the car park, near to the bridge where Neil was standing, he instantly recognised the Mercedes with the tinted windows, and knew it was big Joe.

Dean walked over to the Mercedes, got inside, and simply nodded to the big man; at this, Joe smiled, and leaned forward to speak to his driver.

"Stretch your legs for five minutes, Dave - I'll be all right, now Dean's here." The driver accordingly nodded to Joe, got out of the car, and strolled a short distance away.

"Well, I must admit, I'm stumped," declared Dean. "I know how *I* knew Neil might be here, and how to recognise him after the plastic surgery - but I can't fathom how you worked it out. He looks completely different from when you last saw him."

"I don't know, Dean," confessed Joe, shrugging and shaking his head; "I can't explain it – I only know that I felt he would be here, and when I saw him, I just knew it was Neil. When he rang me to say he'd dealt with the Flynns, and to call off the lads, I just sort of sensed that I may be about to lose him. I lost him once, and I don't want to lose him again."

To anyone else, Joe's words would have made no sense; Dean, however, knew exactly what the big man meant.

"Well, I haven't got your sixth sense," admitted Dean; "but I've been here once before with Neil - so when he rang and mentioned the ship canal, I put two and two together, and guessed that this is where he might be." At Joe's questioning expression, Dean explained further. "You see, Neil and I were here a couple of years ago, dangling a young thug by his ankles, from the top of that very bridge."

Joe threw back his head and laughed. "This is a story I've got to hear!"

"I'll tell you the full version another time," promised Dean, grinning; "but suffice to say, this lad and his mates - who'd been terrorising the estate they live on - keep a very low profile now. We didn't hurt him, but we certainly gave him a fright."

"I look forward to hearing the story," chuckled Joe. "Well, that explains how you guessed the right place - but how did you know that it was Neil?"

"Here, take a look at this." Dean took his phone from his pocket, tapped the screen several times, and handed it to Joe. "When Neil came out of the hospital with Caroline, me and Jonjo were outside the main door, and so we took his photograph. Because that phone you've got is even older than Neil's, I wasn't able to send you the photo; but the warehouse boys, and the wives and girlfriends, have all got Neil's picture on their phone - and as we speak, they're all going up and down the ship canal, searching for him."

"But didn't Neil realise you'd taken his photograph?"

"Jonjo made it look like he was just holding his phone out of the sun, so I don't think Neil cottoned on," explained Dean. He smiled. "What happened next was quite funny. Caroline's car had been clamped while she was in the hospital, and Neil came walking back over to the main entrance to sort it out; anyway, one of the security lads there also does a bit of door work for us, so I went up to him and said 'Have you ever heard of Scouse Neil?' And when he nodded, I put on a really serious face and said 'Well, you've just clamped his car, and he's walking over towards you now!' Needless to say, the security lad's bottle went completely."

"I bet they got that clamp off pretty quickly!" sniggered Joe. "Anyway, how come you were there when Neil got discharged?"

"All the time Neil was in hospital, effectively, there were always two of us on guard, in case the Flynns turned up. We worked a simple rota system, so there were always two warehouse boys there round the clock. I know you had a couple of your lads on duty all the time, as well."

"Yes." Joe's expression became serious. "And after Neil surviving what was done to him, we can't lose him now."

"I know! When he rang me, it wasn't so much what he said - it was something in the sound of his voice that bothered me." Dean shook his head. "That first time we visited the hospital and spoke to his sons, when they told me he'd lost his memory completely, I remember thinking that maybe it wasn't a bad thing. You see, the warehouse boys have always believed that ScouseNeil is the only man we've ever met who's just like us……."

"As far as being brave, fearless and a hell of a fighter, I think you're right," interrupted Joe.

"But the trouble is, Joe, there's one big difference - we're killers, trained to kill. Neil is no killer! When he hit that filth Kieran Flynn in the throat, I could see the horror in Neil's face – and now he's got his memory back, I don't think he can cope with what he's done. He's probably convinced himself that he got what he deserved."

Joe nodded sadly. "What did he say to you, when he rang? He said very little to me."

"First, he just said to tell Tommy that Billy's finally got justice. So I asked him what had happened, and he told me that the Flynns were at the bottom of the Manchester ship canal. That's when it hit me, and I thought, what the hell have we done? What in God's name have we created?"

Joe was shaking his head. "I can't believe it was just about revenge. There must have been more to it than that. It could be that the Flynns tracked him down again, and he had to kill them to stop them."

"I hope you're right, Joe," sighed Dean; "but either way - where do we go from here?"

"We sit and watch, and hope."
....

The fact that Neil had left his phone in the car, switched off, was the worst thing he could have done; because while he had been walking by the canal remembering the last four years, a great many things had been happening at home – things which, if he only knew, would completely change his perspective.

Chapter 20

As Neil had been fighting for his life against the Flynns, Caroline was swimming length after length, oblivious to his danger; yet her mind was not at ease.

When she left the house that morning, she had been extremely concerned at Neil's behaviour. She had believed that things were going in the right direction and, therefore, was at a loss to understand the sudden change in his demeanour. It was not merely the blankness in his eyes; it was the way he had held her – almost, it seemed, as if he knew he was doing it for the last time.

....

Caroline's preoccupation must have been written all over her face as, when Alice opened the front door to her, she could see that there was something wrong.

"Caz?" Alice took her by the hand, and led her into the hall. "Has something happened?"

"Not exactly." Caroline smiled wearily. "I can't hide anything from you, can I? I'm just a bit worried about something – it's difficult to explain."

"Well, you can try and explain it to me," said Alice firmly. "Go inside – the kettle's on, and I'll be back in a minute."

A short time later, when the two women were sitting together in the lounge, Caroline leaned back in her seat, and sighed heavily.

"It was something that happened when I left the house this morning," she began. "Lately, things have been improving between Neil and me – we were getting to be more at ease with each other; even though he still has no memory, I was hopeful that we were making progress, and would get back to the way we used to be. But then, this morning, he was completely different."

"Did you ask him if there was anything wrong?"

"He just said that he was tired, but I don't think it was that." Caroline paused, and seemed to struggle to find the right words. "This is going to sound strange, and it's hard to describe. It was the expression in his eyes; or rather, it was that he had no expression in them at all. They were dull, without any emotion – exactly the same look they had that night when he came back from the site of the hospital, where his dad died." She paused again. "But then, as I was leaving the house, he seemed really sad, and held onto me as if he never wanted to let me go – and I know this sounds stupid, but I couldn't shake the feeling that I wasn't going to see him again."

Alice was silent for a few moments, as she considered what Caroline had told her.

"Maybe it was just tiredness, as he said," she eventually suggested; "but even if it *was* sadness, I can't really blame him. I know he's always been such a positive man - but even someone as tough as Neil can only take so many setbacks. You've got to be the strong one now, to stay cheerful, and keep showing him how much you love him."

"I know," agreed Caroline forlornly. "The trouble is, I've got so many things badly wrong since Neil came out of hospital. What if it's too late, and I've already lost him? I feel the whole thing is, somehow, my fault."

Alice could see how desperately sad Caroline was, wishing that she could do or say something that would lift her spirits; and then she suddenly had a thought.

"I've just remembered something," she announced. "I was talking to our John – you know what he's like, the sort who's always been a great one for standing up for the rights of the underdog – well, when I told him about what had happened to you and Neil, he was appalled that you hadn't been informed of your rights." Alice looked triumphant. "He told me that you're entitled to industrial compensation."

Caroline knew that Alice's son was a solicitor, but she was somewhat confused at Alice's words. "Industrial compensation? You've lost me there, Alice."

"Did I say industrial?" Alice laughed, and shook her head. "I meant *criminal* compensation. John said Neil is definitely entitled to it, and it could be a substantial sum of money - particularly as he hasn't been able to work because of the attack, and is still not working now. According to our John, whoever the senior investigating officer was at the start of the case should have informed you – or, at least, made sure that you were informed."

"Oh, I see," murmured Caroline. "Well, that is good news, certainly – it's true, we are really struggling financially at the moment, and I think Neil blames himself for everything that's gone wrong, and for not being able do anything to put things right."

"Well, with any luck, when you tell him this, it might lift his spirits a little bit, which is certainly what that poor man needs."

Alice could see that this news had been welcome to her friend, but she was no fool; she had known Caroline for enough years to guess that there was more troubling her.

"Caroline," she said carefully, "would I be right in thinking that something else has happened, something which has nothing to do with Neil being attacked?" The expression on Caroline's face told Alice that she was right. "I've thought this for a few weeks now," she continued, "but if it's none of my business, please say so."

Caroline hesitated, as though deciding whether to tell Alice what had been bothering her; then she appeared to come to a decision.

"I haven't told anyone this," she confessed. "If I do decide to tell Neil, I just hope he can find it in his heart to forgive me."

"I'm sorry, Caz – if it's too upsetting, leave it until you feel you can talk about it."

"No," said Caroline decidedly; "I think I'd like to tell you, even though I feel awful whenever I think about what I did."

Caroline twisted and untwisted her fingers, as she recounted the story.

"It all started the night I was at my cousin's wedding. I was really enjoying myself but, stupidly, had a bit too much to drink. Anyway, each time I went out for a cigarette, there happened to be a very nice man out there at the same time, and we got chatting. He was very polite, well mannered, and I have to admit, very handsome and charming. I actually felt a bit sorry for him as well, because of the way his wife had been speaking to him.

"Well, a few days after the wedding, I happened to bump into this same man at the supermarket where I do my shopping. It turned out that his wife normally shopped there, but was unwell, so he was filling in. After we'd both finished our shopping, we went for a cup of coffee in the supermarket's restaurant; we got talking, and he mentioned that he and his wife, together with her friend, were going to a jazz concert in Manchester. As you know, I love jazz, but Neil's not keen on it; anyway, I told this man how much I liked jazz, when he said 'Actually, we've been let down by two friends, so I've got a couple of spare tickets – perhaps you and your husband would like to come with us?' Well, I couldn't resist that - I said that I doubted Neil would be interested, but that I'd be happy to tag along with him and his wife, if that was all right. He said that wouldn't be a problem, because he knew someone else who would take the other spare ticket. So, we exchanged mobile numbers, and then as we parted company in the car park, I gave him a hug - which, on reflection, was a mistake," remarked Caroline ruefully, shaking her head.

"The thing was, I was absolutely overjoyed at being able to go to this particular concert, because I'd tried to get tickets myself, but the concert was sold out. This jazz band is American, been going for many years, and it was probably the last time they would ever visit Britain." Caroline seemed to feel the need to justify herself. "I did ask Neil if he wanted to go to the concert," she continued, "but I wasn't surprised at his answer. He didn't bother saying no, he just laughed! Like I say, he hates jazz, always has – but he encouraged me to go, and told me to enjoy myself, so I felt alright about it.

"The arrangement, as I was told, was to meet up in a particular pub car park, which I didn't know very well, so I just put it in the satnav system in my car. The place in Manchester, though, where the concert was being held, I knew to be very high-class, so I got dressed up to the nines – I was really looking forward to it, when I set off.

"Anyway, as I was following the directions from the satnav, I was getting a bit concerned, because I seemed to be going in the wrong direction, heading away from Manchester, rather than towards it; even so, when I got there, it was the right pub – although, as I turned into the car park, the first thing that struck me was how poorly lit it was, and I felt a bit uneasy. Then I spotted his car, which was a relief - so I got out of my car, walked towards him, and put my arms out to give him a hug. That's when it happened." Caroline hesitated for a moment. "Before I knew it, he had his arms round me, holding me tightly, and tried to kiss me - and then he put his hand on my bottom." Her eyes were lowered, and she seemed to squirm. "With him being so big and strong, it took me two or three seconds to prise him off. As soon as I had, I swung back my hand, because I was going to slap his face - but he immediately stepped back, raised his hands, and was full of apologies, blurting out something about being excited, because he had just been told he was being promoted."

While Caroline had been speaking, a shocked Alice had her hand to her mouth, full of righteous indignation on her friend's behalf.

"Obviously, at that point, I should've simply got back into my car and driven home," said Caroline ruefully. "I was so naïve. I still believed he had tickets for the concert and so, foolishly, was willing to accept his apologies, and his excuse that his hand had 'slipped' onto my bottom – although I did make it clear that, if he dared do something like that again, he would be very sorry. Well, as we walked to his car, I could see there was no sign of his wife or her friend, but he assured me we were picking them up on the way, and would I mind sitting in the front - as they preferred to sit in the back, so that they could chat to each other on the way." Caroline looked embarrassed. "You'd think alarm bells would be ringing by now, wouldn't you? I can't believe how stupid I was." She sighed.

"So, we drove out of the car park; but, instead of turning to go back to the main road, he turned in the other direction, drove a short distance down the country lane, and then turned into what looked like the entrance to a country park. It was absolutely pitch black; he just drove to the far corner, stopped the car, switched the engine off and made a grab for me. I managed to push him away - then he hit me." Alice gasped. "For a split second, I remember noticing a van had pulled into the car park behind us, and I recognised the name of the garage it was from – it's one that Neil uses - so I thought whoever it was might come and help me. But then, the van just swung round and drove away, and I knew I was on my own."

Alice was horrified. How could anyone harm this lovely young woman? A feeling of hatred for this loathsome man was building up inside her, and she knew she would be unable to stem the tears. She closed her eyes, as she waited for Caroline to recount the inevitable conclusion to the story.

"So, naturally," continued Caroline, almost nonchalantly, "I punched him."

Alice opened her eyes in astonishment. "You *punched* him?"

"Too right, I did! I got him with a straight left to the nose. Not one of my best, but it made his nose bleed. Then I got out of the car, slammed the door and stormed off." Caroline was shaking her head. "I was so angry - not just with him, but with myself; my own stupidity had put me in a vulnerable situation. There was no jazz concert - the whole thing was a set-up from start to finish; and if I hadn't been able to look after myself, I dread to think what the consequences could've been. I soon realised that I must have told him a great deal about myself the night of the wedding but, because I was so drunk, I didn't remember; so, bumping into him in my usual supermarket wasn't by chance - and the business over the jazz concert was also rubbish, because I must have told him that I'd tried to get tickets, and that Neil hated jazz."

"So he knew he could invite Neil, knowing full well that he wouldn't go with you." Alice was appalled. "I wouldn't be surprised if this man has done something like this before, and got away with it. Any woman would have difficulty proving rape against him after, apparently, going with him willingly to a lonely place, like that country park."

"Funny you should say that, I had the same thought," admitted Caroline; "and you'll see why, when I tell you who he is." She was not surprised to see the shock on Alice's face, when she revealed the man's name.

"But that's disgraceful!" exclaimed Alice.

"Isn't it just?" remarked Caroline. "Anyway, I haven't told you the next bit. As I stormed off, he got out of the car and came after me; so I stopped, turned round to look him straight in the eye, and told him to walk away while he still could. Make no mistake Alice, if he'd taken another step towards me, he would've regretted it. I was limited for space inside the car - but outside, I'd have taken him with a combination, as well as getting a number of kicks in."

Alice was, by now, almost clapping her hands with delight; this was a whole new side to Caroline that she had never imagined. "Caz! How on earth do you know anything about combination punches?"

Caroline looked slightly sheepish. "Remember me telling you about the training room Neil had installed, about four years ago? I would often sit and watch Neil train, and also watch while he trained the boys; so, when the house is empty, I regularly go up and train there myself." She grinned. "I'm not quite sure what each piece of equipment is called, but I really enjoy using them - and as a result, I'm fitter and stronger now than I've ever been in my life. You don't get biceps like this just by swimming." Caroline rolled up her sleeve, and showed Alice the muscles in her arm.

Alice felt like hugging Caroline; she had always looked upon the younger woman as the daughter she had never had and, at that moment, could not have been more proud of her.

"Well, I'm certainly impressed," declared Alice. "Funnily enough, I could probably tell you the names of the different pieces of equipment - my father was a very good amateur boxer, and when I was a little girl, he sometimes used to take me with him when he went training." She smiled. "My father was a lovely man, an absolute gentleman and, just like Neil, wasn't very confident in the company of women; but if anyone was fool enough to get on the wrong side of him, he was a different man. When we were little, if we were with our daddy, a monster could have come round the corner, and it wouldn't have frightened us. As children, we felt we had the toughest man in the world protecting us."

Caroline now realised why Alice had always had an affection for Neil; she knew exactly what Alice meant as she described her father, as Caroline had always felt the same when she was with Neil.

"So," continued Alice, "what did you use for your training at home?"

"Well, the thing that made my arms a lot stronger is like a big, long bag, which hangs from the ceiling. Punching and kicking that certainly uses up a lot of energy."

"Yes, that's just called the heavy bag."

"Another one I use is ball-shaped, in the middle of an elasticated rope which is connected to the floor and ceiling. As you punch it, it comes back at you at various angles, so you have to be really quick to be able to punch it again. That took some getting used to, but it really speeds up your punches, and encourages you to be able to punch with both hands."

"That's a punchball - you've really got to be on your toes when you're working on that. What else?"

Caroline smiled. "My favourite is the one that's in a sort of frame; it's like a football at one end, and a rugby ball at the other. When the boys were younger, they had to use a small stand to be able to reach it, and I still use the stand now. It's difficult to get into a routine when you first start, but when you do, it really does strengthen your arms."

"Ah yes, that's the speedball," said Alice. "That's what helps you to deliver a reasonably good blow in a confined space – for when you need to give someone a good punch on the nose," she chuckled.

Caroline also giggled. "When I told him to walk away, he looked so stupid with blood running from his nose, and constantly sniffing."

Alice regarded Caroline with open admiration. "With him being so much bigger and stronger than you, weren't you frightened?"

"Strangely enough, no I wasn't," Caroline told her. "I've often sat in the training room, not only watching Neil train the boys, but listening to what he says. He's always said to them that, if someone tries to bully you, you should never show fear, never back down, and never give up. If you fight with everything you've got, Neil says, bullies will always give in. Well, it certainly worked for me - that night, I showed that man that I was more than willing to take him on, regardless of his size; and he, being the typical bully, did back off. I found myself thinking of the sign Neil has on the wall in the training room - it says: 'If you're in the right, then stand and fight!'"

"Well, that is peculiar - my father often said those exact words."

"The trouble was," continued Caroline, "when I got home and looked in the mirror, I realised that my eye was starting to discolour where he'd hit me. By the morning, I knew I was going to have quite a black eye; and, as I hadn't decided whether or not to tell Neil what had happened, I didn't want him to see it, and start asking questions. Anyway, as it happened, Neil was still out working, so I went straight to bed; but I deliberately stayed awake until I heard him come in, then I pretended to be asleep - but made sure I was hiding the side of my face that was starting to bruise. I heard Neil come up to the bedroom, but then I assume he decided not to disturb me, because he went back downstairs to sleep on the couch.

"The following morning, I got up as quietly as I could, crept downstairs, glanced into the living room, and saw that Neil was still asleep; so I took the opportunity to go straight out. I just drove round the block, and parked up at the bottom of our lane. Next to the woods, which are not far from where we live, is a small layby, and that's where I waited; it's a good vantage point - you can see if anyone drives away from our house, but the layby itself is not visible from any of our windows. I glanced at myself in the rear view mirror, and my eye looked awful; so I just sat there, and waited for Neil to go out.

"Anyway, while I was waiting, I got a call from 'guess who.' He was full of apologies, he was so sorry, he misunderstood the situation - and then tried to say I had sent out the wrong messages to him, which really annoyed me. He knew full well that I had made it very clear to him, that day when we were chatting over coffee at the supermarket, how close Neil and I were, how happy we were, and how much we loved each other. I told him not to ring me again." Caroline's mouth was set in a grim line.

"Well, eventually, I saw Neil leave the house, so I was able to go back. I spent some time in the bathroom, trying to disguise the bruising around my eye with make-up, but it was no use – it was still clearly visible. So I gave up, went downstairs and made a brew, and sat in the living room, wondering how I was going to avoid Neil until such time as the bruise faded." Caroline sighed. "Funny, the little things you notice, when your mind is full of something else. Neil's favourite family photo – the one he always carried round in the taxi with him – was face down on the coffee table; I remember wondering why he'd put it there, instead of back up on the fire surround."

Alice shot Caroline a searching look. "Did you ask Neil why he'd put it face down, and not displayed it properly?"

Caroline shook her head. "That's the worst thing," she replied, sadly. "Those last few days before Neil was attacked, we barely spoke; I was keeping out of his way, because of my black eye. The one time I did speak, I was so rude to him, I felt awful. As he came in one evening, I was in the kitchen – and I panicked, because I had to think of some excuse quickly. So, I kept my back to him so that he couldn't see my face, muttered that I wasn't well and was going to bed, and just walked out; but I could see out of the corner of my eye how sad he was, and how much I'd hurt him with my behaviour. I just lay in bed and cried, but I didn't know what else to do." Caroline paused. "You see, the other thing that was bothering me, was that I got another call, and it was far more menacing. Basically, that swine was saying how upsetting it would be for Neil to discover that his 'perfect' wife was seeing someone behind his back; and, although he didn't say it in so many words, he implied that if I was willing to have sex with him, Neil wouldn't get any bad news."

Alice clenched her fists, inwardly cursing that she was not younger, because she would happily tear this man apart; she shook her head. "You said before you felt sorry for him. How could you possibly feel sorry for an animal like this?"

"Well, it sounds ridiculous now, but I felt sorry for him because of the way his wife was speaking to him," confessed Caroline. "At the wedding, she appeared to be deliberately ridiculing him in front of everyone on their table – but, as their table was next to ours, we could hear her as well. Of course, now, I realise that he followed me out, each time I went for a cigarette; after hearing the way his wife spoke to him, I made the mistake of being far too friendly with him."

"Yes, well - maybe his wife is like that towards him because she knows exactly what he's up to behind her back."

"Maybe," mused Caroline. "I probably shouldn't say this – it's a bit catty – but although he's actually very handsome, his wife is incredibly ugly." Caroline looked a little ashamed, but also amused. "The woman could win ugly tournaments."

"Well, who knows what goes on behind closed doors?" remarked Alice. "For all we know, she might have some hold over him."

"Anyway, I can't turn back the clock," said Caroline, and her mood became sombre. "What makes me feel really bad, is that I believe Neil was trying to talk to me about something, the day after all this happened - and of course, I was blanking him. I realised afterwards that, in the end, he gave up trying to speak to me; and then, he was attacked." Her eyes began to fill with tears. "When he was first taken to hospital, I thought, he's going to die - and his last memories will be of me being horrible to him." As she finished speaking, she broke down and wept.

Alice held her and tried to comfort her, desperately sorry for the young woman that she loved like a daughter. As she waited for Caroline's tears to subside, she also began to reflect on what she had been told, and found that there were several things which made her wonder; for instance, was it just a coincidence that the van Caroline saw, as she was being attacked, was from a garage regularly used by Neil? Was it significant that, the following day, Caroline had found Neil's prized family photo left face down on a table? And finally – if what Caroline believed was true – what was it that Neil had been trying to speak to her about, in the days before his attack?

Once Caroline had stopped crying, her distress was replaced by anger.

"What really annoyed me, was that business over the phone call," she asserted. "He did nothing about that information that was passed to him. And I had to lie to the boys - which I hated having to do – because when Michael rang him on my phone, he said 'Hi Caz.' I don't know if he thought I'd had a change of mind. The arrogance of it! There was no chance of that."

Alice frowned. "Hold on, you've lost me – why did you have to lie to the boys?"

"Sorry, I'm not making much sense," apologised Caroline. "I told the boys that I'd given our mobile numbers to the police, and that Benton had just rung me concerning the case – both of which weren't true. But I had to do that, in order to explain the fact that I had Benton's number, and he had mine. Michael, particularly, is like Neil; in a situation like that, Mike would have immediately thought it strange that Benton and I had each other's mobile numbers. I may or may not tell Neil what happened to me; but I don't think I'd ever tell the boys." Caroline paused. "Funnily enough, Michael described him as a slimeball which, of course, was a very accurate description; but when he said it, I had to pretend to be annoyed, because I didn't want the boys to know there was any connection."

"I think not telling the boys would be very wise," said Alice, her expression grim. "If Paul knew what had happened, he would be down to the police headquarters like a shot, and would plaster Benton all over his office walls - they'd probably have to call the riot police to stop him. And if Michael ever found out…….." Alice left the sentence hanging, but shuddered. "Although, I have to say, it would be nothing more than what's deserved."

"Anyway," continued Caroline, "the following morning, Michael rang me to say that nothing had been done about the information he'd passed to them; so I stopped off at the police headquarters, on my way over to the hospital. I wanted Benton off the case for obvious reasons, and hoped that, if it was known that he'd done nothing about the information he received, that would do the trick."

"And was that enough to have him taken off the case?"

"No," replied Caroline. "The Chief Superintendent I spoke to was such an arrogant man, telling me that Detective Superintendent Benton had passed the information on to one of his team, and would remain the senior investigating officer because of his 'superior detective skills'. The pompous fool said that, although I'd withheld information from the police regarding Neil, Benton had discovered the truth."

"What nonsense was he talking about?"

"He was talking about the Spanish villa," explained Caroline. "I hadn't mentioned it to the police because I couldn't see what possible relevance it had to Neil being attacked. Apparently, Benton had convinced his superior officer that Neil was involved in the supply of drugs, and had bought the villa with the proceeds. Well, at that point, I really lost it." Caroline clenched her fist at the memory. "I wiped the floor with him. By the time I'd finished, he was left in no doubt exactly how Benton knew we had a villa in Spain, and everything else he had been up to. I was so angry, I demanded to know if it was the usual behaviour of his senior officers to lure women into lonely country parks to attack them."

Alice smiled, and raised an eyebrow. "I would imagine *that* took the wind out of his sails."

"Well, I've never thought of myself as being scary," said Caroline modestly, "but, by the time I'd finished laying into him, he was almost trembling. What surprised me, though, is that when I really got going, he didn't attempt to defend Benton in any way - which makes me think that you're right, and that he has done this kind of thing before. It makes you wonder if there have been accusations in the past, which have just been brushed under the carpet. Anyway, I was asked if I would like to make an official complaint, but I refused – I just demanded he be taken off Neil's case immediately. Chief Superintendent Turnbull then assured me that Benton would play no further part in the investigation – nor any in the future, he said, if he had anything to do with it. He told me that he was appalled at his senior officer's behaviour, and that the man was an absolute disgrace." Caroline smiled. "I call that a result."

Alice was amazed, but gratified; she had known Caroline for over twenty years and had never realised that, when cornered, Caroline was just as tough as Neil.

"So, not long after I left the police headquarters," resumed Caroline, "as I was driving over to Liverpool, I received a call from Benton - saying that I'd ruined his career, and that he would get even. Once he started swearing and calling me names, I found that laughing at him appeared to annoy him even more. Once he'd finished ranting, I told him to get lost – only in rather stronger language – and rang off. Needless to say, he can't ring me anymore, because I've blocked his number on my phone."

"Good for you," beamed Alice. "I'm so proud of you, you've no idea."

"But I'm not proud of myself, as I should never have let any of it happen in the first place," insisted Caroline. "When I think that, since the night we met, Neil has done everything in his power to protect me, look after me and keep me safe. For me to have been so stupid, I'm not sure if Neil could ever forgive me for that." She shook her head. "And that's why I can't decide whether to tell him."

Alice smiled, and patted Caroline's hand. "Firstly, there's nothing to forgive - and I'm sure Neil would feel the same," she said firmly; "but secondly, even if there was, I can tell you now that Neil would forgive you anything. That man has no control over what he feels for you. I have never seen, in all my years, anyone love someone as much as Neil loves you."

Caroline was unconvinced. "All I can think of is that blank look in his eyes when he left this morning, and the fear – which I can't shake – that he may not be coming back."

Alice looked at Caroline sadly; it was clear that she was at a very low ebb, and it was up to her to try to give her friend the reassurance she needed.

"You know, I can remember the first time I ever met Neil," mused Alice; "it's as clear to me now as if it was yesterday. It was two weeks after you met, and he came to collect you from the hairdressers', because it was your half day."

Caroline managed a faint smile. "It was mean, really," she said; "Neil would've preferred to stay outside in the car, but I'd talked him into coming in to collect me."

"Believe me, I was glad that you did - we all were. Right after the two of you left, you were the talk of the shop; all of us - not just the young girls who worked with you, but us older ones as well - were so envious. It was pretty obvious that he was very shy around women, despite being what I would call a 'real' man; but it was that passionate look he had in his eyes, every time he looked at you, that we all envied."

Caroline sighed. "People often used to tell me that, but I never appreciated it. That's the way he had always looked at me, from when we had the first dance in that club in Liverpool, and I took it for granted; but now, I know what you and everyone else were talking about, because that look in his eyes has gone. When Neil and I got home from the hospital, after they had removed his bandages, of course his face had changed – but I knew something else was not quite right, and it took me a few days to realise what it was. I even asked the boys if they could see the change; but, naturally, they couldn't."

"You *will* see it again," Alice said firmly. "Neil will regain his memory, and when he does, he won't have to tell you – you'll know it from the look in his eyes." Alice squeezed Caroline's hand. "When he picked you up from here last month – before his attack – it was lovely to see that expression was still there when he looked at you, as strong as it was twenty years ago."

Caroline was too far gone to believe that things could ever be as they were between her and Neil; but she was touched by Alice's attempts to lift her spirits, and therefore tried her best to look more cheerful for her benefit.

"So you think I should tell Neil what happened?"

"I think you've got to," replied Alice seriously; "and, what's more, I would do it at the first possible opportunity - even if Neil hasn't regained his memory."

"But how much should I tell him? Should I say that Benton hit me?"

"Absolutely," said Alice emphatically. "Tell him everything that happened - starting with the night of your cousin's wedding reception, right through to the threatening phone call you received after visiting the police headquarters – and leave nothing out. I think you'll find that, like me, Neil will be proud of you for standing up for yourself in the way you did."

Caroline still looked unsure. "One of the reasons I hesitate is because I'm concerned what Neil may do, if I tell him that someone hit me."

"But it's the truth – and it's the only way you can explain your behaviour towards him. As you said, you ignored him, and were even rude to him – he has to know that it wasn't because of anything he'd done." Alice paused. "If Neil *were* to decide to deal with Benton, I'm sure he'd manage to do it discreetly – he's no fool; but I suspect it's more likely that he'd be so impressed with how you handled it yourself that, unless Benton tried to back up his threat of getting even, Neil would leave well alone. Mind you, I have to say, I would love Neil to sort him out; in fact, I'd pay good money to watch." Caroline looked surprised, but Alice had the grace to look guilty. "Alright, I admit that sounds very vindictive," she confessed; "even so, I do hope that - one day - Benton will get his comeuppance, one way or the other."

Caroline considered Alice's words, and realised the wisdom of her advice. After all, with things as they were, what more was there to lose by telling Neil the truth?

"You know, I think you're absolutely right," she said decidedly. "I'll tell him as soon as I get the opportunity. Then, if he ever does get his memory back, he'll know straight away why I acted the way I did."

"Good, that's definitely the right thing to do," said Alice, patting Caroline's hand. "And that other thing I was saying before, about the industrial – " she shook her head in exasperation – "I mean the *criminal* compensation; I'll get our John to ring you, and explain all about it."

Just then, the two women heard a car pulling up outside, followed by the sound of a key in the front door.

"Well, talk of the Devil," remarked Alice; "I'd forgotten he'd said he would call round today."

Caroline had known John almost as long as she had known his mother, and she liked him. He was very serious, precise in the way he spoke, and a great believer in doing everything correctly – but he also had a clear sense of right and wrong, and could be as ferocious intellectually as Neil was physically, when it came to defending the vulnerable. For his part, John appreciated Caroline for her caring attachment to his mother, and Alice knew that he would relish the opportunity to help Caroline and Neil in their predicament.

As John entered the living room, he gave his mother a hug.

"Hello, love," said Alice. "I was just talking about you – were your ears burning? Explain to Caz about the industrial compensation." John raised his eyebrows. "You know what I mean."

Caroline smiled at John. "Your mum said you think you may be able to help?"

"No, that isn't the case." John's expression was so stern that Caroline's heart sank, and Alice looked quite taken aback. "I don't *think* I may be able to help," he continued; "I definitely *know* I can help."

Alice regarded her son with impatience. "John, why do you have to be so bloody precise? You almost upset Caz then."

"Apologies, Caz," said John, turning to Caroline, "but you know me - I do like people to be aware of the exact situation." He sat down. "Neil is definitely entitled to criminal compensation. All I need is the incident number which you would have had from the police, and I would also like your mortgage details. I was appalled when mum told me about that letter they sent you. I can guarantee the next letter you receive from them will be a grovelling apology."

"Well, let me think," said Caroline, rubbing her chin; "the incident number is on a pad by the phone – and the mortgage details should be in Neil's box file, so I'll have a look in there. He keeps all the important documents in that file in alphabetical order, so it's easy to lay his hands on what he needs straight away."

"Excellent, a man after my own heart. When you get home, if you can ring that information through to me, then I can get things sorted out. The British judicial system has its critics, and in many cases quite rightly so; however, it would be quite wrong to allow an innocent victim of a crime to suffer financially, and to possibly lose their home." He shook his head. "I'm very disappointed that the senior investigating officer didn't inform you of this; but frankly, when I discovered it was Benton, I wasn't in any way surprised."

Alice and Caroline exchanged a furtive glance, unnoticed by John.

"Well, as long as we can get it sorted out now, that's all that matters," said Caroline. "I'll just be glad to be able to give Neil some good news, after all he's been through. And thanks, John – I'm grateful for your help, and I know Neil will be as well."

Caroline carefully steered the conversation away from Benton, asking John about his family, before glancing at the clock on the mantelpiece.

"Well, I had no idea that was the time," she remarked, as she rose from her seat. "I'd better get going, and break the good news to Neil."

She hugged Alice and John and, after saying her goodbyes, went out to the car. She tried to ring Neil's mobile but, getting only his voicemail, she set off home.

Chapter 21

The house was empty when Caroline arrived; she therefore went into the kitchen, made a pot of tea, and sat waiting for Neil to return.

As she sat sipping her tea, although Caroline was impatient to tell Neil about the criminal compensation, she could not help but regret that they had not found out about it sooner; there would have been no need to sell the villa. She knew perfectly well that Benton had deliberately withheld the information about the entitlement out of sheer spite, and she despised him even more.

Just then, the home phone rang. Caroline almost leapt to it, hoping that it would be Neil; however, by an odd coincidence, it was the Spanish solicitor. Caroline's voice must have reflected her disappointment.

"What? No…I'm sorry, it's just that I was expecting it to be Neil, and I've got something important to tell him….anyway, is there something you want me to tell him about the sale?" Caroline listened to the voice on the other end of the line and, in a few short minutes, she found herself jumping up and down on the spot. "Oh my God – but that's fantastic!" she said ecstatically. "No really, I'm alright – I just can't wait to tell Neil, he'll be overjoyed! Thank you so much – sorry to cut you short, but I want to let him know as soon as possible…yes, you understand correctly, that's exactly what I mean… and thank you again...bye!"

Caroline rang off, and immediately tried Neil's mobile number again, but found she was still unable to get an answer. Undaunted, she walked through to the dining room with the phone in her hand, repeatedly calling his number; meanwhile, with the other hand, she opened the cupboard containing Neil's box file, made a grab for the box, and promptly dropped it, spilling the contents all over the floor.

"Dammit," she muttered, putting the phone down, and getting on her knees to scoop up the papers. She was putting them back in alphabetical order, with the intention of extracting the mortgage details to give to John, when she noticed something else; her hands were trembling as she picked up and examined some documents, hardly believing what she was seeing. Could this be real? If so………

"Come on, woman, get a grip," she said to herself, getting to her feet. She tried to stay calm as she carefully separated the documents relating to the mortgage, and telephoned John to give him the information he needed; once again, he assured her that he could get everything sorted out. She thanked him and, after she had ended the call, she walked slowly into the kitchen, and sat for some time to take in everything that had just happened.

As she heard the front door opening, Caroline almost sprinted down the hall in the hope that it was Neil; but she was unable to hide her disappointment when she saw that it was Michael.

"That's what I love about coming here," he remarked wryly; "the welcome I receive is just overwhelming."

"Sorry Mike," grinned Caroline, giving her son a hug; "of course I'm glad to see you - it's just that I was really hoping it was your dad. Since he came out of hospital, I've desperately wanted to be able to give him a bit of good news, to lift his spirits. Well - the amount of good news I've got now will knock him off his feet."

"Bet I can beat it," was Michael's surprising response. "I was here for a while this morning, and there were two calls, both for dad; whatever your news is, it won't be in the same league as mine."

"Not a chance, matey," laughed Caroline. "My good news will beat yours to a pulp!"

"Oh, yeah? That sounds like a challenge to me," smiled Michael. "Alright then, age before beauty - you can go first."

"Fair enough," said Caroline, "and less of the 'age', you cheeky sod! Come and have a look at what I found in your dad's file."

The two of them went into the dining room, sat at the table, and then Caroline handed the documents she had found to Michael to examine.

"Dear me," murmured Michael, after he had looked at the papers in front of him; "I've got a few premium bonds at home, but certainly not this many. Have you any idea how much is here?"

Caroline beamed. "Just over fifty-eight thousand pounds!"

Michael shook his head in disbelief. "When I was sorting all the documents out for dad, before he came home from hospital, I don't know how I missed these," he admitted. "Although, now I think about it, I suppose they were filed under the letter P – and I didn't look in that section, because there were no direct debits or standing orders beginning with that letter."

"You're right, that's where they were filed – although I wouldn't have found them myself if I hadn't dropped the file, and everything hadn't fallen out onto the floor. Funny really," reflected his mother; "when I saw what they were, I felt a mixture of joy and anger at the same time."

"Anger?" asked Michael, surprised. "Why?"

"Anger at myself, for not paying proper attention to your dad when he's telling me something," confessed Caroline. "The fact is, he told me about the premium bonds years ago, but because I was only half listening as usual, I'd forgotten about them – until today, when they fell out of the box." She sighed. "To think - he's been so worried about our financial situation, and all the time we had nearly sixty thousand pounds here doing nothing. I could kick myself."

"Don't beat yourself up about it," said Michael; "after all, I should've guessed myself that you had premium bonds. Shortly after I set up my business, dad recommended I put my spare cash into them, so common sense should've told me that he had his own stash of bonds."

"Anyway, that's only the first part of the good news – I've also been told that your dad is entitled to industrial compensation!" Caroline was all smiles.

"Come again?"

"Industrial comp - oh, what the hell am I saying?" Caroline collapsed into giggles. "It's all Alice's fault – I mean *criminal* compensation," she spluttered.

A bemused Michael simply smiled and shook his head as he watched his mother, her shoulders shaking.

"I never knew criminal compensation was so hilarious – stop, my sides are aching," he said wryly, which made her laugh even more.

"But I've saved the best news till last," she said finally, wiping the tears of laughter from her eyes, "and no news you've got is going to beat this. We've still got the villa!"

"It's not been sold? But I thought that was all done and dusted?"

"The solicitor phoned from Spain, to tell us that the sale had fallen through – by which time I already knew about the criminal compensation claim." Caroline grinned. "She must have thought I was insane, the way I reacted – she can't have many clients who get so overjoyed at losing a buyer! Anyway, she asked me if that meant we wanted to take it off the market, and I told her yes."

"So how come the sale fell through?"

"Well, it turns out that the English fella who came to our party at the villa is some sort of conman, and didn't have the money to buy it after all."

"Ha! Dad saw through him straight away," nodded Michael, leaning back and folding his arms; "so did I, for that matter. I knew there was something dodgy about him – I just wasn't quite sure what."

"Anyway," continued Caroline, "as you can imagine, the Spanish solicitor was full of apologies. It turns out that all the property he supposedly owned doesn't exist - it was all one big lie. He was trying to get her involved in buying our villa without parting with any money, and then immediately reselling it for more. Luckily, she cottoned on to him in time to stop the transaction going through."

"You've got to take your hat off to dad, he's a very good judge of character," remarked Michael. "He told me, right after the first time he met that solicitor, that she was sound. But as for that bloke – well, when he was at the party, no sooner had he opened his mouth than dad said to me he neither liked nor trusted him."

"Well, he was spot-on about both of them," agreed Caroline. "And so, let me see: we've got no money worries any more, and we've still got the villa in Spain." Caroline paused for effect.

"Beat that!"

"I must admit, I am quite impressed - but I still reckon my news is better," asserted Michael, grinning. "First thing: dad's still got his taxi plate."

"Really? But how?" Caroline was surprised. "Your dad was told by the council that they were taking back the plate because he'd been off the road longer than their rules allowed, and they weren't interested when he tried to explain. What changed their minds?"

"Listen to this," began Michael. "You know dad's mate Danny?"

"Yes – I think he thought he'd let your dad down over the plate business, so it doesn't surprise me if he had something to do with getting it back for him."

"Well, he tried to phone dad to let him know what happened this afternoon, but when he couldn't get hold of him, he told me instead." Michael smiled. "He only got all the taxi drivers to blockade the council building where the taxi authority is based, so no-one could get in or out. It must have looked really good - there are quite a few entrances and exits to that building's car park, but every one of them was completely blocked by all the cabs. Anyway, it seems that Jacko was bringing a letter, from a Chief Superintendent Turnbull, about dad losing his taxi plate."

"Oh?" Caroline was intrigued. "How did he get involved, then? I only met him once, but he didn't strike me as being particularly sympathetic about your dad's situation."

"Remember the two detectives that came here – the Scottish fella, and the young bloke, the boxer?"

Caroline nodded. "Yes I do, Detective Sergeant Smith - he's a mate of Jacko's, and they call him Tinny. I think the younger lad was called Gary."

"That's them – but what you probably don't know is that when they called here that time, dad happened to mention to them about losing his taxi plate. Anyway, it seems that both Tinny and Gary were so annoyed on dad's behalf that Tinny went to see the top man at the police headquarters - who, from all accounts, wasn't impressed either. So, he wrote a letter to the council, along the lines of how appalled he was that an innocent man should be penalised in this way, that it was an absolute disgrace, and he would speaking to people at the highest level - all that sort of stuff."

Caroline smiled to herself. Could it be, she wondered, that the dressing down she had given Turnbull a few weeks ago might have had some bearing on his sudden righteous indignation at Neil's predicament?

"So they were all waiting for Jacko to appear with this letter," continued Michael, "and when he did, all the cabbies thought it was hilarious, according to Danny – because when Jacko arrived, he wasn't in his cab, he was driving a Porsche!" Michael chuckled.

"Oh, yes – that car belongs to Jacko's brother, the farmer," interjected Caroline. "Oddly enough, it's identical to the one that the young detective drives; I noticed that when he and Tinny called here – because as I saw the car pull up, I assumed it was Jacko's brother John, and was surprised to see the two detectives get out."

"Funny you should say that - because Danny went on to tell me that, no sooner had Jacko pulled up in his brother's Porsche, than Tinny and Gary turned up in Gary's Porsche, and parked up next to Jacko, Then, the four of them – Jacko, Danny, Tinny and Gary - marched across the car park in to the council offices, while the cabbies were all looking on. Boy, I'd have liked to have seen that." Michael was grinning. "Once they were inside, Danny said that the Scottish copper demanded, not very nicely, to see whoever was in charge of taxi licensing - and he wasn't careful about his language, if you know what I mean."

Caroline laughed. "Yes – I can well imagine he'd have an interesting turn of phrase, when needed."

"Well, it worked – at least, it got the council officer they were after to come down, and speak to them. At first, though, they weren't getting anywhere; from Danny's description, Jacko and Tinny were really ripping into this fella, but he was standing his ground - just kept repeating that they were the rules, he couldn't make an exception for dad, because that would open the floodgates, and so on. But then, it appears that Gary asked this council bloke – politely - if he could just have a quiet word." Michael raised one eyebrow. "Danny has no idea what Gary said to this fella - but it did the trick. After speaking to Gary, the council official simply agreed that the taxi plate was still dad's – then disappeared, pretty sharpish. Danny told me that the bloke looked absolutely terrified, so God knows what Gary said to him."

Caroline was shaking her head. "I can't believe everything that's happened today," she said wonderingly. "I just can't wait to tell your dad all this. If only he had his phone switched on – and we can't even go and find him, because I don't know where he is."

"I haven't finished yet, though," Michael told her; "the best bit is still to come. You'll have to bear with me, because there's a lot to tell – but I reckon this will win me the 'good news' competition."

"We'll see!" said Caroline, laughing. "Go on then – let's have it!"

"I got a call from a Chief Inspector Davies," explained Michael. "Again, he'd been unable to get hold of dad, and asked me to pass on what he was going to tell him. The funny thing was, he started by saying we can thank 'Morse' for this – that's Gary's nickname, dreamt up by his colleagues at the station, poor sod. Anyway, I think what Davies told me is good news for two reasons, which I'll explain when I've finished; but to begin at the beginning - the police are now convinced it was mistaken identity after all, and that dad wasn't the intended target."

Caroline leaned forward, frowning. "But……..I was told that, early in the investigation, they looked at that possibility – and got nowhere with it."

"That's right - Gary had suggested it after speaking to Mark and Jill, the two officers who were with you at the hospital. After they'd given him all the information they got from you, he was convinced that someone like dad couldn't possibly have been the real target of an attack like that; but initially, they hit a dead end – Gary and Tinny went through all the records of the various taxi authorities, and didn't find any driver that dad could have been mistaken for."

"So what's changed?"

"Remember when Burnsy went in to speak to them? Well, it was when he was telling them about dad's old taxi firm, and how busy it was, that he let slip the fact that a couple of the drivers didn't have badges. Gary immediately picked up on that; because it gave him the idea that maybe there was a taxi driver working out there, not badged, so the taxi authorities would have no record of him – a driver that dad could have been mistaken for."

"I see," said Caroline, nodding slowly. "I'm surprised, though – why didn't the police tell us about that line of enquiry?"

"That's what D.C.I. Davies meant, when he told me that we could thank 'Morse'," explained Michael. "You see, Gary didn't tell anyone else of his suspicions - he did the investigation in his own time. Night after night he was trawling round all the taxi ranks, checking that the actual drivers matched those in the local authority records; once he'd covered the area dad normally works, he moved on to all the surrounding areas, checking each one, until he was satisfied that there were no unlicensed drivers that resembled dad. I've got to say, I admire his stubbornness," admitted Michael; "he was so convinced that it was mistaken identity, he wasn't willing to give up until he could prove it."

"So I take it he eventually found what he was looking for?"

"Yes he did. He was in Warrington one night when he spotted a man, who looked very similar to dad, driving a taxi; he had all the records of the taxi owners on his laptop - including photos - and the man he saw was definitely not the person on record as being the normal driver of that particular cab. At that point, though, he still didn't tell any of his colleagues in the police, because he wanted to be absolutely sure of his facts before saying anything – so he did some more digging, and it paid off. It turns out that this bogus taxi driver was heavily in debt to a major crime family and, the night before dad was attacked, this bloke had been heard boasting in a pub in Warrington that he owed the McCabes a lot of money, wasn't scared of them, and so on."

"Hm," said Caroline doubtfully; "no offence to Gary – after all, he's worked hard to get to the bottom of what happened - but couldn't it just be coincidence?"

"To be fair, the police did stress that it could be coincidence," admitted Michael. "But as things stand, they've never been able to find any motive for someone to attack dad; whereas this Warrington fella, who looked like dad, had definitely fallen out with the wrong people. You see, last night, when he was coming out of a pub, that man was stabbed and killed and yet, initially, there appeared to be no motive."

"Oh!" Caroline was shocked.

"Nobody's been arrested for it yet," continued Michael, "but the police are almost certain that whoever did it were the same people who attacked dad. It seems that the crew responsible for his attack were pointed in the wrong direction in the first place, by someone called Carl McCabe."

"How do you mean, pointed in the wrong direction?"

"Well, the cab this bloke was driving had the same plate number as dad's – although for the Warrington area, not the area that dad works - the registration number of the two cabs was very similar and, on top of that, he did look like dad. So, the police suspect that Carl McCabe took the opportunity, deliberately, to lead the attackers in dad's direction – because he wanted to get revenge on him."

"Revenge?" Caroline was mystified. "For what?"

"Dad would never tell you about something like this," said Michael sheepishly; "but it seems that this Carl McCabe and a load of his mates kicked off on one of the taxi drivers, just as dad was driving past – and being dad, he went to the rescue. D.C.I. Davies told me how impressed he was with the way dad dealt with them – he saw the whole thing, because it was caught on CCTV. McCabe, supposedly a hard man, was put down with one kick, and didn't have the bottle to get back up again." Michael grinned proudly. "Anyway, the police now suspect that the real gangsters woke up to the fact that Carl McCabe had wasted their resources - because he's never been seen since."

"Wasting resources? I'm sorry Mike, but this is all very complicated," said Caroline, scratching her head. "I think you're going to have to explain everything to me again."

"Okay," said Michael. "To begin with, we've got a man who looked like dad, and he also drove a taxi with the same plate number, and similar registration number. This fella is a heavy gambler, he'd run up a big debt with a family of gangsters called the McCabes, and then got drunk one night and boasted he wasn't going to pay them. People like the McCabes can't allow that to happen; so they'll have arranged for a crew to deal with him, to send a message out to all the other low-lives who owe them money.

"The next thing – so the police believe - dad was attacked, because the gangsters mistook him for the Warrington man; the police also think that Carl McCabe, who is related to these gangsters, encouraged their mistake by feeding them the wrong information, because he wanted to get revenge on dad. Now, the McCabes will have paid this crew to carry out the attack – and wouldn't be very happy to find that Carl McCabe had got them to waste their time attacking dad, the wrong bloke. It can't be coincidence that Carl has now vanished, or that the Warrington cabbie was killed last night.

"Now, D.C.I. Davies did stress to me that all this is only theory and speculation; but he's convinced that it explains everything that happened. If the Warrington police catch whoever killed dad's lookalike, the D.C.I. said the police certainly wouldn't be looking for anyone else in connection with the attack on dad – regardless of whether the attackers ever admit to it."

Caroline was slowly nodding, as if still trying to absorb all this information, and there was silence for a few moments after Michael had finished speaking.

"So," said Michael, "do you want to hear the two reasons I mentioned earlier?"

"What?"

"I said I thought this was good news, for two reasons," he reminded her.

"So you did," replied his mother, smiling. "What are they?"

"First of all – and I feel a bit guilty over this - I did find myself wondering what the hell dad must have done to deserve being beaten so badly, and for someone to want him dead."

Caroline bowed her head. "So did I."

"Well," continued Michael brightly "we now know he didn't do anything – he was completely innocent." Caroline nodded, and her eyes began to fill with tears.

"And the second reason," said Michael, "is because dad is now safe. You see, after it happened, Paul and I wondered when dad's attackers would try again, once they realised they'd failed; we even considered buying a taxi between us, and both working it night and day - so if dad was in trouble, one or other of us wouldn't be very far away. But now we know it won't happen again."

"Because the thugs got the man they were really looking for." Caroline paused; then she got up from her chair, went over to her son, and hugged him tightly. "You're right, you win - yours is the best news by far."

"So, anyway – how come the police didn't tell you straight away about the possibility of criminal compensation?"

Caroline sat down, looking slightly uncomfortable. "Well......from what I can gather, the senior investigating officer should have made sure that we were aware of it; but he didn't, and I don't know why."

Michael grinned. "Are we talking about the slimeball, by any chance?"

Caroline fidgeted as she nodded. "So you would agree that Benton *was* a slimeball?" pressed Michael.

"Alright, yes," agreed Caroline sheepishly. "I can see you're just like your dad – being able to size somebody up, just from a short phone conversation."

Michael looked triumphant. "In that case, I can tell you what happened," he announced. "Benton turned up at the hospital one evening, demanding to talk to dad."

Caroline's stomach turned; could Benton have got his revenge after all, by poisoning Neil's mind against her? However, she gave no sign to Michael of her inner turmoil.

"Oh?" she said, with affected nonchalance; "I wonder what he wanted."

"We'll never know!" Michael was grinning like a schoolboy.

Caroline also forced a smile. "I'm surprised your dad didn't mention speaking to Benton."

Michael shook his head vigorously. "No, you don't understand - what I meant, is that I wouldn't allow Benton to speak to dad. It was one evening in the hospital, just after I took over from you; I was coming out of dad's room, after checking on him, when this Benton character comes marching down the corridor – and the cheeky swine was about to walk straight past me, into the room. Just as well I was there; if he'd arrived ten minutes earlier, you'd probably have let him in."

As she listened to Michael's account, Caroline was still trying to show a degree of indifference; inwardly, however, she was overjoyed.

"I just stood in his way, and said that dad couldn't be disturbed," continued Michael. "I explained that, as far as I knew, only when Dr. Hargraves gave the all clear could anyone speak to dad. At this point, I was being polite and well-mannered, just as my mother taught me." Caroline permitted herself a wry smile.

"That fool told me to step out of the way - he was the 'senior investigating officer', could speak to whoever he liked, didn't need anyone's permission, and who did I think I was interfering in his investigation. He then, stupidly, called me 'son' - there's only one man entitled to do that. *That's* when I got annoyed." Michael paused. "I discovered that as well as being a slimeball, he was also gutless. Basically, I told him to walk away, otherwise I would knock him out; he stepped back a few paces, saying something about how I hadn't heard the last of this - so I stepped forward quickly; and you know what? He almost ran back down the corridor!" Michael was delighted as he recalled the image; but then he remembered who he was talking to, and looked slightly shame-faced. "At the time, if I'd have told you about this, you'd have got really mad with me."

"Well, maybe, maybe not," shrugged Caroline. "If, as you told him, the police weren't allowed to speak to your dad at that time, then you did the right thing. But it's probably just as well he didn't turn up while Paul was there."

"Oh, I don't know about that," chuckled Michael. "When Paul arrived later that night, I told him about Benton. He smiled, rubbed his hands together, and said he hoped Benton would turn up after I left, because there was something he wanted to try out. During the night was when they cleaned and polished the corridor floor so, for a short time, it was very shiny, but a bit slippery; Paul said he could get some markers to put along the wall and, if Benton turned up, he wouldn't bother getting into any sort of conversation with him – he'd just crack him one, and see how far his body slid up the corridor!"

Caroline could not stop herself from giggling, as she pictured such a farcical scene in her mind.

"So I take it he never came back then, after that night?" she asked. "He certainly didn't come to the hospital while I was there."

"Definitely not while I was there, either - and I'm sure Paul would have told me how far Benton slid up the corridor, " added Michael, sniggering, "so it can't have been that important for him to speak to dad."

"Incidentally," said Caroline, "where *is* Paul? I can't get an answer from your dad's phone, and I had no luck calling Paul either."

"He's actually finishing a little job off just outside Warrington - but he left his phone in my van this morning, so I've got no way of contacting him. I would imagine he'll be back within the next hour or so." Michael looked at his mother, as if deciding whether to continue. "I may as well tell you this now - have you realised that Paul has actually moved out? He lives with Jenny, but never quite got round to actually telling you. He was about to tell you just before dad got attacked - but since that happened, I think he was afraid to tell you officially."

"Oh," said Caroline, waving her hand dismissively, "I'm not a complete fool. Do you think I hadn't noticed him taking away more and more of his stuff every time he went to Jenny's, and not bringing it back? It's just such a relief to know that he's settled down with her, and that I don't have to worry about him as much – she's a great girl, and I couldn't be happier for him."

Michael nodded and smiled. "Should have known you'd put two and two together. Sorry, mum – you're not a fool, complete or otherwise!"

They both laughed at this, and then Caroline leaned back in her chair, reflecting on everything that had happened that day.

"Well, that's it - when your dad gets home, I'm going to give him all this good news, and suggest we move to Spain," she declared. "By the way, I forgot to mention before – in that box file of your dad's, as well as the premium bonds, I found the business card of the agent who can rent this house out for us."

Michael smiled at his mother's enthusiasm; but he had one reservation. "What if dad never gets his memory back? What happens then?"

"Then I'll just have to make sure that he falls in love with me all over again. It worked twenty years ago, so if I try my best, it'll work again now. Or, at least," she qualified, as she got up and looked out of the window, "it will if your dad answers his bloody phone! It's starting to go dark now."

………………………………...

Neil was looking down from the high bridge; but in the darkness, he could no longer see the concrete beneath.

After reliving everything that had happened before the attack, he had gone on to ponder, long and hard, over all that had occurred since he came out of hospital – now, of course, with his memory complete. Ironic really, he reflected; in different circumstances, he would have been angry at losing the taxi plate, and depressed at knowing that the sale of his dream villa could have been avoided – given that the existence of the premium bonds, the bank account in Spain, and the money under the shed, would have rendered it unnecessary. Not to mention that the buyer – whose name on the sale documents, emailed by the Spanish solicitor, had meant nothing to him at the time – was none other than that snake that had been boasting about his wealth, at their party at the villa. But so what? None of that was important. In losing Caroline, he had lost the only thing that mattered.

So, what was he to do? Get back involved in the bare knuckle fighting, with the warehouse boys – or go back to Caroline, in the suspicion that she would only be staying with him out of a sense of duty? Neither of these choices were palatable; and, as he looked down into the darkness far below, he knew that there was a third option. Why not?

Then suddenly, he smiled to himself. He knew why not – because he was a fighter. In his life, he had never given up on anything, and had taught others the same philosophy. He now had something new to fight for – different from what he was used to, but a fight all the same – and the prize would be regaining Caroline's love. He took a deep breath, stood up straight, and squared his shoulders; he had never given up on anything – and he was not going to give up on Caroline.

Neil turned, and set off to walk back to his car, when he saw a figure coming towards him; for a moment, he was wary – until, to his surprise, he came face to face with his younger son.

"Paul? What are you doing here?"

"I've been finishing a job off not far from here," explained a smiling Paul, "and felt like a little stroll, before I go home."

Neil decided not to tell his son that he had regained his memory; he was not sure why, but he felt that Caroline should be the first to know.

"Strangely enough, that's what I've been doing," he told Paul; "just having a stroll along the canal, thinking about various things."

Paul nodded. "So, is everything okay? Are you heading home soon?"

"I'm just going back to the car now, and then I'll be driving straight home."

"Great – and…….thanks." Paul held out his hand.

Neil shook his son's hand. "Thanks for what?"

"Thanks for being my dad."

As Paul watched his father walk from the bridge to his car, he nodded to himself, and let out a sigh of relief.

…………………………………………………………………

Driving home, Neil suddenly remembered that he had switched off his phone. Pulling over, he opened the glove box, retrieved the phone and, switching it on, noted that the battery was low; he therefore realised, as he dialled home, that he would need to keep the conversation short.

"Caroline - I'll be home soon."

There was a slight pause on the other end of the line, before she responded.

"Okay."

She carefully put down the receiver and stood, almost rooted to the spot, mentally repeating the words Neil had just spoken. 'Caroline', he had said - not 'Caz.' Could it be? She was now alone – Michael had gone home to get changed – so it would not have mattered if she had given in to the urge to jump up and down; but she tried her best not to get too excited. After all, it might not mean anything. But he had called her Caroline! She sat down on the bottom step of the staircase, and was back on her feet almost instantly.

She began pacing up and down the hallway, then found herself standing in the living room staring out of the window, in the hope of seeing Neil arrive home; as she saw his car turn into the driveway, she almost sprinted into the hall, and waited for him to come through the front door. She was shaking slightly, with a mixture of fear and excitement.

As Neil stepped in to the hallway, his eyes told her all what she needed to know – there it was, that look which had been there from when they first met, a look she had always taken for granted. Neil took a step forward, carefully held her face in his hands, and gently kissed her on the lips, exactly the same way he had kissed her on that first night. She almost launched herself at him - holding him so tightly, it was as if she was afraid he would evaporate if she let him go. Eventually, and almost reluctantly, she released her embrace.

"I've got so much good news to tell you, I'm not sure where to start," she told him; "but before I do, there is something I've got to tell you – and I just hope you can forgive me."

Neil smiled at her; of one thing he was certain – regardless of what she was about to tell him, he could guarantee his forgiveness; there was nothing she could ever do that he would not forgive.

Sometime later, after she had explained everything to him – leaving out none of the details, as

Alice had advised – Caroline looked at him sadly. "So – if you can - please forgive me, for putting myself in such a dangerous situation."

Neil was still smiling, and had decided that he would never tell her that he had been the driver of the van she saw that night; once she had finished her account, he tried to look serious.

"Well, I'm not sure whether I can forgive you or not," he said, shaking his head. "You're asking me to forgive you for being a little bit naive, slightly gullible, and far too trusting of other people. These are three of the things that I love most about you - for me to forgive you would mean they were faults. Which they certainly are not!"

As Caroline hugged Neil again, he felt an overwhelming sense of relief to know that Caroline did love him, had always loved him, and had no feelings for anyone else.

There was something else he now knew. After the death of Patrick Flynn, he had taken the man's mobile phone – remembering that Flynn had been due to receive the details of Neil's address from an informant. Neil still had the phone, and the call had come through, just as he had pulled up outside his house; he was able to mimic Patrick's voice, but had been confused when he recognised the voice of the caller. In light of Caroline's story, it now made sense. He would deal with Benton another time.

And finally – as Caroline was still holding Neil as tightly as she could – he remembered how tightly he had closed his eyes, when he believed that she was betraying him. To think - if only he had been able to watch for five seconds longer then, probably, none of this would have happened.

THE END